THE MERRY
WIVES OF WINDSOR

By
WILLIAM SHAKESPEARE

SAMUEL FRENCH

FRENCH

LONDON

NEW YORK   TORONTO   SYDNEY   HOLLYWOOD

MADE AND PRINTED IN GREAT BRITAIN BY
BUTLER & TANNER LTD, FROME AND LONDON
MADE IN ENGLAND

PERSONS REPRESENTED

SIR JOHN FALSTAFF.

FENTON, a young gentleman.

SHALLOW, a country justice.

SLENDER, cousin to Shallow.

FORD, } two gentlemen dwelling at Windsor.
PAGE,

SIR HUGH EVANS, a Welsh parson.

DOCTOR CAIUS, a French physician.

Host of the Garter Inn.

BARDOLPH,
PISTOL, } followers of Falstaff.
NYM,

ROBIN, page to Falstaff.

SIMPLE, servant to Slender.

RUGBY, servant to Doctor Caius.

MISTRESS FORD.

MISTRESS PAGE.

ANNE PAGE, her daughter.

MISTRESS QUICKLY, servant to Doctor Caius.

Servants to PAGE, FORD, etc.

Scene.—Windsor, and the neighbourhood.

NOTES

"The Merry Wives of Windsor" is a comedy played in 17 different scenes. The first problem that presents itself is to accommodate such settings to the play and to devise such methods of change as will assist the speed of the action and yet maintain a picturesque atmosphere. In addition, a production has to be designed that can be modified to suit different local circumstances, and yet maintain all essential requirements. All these points have been taken into consideration in the plan of this production. The play has been divided into two parts, and the scenes should follow each other without interruption. By this means the action of the play will retain its necessary speed and occupy the desirable limits of time. A pair of traverse curtains, and three sets will suffice to mount the play, or if necessary, only two sets will be needed, the Field and Forest scenes sufficing one for the other by a little rearrangement. Two six-foot tree wings used as backing in last scene, lashed together on the R. and two more sets as wings on the L., a plain backcloth and the hedge will suggest some difference between the Field and the Forest. The sketches have been drawn as means to suggestion only and the scale plan can be adapted to particular requirements.

The producer is advised against introducing any unnecessary business. Business should be a logical development out of a situation and only in such degree as to place a natural emphasis upon a point of drama or character without becoming detached or obtrusive ; or, as in the instance of the ending to Act II, Scene II, where the host conceals himself behind the tapestry to simulate a hidden Falstaff, it can be introduced to close a scene which otherwise would end in a weak manner. The lapses into dumb pantomime which are often relics of traditional business grown to distortion should be studiously avoided.

iii

THE SETS

As planned, the sets occupy a 27-ft. opening and a depth of 25 ft. from curtain-line to backcloth. The house-piece on the right consists of two 4-ft. flats on either side of a 6-ft. one containing the arch, which can also be a beam opening. The flats at the back are 4 ft.—6 ft.—4 ft. and can either be lashed and braced or battened and flied ; the latter being more convenient. The door should be wide enough to give the window-piece a view to its backing in the Inn scene.

The following are the three methods with which to deal with the return-piece, Z^4.

1. A piece of three-ply wood comes down to the level of the floor beam and is pin-hinged to the front flat. From it is bracketed, at right angles, a piece equal in width to that of the projecting beams. This piece drops at an angle towards the backcloth in order to give the perspective to the beams painted on it and it meets the remaining piece that rises up, making the lower storey.

2. The flat carrying the angled corner or " dragon " beam need not be profiled. The space beneath it can be painted in with a shrub reaching to the upper storey and on the return piece, a hedge, window-high, can be painted, terminating in a tall shrub at the other end, the whole being in perspective. This will spoil the line of the house a little but it will serve its purpose.

3. The corner of the house can be perfectly straight and this only requires a straight return.

The shrubs and hedge can also be painted on the front of the house where, in the perspective, the base of the recessed storey does not reach the stage level and also, where the extension of the stone wall from the right requires to be painted in up to the timber, unless it is otherwise covered. In the first instance the intervening space can be filled with grass if the hedge is not desired.

In the event of any further need for condensation of the scene, the ground row, Z^3, can be joined at right angles to Z^4, as full-sized flats and the backcloth flied over its setting-line.

On the left, the pieces consist of a 6-ft. flat above and a 2-ft. flat below the chimney. The top piece contains a window which opens back and forms an entrance or exit for the Inn scene. On the plan the dotted line indicates this.

The chimney consists of two flats joined together. They can rise straight up without any architectural variations. In the bottom of the flat facing the stage, a cut is made following the pattern of the bricks and the canvas stiffened with three-ply. The area thus cut should be fitted so as to take out or be lifted up in order to expose the grate and logs behind for the interior scenes, when the front is given a simple stone facing with a thickness to hide the unevenness of the upstage edge of the cut.

The actual chimney-piece can be eliminated entirely and the same process be applied to the wall of the house.

Or again, the whole can be mounted and firmly fixed together on a wooden base, painted to resemble a hearth and which can be mounted on runners or " domes of silence." This will enable it to be pushed into the scene flush with the wall for one of the scenes or set at any required depth. It will also facilitate the strike to the Field scene.

The front Traverse curtains are blue-grey, matching the colour of the false proscenium and its ceiling. They are used for the various scenes as indicated.

The window-piece, Q, is inserted for Caius' House.

The Garter Inn and Ford's House scenes are made up out of the first scene with the following changes :

The Garter Inn.—The window-piece, Q, is set at the back in front of the door of the house, the door being opened and a street backing placed as in the plan. Blue-grey curtains are lowered, and, being on runners, are adjustable for masking. They should come up to the window itself.

On the R., dark red canvas is hung from the beam concealing the arch and lower piece of wall, the piece covering the arch being separate from the other.

The chimney is arranged as already described.

Beam borders replace the exterior ones, with the exception of the back one, which is covered by the curtains with a beam border in front of them.

Ford's House.—The centre tapestry is taken down revealing the arch over R. The lower piece is reversed and is painted an agreeable green. Another piece of the same colour with a cut for the opening is hung over the piece above the arch.

Antlers are hung over the arch.

At the back, as the house piece for Act I has been finished with, it has been flied, but its backing remains with the steps and is rearranged as in the sketch.

A strong light is thrown in from the window on the L. which, being opened in the Inn scene to make the entrance to the Falstaff's chamber, is now closed. This difference in lighting will greatly assist to alter the aspect of the scene from its former appearance.

If necessary, the fireplace can have a different front or an addition added to it, but this may not be essential. The borders remain the same.

The Frogmore scene requires the left of the former scene to be struck. If the chimney is movable in one piece as has been suggested, it will facilitate this change.

In the plan the backcloth and ground row, T^6, are already set. The return piece, T^3, masks the wall on the R. so that it need not be struck. The curtains can again be used as a backcloth if space demands it, although the more distant view, as in the plan, looks better.

The body of the haystack in the upper wing needs to be in profile but not the top. In the lower wing the entire upper side must be in profile.

As an alternative, tree wings can be set in place of the haystacks. It does not create the atmosphere of a field in the same way as it achieved by the stacks, but it will suffice if circumstances demand it.

For the last scene the stage must be cleared and reset. Upon examination this will be found to be quite easy and can be done without any noise during the scenes which lead up to it.

The gauze curtain hung in front of the backcloth will be found very effective in dimming it down. The effect can be regulated by the distance between the two and also by leaving the trees on the outer piece or by veiling them with one or both of the others. The lighting should be kept downstage as the reflected light will be sufficient to pick out the tree forms with ghostly touch at the back.

Lighting cannot be specified in detail. The plot provided will serve as a working basis and can be adapted to local means. The strength of the lighting, nature and degree of colour, the number of lamps will necessitate the re-adjustment of the plot, but that which is provided will serve to show what is required.

The Furniture, unless specially made in Gothic style, should be plain wood but not upholstered. Trestle tables are quite in period and a tall settle is near enough for its purpose.

The hanging brackets for the candles are very simple to make. The bowls should be of metal, painted blue or one of the other primary colours and screwed or nailed on to the wood. Two of these brackets can be hung if desired, one R. and the other L. The pulley by which each is suspended can hang down on a line behind the border being attached to the border batten.

The tower of Windsor Castle was much lower than at present and was without a flag turret in the fourteenth century. Its present height and additions are of comparatively modern times.

The Borders in the interiors should be brought down as low as possible. Mediaeval rooms were extremely low. The brackets can be brought down below the horizontal beam and the beams can be either simple or plain. A front border can be substituted for the blue curtain one as shown in the plan and sketch. But this is not absolutely necessary. In the sketch the borders have been lifted in order to show the scene. If a decorated border should be used, such as No. I, the space within the arch should be painted in instead of cut unless very deep borders are available to mask behind.

In the first scene a tree border may be found necessary to hang in front of the chimney-piece. This can take tree-branches coming from R. and L. and C. The house-border in this scene must be caught between the house-piece and the wall-piece R. This will keep it in position and need not be struck for the interior scenes. It supplies the thatch of the house. The thatch will be found the more acceptable roofing, because it will be easier to lose among the branches of the border in front, if they have to carry it.

The front pelmet should be kept as low as 14 feet from the stage, if possible.

Lighting battens should be placed behind the borders and hung high enough to clear the line of sight in the region of all borders hanging in that area.

The trees must be leafless, as the play is set in winter-time.

The production given in this book is the arrangement devised by Mr. George Skillan.

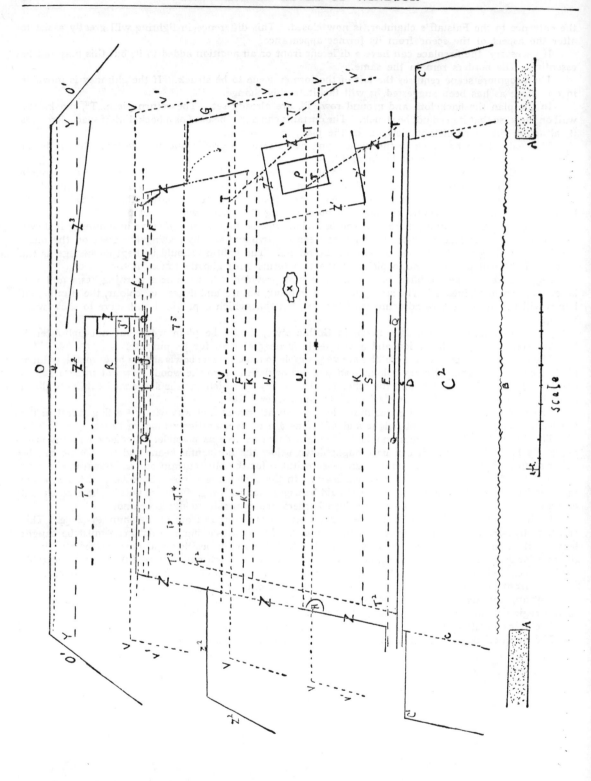

KEY TO PLAN

A.   Proscenium opening.

B.   Curtain line.

C.   False Proscenium.

c^1.   False Proscenium backing.

c^2.   False Proscenium ceiling.

D.   Blue-grey border.

E.   Blue-grey Traverse curtains.

QQ.   Window-piece, Act I, Scene I, and at back for Act I, Scene III.   This must have a practicable window to open up stage on the [stage] L. side.

F.   Beam borders.   The first one will probably have to be brought up stage a little and set as required.

z.   House-pieces, Act I, Scene I.

z^1.   Flats for chimney-piece, Act I, Scene I.

z^2.   Backings for openings in Act I, Scene I.   The arch backing has been moved up stage a little to avoid confusion with other pieces in the drawing.

z^3.   Castle backing, Act I, Scene I.

z^4.   Shrub, Act I, Scene I.

H.   Stone piece, Act I, Scene I.

O.   Sky-cloth to stand for the play.

J.   One or two-tread steps for Act I, Scene I ; also Act II, Scene II.   [J^1].

o^1.   Sky wings to backcloth.

L.   House border Act I, Scene I, which carries sky on L. of the house.

K.   Tree borders Act I, Scene I.

K^1.   Tree piece, Act I, Scene I.

P.   Fire-grate and logs, Act I, Scene II.

N.   Blue-grey curtains, flied, or Traverse if drawn on from the L.

S.   Backing for window, Act I, Scene III.

R.   Backing for window, Act I, Scene II.

TT.   Wing-pieces.

T^2,T^2.   Hedge flats.

T^3,T^3.   Return flat.

T^4.   Stile.

T^5.   Back hedge piece.

T^6.   Ground row behind stile for distant hedge.

T^7.   Tree or sky wing to mask opening made by profile of the front hay-stack wing.

U.   Sky borders.

} Act I, Scene VII.

VV.   Cut-cloths for last scene.

v^1.   Backings for cut-cloth wings.

YY.   Black-gauze cloth, three thicknesses if possible.

W.   " Herne's Oak " treepiece.

G.   Backing for opening in Garter Inn scene.

X.   Tree-stump, Act I, Scene VII.

PROPERTY PLOT

ACT I
Scene I.

Stone piece down R.

Off R.—Tray with chalices or mugs and a flagon for Anne.

Stout staff for Shallow. Smaller one for Evans. Elegant one for Slender. Very stout one for Falstaff.

Letter for Evans.

Scene II.

Two pieces of tapestry, one to hang over arch opening R. and the other to hang on flat below the archpiece. They are painted a red or brown, and on the reverse side a blue-green. They can be fixed to light battens which can be made to fix on to the wall.

Bench by the wall, table and two stools, one at the top and the other L. of table.

Dice and box on the table and drinking-vessels.

Up at back, a bench or chest.

Curtains on the window-piece.

Hanging candle-bracket C., or one R. and another L.

Table over L. by fire.

Mugs on the table.

Log fire on firedogs in chimney. This is set with the chimney in the first Act.

Two letters for Falstaff.

Scene III.

Chair or stool by the window.

Off R.

Sword and some paper, for Rugby.

Off L.

Prepared letter for Caius. Caius can carry an ink-horn round his neck with a quill inserted beside it.

Money for Fenton.

Scene IV.

Stage set the same as Scene I.

Two letters, one for Mrs. Ford and the other for Mrs. Page.

Staff for Ford.

Scene V.

Same as Scene II. The table L. has a white cloth and a pasty and bread on it.

One of the stools has been brought R. of the table L.

Falstaff's hat and staff over on table R.

Scene VI.

Rapier or sword for Caius.

Scene VII.

Tree-stump up L.C.

Gown which Simple carries.

Rapier for Evans, worn sheathed.

ACT II
Scene I. Nil.

Scene II.

Large circular or square basket R.C. Linen in and around the same.

Over L. a table and a settle by the fireplace.

Chair down L. by the wall.

Chest up at back R.

Table over L. by the window.

These properties are merely the rearrangement of those used in the Garter Inn scene and are replaced for use or to dress the stage.

On the wall over L. a pair of antlers are hung over the arch.

The tapestry on the wall down R. is reversed ; the piece taken down from in front of the arch and another hung on the flat above the arch.

Embroidery for Mrs. Ford.

Letter for Mrs. Page.

Poles to basket off R.

Scene III.

Ring and purse for Fenton.

Scene IV.

Chair by the fire.

Table that was L.C. has been moved up to back R.

A stool from over R. has been moved to R. of chair L.

On this stool a drinking-vessel.

Other drinking-vessels are on the table up R. and a cloth for cleaning them.

The curtains attached to the window-piece are drawn together and the candles are alight.

Two drinking-vessels, one a chalice, and the other a " pottle " or quart pot, off R. for Bardolph.

Scene V.

Same as Scene II. Table has been put up L. at the back out of the way.

A piece of linen, a large wimple, off R. for Mrs. Ford.

Scene VI.

Paper missiles and sticks for the crowd.

Scene VII.

Same as Scene II. Table L.C. lengthwise across the stage.

Scene VIII.

Exactly the same as Scene IV.

Falstaff's hat hangs on back of chair L. and his stick leans beside it.

Scene IX.

Masks for Page, Shallow, Evans, which they carry.

Scene X.

Pair of horns and chains for Falstaff.

Grotesque masks for the principals taking part in the dance.

LIGHTING PLOT

ACT I

Scenes I and IV.

Floats.—Amber full, three-quarter white.

Battens.—Amber three-quarter white ; half, up to the house ; then full up.

On Stage, R.—A weak light coming through the arch from a strip.

On Stage, up at back.—Flood behind backing Z^2 to light the backcloth and backing Z^3 and to catch entrances from L. This may require two floods. White and amber strip behind backing Z^3 on backcloth.

On Stage, L.—White flood on backcloth ; another on the backing Z^3 and to strike through window in Z, flooding the backing Z^2.

Perches, P —One straw flood. One straw focus head-high C.

Perches, L.—One C. ; one flood.

Scenes II and V.

Floats.—Full amber and a quarter or half white.

Battens.—Nil.

On Stage, R.—Nil.

On Stage, at back.—The flood on the L., used in Scene I, strikes through the window on to backing. Nothing in the entrances. Red or light amber flood from the fireplace.

Perches, R.—Straw focused on table and chair L. Another head-high C. and a straw flood.

Perches, L.—Straw focused on table R. and another on chair L. Don't flood from this side. This will help to make the scene distinct from Ford's House.

Scene III.

Floats.—Full amber and half white.

Perches.—Straw floods either side.

Battens.—None in the scene, but number one full up amber and white to light backing.

Scene VI.

Same as Scene III without backing.

Scene VII.

Floats.—Full amber and white.

Battens.—Full amber and white.

On Stage, R. and L.—Floods on the backcloth and stage and in the wings L. Those in the wings should be straw. White length behind the hedge.

Perches, R.—Straw flood and focus head-high C.

Perches, L.—Straw flood and focus head-high C.

ACT II

Scene I.

Same as Act I, Scene VI.

Scene II.

Floats.—Full amber and three-quarter white.

Battens.—Nil.

On Stage, R.—Medium strength amber flood in arch.

On Stage, at back.—From the R. a medium straw flood to light the entrances from the C.

Over R.—Strong white flood from the window. Deep amber flood from the fireplace.

Perches, R.—Straw focus on seat L. and another head-high C.

Perches, L.—Straw focus C. and amber flood.

Scene III.

Same as Act I, Scene VI.

Scene IV.

Same as Act I, Scene II.

The floats are full amber only and the floods are a darker amber. No lighting at the back.

Scene V.

Same as Act II, Scene II.

Scene VI.

Same as Act II, Scene I.

Scene VII.

Same as Act II, Scene II.

Scene VIII.

Same as Act I, Scene II.

Scene IX.

2 light blue floods from either perch.
Floats full blue and half white.

Scene X.

The lighting of this scene should be kept as much downstage as possible. From either perch a light-blue focus should be trained on the area occupied by Falstaff. Another focus from each perch lights R.C. and L.C. respectively. If possible, a spot light should be set in the floats and trained on Falstaff's face, but not travelling beyond the tree-piece, otherwise a shadow will be cast. A cut cardboard will regulate the size. This lighting will reflect on the surrounding scenery and at the same time keep the stage in shadow to help the various appearances of the other characters. The fairies can carry lanterns lit electrically by electric candles, which on being applied to the lanterns can be switched on when required.

Perch lights are always frosted. The choice between thick or thin frost must be left to the producer.

Flood lights are usually unfrosted.

A flood light should be placed close up to the backing of an entrance and preferably on a pair of steps. This prevents the casting of shadow by those making their entrances or exits.

A focus light is always trained on the faces of characters unless otherwise stated. Thus the lighting in the Inn and Ford's House scenes is set on the groups or individuals at the tables or in the chairs.

Always keep the focus lighting off the scenery as much as possible. Furniture should be set so as to enable characters to be lit on the sides of the stage by the near-side perches, if this should be necessary, without the light striking the false proscenium or returns.

THE MERRY WIVES OF WINDSOR

ILLUSTRATION No. 1
This scene stands for Act I, Scenes I and IV

ACT THE FIRST

SCENE I

Windsor. Before PAGE'S *house.*

¹ *Enter* JUSTICE SHALLOW, SLENDER, *and* SIR HUGH EVANS.

SHALLOW. Sir Hugh, persuade me not ; I will make a Star-chamber matter of it : if he were twenty Sir John Falstaffs, he shall not abuse Robert Shallow, esquire.

SLENDER. In the county of Gloucester, justice of peace and "Coram."

² SHALLOW. Ay, cousin Slender, and "Custalorum."

SLENDER. Ay, and "Rato-lorum" too ; and a gentleman born, master parson ; who writes himself "Armigero," in any bill, warrant, quittance, or obligation, "Armigero."

SHALLOW. Ay, that I do ; and have done any time these three hundred years.

SLENDER. All his successors gone before him hath done't ; and all his ancestors that come after him may : they may give the dozen white luces in their coat.

SHALLOW. It is an old coat.

EVANS. The dozen white louses do become an old coat well ; it

ACT I, SC. I

ACT I
SCENE I
Windsor. Before PAGE'S *house.*

[1] SHALLOW *commences to speak off-stage* R., *coming through arch on his last line, so that* SLENDER *follows and speaks his line as he enters with* EVANS *on his* L.

[2] *They work* O.

1

ACT I, SC. I

[1] SLENDER *sighs and turns up* R. *and, standing with his back to the wall, looks wistfully at the window; the other two move a little over* L.

[2] *Emphasize "Council" and "riot." The two elderly men can become very emphatic and full of spirit in stating their respective points. Thus a picture can be obtained of the two old gentlemen strong in debate down* L. *and the languid attitude of the musing* SLENDER *up* L.

[3] *This is a big outburst, which is tactfully soothed by* EVANS *with the introduction of another subject very near to* SHALLOW'S *heart and possibly his pocket.*

[4] *This brings* SLENDER *down into the scene.*

[5] EVANS *is valiantly at work, painting these advantages to soothe the irate* SHALLOW, *and this makes his parenthesis (a) very funny.*

[6] SLENDER *becomes very much alive to this qualification, and seemingly it develops his affection, as his next line indicates.*

[7] EVANS *has succeeded, and* SHALLOW'S *temper lies subdued under his efforts.*
[8] *A laugh is heard from within the house, from the assembled company. As the three are about to go up to the house, they stop at the laugh, and* SHALLOW *suddenly returns to his old mood.*
[9] *Here comes a big guffaw from* FALSTAFF. EVANS, *who was about to make a humouring remark, finds himself plundered by this situation. He has no resource except these bold platitudes with which he does his bravest and best.*
[10] SHALLOW *makes a movement of anger up towards the door.* SLENDER *almost springs behind tree up* R. EVANS, *of course, restrains* SHALLOW *and suggests the happy idea of knocking at the door and taking matters in hand in a congenial manner.*
[11] SHALLOW *bangs his stick on the ground and moves away down* L. *in anger.*
[12] PAGE *enters through the door of his house up* C. *He is a very genial soul and must be played as such as a contrast with* FORD. *He shakes hands with* EVANS.
[13] SLENDER, *who has begun to come from behind the tree, slips back as his name is mentioned.*
[14] PAGE *comes down to* SHALLOW *and* EVANS *moves over to the tree* R. *and pulls* SLENDER *into view, bringing him down* R. *and on his right-hand side.*
[15] PAGE *turns to* SLENDER, *who is all confusion and nothing else.* EVANS *stands up* R., *watching a little anxiously.*

agrees well, passant; [it is a familiar beast to man, and signifies love.

SHALLOW. The luce is the fresh fish; the salt fish is an old coat.]

SLENDER. I may quarter, coz.

SHALLOW. You may, by marrying.[1]

EVANS. [It is marring indeed, if he quarter it.

SHALLOW. Not a whit.

EVANS. Yes, py'r lady; if he has a quarter of your coat, there is but three skirts for yourself, in my simple conjectures: but that is all one.] If Sir John Falstaff have committed disparagements unto you, I am of the church, and will be glad to do my benevolence to make atonements and compremises between you.

SHALLOW.[2] The council shall hear it; it is a riot.

EVANS. It is not meet the council hear a riot; there is no fear of Got in a riot: the council, look you, shall desire to hear the fear of Got, and not to hear a riot; [take your vizaments in that.]

SHALLOW. Ha! o' my life, if I were young again, the [3] sword should end it.

EVANS. It is petter that friends is the sword, and end it: and there is also another device in my prain, which peradventure prings goot discretions with it: there is Anne Page, which is daughter to Master Thomas Page, which is pretty virginity.

[4] SLENDER. Mistress Anne Page? She has brown hair, and speaks small like a woman.

[5] EVANS. It is that fery person for all the orld, as just as you will desire; and seven hundred pounds of moneys, and gold and silver, is her grandsire upon his death's-bed—(a)Got deliver to a joyful resurrections!—give, when she is able to overtake seventeen years old: it were a goot motion if we leave our pribbles and prabbles, and desire a marriage between Master Abraham and Mistress Anne Page.

SLENDER.[6] Did her grandsire leave her seven hundred pound?

EVANS. Ay, and her father is make her a petter penny.

SLENDER. I know the young gentlewoman; she has good gifts.

EVANS. Seven hundred pounds and possibilities is goot gifts.

SHALLOW.[7] Well, let us see honest Master Page.[8] Is Falstaff there? [9]

EVANS. Shall I tell you a lie? I do despise a liar as I do despise one that is false, or as I despise one that is not true. The knight, Sir John, is there; [10] and, I beseech you, be ruled by your well-willers. I will peat the door for Master Page.[11] [*Knocks.*] What, hoa! Got pless your house here!

PAGE [*within*]. Who's there?

Enter PAGE.[12]

EVANS. Here is Got's plessing, and your friend, and Justice Shallow; and here young Master Slender, that peradventures shall tell you another [13] tale, if matters grow to your likings.

[14] PAGE. I am glad to see your worships well. I thank you for my venison, Master Shallow.

SHALLOW. Master Page, I am glad to see you: much good do it your good heart! I wished your venison better; it was ill killed. How doth good Mistress Page?—and I thank you always with my heart, la! with my heart.

PAGE. Sir, I thank you.

SHALLOW. Sir, I thank you; by yea and no, I do.

[15] PAGE. I am glad to see you, good Master Slender.

SLENDER. How does your fallow greyhound, sir? I heard say he was outrun on Cotsall.

PAGE. It could not be judged, sir.

SLENDER. You'll not confess, you'll not confess.

SHALLOW. That he will not. 'Tis your fault, 'tis your fault ; 'tis a good dog.

PAGE. A cur, sir.

SHALLOW. Sir, he's a good dog, and a fair dog : can there be more said? he is good and fair.[1] Is Sir John Falstaff here?

PAGE. Sir, he is within ; and I would I could do a good office between you.

[2] EVANS. It is spoke as a Christians ought to speak.

SHALLOW. He hath wronged me, Master Page.

PAGE. Sir, he doth in some sort confess it.

[3] SHALLOW. If it be confessed, it is not redressed : is not that so, Master Page? He hath wronged me ; indeed he hath ; at a word, he hath, believe me : Robert Shallow, esquire, saith, he is wronged.[4]

PAGE. Here comes Sir John.

Enter SIR JOHN FALSTAFF, BARDOLPH, NYM, *and* PISTOL.

FALSTAFF. Now, Master Shallow, you'll complain of me to the king?

[5] SHALLOW. Knight, you have beaten my men, killed my deer, and broke open my lodge.

[6] FALSTAFF. But not kissed your keeper's daughter?

SHALLOW. Tut, a pin! this shall be answered.

FALSTAFF. I will answer it straight ; I have done all this. That is now answered.

SHALLOW. The council shall know this.

FALSTAFF. 'Twere better for you if it were known in counsel : you'll be laughed at.

EVANS. Pauca verba, Sir John ; goot worts.

FALSTAFF. Good worts! good cabbage.[7] Slender, I broke your head : what matter have you against me?

SLENDER. Marry, sir, I have matter in my head against you ; and against your cony-catching rascals, Bardolph, Nym, and Pistol.

BARDOLPH. You Banbury cheese!

SLENDER. Ay, it is no matter.

PISTOL.[8] How now, Mephostophilus!

SLENDER. Ay, it is no matter.

[9] NYM. Slice, I say! pauca, pauca : slice! that's my humour.

SLENDER. Where's Simple, my man? [Can you tell, cousin?

EVANS. Peace, I pray you. Now let us understand. There is three umpires in this matter, as I understand ; that is, Master Page, fidelicet Master Page ; and there is myself, fidelicet myself ; and the three party is, lastly and finally, mine host of the Garter.

PAGE. We three, to hear it and end it between them.

EVANS. Fery goot : I will make a prief of it in my note-book ; and we will afterwards ork upon the cause with as great discreetly as we can.

FALSTAFF. Pistol!

PISTOL. He hears with ears.

EVANS. The tevil and his tam! what phrase is this, ' He hears with ear' ? why, it is affectations.]

FALSTAFF.[10] Pistol, did you pick Master Slender's purse?

SLENDER. Ay, by these gloves, did he, or I would I might never come in mine own great chamber again else, of seven groats in mill-sixpences, and two Edward shovel-boards, that cost me two shilling and two pence a-piece of Yead Miller, by these gloves.

[1] *Another laugh from the house.* SHALLOW *immediately fires up.* SLENDER *runs over into the arch over* R. EVANS *comes down* R. *to help keep the peace.* PAGE, *seeing the hint of trouble, quietly and genially takes* SHALLOW *over* R.

[2] EVANS *slips his line in with great approval.*

[3] SHALLOW *gets very angry.*

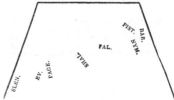

[4] *Door of house opens and enter* FALSTAFF, *followed by* PISTOL, NYM, BARDOLPH. SLENDER *retires down* R. *at their entrance.*

[5] SHALLOW *goes boldly up to* FALSTAFF.

[6] FALSTAFF'S *followers laugh and also* PAGE.

[7] PAGE, *seeing that the old gentlemen are getting a rough handling, takes them up* R. *to soothe them. At this movement,* FALSTAFF *sees* SLENDER *down* R.

[8] PISTOL *comes down* L. *At each of these assaults,* SLENDER'S *courage becomes weaker, until he cries for* SIMPLE.

[9] NYM *comes forward from behind* PISTOL.

[10] PAGE, EVANS *and* SHALLOW *turn round to watch this scene.*

ACT I, SC.

[1] EVANS *comes down* R.

[2] PISTOL *crosses in front of* FALSTAFF *at the which* EVANS *retires hastily back to* PAGE.

[3] PISTOL, *thus satisfied, retires up stage* R. *to a position in front of the window.*

[4] NYM *goes round at back of* FALSTAFF *and joins* PISTOL. *They both stand looking at* SLENDER *in a threatening manner.*

[5] FALSTAFF *moves over to* BARDOLPH, *who stands in a sleepy condition, and just touches him with his stick to wake him up.* BARDOLPH *goes into the corner of the chimney and wall and gets a warm.*

[6] PISTOL *and* NYM *make a movement and noise of a threatening kind, which is stopped by both* FALSTAFF *and* PAGE ; *the former crossing over on his line and the others moving down.*

[7] ANNE *appears at the doorway and comes on stage just a few steps and exits at cue.*

[8] *Sinks on to stone down* R. *The thought that he has to woo her overcomes him. As he sinks* **enter the Wives,** MRS. FORD *on* L. *of* MRS. PAGE.

[9] PAGE *comes behind* FALSTAFF *and greets* MRS. FORD *with a handshake, passing her across to* FALSTAFF, *and goes up to his wife. The two women come in laughing. All eyes are on them except* SLENDER'S *and* BARDOLPH'S. SLENDER *being preoccupied with other thoughts and* BARDOLPH *asleep.*

[10] *All laugh.*

[11] *She crosses over to the group* R. *and curtsies to them. They bow and laugh and talk, also* FALSTAFF *and* MRS. FORD, C.

[12] PAGE *goes down to* BARDOLPH *and wakes him up with this line.*

[13] *Going up to his door again. Gentlemen indicate to* MRS. PAGE *to enter ; she is followed by* MRS. FORD, FALSTAFF *and the others,* PAGE *being last.* SLENDER *is left, very disconsolate, on the seat over* R.

[14] SIMPLE *enters from up* L., *comes down* R. *and sneezes.*

[15] SLENDER *moves a little over* R. *impatient at the loan of his book.*

[16] *Re-enter from house,* SHALLOW *and* EVANS. SHALLOW *comes down* R. *of* SLENDER, EVANS *down* L. SIMPLE *goes over to the same corner as was occupied by* BARDOLPH, *and gets warm.*

[17] SHALLOW *and* EVANS *bring* SLENDER *well down stage so as to be well away from the house.*

FALSTAFF. Is this true, Pistol?

EVANS.[1] No ; it is false, if it is a pick-purse.

[2] PISTOL. Ha, thou mountain-foreigner! Sir John and master mine,

I combat challenge of this latten bilbo.

Word of denial in thy labras here!

Word of denial : froth and scum, thou liest!

SLENDER. By these gloves, then, 'twas he.[3]

NYM. Be avised, sir, and pass good humours : I will say " marry trap " with you, if you run the nuthooks humour on me ; that is the very note of it.

SLENDER. By this hat, then, he in the red face had it[4] ; for though I cannot remember what I did when you made me drunk, yet I am not altogether an ass.

FALSTAFF. What say you, Scarlet and John?[5]

BARDOLPH. Why, sir, for my part, I say the gentleman had drunk himself out of his five sentences.

EVANS. [It is his five senses : fie, what the ignorance is!

BARDOLPH. And being fap, sir, was, as they say, cashiered ; and so conclusions passed the careires.

SLENDER. Ay, you spake in Latin then too ; but] 'tis no matter : I'll ne'er be drunk whilst I live again, but in honest, civil, godly company, for this trick : if I be drunk, I'll be drunk with those that have the fear of God, and not with drunken knaves.[6]

EVANS. [So Got udge me, that is a virtuous mind.]

FALSTAFF. You hear all these matters denied gentlemen ; you hear it.[7]

Enter ANNE PAGE, *with wine.*

PAGE. Nay, daughter, carry the wine in ; we'll drink within.
                                        [*Exit* ANNE PAGE.

SLENDER. O heaven! this is Mistress Anne Page.[8]

[9] PAGE. How now, Mistress Ford!

FALSTAFF. Mistress Ford, by my troth, you are very well met : by your leave, good mistress. [*Kisses her.*[10]

PAGE. Wife, bid these gentlemen welcome[11] [12] Come, we have a hot venison pasty to dinner : [13] come, gentlemen, I hope we shall drink down all unkindness.
                [*Exeunt all except* SHALLOW, SLENDER, *and* EVANS.

SLENDER. I had rather than forty shillings I had my Book of Songs and Sonnets here.

[14]*Enter* SIMPLE.

How now, Simple! where have you been? I must wait on myself, must I? You have not the Book of Riddles about you, have you?

SIMPLE. Book of Riddles! why, did you not lend it to Alice Shortcake upon All-hallowmas last, a fortnight afore Michaelmas?[15]

[16] SHALLOW. Come, coz ; come, coz ; we stay for you.

[17] A word with you, coz ; marry, this, coz : there is, as 'twere, a tender, a kind of tender, made afar off by Sir Hugh here. Do you understand me?

SLENDER. Ay, sir, you shall find me reasonable ; if it be so, I shall do that that is reason.

SHALLOW. Nay, but understand me.

SLENDER. So I do, sir.

EVANS. Give ear to his motions, Master Slender : I will description the matter to you, if you be capacity of it.

SLENDER. Nay, I will do as my cousin Shallow says : I pray you, pardon me ; he's a justice of peace in his country, simple though I stand here.

EVANS. But that is not the question : the question is concerning your marriage.

SHALLOW. Ay, there's the point, sir.

EVANS. Marry, is it ; the very point of it ; to Mistress Anne Page.

SLENDER. Why, if it be so, I will marry her upon any reasonable demands.

EVANS. But can you affection the 'oman? [Let us command to know that of your mouth or of your lips ; for divers philosophers hold that the lips is parcel of the mouth. Therefore, precisely,] can you carry your good will to the maid?

SHALLOW. Cousin Abraham Slender, can you love her?

SLENDER. I hope, sir, I will do as it shall become one that would do reason.

EVANS. [Nay, Got's lords and his ladies! you must speak possitable, if you can carry her your desires towards her.

SHALLOW. That you must.] Will you, upon good dowry, marry her?

SLENDER. I will do a greater thing than that, upon your request cousin, in any reason.

SHALLOW. Nay, conceive me, conceive me, sweet coz : what I do is to pleasure you, coz. Can you love the maid?

SLENDER. I will marry her, sir, at your request : but if there be no great love in the beginning, yet heaven may decrease it upon better acquaintance, when we are married and have more occasion to know one another ; I hope, upon familiarity will grow more contempt : but if you say, "Marry her," I will marry her ; that I am freely dissolved, and dissolutely.[1]

EVANS.[2] It is a fery discretion answer ; save the fall is in the ort "dissolutely :"[3] the ort is, according to our meaning, "resolutely :" his meaning is good.

SHALLOW. Ay, I think my cousin meant well.[4]

SLENDER. Ay, or else I would I might be hanged, la!

SHALLOW. Here comes fair Mistress Anne.[5]

Re-enter ANNE PAGE.

Would I were young for your sake, Mistress Anne!

ANNE. The dinner is on the table ; my father desires your worships' company.[6]

SHALLOW. I will wait on him, fair Mistress Anne.[7]

EVANS.[8] Od's plessed will! I will not be absence at the grace.
[*Exeunt* SHALLOW *and* EVANS.

ANNE. Will't please your worship to come in, sir?

SLENDER.[9] No, I thank you, forsooth, heartily ; I am very well.

ANNE. The dinner attends you, sir.[10]

SLENDER. I am not a-hungry, I thank you, forsooth. Go, sirrah, for all you are my man, go wait upon my cousin Shallow. [*Exit* SIMPLE.] A justice of peace sometimes may be beholding to his friend for a man. I keep but three men and a boy yet, till my mother be dead : but what though? yet I live like a poor gentleman born.

[11] ANNE. I may not go in without your worship : they will not sit till you come.

SLENDER. I' faith, I'll eat nothing ; I thank you as much as though I did.

ANNE. I pray you, sir, walk in.

[1] SLENDER *comes over to* R., *being very resolute.*
[2] *Both turn and go up towards house.*
[3] *Stops to explain the meaning of the "ort".*

[4] *They continue towards the house.*

[5] EVANS, *who is on* SHALLOW'S R., *both having their backs to the audience, goes on a little and turns, whilst* SHALLOW *crosses to* ANNE.

[6] ANNE *curtseys.*

[7] *Exit* SHALLOW.

[8] *Said round to audience.*

[9] SLENDER *is over* R.
[10] *At this line,* SIMPLE *comes out of his corner, sniffing the air, and exits behind* ANNE—*who has come down a little to speak to* SLENDER—*into the house. These two retain the distance between themselves,* ANNE *being quite placid and well disciplined and* SLENDER *becoming more and more imbecile.*

[11] *Quietly ignoring his remarks.*

ACT I, SC. I.

[1] ANNE *gives a slight sign of her thoughts in a sigh.*

[2] *Dog's bark heard from behind the house.*

[3] *Coming down to him.*

[4] *Taking his arm and pulling him.*

[5] *At the door of his house and exits.*
[6] SLENDER *is following hesitatingly, then stops on a level with* ANNE.
[7] *Meaning " now you have started, don't stop ! "*

[8] *Desperately ; almost with anger, which rather troubles* SLENDER.
[9] *Goes up to the door, then stops and turns.* ANNE, *thinking that she had succeeded at last, is getting him in, is about to follow, but stops abruptly with a look of despair. He flings out his final line like a child having to do something against its will. ANNE turns to the audience, gives a laugh, and follows him in. Shouts heard within. A little incidental music plays after her exit, merely a few bars to mark lapse of time ; and then enter EVANS and SIMPLE. The music dies down as EVANS speaks. EVANS enters with SIMPLE on his L.*

[10] SIMPLE *exits up* L. *Music begins softly, swelling up on last line, which is said with great relish to audience.*
Music continues to play during the change and fades away at rise of curtain.

SLENDER. I had rather walk here, I thank you.[1] I bruised my shin th' other day with playing at sword and dagger with a master of fence ; three veneys for a dish of stewed prunes ; and, by my troth, I cannot abide the smell of hot meat since.[2] Why do your dogs bark so? be there bears i' the town?

ANNE. I think there are, sir ; I heard them talked of.

SLENDER. I love the sport well ; but I shall as soon quarrel at it as any man in England. You are afraid, if you see the bear loose, are you not?

ANNE. Ay, indeed, sir.

SLENDER. That's meat and drink to me, now. I have seen Sackerson loose twenty times, and have taken him by the chain ; but, I warrant you, the women have so cried and shrieked at it, that it passed : but women, indeed, cannot abide 'em ; they are very ill-favoured rough things.

Re-enter PAGE.

PAGE. Come, gentle Master Slender, come ; we stay for you.[3]

SLENDER. I'll eat nothing, I thank you, sir.

PAGE. By cock and pie, you shall not choose, sir! come, come.[4]

SLENDER. Nay, pray you, lead the way.

PAGE. Come on, sir.[5]

[6] SLENDER. Mistress Anne, yourself shall go first.

ANNE. Not I, sir ; pray you, keep on.[7]

SLENDER. Truly, I will not go first ; truly, la! I will not do you that wrong.

ANNE. I pray you, sir.[8]

SLENDER. I'll rather be unmannerly than troublesome.[9] You do yourself wrong, indeed, la! [*Exeunt.*

Enter SIR HUGH EVANS *and* SIMPLE.

EVANS. Go your ways, and ask of Doctor Caius' house which is the way : and there dwells one Mistress Quickly which is in the manner of his nurse, or his dry nurse, or his cook, or his laundry, his washer, and his wringer.

SIMPLE. Well, sir.

EVANS. Nay, it is petter yet. Give her this letter ; for it is a 'oman that altogether's acquaintance with Mistress Anne Page : and the letter is, to desire and require her to solicit your master's desires to Mistress Anne Page. I pray you, be gone.[10] I will make an end of my dinner ; there's pippins and cheese to come. [*Exeunt.*

ILLUSTRATION No. 2

This scene stands for Act I, Scenes II and V, and Act II, Scenes IV and VIII

SCENE II

A room in the Garter Inn.[1]

FALSTAFF.   Mine host of the Garter!

HOST.   What says my bully-rook? speak scholarly and wisely.

FALSTAFF.   Truly, mine host, I must turn away some of my followers.

HOST.   Discard, bully Hercules ; cashier : let them wag ; trot, trot.

FALSTAFF.   I sit at ten pounds a week.

HOST.[2]   Thou'rt an emperor, Cæsar, Keisar, and Pheezar.[3]   I will entertain Bardolph ; he shall draw, he shall tap : said I well, bully Hector?

FALSTAFF.   Do so, good mine host.

HOST.   I have spoke ; let him follow. [*To* BARDOLPH.]   Let me see thee froth and lime : I am at a word ; follow.[4]   [*Exit.*

FALSTAFF.[5]   Bardolph, follow him.   A tapster is a good trade : an old cloak makes a new jerkin ; a withered serving-man a fresh tapster.   Go ; adieu.

BARDOLPH.   It is a life that I have desired : I will thrive.[6]

PISTOL.   O base Hungarian wight! wilt thou the spigot wield?

          [*Exit* BARDOLPH.

NYM.   He was gotten in drink : is not the humour conceited?

FALSTAFF.   I am glad I am so acquit of this tinderbox : his thefts were too open ; his filching was like an unskilful singer ; he kept not time.

NYM.   The good humour is to steal at a minute's rest.

ACT I, SC. II
SCENE II
A room in the Garter Inn

[1] FALSTAFF *discovered seated in chair over* L. *and on* L. *of table.* ROBIN *sits on a chest up* C., *looking out of window. At table on* R. *sit* BARDOLPH *at top, and below him on his* R. PISTOL ; *below* PISTOL, NYM. *Host watches them play dice standing up by* BARDOLPH. FALSTAFF *has his hat on the table, and his staff.*

[2] *Comes* C. *to* FALSTAFF.
[3] *Turns and looks at them all three before making his choice.* BARDOLPH *is very pleased with the choice.*

[4] *Up and off* R.
[5] BARDOLPH *rises and comes* C.

[6] *Turns up* R. *and feels inclined to make a rude remark to* PISTOL, *but pulls a face instead and with a grin exits off* R.

B

ACT I, SC. II

[1] FALSTAFF *beckons to them and they come across to him.* PISTOL *comes up behind* FALSTAFF'S *chair and leans over behind it on the left corner,* NYM *sits on table facing fire.*
[2] *Laugh from both.*

PISTOL. "Convey," the wise it call. "Steal!" foh! a fico for the phrase!

FALSTAFF. Well, sirs, I am almost out at heels.

PISTOL. Why, then, let kibes ensue.

FALSTAFF. There is no remedy ; I must cony-catch ; I must shift.

PISTOL. Young ravens must have food.

[1] FALSTAFF. Which of you know Ford of this town?

PISTOL. I ken the wight : he is of substance good.

FALSTAFF. My honest lads, I will tell you what I am about.

PISTOL. Two yards and more.[2]

FALSTAFF. No quips now, Pistol! Indeed, I am in the waist two yards about ; but I am now about no waste ; I am about thrift. Briefly, I do mean to make love to Ford's wife : I spy entertainment in her ; she discourses, she carves, she gives the leer of invitation : I can construe the action of her familiar style ; and the hardest voice of her behaviour, to be Englished rightly, is, "I am Sir John Falstaff's."

PISTOL. He hath studied her will, and translated her will, out of honesty into English.

NYM. [The anchor is deep : will that humour pass?]

FALSTAFF. Now, the report goes she has all the rule of her husband's purse ; he hath a legion of angels.

PISTOL. As many devils entertain ; and "To her, boy," say I.

NYM. The humour rises ; it is good : humour me the angels.

FALSTAFF. I have writ me here a letter to her : and here another to Page's wife, who even now gave me good eyes too, examined my parts with most judicious œillades ; sometimes the beam of her view gilded my foot, sometimes my portly belly.

PISTOL. Then did the sun on dunghill shine.

NYM. I thank thee for that humour.

FALSTAFF. O, she did so course o'er my exteriors with such a greedy intention, that the appetite of her eye did seem to scorch me up like a burning-glass! Here's another letter to her : she bears the purse too ; she is a region in Guiana, all gold and bounty. [I will be cheater to them both, and they shall be exchequers to me] ; they shall be my East and West Indies, and I will trade to them both.[3] Go bear thou this letter to Mistress Page ; and thou this to Mistress Ford : [4] we will thrive, lads, we will thrive.

[5] PISTOL. Shall I Sir Pandarus of Troy become,
And by my side wear steel? then, Lucifer take all! [6]

NYM. I will run no base humour : [7] here, take the humour-letter : [8] I will keep the haviour of reputation.[9]

FALSTAFF [*to* ROBIN]. Hold, sirrah [10] bear you these letters tightly ; Sail like my pinnace to these golden shores.[11]
[12] Rogues, hence, avaunt! vanish like hailstones, go ; [13]
[14] Trudge, plod away o' the hoof ; seek shelter, pack!
Falstaff will learn the humour of the age,[15]
[16] French thrift, you rogues ; myself and skirted page.

[*Exeunt* FALSTAFF *and* ROBIN.

[17] PISTOL. Let vultures gripe thy guts! for gourd and fullam holds,
And high and low beguiles the rich and poor :
Tester I'll have in pouch when thou shalt lack,
[18] Base Phrygian Turk!

[19] NYM. I have operations which be humours of revenge.

PISTOL. Wilt thou revenge?

NYM. By welkin and her star!

PISTOL. With wit or steel?

[3] FALSTAFF *rises.* PISTOL *comes down on his* L. *and receives the first letter, and* NYM, *being on his* R., *the second.*
[4] FALSTAFF *crosses to* C., *whilst the two read the addresses.*
[5] PISTOL *comes up to* FALSTAFF.
[6] *On the last word he finishes his flourish with the letter held up above his head and then very grandly throws it down at* FALSTAFF'S *feet and struts in front of him across* R.
[7] *Throws the letter down and runs across* FALSTAFF.
[8] *Turns and speaks to* FALSTAFF *from* R.
[9] *Moves over to* PISTOL R.
[10] ROBIN *comes down from bench up* C., *and picks up the letters.*
[11] ROBIN *runs off* R.
[12] FALSTAFF *moves over to them with threatening gestures. They crouch behind table.*
[13] *Turns up* R.
[14] *Turns round on them again.*
[15] *Turns up to make exit.*
[16] *Turns to them for final line and exit.*
[17] *Runs up* C.; *bawls this out after* FALSTAFF.
[18] *Comes down* L. *and sits in exaggerated pose of fury and meditation on front of table, facing audience.*
[19] NYM *swiftly runs over to* L. *Both play quickly and intensely.*

NYM. With both the humours, I :
I will discuss the humour of this love to Page.

 PISTOL. And I to Ford shall eke unfold
    How Falstaff, varlet vile,
   His dove will prove, his gold will hold,
    And his soft couch defile.

 NYM. My humour shall not cool : I will incense Page to deal with poison ; I will possess him with [1] yellowness, for the revolt of mine is dangerous : that is my true humour.

 PISTOL.[2] **Thou art the Mars of malecontents : I** [3] **second thee ;** [4] **troop on.**[5]   [*Exeunt.*

[1] *This speech gives* PISTOL *great satisfaction, who registers every point with growing glee, which culminates in his own speech.*
[2] *Rise.*
[3] *Brings his hand with a big sweep and smack to meet* NYM'S.
[4] *With big gesture point off* R.
[5] *They go off, arm in arm. Curtain as they go up, and music during the change.*

ILLUSTRATION No. 3
Act I, Scene III

ACT I, SC. III
SCENE III

A room in DOCTOR CAIUS'S *house*
[1] RUGBY *discovered over* L. *seated on stool dozing.* *Enter* QUICKLY *from* R. *followed by* SIMPLE.

[2] RUGBY *starts up thinking it to be* CAIUS.

[3] *Runs over* R., *but does not exit.*

[4] RUGBY'S *face brightens and he exits* R.

SCENE III

[1] *A room in* DOCTOR CAIUS'S *house.*

Enter MISTRESS QUICKLY, *and* SIMPLE.

QUICKLY. What, John Rugby! [2] I pray thee, go to the casement, and see if you can see my master, Master Doctor Caius, coming. If he do, i' faith, and find any body in the house, here will be an old abusing of God's patience and the king's English.

[3] RUGBY. I'll go watch.

QUICKLY. Go ; and we'll have a posset for 't soon at night, in faith, at the latter end of a sea-coal fire.[4] [*Exit* RUGBY.] An honest, willing, kind fellow, as ever servant shall come in house withal, and, I warrant you, no tell-tale nor no breed-bate : his worst fault is, that he is given to prayer ; he is something peevish that way : but nobody but has his fault ; but let that pass. Peter Simple, you say your name is?

SIMPLE. Ay, for fault of a better.

QUICKLY. And Master Slender's your master?

SIMPLE. Ay, forsooth.

QUICKLY. Does he not wear a great round beard, like a glover's paring-knife?

SIMPLE. No, forsooth : he hath but a little wee face, with a little yellow beard, a Cain-coloured beard.

QUICKLY. A softly-sprighted man, is he not?

SIMPLE. Ay, forsooth : but he is as tall a man of his hands as any is between this and his head ; he hath fought with a warrener.

QUICKLY. How say you? O, I should remember him : does he not hold up his head, as it were, and strut in his gait?

SIMPLE. Yes, indeed, does he.

QUICKLY. Well, heaven send Anne Page no worse fortune! Tell Master Parson Evans I will do what I can for your master : Anne is a good girl, and I wish—

Re-enter RUGBY.[1]

RUGBY. Out, alas! here comes my master.

QUICKLY. We shall all be shent. Run in here,[2] good young man ; go into this closet : he will not stay long. [*Shuts* SIMPLE *in the closet.*] What, John Rugby! John! what, John, I say! Go, John, go [3] inquire for my master ; I doubt he be not well, that he comes not home.

[*Singing*] And down, down, adown-a, etc.[4]

Enter DOCTOR CAIUS.[5]

CAIUS. Vat is you sing? I do not like des toys.[6] Pray you, go and vetch me in my closet un boitier vert, a box, a green-a box : [7] do intend vat I speak? a green-a box.

QUICKLY.[8] Ay, forsooth ; I'll fetch it you.[9] [*Aside.*] I am glad he went not in himself : if he had found the young man, he would have been horn-mad.

[10] CAIUS. Fe, fe, fe, fe! ma foi, il fait fort chaud. Je m'en vais a la cour—la grande affaire.[11]

[12] QUICKLY. Is it this, sir?

[13] CAIUS. Oui ; mette le au mon pocket : depeche, quickly. Vere is dat knave Rugby?

[14] QUICKLY. What, John Rugby! John!

[15] RUGBY. Here, sir!

CAIUS. You are John Rugby, and you are Jack Rugby.[16] Come, take-a your rapier, and come after my heel to the court.

RUGBY. 'Tis ready, sir, here in the porch.

CAIUS. By my trot, I tarry too long.[17] Od's me! Qu'ai-j'oublie! dere is some simples in my closet,[18] dat I vill not for the varld I shall leave behind.[19]

QUICKLY. Ay me, he'll find the young man there, and be mad!

CAIUS. O diable, diable! vat is in my closet? Villain! larron! [*Pulling* [20] SIMPLE *out.*] Rugby, my rapier! [21]

QUICKLY. Good master, be content.

CAIUS. Wherefore shall I be content-a?

QUICKLY. The young man is an honest man.

CAIUS.[22] What shall de honest man do in my closet? dere is no honest man dat shall come in my closet.

QUICKLY. I beseech you, be not so phlegmatic. Hear the truth of it : he came of an errand to me from Parson Hugh.

CAIUS. Vell.

SIMPLE. Ay, forsooth ; to desire her to—

QUICKLY. Peace, I pray you.

CAIUS. Peace-a your tongue. Speak-a your tale.

SIMPLE.[23] To desire this honest gentlewoman, your maid, to speak a good word to Mistress Anne Page for my master in the way of marriage.

QUICKLY. This is all, indeed, la! but I'll ne'er put my finger in the fire, and need not.

[1] *Enter* RUGBY *very excitedly from* R.

[2] *Takes* SIMPLE, *who is on her* R., *and pushes him off* L.

[3] *Spoken with affected concern. They both live in terror of the doctor and this must be evidenced throughout the scene. It makes for comedy.*
[4] *Quickly moves up to window looking out.* RUGBY *stands* R.C. *very nervous. After a moment, enter* CAIUS.
[5] *She drops a curtesy. He comes and speaks right into her face.*
[6] *Triflings. The allusion is to her not having anything better to do than singing.*
[7] *She does not move, thinking of* SIMPLE *in the closet!*

[8] *Suddenly pulls herself together and curtseys and moves over* L.
[9] *Stops and turns to audience.*

[10] *Moves over* R. *and back to* C. CAIUS *is hardly ever still. As he speaks,* SIMPLE *nods his head in a wooden way, answering "yes" in his nod.*
[11] *Brings* CAIUS C.
[12] *Re-enter from* L. *and with great anxiety that it should be the one.*
[13] MRS. QUICKLY *puts it in his pouch.*
[14] *Spoken very sharply.*
[15] *Spoken with a tremor of fear as he advances.*
[16] *Of course, they laugh at his little joke very nervously, hoping it is the right thing to do. Also* SIMPLE *is in the closet.*
[17] *Moves to go off* R., *passes* RUGBY. *Then stops and turns.*
[18] *Emphasize "closet." Both the servants look scared.*
[19] *Crosses and exits* L. *Both the others put their fingers to their ears and wait. Squeals heard off* L. *and then* CAIUS *appears dragging on* SIMPLE *by up-stage ear and throat, after his first line, which is heard off.*
[20] *Appears pulling out* SIMPLE *as described. They come* L. C. *where* CAIUS *draws* RUGBY *round to* R.
[21] RUGBY *rushes out* R. *for rapier and returns standing beside* QUICKLY, *who waves him with her hand to stay there and not be seen, while she is talking.*
[22] *Still holding his ear.*

[23] *Very much out of breath and frightened for his life.*

ACT I, SC. III

[1] *Very big.*
[2] RUGBY *jumps forward ready to deliver the rapier, but it is paper he asks for.*
[3] CAIUS *goes to exit* L. *Stops and turns.*
[4] *Exit* L. RUGBY *rushes off* R. *at the order and almost instantaneously re-appears with paper and without the rapier, and runs very quickly across and off* L.
[5] QUICKLY *draws* SIMPLE, *who is like a jelly and not altogether helped by* RUGBY'S *swift excursions, over to* C.
[6] SIMPLE'S *eyes almost drop out of his head at this remark.*

[7] *A blank look from* SIMPLE.

[8] RUGBY *comes out.* QUICKLY *and* SIMPLE *stand back.*
[9] SIMPLE *shrivels as this is hurled at him.*
[10] *Another terrifying effort on the part of* CAIUS *and with a general success.*
[11] SIMPLE *can't move.*
[12] *He goes up to* SIMPLE *and puts his face right up to his.* SIMPLE *turns his head slowly, sees the face, and bolts. This pleases* CAIUS.

[13] CAIUS *crosses to* R.

[14] RUGBY *crosses to him.*
[15] *This is said moving up to him and looking at him so as to cause* RUGBY *to back.*
[16] *Emphasize "follow." Turns sharply and exits swiftly, followed by* RUGBY.
[17] *Moves over after him to* R.
[18] *Spoken to audience.*

[19] *From behind cloth* L.
[20] *Goes up to window and opens it.*

[21] *Comes to window from* L.

[1] CAIUS. Sir Hugh send-a you? [2] Rugby, baille me some paper.[3] Tarry you a little-a while.[4]   [*Writes.*

QUICKLY [5] [*aside to* SIMPLE]. I am glad he is so quiet[6] : if he had been thoroughly moved, you should have heard him so loud and so melancholy. But notwithstanding, man, I'll do you your master what good I can : and the very yea and the no is, the French doctor, my master,—I may call him my master, look you, for I keep his house ; and I wash, wring, brew, bake, scour, dress meat and drink, make the beds, and do all myself,—

SIMPLE [*aside to* QUICKLY]. 'Tis a great charge to come under one body's hand.

QUICKLY [*aside to* SIMPLE]. Are you avised o' that? you shall find it a great charge : and to be up early and down late ; but notwithstanding,—to tell you in your ear ; I would have no words of it,—my master himself is in love with Mistress Anne Page :[7] but notwithstanding that, I know Anne's mind,—that's neither here nor there.[8]

CAIUS. You jack'nape,[9] gives a this letter to Sir Hugh ; by gar, it is a shallenge[10] : I will cut his troat in de park ; and I will teach a scurvy jack-a-nape priest to meddle or make. You may be gone,[11] it is not good [12] you tarry here. [By gar, he shall not have a stone to throw at his dog.]   [*Exit* SIMPLE.

QUICKLY. Alas, he speaks but for his friend.

CAIUS. It is no matter-a ver dat : do not you tell-a me dat I shall have Anne Page for myself? By gar, I vill kill de Jack priest ; and I have appointed mine host of de Jarteer to measure our weapon.[13] By gar, I will myself have Anne Page.

QUICKLY. Sir, the maid loves you, and all shall be well. We must give folks leave to prate : what, the good-jer!

CAIUS. Rugby, come to the court with me.[14] By gar, if I have not Anne Page, I shall turn your head out of my door.[15] Follow [16] my heels, Rugby.   [*Exeunt* CAIUS *and* RUGBY.

QUICKLY.[17] You shall have An fool's-head of your own.[18] No, I know Anne's mind for that : never a woman in Windsor knows more of Anne's mind than I do ; nor can do more than I do with her, I thank heaven.

FENTON [*within*]. Who's within there? ho! [19]

[20] QUICKLY. Who's there, I trow! Come near the house, I pray you.

Enter FENTON.[21]

FENTON. How now, good woman! how dost thou?

QUICKLY. The better that it pleases your good worship to ask.

FENTON. What news? how does pretty Mistress Anne?

QUICKLY. In truth, sir, and she is pretty, and honest, and gentle ; and one that is your friend, I can tell you that by the way ; I praise heaven for it.

FENTON. Shall I do any good, thinkest thou? shall I not lose my suit?

QUICKLY. Troth, sir, all is in his hands above : but notwithstanding, Master Fenton, I'll be sworn on a book, she loves you. Have not your worship a wart above your eye?

FENTON. Yes, marry, have I ; what of that?

QUICKLY. Well, thereby hangs a tale : good faith, it is such another Nan ; but, I detest, an honest maid as ever broke bread : we had an hour's talk of that wart. I shall never laugh but in that maid's company! But indeed she is given too much to allicholy and musing : but for you—well, go to.

FENTON. Well, I shall see her to-day. Hold, there's money for thee ; let me have thy voice in my behalf : if thou seest her before me, commend me.

QUICKLY. Will I? i' faith, that we will ; and I will tell your worship more of the wart the next time we have confidence ; and of other wooers.

FENTON. Well, farewell ; I am in great haste now.

QUICKLY. Farewell to your worship. [*Exit* FENTON.] [1] Truly, an honest gentleman : but Anne loves him not ; for I know Anne's mind as well as another does. Out upon 't! what have I forgot? [2]
[*Exit.*

[1] *Closing window.*

[2] *Going off* R.
*Music swells up at her exit and continues
during the change.*

SCENE IV
Before PAGE'S *house
See Illustration No. 1, p. 1.*

[3] *Enter from house and come* C.

SCENE IV

Before PAGE'S *house.* [3]

Enter MISTRESS PAGE, *with a letter.*

MRS. PAGE.   What, have I 'scaped love-letters in the holiday-time of my beauty, and am I now a subject for them? Let me see. [*Reads.*
" *Ask me no reason why I love you ; for though Love use Reason for his physician, he admits not for his counsellor. You are not young, no more am I ; go to then, there's sympathy : you are merry, so am I ; ha, ha ! then there's more sympathy : you love sack, and so do I ; would you desire better sympathy ? Let it suffice thee, Mistress Page,—at the least, if the love of soldier can suffice,—that I love thee. I will not say, pity me ; 'tis not a soldier-like phrase : but I say, love me. By me,*

> *Thine own true knight,*
> *By day or night,*
> *Or any kind of light,*
> *With all his might*
> *For thee to fight,* JOHN FALSTAFF."

What a Herod of Jewry is this! O wicked, wicked world! One that is well-nigh worn to pieces with age to show himself a young gallant! What an unweighed behaviour hath this Flemish drunkard picked— with the devil's name!—out of my conversation, that he dares in this manner assay me? Why, he hath not been thrice in my company! What should I say to him? I was then frugal of my mirth : Heaven forgive me! Why, I'll exhibit a bill in the parliament for the putting down of men. How shall I be revenged on him? for revenged I will be, as sure as [his guts are made of puddings.]

Enter MISTRESS FORD. [4]

MRS. FORD.   Mistress Page! trust me, I was going to your house.

MRS. PAGE.   And, trust me, I was coming to you. You look very ill.

MRS. FORD.   Nay, I'll ne'er believe that ; I have to show to the contrary.

MRS. PAGE.   Faith, but you do, in my mind.

MRS. FORD.   Well, I do then ; yet I say I could show you to the contrary. O Mistress Page, give me some counsel!

MRS. PAGE.   What's the matter, woman?

MRS. FORD.   O woman, if it were not for one trifling respect, I could come to such honour!

ACT I, SC. IV

[1] MRS. PAGE *curtesys.*

[2] RS. FORD *hands her letter to* MRS. PAGE.

[3] MRS. PAGE *must make a point of this.*

[4] *Hands her letter to* MRS. FORD. *It does not take long for her to realize that they are identical.*

[5] *Move over* R.
[6] *Turns and looks off* L.

[7] *Off through arch* R.

[8] *From up* L. FORD *and* PISTOL *come down* R. PISTOL *being on* FORD'S L. PAGE *and* NYM *remain up* L., *having come on just after and not with the others.* NYM *is on* PAGE'S L.

MRS. PAGE. Hang the trifle, woman! take the honour. What is it? dispense with trifles; what is it?

MRS. FORD. If I would but go to hell for an eternal moment or so, I could be knighted.

MRS. PAGE. What? thou liest! Sir Alice Ford! [1] [These knights will hack; and so thou shouldst not alter the article of thy gentry.]

MRS. FORD. We burn daylight [2]: here, read, read; perceive how I might be knighted. I shall think the worse of fat men, as long as I have an eye to make difference of men's liking: and yet he would not swear; praised women's modesty; and gave such orderly and well-behaved reproof to all uncomeliness, that I would have sworn his disposition would have gone to the truth of his words; but they do no more adhere and keep place together than the Hundredth Psalm to the tune of "Green Sleeves." [What tempest, I trow, threw this whale, with so many tuns of oil in his belly, ashore at Windsor?] How shall I be revenged on him? I think the best way were to entertain him with hope, till the wicked fire of lust have melted him in his own grease. Did you ever hear the like?

[3] MRS. PAGE. Letter for letter, but that the name of Page and Ford differs! To thy great comfort in this mystery of ill opinions, here's the twin-brother [4] of thy letter: [but let thine inherit first; for, I protest, mine never shall.] I warrant he hath a thousand of these letters, writ with blank space for different names,—[sure, more,—and these are of the second edition: he will print them, out of doubt; for he cares not what he puts into the press, when he would put us two. I had rather be a giantess, and lie under Mount Pelion. Well, I will find you twenty lascivious turtles ere one chaste man.]

MRS. FORD. Why, this is the very same; the very hand, the very words. What doth he think of us?

MRS. PAGE. Nay, I know not: it makes me almost ready to wrangle with mine own honesty. [I'll entertain myself like one that I am not acquainted withal; for, sure, unless he know some strain in me, that I know not myself, he would never have boarded me in this fury.

MRS. FORD. "Boarding," call you it? I'll be sure to keep him above deck.

MRS. PAGE. So will I: if he come under my hatches, I'll never to sea again.] Let's be revenged on him: let's appoint him a meeting; give him a show of comfort in his suit and lead him on with a fine-baited delay, till he hath pawned his horses to mine host of the Garter.

MRS. FORD. Nay, I will consent to act any villany against him, that may not sully the chariness of our honesty. O, that my husband saw this [5] letter! it would give eternal food to his jealousy.

[6] MRS. PAGE. Why, look where he comes; and my good man too: he's as far from jealousy as I am from giving him cause; and that I hope is an unmeasurable distance.

MRS. FORD. You are the happier woman.

MRS. PAGE. Let's consult together against this greasy knight. Come hither. [*They retire.* [7]]

Enter FORD *with* PISTOL, *and* PAGE *with* NYM. [8]

FORD. Well, I hope it be not so.

PISTOL. Hope is a curtal dog in some affairs:
Sir John affects thy wife.

FORD. Why, sir, my wife is not young.

PISTOL.   He wooes both high and low, both rich and poor,
Both young and old, one with another, Ford ;
He loves the gallimaufry : Ford, perpend.

FORD.   Love my wife!

PISTOL.   With liver burning hot.   Prevent, or go thou,
Like Sir Actæon he, with Ringwood at thy heels :
[O, odious is the name!

FORD.   What name, sir?

PISTOL.   The horn, I say.]   Farewell.
Take heed, have open eye, for thieves do foot by night :
Take heed, ere summer comes or cuckoo-birds do sing.
[1] Away, Sir Corporal Nym!
Believe it, Page ; he speaks sense.   [*Exit.*

FORD [*aside*].   I will be patient ; I will find out this.[2]

[3] NYM [*to* PAGE].   And this is true ; I like not the humour of
lying.   He hath wronged me in some humours : I should have
borne the humoured letter to her ; but I have a sword and it shall
bite upon my necessity.   He loves your wife ; there's the short
and the long.   My name is Corporal Nym ; I speak and I avouch ;
'tis true : my name is Nym and Falstaff loves your wife.   [4] Adieu.
[5] I love not the humour of bread and cheese, and there's the humour
of it.   Adieu.   [*Exit.*

[6] PAGE.   "The humour of it," quoth a'! here's a fellow frights
English out of his wits.

FORD.   I will seek out Falstaff.

[7] PAGE.   I never heard such a drawling, affecting rogue.

FORD.   If I do find it : well.

PAGE.   I will not believe such a Cataian, though [8] the priest o'
the town commended him for a true man.

[9] FORD.   'Twas a good sensible fellow : well.

PAGE.   How now, Meg!
                    [MRS. PAGE *and* MRS. FORD *come forward.*

[10] MRS. PAGE.   Whither go you, George?   Hark you.

[11] MRS. FORD.   How now, sweet Frank! why art thou melancholy?

FORD.   I melancholy!   I am not melancholy.   Get you home, go.

MRS. FORD.   Faith, thou hast some crotchets in thy head.[12]   Now,
will you go, Mistress Page? [13]

MRS. PAGE.   Have with you.[14]   You'll come to dinner, George.
[*Aside to* MRS. FORD.]   Look who comes yonder : she shall be our
messenger to this paltry knight.

MRS. FORD [*aside to* MRS. PAGE].   Trust me, I thought on her :
she'll fit it.

Enter MISTRESS QUICKLY.

[15] MRS. PAGE.   You are come to see my daughter Anne?

QUICKLY.   Ay, forsooth ; and, I pray, how does good Mistress
Anne?

MRS. PAGE.   Go in with us and see : we have an hour's talk with
you.[16]
                    [*Exeunt* MRS. PAGE, MRS. FORD, *and* MRS. QUICKLY.

PAGE.   How now, Master Ford!

FORD.   You heard what this knave told me, did you not?

PAGE.   Yes : and you heard what the other told me?

FORD.   Do you think there is truth in them?

PAGE.   Hang 'em, slaves!   I do not think the knight would offer
it : but these that accuse him in his intent towards our wives are
a yoke of his discarded men ; very rogues, now they be out of service.

[1] *Turning up to* NYM.

[2] *Goes down* R. *and puts one foot on stone.*
PISTOL *exits up* L.

[3] *They come down to* C.

[4] *Going up* L.

[5] *Turns and speaks from up* L.

[6] PAGE *goes up* L. *laughing at* NYM.
FORD *is darkly meditating down* R.
*The two wives slip on and watch, rather
amused.*

[7] *Still looking after* NYM. *These lines
must be played rather quickly.*

[8] *Coming down at the end of his speech.*

[9] FORD *takes his foot down from stone and
turns as though he had quite made up
his mind.*

[10] *She comes forward to* PAGE. *They
stand talking together.*
[11] *Turns down to* FORD R.

[12] MRS. PAGE *leaves her husband to whom
she has been speaking about the letter
business.   He goes round to tree up* R.
looking down at FORD. *She comes
down* C.
[13] MRS. FORD *turns to her.*
[14] *They turn in together, and she speaks
her line to* PAGE *as they go up.   As
they are about to go in they see* MRS.
QUICKLY.   MRS. FORD *turns round to*
MRS. PAGE *at the door.*

[15] MRS. QUICKLY *enters from up* L. *and
comes to the two wives,* MRS. FORD R.,
MRS. PAGE C. *and* MRS. QUICKLY L.

[16] *Exit* MRS. PAGE *first and then* MRS. FORD
takes QUICKLY'S *arm and they go in,
having paused for a moment whilst* MRS.
FORD *whispers something in* QUICKLY'S
ear, at which they both laugh. PAGE,
*who has been watching and knows what
is hatching, quietly enjoys it all.   He
comes down to* FORD *on his line.* FORD
*has been involved in dark doubts.   This
scene must be played with the contrast
in character between the two men ; the
one jovial, open and honest ; the other
nettled by jealousy and suspicion.*

[1] *Laughing off stage up* L.

[2] *Enters up* L.

[3] *Turns and beckons to* SHALLOW.

[4] HOST *goes across the stage laughing as* PAGE *goes up to greet* SHALLOW.

[5] *Comes to* R. *of* PAGE, *who has come down stage* R.C.

[6] *Takes him up* R.

[7] *They go up to the door of the house, whilst the others come down* R.

[8] *Coming down and across* L.

[9] *During this speech* PAGE *and* SHALLOW *move over to* R.C. *They have been discussing Evans who lives just off* R. *and they are going to see him about the fight.* PAGE *will be* R. *and* SHALLOW *on his* L.

[10] *Making cuts with his sword that look dangerous if prolonged.*

[11] *Exeunt through arch* R. *laughing and* SHALLOW *still active with his sword-stick.*
[12] FORD *is over* L.C. *He goes up* C. *and looks after* PAGE *as he begins his speech.*

[13] *Going up* L.
[14] *Stop and turn front.*
Music to strike up at end of scene for change.

FORD. Were they his men?

PAGE. Marry, were they.

FORD. I like it never the better for that. Does he lie at the Garter?

PAGE. Ay, marry, does he. If he should intend this voyage towards my wife, I would turn her loose to him ; and what he gets more of her than sharp words, let it lie on my head.

FORD. I do not misdoubt my wife ; but I would be loath to turn them together. A man may be too confident : I would have nothing lie on my head : I cannot be thus satisfied.[1]

PAGE. Look where my ranting host of the Garter comes : there is either liquor in his pate or money in his purse when he looks so merrily.

Enter HOST.[2]

How now, mine host!

HOST. How now, bully-rook! thou'rt a gentleman.[3] Cavaleiro-justice, I say!

Enter SHALLOW.[4]

SHALLOW. I follow, mine host, I follow. Good even and twenty, good Master Page! Master Page, will you go with us? we have sport in hand.

HOST.[5] Tell him, cavaleiro-justice ; tell him, bully-rook.

SHALLOW. Sir, there is a fray to be fought between Sir Hugh the Welsh priest and Caius the French doctor.

FORD. Good mine host o' the Garter, a word with you.[6]
                                                [Drawing him aside.

HOST. What sayest thou, my bully-rook?

SHALLOW [*to* PAGE]. Will you go with us to behold it? My merry host hath had the measuring of their weapons ; and, I think, hath appointed them contrary places ; for, believe me, I hear the parson is no jester. Hark! I will tell you what our sport shall be.[7]
                                                [They converse apart.

HOST. Hast thou no suit against my knight, my guest-cavaleire?[8]

[9] FORD. None, I protest : but I'll give you a pottle of burnt sack to give me recourse to him and tell him my name is Brook ; only for a jest.

HOST. My hand, bully ; thou shalt have egress and regress ;—said I well?—and thy name shall be Brook. It is a merry knight. Will you go, An-heires?

SHALLOW. Have with you, mine host.

PAGE. I have heard the Frenchman hath good skill in his rapier.

SHALLOW. Tut, sir, I could have told you more. In these times you stand on distance, your passes, stoccadoes, and I know not what : 'tis the heart, Master Page ; 'tis here, 'tis here. I have seen the time, with my long sword I would have made you [10] four tall fellows skip like rats.

HOST. Here, boys, here, here! shall we wag?

PAGE. Have with you. I had rather hear them scold than fight.
                                    [11] [*Exeunt* HOST, SHALLOW *and* PAGE.

[12] FORD. Though Page be a secure fool, and stands so firmly on his wife's frailty, yet I cannot put off my opinion so easily : she was in his company at Page's house ; and what they made there, I know not. Well, I [13] will look further into 'it : [14] and I have a disguise to sound Falstaff. If I find her honest, I lose not my labour ; if she be otherwise, 'tis labour well bestowed.   [*Exit.*

SCENE V

A room in the Garter Inn.[1]

FALSTAFF.[2] I will not lend thee a penny.

PISTOL.[3] Why, then the world's mine oyster,
Which I with sword will open.

FALSTAFF.[4] Not a penny. I have been content, sir, you should lay my countenance to pawn : I have grated upon my good friends for three reprieves for you and your coach-fellow Nym ; or else you had looked through the grate, like a geminy of baboons. I am damned in hell for swearing to gentlemen my friends, you were good soldiers and tall fellows ; and when Mrs. Bridget lost the handle of her fan, I took't upon mine honour thou hadst it not.

[5] PISTOL. Didst not thou share? hadst thou not fifteen pence?

FALSTAFF. Reason, you rogue, reason : thinkest thou I'll endanger my soul gratis? At a word, hang no more about me, I am no gibbet for you. Go. A short knife and a throng! To your manor of Pickthatch![6] Go. You'll not bear a letter for me, you rogue! you stand upon your honour. Why, thou unconfinable baseness, it is as much as I can do to keep the terms of my honour precise : I, I, I myself sometimes, leaving the fear of God on the left hand and hiding mine honour in my necessity, am fain to shuffle, to hedge and to lurch ; and yet you, rogue, will ensconce [7] your rags, your cat-a-mountain looks, your red-lattice phrases, and your bold-beating oaths under the shelter of your honour! You will not do it, you! [8]

PISTOL. I do relent : what would thou more of man?

Enter ROBIN.[9]

ROBIN. Sir, here's a woman would speak with you.

FALSTAFF. Let her approach.[10]

Enter MISTRESS QUICKLY.

QUICKLY. Give your worship good morrow.

FALSTAFF. Good morrow, good wife.

QUICKLY. Not so, an't please your worship.

FALSTAFF. Good maid, then.

QUICKLY. I'll be sworn,
As my mother was, the first hour I was born.

FALSTAFF. I do believe the swearer. What with me?

QUICKLY. Shall I vouchsafe your worship a word or two?

FALSTAFF. Two thousand, fair woman : and I'll vouchsafe thee the hearing.

QUICKLY. There is one Mistress Ford, sir : [11]—I pray, come a little nearer this ways :—I myself dwell with Master Doctor Caius,—

FALSTAFF. Well, on : Mistress Ford, you say,—

QUICKLY. Your worship says very true : [12] I pray your worship, come a little nearer this ways.

[13] FALSTAFF. I warrant thee, nobody hears ; mine own people, mine own people.

QUICKLY. Are they so? God bless them and make them his servants!

FALSTAFF. Well, Mistress Ford ; what of her?

QUICKLY. Why, sir, she's a good creature. Lord, Lord! your worship's a wanton! Well, heaven forgive you and all of us, I pray!

FALSTAFF. Mistress Ford ; come, Mistress Ford,—

ACT I, SC. V

SCENE V

A room in the Garter Inn
See Illustration No. 2, p. 7.

[1] FALSTAFF *seated at* L. *of table over* L. *eating a pasty and drinking. He is facing* PISTOL *who sits* R. *of the table looking the picture of misery.*

[2] FALSTAFF *leans over the table and thumps this out as the definite conclusion of a preceding conversation.*

[3] *Rises and takes stage* C. *with his old swagger and announcing this desperate attempt upon the world's security, which, fortunately, the world does not hear, as the result of* FALSTAFF'S *meanness.*

[4] FALSTAFF *is not at all awed.* PISTOL'S *attempt collapses at once.*

[5] PISTOL *points this out to be the sufficient reason for* FALSTAFF'S *act of apparent kindness to his follower. And it is on this that the great comedy of* FALSTAFF'S *following line is built.*

[6] FALSTAFF *rises and advances to* PISTOL, *who stands trembling.*

[7] PISTOL, *getting more terrified, drops on his knees.*

[8] *Pushes him over with his foot.*

[9] ROBIN *runs on from up* R. *and comes down* L. *of* FALSTAFF. *The announcement of a lady interrupts* FALSTAFF'S *further pillorying of* PISTOL *and he goes over* L., *but keeps* R. *of table.*

[10] ROBIN *goes up to exit and beckons* QUICKLY *on. She comes down* R. *of* FALSTAFF. PISTOL *gets up and moves round the back to the other end of table, where he gets busy with the food.* ROBIN *comes down to top of table* R. *and sits on stool.*

[11] *At the mention of* MRS. FORD, PISTOL'S *head comes up with a jerk and this attracts* MRS. QUICKLY'S *attention. She takes* FALSTAFF *over* R. *At this* PISTOL *also goes over* R., *taking the food with him and sits at* L. *of table, and* ROBIN *on his right. This also* MRS. QUICKLY *sees, watching him go* L. *to* R. *and then turns and looks over her* R. *shoulder up at* PISTOL.

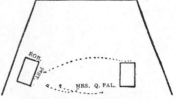

[12] *She then moves* FALSTAFF *back* L. *This rather annoys* FALSTAFF *and his line*

[13] *spoken with irritation.*

ACT I, SC. V

[1] PISTOL *is listening intently all the while.*

[2] *Emphasize " me."*

[3] FALSTAFF *now begins to take some interest in he conversation and utters a satisfied " Ah."*

[4] *Both laugh.*

[5] FALSTAFF *attempts to affect modesty, with a little " Oh !"*

[6] *Grunt from* FALSTAFF.

QUICKLY.[1] Marry, this is the short and the long of it ; you have brought her into such a canaries as 'tis wonderful. The best courtier of them all, when the court lay at Windsor, could never have brought her to such a canary. Yet there has been knights, and lords, and gentlemen, with their coaches, I warrant you, coach after coach, letter after letter, gift after gift ; smelling so sweetly, all musk, and so rushling, I warrant you, in silk and gold ; and in such alligant terms ; and in such wine and sugar of the best and the fairest, that would have won any woman's heart ; and, I warrant you, they could never get an eye-wink of her : I had myself twenty angels given me this morning ; but I defy all angels, in any such sort, as they say, but in the way of honesty : and, I warrant you, they could never get her so much as sip on a cup with the proudest of them all : and yet there has been earls, nay, which is more, pensioners ; but, I warrant you, all is one with her.

FALSTAFF. But what says she to me?[2] be brief, my good she-Murcury.

QUICKLY. Marry, she hath received your letter, for the which she thanks you a thousand times ; and she gives you to notify that her husband will be absence from his house between ten and eleven.[3]

FALSTAFF. Ten and eleven?

QUICKLY. Ay, forsooth ; and then you may come and see the picture, she says, that you wot of :[4] Master Ford, her husband, will be from home. Alas ! the sweet woman leads an ill life with him : he's a very jealousy man : she leads a very frampold life with him, good heart.

FALSTAFF. Ten and eleven. Woman, commend me to her ; I will not fail her.

QUICKLY. Why, you say well. But I have another messenger to your worship. Mistress Page hath her hearty commendations to you too : and let me tell you in your ear, she's as fartuous a civil modest wife, and one, I tell you, that will not miss you morning nor evening prayer, as any is in Windsor, whoe'er be the other : and she bade me tell your worship that her husband is seldom from home ; but she hopes there will come a time. I never knew a woman so dote upon a man : surely I think you have charms, la ;[5] yes, in truth.

FALSTAFF. Not I, I assure thee : setting the attraction of my good parts aside I have no other charms.

QUICKLY. Blessing on your heart for 't !

FALSTAFF. But, I pray thee, tell me this : has Ford's wife and Page's wife acquainted each other how they love me?

QUICKLY. That were a jest indeed ! they have not so little grace, I hope : that were a trick indeed ! But Mistress Page would desire you to send her your little page, of all loves : her husband has a marvellous infection to the little page ; and truly Master Page is an honest man. Never a wife in Windsor leads a better life than she does : do what she will, say what she will, take all, pay all, go to bed when she list, rise when she list, all is as she will : and truly she deserves it ; for if there be a kind woman in Windsor, she is one. You must send her your page ; no remedy.

FALSTAFF. Why, I will.

QUICKLY. Nay, but do so, then : and, look you, he may come and go between you both ; and in any case have a nay-word, that you may know one another's mind ; and the boy never need to understand any thing ; for 'tis not good that children should know any wickedness :[6] old folks, you know, have discretion, as they say, and know the world.

FALSTAFF. Fare thee well : commend me to them both : there's [1] my purse ; I am yet thy debtor. [2] Boy, go along with this woman. [*Exeunt* MISTRESS QUICKLY *and* ROBIN.] [3] This news distracts me!

PISTOL. This punk is one of Cupid's carriers : [4] [Clap on more sails ; pursue ; up with your fights : Give fire : she is my prize, or ocean whelm them all!]   [*Exit.*

FALSTAFF. Sayest thou so, old Jack? go thy ways ; I'll make more of thy old body than I have done. Will they yet look after thee? Wilt thou, after the expense of so much money, be now a gainer? Good body, I thank thee. Let them say 'tis grossly done ; so it be fairly done, no matter.

Enter BARDOLPH.[5]

BARDOLPH. Sir John, there's one Master Brook below would fain speak with you, and be acquainted with you ; and hath sent your worship a morning's draught of sack.

FALSTAFF. Brook is his name?

BARDOLPH. Ay, sir.

FALSTAFF. Call him in. [*Exit* BARDOLPH.] Such Brooks are welcome to me, that o'erflow such liquor. Ah, ha! Mistress Ford and Mistress Page, have I encompassed you? go to ; via!

Re-enter BARDOLPH, *with* FORD *disguised.*[6]

FORD. Bless you, sir!

FALSTAFF. And you, sir! Would you speak with me?

FORD. I make bold to press with so little preparation upon you.

FALSTAFF. You're welcome.[7] What's your will? Give us leave, drawer.   [*Exit* BARDOLPH.

FORD. Sir, I am a gentleman that have spent much : my name is Brook.

FALSTAFF. Good Master Brook, I desire more acquaintance of you.

FORD. Good Sir John, I sue for yours : not to charge you ; for I must let you understand I think myself in better plight for a lender than you are : the which hath something emboldened me to this unseasoned intrusion ; for they say, if money go before, all ways do lie open.

FALSTAFF. Money is a good soldier, sir, and will on.

FORD. Troth, and I have a bag of money here troubles me : if you will help me to bear it, Sir John, take all, or half, for easing me of the carriage.

FALSTAFF. Sir, I know not how I may deserve to be your porter.

FORD. I will tell you, sir, if you will give me the hearing.

FALSTAFF. Speak, good Master Brook : I shall be glad to be your servant.

FORD. Sir, I hear you are a scholar,—I will be brief with you,— and you have been a man long known to me, though I had never so good means, as desire, to make myself acquainted with you. I shall discover a thing to you, wherein I must very much lay open mine own imperfection : but, good Sir John, as you have one eye upon my follies, as you hear them unfolded, turn another into the register of your own ; that I may pass with a reproof the easier, sith you yourself know [8] how easy it is to be such an offender.

FALSTAFF. Very well, sir ; proceed.

FORD. There is a gentlewoman in this town ; her husband's name is Ford.

FALSTAFF.[9] Well, sir.

[1] *Look of amazement from* PISTOL *to see a purse given to* QUICKLY *when he was denied a penny. This resolves him to follow her and, in a few words, do a little blackmailing.*

[2] ROBIN *comes from his seat and exits with* QUICKLY *up* R.

[3] *Crossing back to his chair* L. *of table.*

[4] *Simultaneously* PISTOL *slinks up to the back ; mutters his final line and follows the others off* R.

[5] *From up* R. *with a pot which he hands to* FALSTAFF.

[6] *In a cloak and hood.*

[7] *Indicates to* FORD *to sit on stool* R. *of table.* BARDOLPH *exits up* R.

[8] *A veiled indictment of* FALSTAFF *by* FORD. *Play it with relish, but not too obviously.*

[9] FALSTAFF, *who is about to drink, suddenly stops.* FORD *watches him closely.*

ACT I, SC. V

[1] *Hinting to* FALSTAFF *that there is no satisfaction in the flights of love.*

[2] *Turning to him in mild amazement.*

[3] *Very flattered.*
[4] *At this point* FALSTAFF'S *hand must be on his knee. At the mention of money his hand begins to open and close.*
[5] *It comes up to the table but falls back on the arm of his chair, and at each successive " spends " he repeats the action until finally it gets to the table. When he does this,* FORD *keeps his hand on the bag.*

[6] FALSTAFF *begins to play with the money-bag which* FORD *has gently pushed over to him just previously.*

[7] *Takes the money and puts it in his wallet with a satisfied sigh.*
[8] *Rises and extends his hand to* FORD.

[9] *Very assured and crossing over to table* R. *for hat and stick.*
[10] *At table* R. *Says this with a laugh.*
[11] *Coming back to* FORD.

FORD. I have long loved her, and I protest to you, bestowed much on her ; followed her with a doting observance ; engrossed opportunities to meet her ; fee'd every slight occasion that could but niggardly give me sight of her ; not only bought many presents to give her, but have given largely to many to know what she would have given ; briefly, I have pursued her as love hath pursued me ; which hath been on the wing of all occasions. But whatsoever I have merited, either in my mind or in my means, meed, I am sure, I have received none ; unless experience be a jewel that I have [1] purchased at an infinite rate, and that hath taught me to say this :
" *Love like a shadow flies when substance love pursues ;*
    Pursuing that that flies, and flying what pursues."

FALSTAFF. Have you received no promise of satisfaction at her hands ?

FORD. Never.

FALSTAFF. Have you importuned her to such a purpose ?

FORD. Never.

FALSTAFF. Of what quality was your love, then ? [2]

FORD. Like a fair house built on another man's ground ; so that I have lost my edifice by mistaking the place where I erected it.

FALSTAFF. To what purpose have you unfolded this to me ?

FORD. When I have told you that, I have told you all. Some say, that though she appear honest to me, yet in other places she enlargeth her mirth so far that there is shrewd construction made of her. Now, Sir John, here is the heart of my purpose : you are a gentleman of excellent breeding, admirable discourse, of great admittance, authentic in your place and person, generally allowed for your many war-like, court-like, and learned preparations.

FALSTAFF. O, sir ! [3]

FORD. Believe it, for you know it. There is [4] money ; spend [5] it, spend it ; spend more ; spend all I have ; only give me so much of your time in exchange of it, as to lay an amiable siege to the honesty of this Ford's wife : use your art of wooing ; win her to consent to you ; if any man may, you may as soon as any.

FALSTAFF. Would it apply well to the vehemency of your affection, that I should win what you would enjoy ? Methinks you prescribe to yourself very preposterously.

FORD. O, understand my drift. She dwells so securely on the excellency of her honour, that the folly of my soul dares not present itself : she is too bright to be looked against. Now, could I come to her with any detection in my hand, my desires had instance and argument to commend themselves [6] : I could drive her then from the ward of her purity, her reputation, her marriage-vow, and a thousand other her defences, which now are too too strongly embattled against me. What say you to 't, Sir John ?

FALSTAFF. Master Brook, I will first make bold with [7] your money ; [8] next, give me your hand ; and last, as I am a gentleman, you shall, if you will, enjoy Ford's wife.

FORD. O good sir !

FALSTAFF. I say you shall. [9]

FORD. Want no money, Sir John ; you shall want none.

FALSTAFF. Want no Mistress Ford, [10] Master Brook ; you shall want none. [11] I shall be with her, I may tell you, by her own appointment ; even as you came in to me, her assistant or go-between parted from me. I say I shall be with her between ten and eleven ; for at that time the jealous rascally knave her husband will be forth. Come you to me at night ; you shall know how I speed.

FORD.   I am blest in your acquaintance.   Do you know Ford, sir?

FALSTAFF.   Hang him, poor [cuckoldly] knave!   I know him not : yet I wrong him to call him poor ; they say the jealous wittolly knave hath masses of money ; for the which his wife seems to me well-favoured.   I will use her as the key of the [cuckoldly] rogue's coffer ; and there's my harvest-home.

FORD.   I would you knew Ford, sir, that you might avoid him if you saw him.

FALSTAFF.   Hang him, mechanical salt-butter rogue!   I will stare him out of his wits ; I will awe him with my cudgel [1] : it shall hang like a meteor o'er the cuckold's horns.   Master Brook, thou shalt know I will predominate over the peasant, and thou shalt lie with his wife.   Come to me soon at night. [2]   Ford's a knave, and I will aggravate his style ; thou, Master Brook, shalt know him for knave and cuckold.   Come to me soon at night. [3]   [*Exit.*

FORD.   What a damned Epicurean rascal is this!   My heart is ready to crack with impatience.   Who says this is improvident jealousy?   my wife hath sent to him ; the hour is fixed ; the match is made.   Would any man have thought this?   See the hell of having a false woman!   My bed shall be abused, my coffers ransacked, my reputation gnawn at ; and I shall not only receive this villanous wrong, but stand under the adoption of abominable terms, and by him that does me this wrong.   Terms! names!   Amaimon sounds well ; Lucifer, well ; Barbason, well ; yet they are devils' additions, the names of fiends : but Cuckold! Wittol!—Cuckold! the devil himself hath not such a name.   Page is an ass, a secure ass : he will trust his wife ; he will not be jealous.   I will rather trust a Fleming with my butter, Parson Hugh the Welshman with my cheese, an Irishman with my aqua-vitæ bottle, or a thief to walk my ambling gelding, than my wife with herself ; then she plots, then she ruminates, then she devises ; and what they think in their hearts they may effect, they will break their hearts but they will effect.   God be praised for my jealousy!   Eleven o'clock the hour.   I will prevent this, detect my wife, be revenged on Falstaff, and laugh at Page. I will about it ; [4] better three hours too soon than a minute too late.   [Fie, fie, fie! cuckold! cuckold! cuckold!]   [*Exit.*

[1] *Lifting up his stick.*

[2] *Turns up* R. *a few steps.   Then stops and turns.*

[3] *Turns and goes off* R. *saying this.*

[4] *Going up* R.   *Then stop and turn. Music to play during the change and commencing on fall of curtain.*

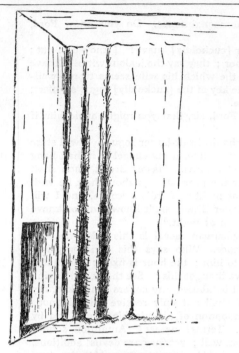

ILLUSTRATION No. 4

This scene stands for Act I, Scene VI, and Act II, Scenes I, III, VI and IX

ACT I, SC. VI
SCENE VI
A field near Windsor

[1] *Enter from* L. CAIUS *first with hands behind back, deep in thought.* RUGBY *follows.* CAIUS *comes* C. *and carries his sword behind him in his hands. It is unsheathed.*

SCENE VI

A field near Windsor.[1]

Enter CAIUS *and* RUGBY.

CAIUS. Jack Rugby!

RUGBY. Sir?

CAIUS. Vat is de clock, Jack?

RUGBY. 'Tis past the hour, sir, that Sir Hugh promised to meet.

CAIUS. By gar, he has save his soul, dat he is no come ; he has pray his Pible well, dat he is no come : by gar, Jack Rugby, he is dead already, if he be come.

RUGBY. He is wise, sir ; he knew your worship would kill him, if he came.

CAIUS. By gar, de herring is no dead so as I vill kill him. Take your rapier, Jack ; I vill tell you how I vill kill him.

[2] *Very frightened.*

[3] CAIUS *is about to draw* RUGBY'S *sword when the others come on.*

RUGBY. Alas, sir, I cannot fence.[2]

CAIUS. Villany, take your rapier.[3]

RUGBY. Forbear ; here's company.

[4] *Enter from* R. HOST *first, then* SHALLOW, PAGE, SLENDER.

Enter HOST, SHALLOW, SLENDER, *and* PAGE.[4]

HOST. Bless thee, bully doctor!

SHALLOW. Save you, Master Doctor Caius!

PAGE. Now, good master doctor!

SLENDER. Give you good morrow, sir.

CAIUS. Vat be all you, one, two, tree, four, come for?

[5] HOST *can, if desired, make the motions of these passes with sword which he takes from* CAIUS.

HOST. To see thee fight, to see thee foin, to see thee traverse ; to see thee here, to see thee there ; to see thee pass thy punto, thy stock, thy reverse,[5] thy distance, thy montant. Is he dead, my Ethiopian? is he dead, my Francisco? ha, bully! What says my

Æsculapius? my Galen? my heart of elder? ha! is he dead, bully stale? is he dead?

CAIUS.   By gar, he is de coward Jack priest of [1] de vorld ; he is not show his face.

HOST.   Thou art [a Castalion-King-Urinal.]   Hector of Greece, my boy! [2]

CAIUS.   I pray you, bear vitness that me have stay six or seven, two, tree hours for him, and he is no come.

SHALLOW.   He is the wiser man, master doctor : he is a curer of souls, and you a curer of bodies ; if you should fight, you go against the hair of your professions.   Is it not true, Master Page?

PAGE.   Master Shallow, you have yourself been a greater fighter, though now a man of peace.

SHALLOW.   Bodykins, Master Page, though I now be old and of the peace, if I see a sword out, my finger itches to make one.[3]   Though we are justices and doctors and churchmen, Master Page, we have some salt of our youth in us ; we are the sons of women, Master Page.

PAGE.   'Tis true, Master Shallow.

SHALLOW.   It will be found so, Master Page.[4]   Master Doctor Caius, I am come to fetch you home.   I am sworn of the peace : you have showed yourself a wise physician, and Sir Hugh hath shown himself a wise and patient churchman.   You must go with me, master doctor.

HOST.   Pardon, guest-justice.[5]   A word, Mounseur Mockwater.

CAIUS.   Mock-vater! vat is dat?

HOST.   Mock-water, in our English tongue, is valour, bully.

CAIUS.   By gar, den, I have as mush mock-vater as de Englishman. Scurvy jack-dog priest! by gar, me vill cut his ears.

HOST.   He will clapper-claw thee tightly, bully.

CAIUS.   Clapper-de-claw! vat is dat?

HOST.   That is, he will make thee amends.

CAIUS.   By gar, me do look he shall clapper-de-claw me ; for, by gar, me vill have it.

HOST.   And I will provoke him to't, or let him wag.

CAIUS.   Me tank you for dat.[6]

HOST.   And, moreover, bully,—but first, master guest, and Master Page, and eke Cavaleiro Slender, go you through the town to Frog-more.   [Aside to them.

PAGE.   Sir Hugh is there, is he?

HOST.   He is there : see what humour he is in ; and I will bring the doctor about by the fields.   Will it do well?

SHALLOW.   We will do it.

PAGE, SHALLOW, and SLENDER.   Adieu, good master doctor.[7]

            [Exeunt PAGE, SHALLOW, and SLENDER.[7]

CAIUS.[8]   By gar, me vill kill de priest ; for he speak for a jack-an-ape to Anne Page.

HOST.   Let him die : sheathe thy impatience, throw cold water on thy choler : go about the fields with me through Frogmore : I will bring thee where Mistress Anne Page is, at a farm-house a-feasting [9] : and thou shalt woo her.   Cried I aim?   said I well?

CAIUS.   By gar, me dank you for dat : by gar, I love you,[10] and I shall procure-a you de good guest, de earl, de knight, de lords, de gentlemen, my patients.

HOST.   For the which I will be thy adversary toward Anne Page. Said I well?

CAIUS.   By gar, 'tis good ; vell said.[11]

HOST.   Let us wag, then.[12]

CAIUS.   Come at my heels, Jack Rugby.   [Exeunt.

[1]   *Full of temperament.*

[2]   *Claps him on shoulder.*

[3]   *Is just going to throw himself into fighting attitude when* PAGE *soothes him.* CAIUS *and* HOST *busy discussing* EVANS' *absence.*

[4]   *Cross over to* CAIUS.

[5]   *Crossing* SHALLOW *to* CAIUS, *and taking him over* L.

[6]   *Laughs in a very satisfied way and turns to tell* RUGBY *how he will exact his "clapper-de-claw," at which* HOST *leaves him and turns to the others, speaking rapidly and softly.*

[7]   *Off* R.

[8]   *Turns to* HOST *as he comes over to him.*

[9]   *This puts* EVANS *out of his mind and sweetens him considerably.*

[10]   *Hug and kiss* HOST.

[11]   CAIUS *makes another attempt to kiss* HOST, *but does not succeed.*

[12]   HOST *crosses* L. *rather hurriedly, on his line.   Then* CAIUS *runs after him and hears a snigger from* RUGBY, *to whom he turns and becomes the master and doctor.*

C

ILLUSTRATION No. 5
Act I, Scene VII

ACT I, SC. VII
SCENE VII
A field near Frogmore

[1] EVANS *in doublet and hose, looking very fragile and cold, is seated on tree stump* L. ; *hands on his knees and face held between his hands.* SIMPLE *stands* C., *blowing his nails and also looking somewhat cold. They can both be a little red about the nose.*
[2] *Point off up* R.
[3] *Points behind him.*
[4] *Wide gesture.*
[5] *Points in front.*
[6] *Points off* L.

[7] *Off* L. *in front of* EVANS.

[8] *Rising, shivering and looking extremely miserable.*

[9] *Looking round for someone to come.*

[10] *Shivering with cold and fright. Moving* R.

[11] *Begins to walk about to warm both body and soul. Moving up to stile, stops singing as he looks over to see if he can see anybody, and resumes singing as he comes down to tree stump at* [12].

[13] *Sits on the tree-stump.*

[14] *As* SIMPLE *runs in down* L., EVANS *springs up and almost jumps to* C. *with hand on rapier, thinking it to be* CAIUS.

SCENE VII

A field near Frogmore.

EVANS.[1] I pray you now, good Master Slender's serving-man, and friend Simple by your name, which way have you looked for Master Caius, that calls himself doctor of physic?

SIMPLE. Marry, sir, the [2] pittie-ward, the [3] park-ward, [4] every way ; old Windsor-way,[5] and every way but the town way.[6]

EVANS. I most fehemently desire you you will also look that way.

SIMPLE. I will, sir.   [*Exit.*[7]

EVANS. 'Pless my soul, how full of chollors I am,[8] and trempling of mind ! I shall be glad if he have deceived me. How melancholies I am.[9] [I will knog his urinals about his knave's costard when I have good opportunities for the ork.] 'Pless my soul ![10]   [*Sings.*

> [11] *To shallow rivers, to whose falls*
> *Melodious birds sings madrigals ;*
> *There will we make our peds of roses,*[12]
> *And a thousand fragrant posies.*
> *To shallow—*

Mercy on me ! I have a great dispositions to cry.[13]   [*Sings.*

> *Melodious birds sing madrigals—*
> *When as I sat in Pabylon—*
> *And a thousand vagram posies.*
> *To shallow, etc.*

Re-enter SIMPLE.[14]

SIMPLE. Yonder he is coming, this way, Sir Hugh.

EVANS. He's welcome.[1]   [*Sings.*

[2] *To shallow rivers, to whose falls—*

[3] Heaven prosper the right! [4] What weapons is he?

SIMPLE. No weapons, sir.[5] There comes my master, Master Shallow, and another gentleman, from Frogmore, over the stile, this way.

[6] EVANS. Pray you, give me my gown ; or else keep it in your arms.

Enter PAGE, SHALLOW, *and* SLENDER.[7]

SHALLOW. How now, master Parson! Good morrow, good Sir Hugh. Keep a gamester from the dice, and a good student from his book, and it is wonderful.

SLENDER.[8] [*aside*]. Ah, sweet Anne Page!

PAGE.[9] 'Save you, good Sir Hugh!

EVANS. 'Pless you from his mercy sake, all of you!

SHALLOW. What, the sword and the word! do you study them both, master parson?

PAGE. And youthful still! in your doublet and hose this raw rheumatic day!

EVANS.[10] There is reasons and causes for it.

PAGE. We are come to you to do a good office, master parson.

EVANS. Fery well : what is it?

PAGE. Yonder is a most reverend gentleman, who, belike having received wrong by some person, is at most odds with his own gravity and patience that ever you saw.

SHALLOW. I have lived fourscore years and upward ; I never heard a man of his place, gravity and learning, so wide of his own respect.

EVANS. What is he?

PAGE. I think you know him ; Master Doctor Caius, the renowned French physician.

EVANS.[11] Got's will, and his passion of my heart! I had as lief you would tell me of a mess of porridge.

PAGE. Why?

EVANS.[12] He has no more knowledge in Hibocrates and Galen,—and he is a knave besides ; a cowardly knave as you would desires to be acquainted withal.[13]

PAGE. I warrant you, he's the man should fight with him.

SLENDER [*aside*]. O sweet Anne Page!

SHALLOW. It appears so by his weapons. Keep them asunder : here comes Doctor Caius.[14]

Enter HOST, CAIUS, *and* RUGBY.[15]

PAGE. Nay, good master parson, keep in your weapon.

SHALLOW. So do you, good master doctor.

HOST. Disarm them, and let them question : let them keep their limbs whole and hack our English.[16]

CAIUS. I pray you, let-a me speak a word with your ear. Wherefore vill you not meet-a me?

EVANS [*aside to* CAIUS]. Pray you, use your patience : in good time.

CAIUS. By gar, you are de coward,[17] de Jack dog,[18] John ape.

EVANS [*aside to* CAIUS]. Pray you, let us not be laughing-stocks to other men's humours ; I desire you in friendship, and I will one

[1] *Becomes limp in reaction.*

[2] *Commences to walk over* R.

[3] *Stops.*

[4] *Comes over to* RUGBY *who is* L. *and asks a fearful but necessary question.*

[5] *Sighs relieved. Others appear at stile.*

[6] *Takes the gown and gives it back on the next line.*

[7] EVANS *remains down* L. SHALLOW *comes down to him,* PAGE *a little later comes down* R.C., *and* SLENDER *remains seated on stile looking back in the direction from which they came, i.e. off* R.

[8] *On the stile sitting.* SIMPLE *retires up stage* C.

[9] *Coming down* R.C.

[10] *Comes between them.*

[11] *Very irate, cross* R. *and keep moving, and return up stage so that he arrives on a level with* PAGE *and on* PAGE'S R. *at* [12].

[13] *Moves up* R.C. *to hedge, very agitated. The dialogue between* PAGE *and* SHALLOW *is slipped in between* EVANS'S *walk up and back.*

[14] PAGE, *anticipating trouble, goes up* R. *behind* EVANS, *ready to seize him.* EVANS *arrives* R.C. *on this line, hears the line and makes to draw his sword. He is held by* PAGE *from behind.*

[15] *Enter from down* L. *in front of haystack.* HOST *enters, followed by* CAIUS *and* RUGBY. HOST *carries* CAIUS'S *rapier. As soon as* CAIUS *sees* EVANS *he lets out one yell, snatches the rapier from* HOST *and makes a dash at* EVANS, *but is held back by* HOST, *who slips behind him as he passes.* EVANS *is trying hard to get at his sword in sheer desperation.* CAIUS *is yelling and kicking;* SHALLOW *is trying to pacify him, going over to* CAIUS *receives a spit in the face intended for* EVANS. *The others are hanging on laughing.*

[16] SHALLOW *disarms* CAIUS *first, then goes over to* EVANS *and draws his sword out of his scabbard and takes it away. Then* PAGE *and* HOST *allow the two to come nearer, but still holding them. They let them get near enough so that their noses almost touch each other. The drawing near is mostly done by* CAIUS.

[17] *Right in* EVANS'S *face, and again on next phrase* [18] *and finally after the third, a spit. Though both are held firmly,* EVANS *does his best to get private talk with* CAIUS *and through all the abuse hurled against him.*

ACT I, SC. VII

[1] CAIUS *gives another spit. This rouses* EVANS.
[2] CAIUS *leaps into the air—free.*
[3] *Comes down to earth—gives another leap with a loud yell.* EVANS *collapses.* CAIUS *turns across to* RUGBY *excitedly, who also nearly collapses.*
[4] *Goes up to* L. *of* HOST, *who is laughing heartily.* PAGE *has released his hold of* EVANS. *As* CAIUS *yells* SHALLOW *has taken a step back.*
[5] *Brings* CAIUS C. *and reaches out for* EVANS, *whom he brings on his* R. HOST *puts his arm round the neck of each.*
[6] *Laughs.* EVANS *also, very feebly.*
[7] *Puts his* R. *hand out and takes* CAIUS's *hand.*
[8] *Takes* EVANS'S *hand with his left one.*
[9] *He draws their hands up in the air on "both" and enjoys the joke very much. They do not.*
[10] *Slapping them on their backs.*
[11] HOST *goes over to exit* L. *Turns at "Follow, follow, follow," goes off, followed by the others, laughing.* SLENDER *comes down off his stile, crosses over to the exit* L., *turns, and with a last fond look off over* R., *speaks his last line.*
[12] *Both are left looking at each other. When the others are off,* CAIUS *suddenly sees the situation and startles the audience with his remark.*
[13] *Shouts after* HOST. *His* ha, ha, ha! *is a mocking laughing and full of anything but humour.*
[14] EVANS *meekly goes up to him, very glad to be able to share a common grievance with him.*
[15] *They embrace, and* EVANS *is very happy indeed.* CAIUS *is* L., EVANS R.
[16] *Now, feeling very warlike, he almost rushes across* CAIUS *as though to pursue* HOST. *Then turns and invites the doctor to see him do it.*
The scene closes with lively music, which swells up as curtain falls.

way or other make you amends.[1] [*Aloud.*]   I will knog your knave's cogscomb for missing your meetings and appointments.

CAIUS.[2]   Diable![3]   Jack Rugby,[4] mine host de Jarteer,—have I not stay for him to kill him? have I not, at de place I did appoint?

EVANS.   As I am a Christians soul now, look you, this is the place appointed : I'll be judgement by mine host of the Garter.

[5] HOST.   Peace, I say, Gallia and Gaul, French and Welsh, soul-curer and body-curer!

CAIUS.   Ay, dat is very good ; excellent.[6]

HOST.   Peace, I say! hear mine host of the Garter.   Am I politic? am I subtle? am I a Machiavel?   Shall I lose my doctor? no ; he gives me the potions and the motions.   Shall I lose my parson, my priest, my Sir Hugh? no ; he gives me the proverbs and the no-verbs. Give me thy hand, terrestrial ; so.[7]   Give me thy hand, celestial,[8] so. Boys of art, I have deceived you both ;[9] I have directed you to wrong places : your hearts are mighty, your skins are whole, and let burnt sack be the issue.[10]   Come,[11] lay their swords to pawn. Follow me, lads of peace ; follow, follow, follow.

SHALLOW.   Trust me, a mad host.   Follow, gentlemen, follow.

SLENDER [*aside*].   O sweet Anne Page!

[*Exeunt* SHALLOW, SLENDER, PAGE, *and* HOST.

[12] CAIUS.   Ha, do I perceive dat?[13] have you make-a de sot of us, ha, ha?

[14] EVANS.   This is well ; he has made us his vlouting-stog.   I desire you that we may be friends ; and let us knog our prains together to be revenge on this same scall, scurvy, cogging companion, the host of the Garter.

CAIUS.   By gar, with all my heart.[15]   He promise to bring me where is Anne Page ; by gar, he deceive me too.

[16] EVANS.   Well, I will smite his noddles.   Pray you, follow.

[*Exeunt.*

ACT II
SCENE I

A street.

Enter MISTRESS PAGE *and* ROBIN.[1]

MRS. PAGE.   Nay, keep your way, little gallant ; you were wont
to be a follower, but now you are a leader.   [Whether had you rather
lead mine eyes, or eye your master's heels?

ROBIN.   I had rather, forsooth, go before you like a man than
follow him like a dwarf.

MRS. PAGE.   O, you are a flattering boy : now I see you'll be
a courtier.]

Enter FORD.[2]

FORD.   Well met, Mistress Page.   Whither go you?

MRS. PAGE.   Truly, sir, to see your wife.   Is she at home?

FORD.   Ay ; and as idle as she may hang together, for want of
company.   I think, if your husbands were dead, you two would
marry.

MRS. PAGE.   Be sure of that,—two other husbands.

FORD.   Where had you this pretty weathercock?

MRS. PAGE.   I cannot tell what the dickens his name is my husband
had him of.   What do you call your knight's name, sirrah?

ROBIN.   Sir John Falstaff.

FORD.   Sir John Falstaff![3]

MRS. PAGE.[4]   He, he ; I can never hit on's name.   There is such
a league between my good man and he!   Is your wife at home
indeed?

FORD.   Indeed she is.

MRS. PAGE.   By your leave, sir :[5] I am sick till I see her.

[*Exeunt* MRS. PAGE *and* ROBIN.[6]

FORD.   Has Page any brains? hath he any eyes? hath he any
thinking?   Sure, they sleep ; he hath no use of them.   Why, this
boy will carry a letter twenty mile, as easy as a cannon will shoot
point-blank twelve score.   He pieces out his wife's inclination ; he
gives her folly motion and advantage : and now she's going to my
wife, and Falstaff's boy with her.   [A man may hear this shower
sing in the wind.]   And Falstaff's boy with her!   [Good plots, they
are laid ; and our revolted wives share damnation together.]   Well ;
I will take him, then torture my wife, pluck the borrowed veil of
modesty from the so seeming Mistress Page, divulge Page himself
for a secure and wilful Actæon ; and to these violent proceedings
all my neighbours shall cry aim.[7]   [*Clock heard.*]   [The clock gives
me my cue, and my assurance bids me search : there I shall find
Falstaff : I shall be rather praised for this than mocked ; for it is
as positive as the earth is firm that Falstaff is there : I will go.]

ACT II
SCENE I
A street
See Illustration No. 4, p. 22.

[1] *Enter from* R., *and come* C.

[2] *From* L.

[3] *Aside to audience in strong, jealous
        surprise.*
[4] *Light giggle at* FORD.

[5] *Crossing over to* L. *with* ROBIN.

[6] *Both exit* L., *smothering their laughter.*

[7] *Exit* L. *on black-out.*

ILLUSTRATION No. 6
This scene stands for Act II, Scenes II, V and VII

ACT II, SC. II
SCENE II
A room in FORD'S *house*

[1] *As curtains open* MRS. FORD *and* MRS. PAGE *are discovered addressing the servants who stand over* R. *by the basket.*

Note: Entrances or exits marked R. *in these two* FORD'S *house scenes refer to the opening above the arch, concealed behind the arras.*

[2] *Keep the scene spirited and full of suppressed excitement.*

[3] *Enter* ROBIN *from* R. *excitedly.* MRS. PAGE *goes up to him.*

[4] *She moves them off* R. *quickly. Then speaks to* ROBIN.

[5] ROBIN *comes down to* MRS. FORD. MRS. PAGE *comes on his* R.
[6] *The two wives appreciate the full humour of this remark.*

SCENE II

A room in FORD'S *house.*[1]

MRS. FORD. [What, John! What, Robert!
MRS. PAGE. Quickly, quickly! Is the buck-basket—
MRS. FORD. I warrant. What, Robin, I say!

Enter SERVANTS *with a basket.*

MRS. PAGE. Come, come, come.
MRS. FORD. Here, set it down.]
MRS. PAGE. Give your men the charge; we[2] must be brief.
MRS. FORD. Marry, as I told you before, John and Robert, be ready here hard by in the brew-house : and when I suddenly call you, come forth, and without any pause or staggering take this basket on your shoulders : that done, trudge with it in all haste, and carry it among the whitsters in Datchet-mead, and there empty it in the muddy ditch close by the Thames side.[3]
MRS PAGE. You will do it?
MRS. FORD. I ha' told them over and over ; they lack no direction. Be gone, and come when[4] you are called. [*Exeunt* SERVANTS.
MRS. PAGE. [Here comes little Robin.]
MRS. FORD. How now, my eyas-musket! what news with you?
ROBIN.[5] My master, Sir John, is come in at your backdoor, Mistress Ford, and requests your company.[6]
MRS. PAGE. You little Jack-a-Lent, have you been true to us?
ROBIN. Ay, I'll be sworn. My master knows not of your being here and hath threatened to put me into everlasting liberty if I tell you of it ; for he swears he'll turn me away.

MRS. PAGE.   Thou'rt a good boy ; this secrecy of thine shall be a tailor to thee and shall make thee a new doublet and hose.   I'll go hide me.[1]

MRS. FORD.   Do so.   Go tell thy master I am alone.   [*Exit* ROBIN.][2]   Mistress Page, remember you your cue.[3]

MRS. PAGE.   I warrant thee ; if I do not act it, hiss me.

[*Exit.*

MRS. FORD.   Go to, then : [we'll use this unwholesome humidity, this gross watery pumpion ;] we'll teach him to know turtles from jays.[4]

Enter FALSTAFF.[5]

FALSTAFF.   Have I caught thee, my heavenly jewel?[6]   Why, now let me die, for I have lived long enough : this is the period of my ambition : O this blessed hour !

MRS. FORD.   O sweet Sir John ![7]

FALSTAFF.   Mistress Ford, I cannot cog, I cannot prate, Mistress Ford.[8]   [9]Now shall I sin in my wish : I would thy husband were dead : I'll speak it before the best lord,[10] I would make thee my lady.

MRS. FORD.   I your lady, Sir John! alas, I should be a pitiful lady !

FALSTAFF.   Let the court of France show me such another.   I see how thine eye would emulate the diamond: thou hast the right arched beauty of the brow that becomes the ship-tire, the tire-valiant, or any tire of Venetian admittance.

MRS. FORD.[11]   A plain kerchief, Sir John : my brows become nothing else ; nor that well neither.

FALSTAFF.   By the Lord, thou art a traitor to say so : thou wouldst make an absolute courtier ; [and the firm fixture of thy foot would give an excellent motion to thy gait in a semi-circled farthingale. I see what thou wert, if Fortune thy foe were not, Nature thy friend. Come, thou canst not hide it.]

MRS. FORD.   Believe me, there's no such thing in me.

FALSTAFF.   What made me love thee? let that persuade thee there's something extraordinary in thee.   Come, I cannot cog and say thou art this and that, like a many of these lisping hawthorn-buds, that come like women in men's apparel, and smell like Bucklersbury in simple time ; I cannot : but I love thee ; none but thee ; and thou deservest it.

MRS. FORD.   Do not betray me, sir.   I fear you love Mistress Page.[12]

FALSTAFF.   Thou mightst as well say I love to walk by the Counter-gate, which is as hateful to me as the reek of a lime-kiln.

[13]MRS. FORD.   Well, heaven knows how I love you ;[14] and you shall one day find it.

FALSTAFF.   Keep in that mind ; I'll deserve it.[15]

MRS. FORD.   Nay, I must tell you, so you do ; or else I could not be in that mind.[16]

ROBIN [*within*].   Mistress Ford, Mistress Ford! here's Mistress Page at the door, sweating and blowing and looking wildly, and would needs speak with you presently.[17]

FALSTAFF.   She shall not see me :[18] I will ensconce me behind the arras.[19]

MRS. FORD.   Pray you, do so : she's a very tattling woman.

[FALSTAFF *hides himself.*

Re-enter MISTRESS PAGE *and* ROBIN.

[1] *Goes up to the opening* C.

[2] ROBIN *runs off* R.
[3] *Going up to the opening* C.   MRS. PAGE *exits in the* R. *of this opening.*

[4] *Keep the scene full of sparkle and excitement up to this point.*
    MRS. FORD *runs down to the settle by the fireplace and takes up her embroidery.* ROBIN *comes in cautiously to see that all is ready, and sees* MRS. FORD *sitting quietly at work.   He then looks off* R., *and points with his finger several times over to* MRS. FORD, *after which* FALSTAFF *enters.   As the latter advances* C., ROBIN *makes a deceptive movement as though to exit* R., *and then quickly slips into the opening* C., *where he goes off* R.
[5] *As* FALSTAFF *reaches* C., MRS. FORD *utters a deep sigh simulating a pining desire and letting her work fall into her lap. This pleases* FALSTAFF, *and she is apparently unconscious of his presence.*
[6] *She rises suddenly as though embarrassed. She remains* L. *of table.*
[7] *Very seductively—but on the other side of the table.* MRS. PAGE *and* ROBIN *are watching from behind the opening* C.
[8] FALSTAFF *makes as if to come to her, but she coyly puts out her finger to stop him.   He commences to dodge her round the table and ends up by coming round* L. *while she runs round its upper end and comes* C.   *As she does so they at the back beat a hasty retreat.*
[9] FALSTAFF *speaks this line out of his disappointment at not having reached* MRS. FORD.
[10] *Coming to* C. *as he does so,* MRS. FORD *retires behind the buck-basket and playfully arranges the linen to accommodate him !* MRS. PAGE *has again re-appeared and sees what she is doing and enjoys the situation.*
[11] *Still playing with the linen.*

[12] *Coming down below the basket.*
[13] *She is now leading him on, and must be very seductive and subtle.   She is preparing for the coming trick.*
[14] FALSTAFF *feels that the door is open and is about to walk in, but she lets down the barrier so that he only gets a view behind the promise of a future day.*
[15] *Falling to her bait and coming over to her.*
[16] *This time she comes out to him and acts in a most amatory way.   This is the "cue" arranged with* MRS. PAGE.   *Just as* FALSTAFF *is about to embrace her, in rushes* ROBIN, *pushed by* MRS. PAGE, *speaking as instructed, very excitedly, and, of course, breaking off* FALSTAFF'S *hope of enjoyment.*
[17] *Runs off* C. *as he shouts out "presently."*
[18] *Turning round and looking for somewhere to hide.*
[19] *Goes up and hides behind arras* R. *of door* C., *assisted by* MRS. FORD, *who, as soon as she has finished covering him, runs down* L.U.   MRS. PAGE *and* ROBIN *come running on.* MRS. PAGE *comes down* R. *of* MRS. FORD.   ROBIN *remains up* R.
    The following scene is played so that FALSTAFF *hears all.*

ACT II, SC. II

[1] MRS. PAGE *pushes* MRS. FORD *over to the settle over* L. *This leaves the view of* FALSTAFF *clear. As they sit,* MRS. FORD *gives her own letter to* MRS. PAGE, *which she puts in her wallet.*

[2] *Groan from* FALSTAFF *and laugh from the two wives.*

[3] *Speak this well out. It is answered by a slight groan from* FALSTAFF.
The scene must be over-acted—but not too much so. And as they are on the settle they can laugh as much as they like without being seen by FALSTAFF, *who has begun to look out round the arras. The remark about the husband's coming must be the rubbing of salt into the wound.*

[4] *Going over to the basket* R. MRS. FORD *rises and comes* L.

[5] MRS FORD *turns away* L. *and hides her face as though ashamed at the discovery. As he goes to the basket he is confronted by* MRS. PAGE *and the letters.*

[6] *Accent " thee." All he can do to ease the situation is to whisper in her ear that it is she he loves.* MRS. FORD *bursts out laughing.* MRS. PAGE, *assisted by* MRS. FORD, *turn him round so that he sits on the edge and then push him back into the basket, so that his legs go up into the air.*

[7] ROBIN *comes down from* R. *and assists.*

[8] *Voices are heard off* R. MRS. PAGE *takes* ROBIN *and sends him off up* R., *then comes down and speaks in a loud whisper to* MRS. FORD *to call her men, and, throwing a piece of linen on to* FALSTAFF, *crosses over* L. *as* MRS. FORD *goes up and calls the men. She comes down* L. *Having addressed them she goes over to the settle* L., *taking* MRS. PAGE *with her. There she takes up her needlework and begins to sew. The men put the poles in the basket. This must all be spoken and performed with precision. As they are lifting the basket on their shoulders and the two women are seated calmly and placidly over* L., *the voices outside come near and in bursts* FORD *and the others. He rushes on to* C. *from the arch. He commences his speech just off stage so that he enters at " I deserve it." He looks for a moment at the basket and everyone becomes silent.*

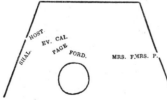

[9] MRS. FORD *rises very indignantly and comes* L.

[10] FORD *is worked up to comic pitch of excitement.*

What's the matter? how now!

MRS. PAGE. O Mistress Ford, what have you done? You're shamed, you're overthrown, you're undone for ever!

MRS. FORD. What's the matter, good Mistress Page?

MRS. PAGE. O well-a-day, Mistress Ford! having an honest man to your husband, to give him such [1] cause of suspicion!

MRS. FORD. What cause of suspicion?

MRS. PAGE. What cause of suspicion! Out upon you! how am I mistook in you!

MRS. FORD. Why, alas, what's the matter?

MRS. PAGE. Your husband's coming hither, woman, with all the officers in Windsor, to search for a gentleman that he says is here now in the house by your consent, to take an ill advantage of his absence : you are undone. [2]

MRS. FORD. 'Tis not so, I hope.

MRS. PAGE. Pray heaven it be not so, that you have such a man here! but 'tis most certain your husband's coming, with half Windsor at his heels, [3] to search for such a one. I come before to tell you. If you know yourself clear, why, I am glad of it ; but if you have a friend here, convey, convey him out. [Be not amazed ; call all your senses to you ; defend your reputation, or bid farewell to your good life for ever.]

MRS. FORD. What shall I do? There is a gentleman my dear friend ; and I fear not mine own shame so much as his peril : I had rather than a thousand pound he were out of the house.

MRS. PAGE. For shame! never stand "you had rather" and "you had rather : " your husband's here at hand ; bethink you of some conveyance : in the house you cannot hide him. O, how have you deceived me! Look, here is a basket : [4] if he be of any reasonable stature, he may creep in here ; and throw foul linen upon him, as if it were going to bucking : or—it is whiting-time—send him by your two men to Datchet-mead.

MRS. FORD. He's too big to go in there. What shall I do?

FALSTAFF [*coming forward*]. Let me see 't, let me see 't, O, let me see 't! I'll in, I'll in. Follow [5] your friend's counsel. I'll in.

MRS. PAGE. What, Sir John Falstaff! Are these your letters, knight?

FALSTAFF. I love thee. [6] Help me away. Let me creep in here. I'll never—

[Gets into the basket ; they cover him with foul linen.

MRS. PAGE. Help to cover your master, boy. [7] [8] Call your men, Mistress Ford. You dissembling knight!

MRS. FORD. What, John! Robert! John!   [*Exit* ROBIN.

Re-enter SERVANTS.

Go take up these clothes here quickly. [Where's the cowl-staff? look, how you drumble]! Carry them to the laundress in Datchet-mead ; quickly, come.

Enter FORD, PAGE, CAIUS, *and* SIR HUGH EVANS.

FORD. Pray you, come near : if I suspect without cause, why then make sport at me ; then let me be your jest ; I deserve it. How now! whither bear you this?

SERVANT. To the laundress, forsooth.

[9] MRS. FORD. Why, what have you to do whither they bear it? You were best meddle with buck-washing.

FORD. Buck! I would I could wash myself of the buck! [10] Buck,

buck, buck ! [1] Ay, buck ; I warrant you, buck ; and of the season too, it shall appear. [*Exeunt* SERVANTS *with the basket.*][2] Gentlemen, I have dreamed to-night ; I'll tell you my dream. Here, here, here be my keys : ascend my chambers ; search, seek, find out : [3] I'll warrant we'll unkennel the fox. [Let me stop this way first. [*Locking the door.*] So, now uncape.]

PAGE.   Good Master Ford, be contented ; you wrong yourself too much.

FORD.[4]   True, Master Page.[5]   Up, gentlemen ; you shall see sport anon : follow me, gentlemen.   [*Exit.*

EVANS.   This is fery fantastical humours and jealousies.[6]

CAIUS.   By gar, 'tis no the fashion of France ; it is not jealous in France.

PAGE.   Nay, follow him, gentlemen ; see the issue of his search.
                                   [*Exeunt* PAGE, CAIUS, *and* EVANS.[7]

MRS. PAGE.   Is there not a double excellency in this? [8]

MRS. FORD.   I know not which pleases me better, that my husband is deceived, or Sir John.

MRS. PAGE.   What a taking was he in when your husband asked who was in the basket ! (*a*).

MRS. FORD.   I am half afraid he will have need of washing ; so throwing him into the water will do him a benefit.

MRS. PAGE.   Hang him, dishonest rascal !   I would all of the same strain were in the same distress.

MRS. FORD.   I think my husband hath some special suspicion of Falstaff's being here ; for I never saw him so gross in his jealousy till now.

MRS. PAGE.   I will lay a plot to try that ; and we will yet have more tricks with Falstaff : [his dissolute disease will scarce obey this medicine.]

MRS. FORD.   Shall we send that foolish carrion, Mistress Quickly, to him, and excuse his throwing into the water ; and give him another hope, to betray him to another punishment?

MRS. PAGE.   We will do it : let him be sent for to-morrow, eight o'clock, to have amends.

Re-enter FORD,[9] PAGE, CAIUS, *and* SIR HUGH EVANS.

FORD.   I cannot find him : may be the knave bragged of that he could not compass.[10]

MRS. PAGE [*aside to* MRS. FORD].   Heard you that?

MRS. FORD.   You use me well, Master Ford, do you?

FORD.   Ay, I do so.

MRS. FORD.   Heaven make you better than your [11] thoughts !

FORD.   Amen !

MRS. PAGE.   You do yourself mighty wrong, Master Ford.[12]

FORD.   Ay, ay ; I must bear it.

EVANS.[13]   If there be any pody in the house, and in the chambers, and in the coffers, and in the presses, heaven forgive my sins at the day of judgement !

CAIUS.[14]   By gar, nor I too : there is no bodies.

PAGE.   Fie, fie, Master Ford !   are you not ashamed?   What spirit, what devil suggests this imagination?   I would not ha' your distemper in this kind for the wealth of Windsor Castle.

FORD.   'Tis my fault, Master Page : I suffer for it.

EVANS.   You suffer for a pad conscience : your wife is as honest a 'omans as I will desires among five thousand, and five hundred too.

ACT II, SC. II

[1] *Holds a piece of dirty linen up and drops it in disgust, rubbing his hands. The servants exeunt through arch.* MRS. FORD *retires patiently up to the settle and sits. They both sit with expressionless faces.*

[2] *Turns to the men* R. *and they all come down, and turn and laugh at each other.*

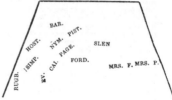

[3] *Turns and goes up to stairs up* C.

[4] *Turns at the stairs and speaks this, meaning that he is wronging himself by trusting his wife. As he turns,* SLEN- DER, *who is behind him, scuttles out of the way.*

[5] *Said looking down at the two women, with sinister meaning.*

[6] *The two old gentlemen are arm in arm over* R. PAGE *goes up to the stairs to follow, and turns to others.*

[7] *All exeunt up the stairs.*

[8] *Both the wives, as soon as the company have gone off, suddenly become convulsed. Up to* (*a*) *the dialogue is spoken to laughter.*

[9] *As* FORD *enters,* MRS. FORD *commences to whimper, as though she has been crying all the time.* MRS. PAGE *looks very solemn.*

[10] *Come well* C. PAGE *comes on his* R.

[11] *Very indignant.*

[12] *More indignant still.*

[13] *Coming down the stairs, followed by* CAIUS. *They come down* L., CAIUS L. *of* EVANS. *Rest of the company dress the stage, but* HOST, *screened by* PISTOL *and* BARDOLPH, *crosses over* R. *and conceals himself behind the arras below the arch.* SLENDER *moves over to* R. *ready for some coming business.*

[14] *Each looks at* MRS. FORD *wiping her eyes as they speak.* CAIUS *goes over to her and comforts her at "By gar, I see it is an honest woman."*

ACT II, SC. II

[1] *Speaks very confidentially as though he really had a subtle and very clever reason for doing what he has done and that he knew all the time that there was not a man on the premises.*

[2] MRS. FORD *rises and comes up to him, sobbing.* MRS. PAGE *rises, but will not come.* SLENDER, *who is over* R., *sees* HOST *behind the arras down* R. *and pulls* FORD'S *cloak. He turns and sees* 8 ENDER *pointing to the figure behind the arras. Everybody looks on in dead silence whilst* FORD *approaches and then darts his hand behind the arras and drags out the* HOST. *Everybody shouts with laughter, and* FORD *stamps off through arch, followed by the company, whilst the two women return to the settle and collapse with laughter. The curtain falls on this picture.*
Music commences as the curtain falls and continues until it rises on next scene.

CAIUS. By gar, I see 'tis an honest woman.

FORD. Well, I promised you a dinner. Come, come, walk in the Park : [1] I pray you, pardon me ; I will hereafter make known to you why I have done this. Come, wife,[2] come, Mistress Page. I pray you, pardon me ; pray heartily, pardon me.

PAGE. [Let's go in, gentlemen ; but, trust me, we'll mock him. I do invite you to-morrow morning to my house to breakfast : after we'll a-birding together ; I have a fine hawk for the bush. Shall it be so?

FORD. Any thing.

EVANS. If there is one, I shall make two in the company.

CAIUS. If dere be one or two, I shall make-a the turd.

FORD. Pray you, go, Master Page.

EVANS. I pray you now, remembrance to-morrow on the lousy knave, mine host.

CAIUS. Dat is good : by gar, with all my heart!

EVANS. A lousy knave, to have his gibes and his mockeries!]

[*Exeunt.*

SCENE III

A room in PAGE'S *house*
See Illustration No. 4, p. 22.

[3] *Enter from* R. *and come* C. FENTON *being on the* L. *of* ANNE.

SCENE III

A room in PAGE'S *house.*

Enter FENTON *and* ANNE PAGE.[3]

FENTON. I see I cannot get thy father's love ;
Therefore no more turn me to him, sweet Nan.

ANNE. Alas, how then?

FENTON.   Why, thou must be thyself.
He doth object I am too great of birth ;
And that, my state being gall'd with my expense,
I seek to heal it only by his wealth :
Besides these, other bars he lays before me,
My riots past, my wild societies ;
And tells me 'tis a thing impossible
I should love thee but as a property.

ANNE. May be he tells you true.

FENTON. No, heaven so speed me in my time to come!
Albeit I will confess thy father's wealth
Was the first motive that I woo'd thee, Anne :
Yet, wooing thee, I found thee of more value
Than stamps in gold or sums in sealed bags ;
And 'tis the very riches of thyself
That now I aim at.

ANNE.   Gentle Master Fenton,
Yet seek my father's love ; still seek it, sir :
If opportunity and humblest suit
Cannot attain it, why, then,—hark you hither![4]

[*They converse apart.*

[4] *Move over to* L.C.

[5] *From* R.: 1 QUICKLY, 2 SHALLOW, 3 SLENDER.

[6] *She crosses over to* ANNE, *who is on* FENTON'S R. *and coughs once or twice during the dialogue, to try and attract her attention. Finally at* [7] *she plucks her sleeve.*

Enter SHALLOW, SLENDER, *and* MISTRESS QUICKLY.[5]

SHALLOW. Break their talk, Mistress Quickly : my kinsman shall speak for himself.[6]

SLENDER. I'll make a shaft or a bolt on 't : 'slid, 'tis but venturing.

SHALLOW. Be not dismayed.

SLENDER. No, she shall not dismay me : I care not for that, but that I am afeard.

QUICKLY.[7] Hark ye ; Master Slender would speak a word with you.

ANNE. I come to him. [*Aside.*][1] This is my father's choice.
O, what a world of vile ill-favour'd faults
Looks handsome in three hundred pounds a-year!
QUICKLY.[2] And how does good Master Fenton? [3]Pray you, a
word with you.
SHALLOW. She's coming ; to her, coz.[4] O boy, thou hadst a
father!
SLENDER. I had a father, Mistress Anne ; my uncle can tell you
good jests of him. Pray you, uncle, tell Mistress Anne the jest,
how my father stole two geese out of a pen, good uncle.
SHALLOW.[5] Mistress Anne, my cousin loves you.
SLENDER. Ay, that I do ; as well as I love any woman in Glouces-
tershire.
SHALLOW. He will maintain you like a gentlewoman.
SLENDER. Ay, that I will, come cut and long-tail, under the
degree of a squire.
SHALLOW. He will make you a hundred and fifty pounds jointure.
ANNE. Good Master Shallow, let him woo for himself.
SHALLOW. Marry, I thank you for it ; I thank you for that good
comfort.[6] She calls you, coz :[7] I'll leave you.
ANNE.[8] Now, Master Slender,—
SLENDER.[9] Now, good Mistress Anne,—
ANNE. What is your will?
SLENDER. My will! 'od's heartlings, that's a pretty jest indeed!
I ne'er made my will yet, I thank heaven ; I am not such a sickly
creature, I give [10] heaven praise.
ANNE. I mean, Master Slender, what would [11] you with me?
SLENDER. Truly, for mine own part, I would little [12] or nothing
with you. Your father and my uncle hath made motions : if it
be my luck, so ; if not, happy man be his dole! They can tell you
how things go better than I can : you may ask your father ; here
he comes.

Enter PAGE *and* MISTRESS PAGE.

PAGE. Now, Master [13] Slender : love him, daughter Anne.
Why, how now! what does Master Fenton here?
[14] You wrong me, sir, thus still to haunt my house :
I told you, sir, my daughter is disposed of.
FENTON. Nay, Master Page, be not impatient.
MRS. PAGE.[15] Good Master Fenton, come not to my child.
PAGE. She is no match for you.
FENTON. Sir, will you hear me?
PAGE.   No, good Master Fenton.
Come, Master Shallow ; come, son Slender, in.[16]
Knowing my mind, you wrong me, Master Fenton.
                [*Exeunt* PAGE, SHALLOW, *and* SLENDER.[17]
QUICKLY.[18] Speak to Mistress Page.
FENTON. Good Mistress Page, for that I love your daughter
In such a righteous fashion as I do,
Perforce, against all checks, rebukes and manners,
I must advance the colours of my love
And not retire : let me have your good will.
ANNE. Good mother, do not marry me to yond fool.
MRS. PAGE. I mean it not ; I seek you a better husband.
QUICKLY. That's my master, master doctor.
ANNE. Alas, I had rather be set quick i' the earth
And bowl'd to death with turnips![19]

ACT II, SC. III

[1] *Sighs and speaks her following lines to* FENTON.

[2] QUICKLY, *seeing that she is still talking to* FENTON, *butts in between them.*
[3] *Takes him off* L. ANNE *thus left, goes reluctantly over to* C.
[4] *Tries to move him across, but he won't go.*

[5] SHALLOW, *who is* L. *of* SLENDER, *turns and comes to her in a desperate attempt to save the situation.*

[6] *Goes over to him.*
[7] *Crosses him and turns to him and speaks his line very playfully, as though he were leaving two lovers to their wooing.*
[8] *A pause before she speaks.* SLENDER *looking more and more uncomfortable and* ANNE *watching him with quiet amusement.*
[9] *Another pause after she speaks, and all that he can think to say is to repeat her question.*
[10] *Here he suddenly feels that he has been very under-rated, and this awakens his spirit.*
[11] *Calmly putting the situation clear.*
[12] *He is getting angry as far as it is possible for him to do so. His nerves here get the better of him.* SHALLOW *re-enters after* PAGE *and* MRS. PAGE.

[13] *Puts his hand on his* R. *shoulder, then crosses over to* ANNE. *As they enter, so* QUICKLY *and* FENTON *re-enter from* L. FENTON *above* QUICKLY.
[14] PAGE *goes up to* FENTON. MRS. PAGE *has come to* ANNE'S R. *And* SHALLOW *remains by* SLENDER'S R.

[15] *Crosses to behind* PAGE *and turns to* ANNE *after her line.*

[16] *Crosses over to exit* L. *Turns and speaks to* FENTON, *and then exit. By the time he has reached the door,* SHALLOW *and* SLENDER *reach* C. *They stop as* PAGE *speaks to* FENTON.
[17] *Exeunt* L.
[18] MRS. QUICKLY, *who has been standing well back by* FENTON R., *whispers in his ear as* MRS. PAGE *is crossing with* ANNE.

[19] *Stamping her foot in anger and then covering her face with her hands.*

ACT II, SC. III
[1] *Putting her arm round her.*

[2] *They exeunt L. FENTON gives a sigh of happiness and crosses over to R., forgetful of QUICKLY, but she touches his arm as he passes and speaks for herself, and he stops and turns.*

[3] *Gives her money as well.*

[4] *Moving over R. Accent the names " Master," " Slender," and " Fenton."*

[5] *Stops and considers and announces her way out of the difficulty with a sweet smile.*
[6] *Makes a false exit and comes back at once and over her L. shoulder sends out her last line and exits.*
Music as before, between the change.

SCENE IV

A room in the Garter Inn
See Illustration No. 2, p. 7.

[7] *FALSTAFF discovered seated L. by the fire. A stool is on his R. to take his mug of liquor. The table is up at the back, R. of the window. Here BARDOLPH is at work sitting on the table cleaning the pots, etc.*
   The fire is alight, and FALSTAFF has a slight cold.
[8] *Still sitting.*
[9] *BARDOLPH somewhat resents this interference with his work, but gets up, places pot on table and exits off R.*

[10] *And comes down to FALSTAFF.*

[11] *FALSTAFF utters a grunt of disgust at the mention of her name.*
[12] *Drinks half his mug of sack.*
[13] *BARDOLPH goes up to back and bawls to her off R. FALSTAFF resumes his drink after he has got his breath. She enters and comes down C. His drink lasts till some moments after her speech. She is well cloaked and hooded.*

[14] *BARDOLPH comes down and collects the pots and exits at [15].*

MRS. PAGE. Come, trouble not yourself.[1] Good Master Fenton,
I will not be your friend nor enemy :
My daughter will I question how she loves you,
And as I find her, so am I affected.
Till then farewell, sir : she must needs go in ;
Her father will be angry.
   FENTON. Farewell, gentle mistress : farewell, Nan.
                              [*Exeunt* MRS. PAGE *and* ANNE.[2]
   QUICKLY. This is my doing, now : " Nay," said I, " will you
cast away your child on a fool, and a physician? Look on Master
Fenton : '' this is my doing.
   FENTON. I thank thee ; and I pray thee, once to-night
Give my sweet Nan this ring : there's for thy pains.[3]
   QUICKLY. Now heaven send thee good fortune! [*Exit* FENTON.]
A kind heart he hath : a woman would run through fire and water
for such a kind heart. But yet I would my master had Mistress [4]
Anne ; or I would Master Slender had her ; or, in sooth, I would
Master Fenton had her : [5] I will do what I can for them all three ;
for so I have promised, and I'll be as good as my word : [6] but speciously
for Master Fenton. [Well, I must be of another errand to Sir John
Falstaff from my two mistresses : what a beast am I to slack it!]
                                                              [*Exit.*

SCENE IV

A room in the Garter Inn.[7]

   FALSTAFF. Bardolph, I say,—
   BARDOLPH. Here, sir.[8]
   FALSTAFF. Go fetch me a quart of sack ; put a toast in 't.[9]
[*Exit* BARDOLPH.] Have I lived to be carried in a basket, like a
barrow of butcher's offal, and to be thrown in the Thames? Well,
if I be served such another trick, I'll have my brains ta'en out and
buttered, and give them to a dog for a new-year's gift. The rogues
slighted me into the river with as little remorse as they would have
drowned a blind bitch's puppies, fifteen i' the litter : and you may
know by my size that I have a kind of alacrity in sinking ; if the
bottom were as deep as hell, I should down. I had been drowned,
but that the shore was shelvy and shallow,—a death that I abhor ;
for the water swells a man ; and what a thing should I have been
when I had been swelled ! I should have been a mountain of mummy.

Re-enter BARDOLPH *with sack.*[10]

   BARDOLPH. Here's Mistress Quickly, sir, to speak with you.
   FALSTAFF.[11] Come, let me pour in some sack to the Thames
water ; for my belly's as cold as if I had swallowed snowballs for pills
to cool the reins.[12] Call her in.[13]
   BARDOLPH. Come in, woman!

Enter MISTRESS QUICKLY.

   QUICKLY. By your leave ; I cry you mercy : give your worship
good morrow.
   FALSTAFF. Take away these chalices.[14] Go brew me a pottle of
sack finely.
   BARDOLPH. With eggs, sir?
   FALSTAFF. Simple of itself ; I'll no pullet-sperm in my brewage.[15]
[*Exit* BARDOLPH.] How now!

QUICKLY. Marry, sir, I come to your worship from Mistress Ford.

FALSTAFF. Mistress Ford! I have had ford enough ; [1] I was thrown into the ford ; I have my belly full of ford.

QUICKLY. Alas the day! good heart, that was not her fault : [she does so take on with her men ; they mistook their erection.

FALSTAFF. So did I mine, to build upon a foolish woman's promise.

QUICKLY. Well,] she laments, sir, for it, that it would yearn your heart to see it. [2] Her husband goes this morning a-birding ; [3] she desires you once more to come to her between eight and nine : I must carry her word quickly: [4] she'll make you amends, I warrant you.

FALSTAFF. [5] Well, I will visit her : tell her so ; and bid her think what a man is : let her consider his frailty, and then judge of my merit.

QUICKLY. I will tell her. [6]

FALSTAFF. Do so. [7] Between nine and ten, sayest thou?

QUICKLY. Eight and nine, sir. [8]

FALSTAFF. Well, be gone : I will not miss her.

QUICKLY. Peace be with you, sir. [9]   [*Exit.*

FALSTAFF. [10] I marvel I hear not of Master Brook ; he sent me word to stay within : I like his money well. O, here he comes. [11]

Enter FORD.

FORD. Bless you, sir!

FALSTAFF. [12] Now, Master Brook, you come to know what hath passed between me and Ford's wife?

FORD. [13] That, indeed, Sir John, is my business.

FALSTAFF. Master Brook, I will not lie to you : I was at her house the hour she appointed me.

FORD. And sped you, sir?

FALSTAFF. Very ill-favouredly, Master Brook.

FORD. How so, sir? Did she change her determination?

FALSTAFF. No, Master Brook ; but the peaking Cornuto her husband, Master Brook, dwelling in a continual 'larum of jealousy, comes me in the instant of our encounter, after we had embraced, [14] kissed, protested, and, as it were, spoke the prologue of our comedy ; and at his heels a rabble of his companions, thither provoked and instigated by his distemper, and, forsooth, to search his house for his wife's love.

FORD. What, while you were there? [15]

FALSTAFF. While I was there. [16]

FORD. [17] And did he search for you, and could not find you?

FALSTAFF. You shall hear. [18] As good luck would have it, comes in one Mistress Page : gives intelligence of Ford's approach : and, in her invention and Ford's wife's distraction, they conveyed me into a buck-basket.

FORD. A buck-basket. [19]

FALSTAFF. [20] By the Lord, a buck-basket : [21] rammed me in with foul shirts and smocks, socks, foul stockings, greasy napkins ; that, Master Brook, there was the rankest compound of villanous smell that ever offended nostril. [22]

FORD. And how long lay you there?

FALSTAFF. Nay, you shall hear, Master Brook, what I have suffered to bring this woman to evil for your good. Being thus crammed in the basket, a couple of Ford's knaves, his hinds, were

[1] *Roaring with indignation.*

[2] MRS. QUICKLY *is a very good actress and makes him believe that* MRS. FORD *is very anxious to see him and very sorry that the last meeting was so abruptly concluded. The producer must keep this well in mind.* QUICKLY'S *character must be handled very carefully.*
  At [3] *she pushes out her sly bait. He looks round with a sly look and the old feeling slowly coming back.*
[4] *Thrust this in as a bit of her own personal re-assurance.*
[5] *He looks and considers, and at her look, melts into acquiesence and agrees.*
[6] *Drops a small curtesy and smiles at her triumph and his own foolishness.*
[7] *Turns up* R.
[8] *Turns and corrects him immediately.*
[9] *Another bob, and giving him an amused look, exits off* R.
[10] FALSTAFF *sits pondering for a few moments, and eventually gives a grunt of satisfaction.*
[11] *Takes up his pot and drinks.* FORD *enters up* R. *The possibility of* FORD *meeting with* QUICKLY *is a weakness in the play, as he would very possibly suspect her. However, as they would both be cloaked and hooded, and eager to avoid seeing anybody, they would probably pass each other and not discover the identity of either.*
[12] *Very pleasantly surprised to see him.*
[13] FORD *does not sit yet.*

[14] *Amazement on* FORD'S *part.*

[15] *As though he can't quite grasp that it was so.*
[16] *Hurled out of all his experiences of being there when* FORD *came.*
[17] *Perplexed at the mystery of not finding* FALSTAFF *after such a thorough search.*
[18] FORD *puts one foot on the stool and leans his chin on his hand and elbows on knees, determined that he will hear.*

[19] *The truth in a flash! and turns away down* R *to realize it.*
[20] FALSTAFF *brings his fist down with a whack on the arm of his chair.*
[21] *As* FORD *moves over* R. BARDOLPH *comes in with the sack and reaches* FALSTAFF *just at the end of his speech, so that he takes it and drinks deep to efface the bad taste of the story.*
[22] *Whilst* FALSTAFF *is drinking,* FORD *returns, quietly draws the stool a little* R. *and sits on it and looks at* FALSTAFF—*very interested, calm but furtive. He waits a little while and then speaks.*

[1] *Puts the pot to his lips and gurgles the last few words into it.*
[2] *FORD turns away with a sigh of satisfaction at what FALSTAFF has experienced.*

[3] *Stops drinking, wipes his beard and moustache, and speaks firmly.*
[4] *Rises and beckons FORD with a nod. They come together.*
[5] *FORD'S eyes open and his face begins to quiver.*
[6] *Nudges him with a sly laugh.*
[7] *Goes up to table at back, puts down pot and picks up hat and stick. FORD stands motionless—overcome.*
[8] *Goes over R. very cheerily.*
[9] *Stops and gives him every hope in a cheerful " adieu," etc.*
[10] *Exit chuckling.*
[11] *After some moments, FORD, who has been looking steadily out to front, sits suddenly on his stool, still looking like a stone. Then he begins to grow conscious of the situation.*

[12] *Rises fully awake. Utters a cry and goes up R. All his jealous feelings get to work and swell up into a crescendo on his last phrase, which takes him off R.*

[13] *Accent " it " and " be " [15] and substitute " me " for " one " [14]. Music takes up at the fall of curtain.*

SCENE V

A room in FORD'S *house*
See Illustration No. 6, p. 28.

[16] *Enter from C. opening, FALSTAFF on L. of MRS. FORD. They come down R.C.*

called forth by their mistress to carry me in the name of foul clothes to Datchet-lane : they took me on their shoulders ; met the jealous knave their master in the door, who asked them once or twice what they had in their basket : I quaked for fear, lest the lunatic knave would have searched it ; but fate, ordaining he should be a cuckold, held his hand. Well : on went he for a search, and away went I for foul clothes. But mark the sequel, Master Brook : I suffered the pangs of three several deaths ; first, an intolerable fright, to be detected with a jealous rotten bell-wether ; next, to be compassed, like a good bilbo, in the circumference of a peck, hilt to point, heel to head ; and then, to be stopped in, like a strong distillation, with stinking clothes that fretted in their own grease : think of that,—a man of my kidney,—think of that,—that am as subject to heat as butter ; a man of continual dissolution and thaw : it was a miracle to 'scape suffocation. And in the height of this bath, when I was more than half stewed in grease, like a Dutch dish, to be thrown into the Thames, and cooled, glowing hot, in that surge, like a horse-shoe ; think of that,—hissing hot,[1]—think of that, Master Brook.

FORD.[2] In good sadness, sir, I am sorry that for my sake you have suffered all this. My suit then is desperate ; you'll undertake her no more?

FALSTAFF.[3]. Master Brook, I will be thrown into Etna, as I have been into Thames, ere I will leave her thus.[4] Her husband is this morning gone a-birding.[5] I have received from her another embassy of meeting : [6] 'twixt eight and nine is the hour, Master Brook.

FORD. 'Tis past eight already, sir.

FALSTAFF. Is it?[7] I will then address me to my appointment. Come to me at your convenient leisure, and you shall know how I speed ; and the conclusion shall be crowned with your enjoying her.[8] [9] Adieu. You shall have her, Master Brook ; Master Brook, you shall cuckold Ford.[10]   [*Exit.*

FORD.[11] Hum! ha! is this a vision? is this a dream? do I sleep? Master Ford, awake! awake. Master Ford! there's a hole made in your best coat, Master Ford. This 'tis to be married! this 'tis to have linen and buck-baskets![12] Well, I will proclaim myself what I am : I will now take the lecher ; he is at my house ; he cannot 'scape me ; 'tis impossible he should ; he cannot creep into a half-penny purse, nor into a pepper-box : but, lest the devil that guides him should aid him, I will search impossible places. Though what I am I cannot avoid, yet to be what I would not shall not make me tame: if[13] I have horns to make one [14] mad, let the proverb go with me : I'll be [15] horn-mad.   [*Exit.*

SCENE V

A room in FORD'S *house.*

Enter FALSTAFF *and* MISTRESS FORD.[16]

FALSTAFF. Mistress Ford, your sorrow hath eaten up my sufferance. I see you are obsequious in your love, and I profess requital to a hair's breadth ; not only, Mistress Ford, in the simple office of love, but in all the accoutrement, complement and ceremony of it. But are you sure of your husband now?

MRS. FORD.   He's a-birding, sweet Sir John.[1]

MRS. PAGE.[2]   [within].   What, ho, gossip Ford! what, ho!

MRS. FORD.   Step into the chamber, Sir John.[3]

Enter MISTRESS PAGE.[4]

MRS. PAGE.   How now, sweetheart! who's at home besides yourself?

MRS. FORD.   Why, none but mine own people.

MRS. PAGE.   Indeed!

MRS. FORD.   No, certainly.   [*Aside to her.*]   Speak louder.

MRS. PAGE.   Truly, I am so glad you have nobody here.

MRS. FORD.   Why?

MRS. PAGE.   Why, woman, your husband is in his old lunes again : he so takes on yonder with my husband ; so rails against all married mankind ; [so curses all Eve's daughters, of what complexion soever ; and so buffets himself on the forehead, crying " Peer out, peer out "] that any madness I ever yet beheld seemed but tameness, civility and patience, to this his distemper he is in now : I am glad the fat knight is not here.[5]

MRS. FORD.   Why, does he talk of him?

MRS. PAGE.   Of none but him ; and swears he was carried out, the last time he searched for him, in a basket ;[6] protests to my husband he is now here, and hath drawn him and the rest of their company from their sport, to make another experiment of his suspicion : but I am glad the knight is not here ; now he shall see his own foolery.

MRS. FORD.   How near is he, Mistress Page?

MRS. PAGE.   Hard by ; at street end ; he will be here anon.[7]

MRS. PAGE.   I am undone! The knight is here.

MRS. PAGE.   Why then you are utterly shamed, and he's but a dead man. What a woman are you!—Away with him, away with him! better shame than murder.[8]

MRS. FORD.   Which way should he go? how should I bestow him? Shall I put him into the basket again?

Re-enter FALSTAFF.[9]

FALSTAFF.   No, I'll come no more i' the basket. May I not go out ere he come?

MRS PAGE.   Alas, three of Master Ford's brothers watch the door with pistols, that none shall issue out ; otherwise you might slip away ere he came. But what make you here?

FALSTAFF.   What shall I do? I'll creep up into the chimney.[10]

MRS. FORD.   There they always use to discharge their birding-pieces. Creep into the kiln-hole.

FALSTAFF.   Where is it?

MRS. FORD.   He will seek there, on my word. [Neither press, coffer, chest, trunk, well, vault, but he hath an abstract for the remembrance of such places, and goes to them by his note :] there is no hiding you in the house.

FALSTAFF.   I'll go out then.[11]

MRS. PAGE.   If you go out in your own semblance, you die, Sir John.[12] Unless you go out disguised—

MRS. FORD.   How might we disguise him?[13]

MRS. PAGE.   Alas the day, I know not! There is no woman's[14] gown big enough for him ; otherwise he might put on a hat, a muffler and a kerchief, and so[15] escape.

FALSTAFF.   Good hearts, devise something : any extremity rather than a mischief.

---

[1] *Very sweetly and invitingly.*

[2] *From off* R.

[3] *She moves him up* R. *and he exits. Slight pause before* MRS. PAGE *enters. She waits for* MRS. FORD *to beckon her on.*

[4] *Enter through arch. She crosses over to* L. *as she enters and turns sharply on* " Indeed."

[5] *Spoken up in* FALSTAFF'S *direction.*

[6] FALSTAFF *can be seen peeping out from the tapestry, and the wives move a little over* L.

[7] *By this time* FALSTAFF *has forgotten himself and come on to the stage. The wives, knowing this, do not see him.* MRS. FORD *moves over* R. *on her line,* " I am undone."

[8] *Signs of great agitation from* FALSTAFF.

[9] FALSTAFF *comes down* C. *between the two wives.*

[10] *About to cross* L. *when* MRS. FORD *stops him.*

[11] *Turns and goes up* C. *to level with stairs. They follow up on either side of him.*

[12] *He stops and turns, groaning.*

[13] *Accent* " him."

[14] *Accent* " woman's."

[15] *Accent* " so."

ACT II, SC. V

[1] *Pushing him up the stairs.*

[2] *Up stairs.*
[3] *Both come down stage a little, laughing. Their manner changes from the artificial to the real. But keep the scene going quickly.*

[4] *Off* R.
[5] *Exit upstairs* L.
[6] *From* R. *and come* C. *speaking as she enters so that they go straight down to it. They bring the poles on with them. She carries a piece of linen.*
[7] *Up stair* C.
[8] *The servants take the basket up on "take it up."*
[9] *Beginning to move off through arch* R.
[10] FORD *enters on word cue, sees them with the basket, and gives one long "Ah!" as much as to say "Here is the basket and Falstaff."*

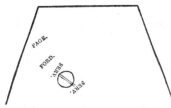

[11] *Having set down the basket and taken out the pole, they retreat from* FORD *to* C. *Then seeing his cudgel beginning to swing, they make a dash for the exit up* R., *and he runs after them. Then he turns and goes up* C. *to stairs and calls off to* MRS. FORD. *The rest enter, having been standing in the arch, during the first few lines of the scene.*
[12] *Coming down and hitting the basket with his stick.*
[13] *Snapping at him.*
[14] *Down stairs and come down to* FORD. *He moderates his tone but not his feeling.*

MRS. FORD. My maid's aunt, the fat woman of Brentford, has a gown above.

MRS. PAGE. On my word, it will serve him ; she's as big as he is : and there's her thrummed hat and her muffler too. Run up, Sir John.[1]

MRS. FORD. Go, go, sweet Sir John : Mistress Page and I will look some linen for your head.

MRS. PAGE. Quick, quick ! we'll come dress you straight : put on the gown the while. [*Exit* FALSTAFF.[2]

MRS. FORD. I would my husband would meet [3] him in this shape : he cannot abide the old woman of Brentford ; he swears she's a witch ; forbade her my house and hath threatened to beat her.

MRS. PAGE. Heaven guide him to thy husband's cudgel, and the devil guide his cudgel afterwards !

MRS. FORD. But is my husband coming ?

MRS. PAGE. Ay, in good sadness, is he ; and talks of the basket too, howsoever he hath had intelligence.

MRS. FORD. We'll try that ; for I'll appoint my men to carry the basket again, to meet him at the door with it, as they did last time.

MRS. PAGE. Nay, but he'll be here presently : let's go dress him like the witch of Brentford.

MRS. FORD. I'll first direct my men what they shall do with the basket. Go up ; I'll bring linen for him straight. [*Exit.*[4]

MRS. PAGE. Hang him, dishonest varlet ! we cannot misuse him enough.

We'll leave a proof, by that which we will do,
Wives may be merry, and yet honest too ;
[We do not act that often jest and laugh ;
'Tis old, but true, Still swine eat all the draff.] [*Exit.*[5]

Re-enter MISTRESS FORD *with two* SERVANTS.[6]

MRS. FORD. Go, sirs, take the basket again on your shoulders : your master is hard at door ; if he bid you set it down, obey him : quickly, dispatch. [*Exit.*[7]

FIRST SERVANT. Come, come, take it up.[8]

SECOND SERVANT. Pray heaven it be not full of knight again.

FIRST SERVANT.[9] I hope not ; I had as lief bear so much lead.[10]

Enter FORD, PAGE, SHALLOW, CAIUS, *and* SIR HUGH EVANS.

FORD. [Ay, but if it prove true, Master Page, have you any way then to unfool me again?] Set down the basket, villain ! Somebody call my wife. Youth in a basket ![11] O you panderly rascals ! there's a knot, a ging, a pack, a conspiracy against me : now shall the devil be shamed. What, wife, I say ! Come, come forth ! Behold what honest clothes you send forth to bleaching ![12]

PAGE. Why, this passes, Master Ford ; you are not to go loose any longer ; you must be pinioned.

EVANS. Why, this is lunatics ! this is mad as a mad dog !

SHALLOW. Indeed, Master Ford, this is not well, indeed.

[13] FORD. So say I too, sir.

Re-enter MISTRESS FORD.[14].

Come hither, Mistress Ford ; Mistress Ford, the honest woman, the modest wife, the virtuous creature, that hath the jealous fool to her husband ! I suspect without cause, mistress, do I ?

MRS. FORD.   Heaven be my witness you do, if you suspect me in any dishonesty.

FORD.   Well said, brazen-face! hold it out.[1] Come forth, sirrah! [*Pulling clothes out of the basket.*

PAGE.   This passes![2]

MRS. FORD.   Are you not ashamed? let the clothes alone.

FORD.   I shall find you anon.

EVANS.   ['Tis unreasonable! Will you take up your wife's clothes? Come away.]

FORD.   Empty the basket, I say![3]

MRS. FORD.   Why, man, why?

FORD.[4]   Master Page, as I am a man, there was one conveyed out of my house yesterday in this basket : why may not he be there again? In my house I am sure he is : my intelligence is true ; my jealousy is reasonable. Pluck me out all the linen.[5]

MRS. FORD.   If you find a man there, he shall die a flea's death.

PAGE.   Here's no man.[6]

SHALLOW.   By my fidelity, this is not well, Master Ford ; this wrongs you.

EVANS.   Master Ford, you must pray, and not follow the imaginations of your own heart : this is jealousies.

FORD.   Well, he's not here I seek for.

PAGE.   No, nor nowhere else but in your brain.

FORD.   Help to search my house this one time.[7] If I find not what I seek, show no colour for my extremity ; let me for ever be your table-sport ; let them say of me, " As jealous as Ford, that searched a hollow walnut for his wife's leman."[8] Satisfy me once more ; once more search with me.[9]

MRS. FORD.   What, ho, Mistress Page! come you and the old woman down ; my husband will come into the chamber.

FORD.   Old woman! what old woman's that?

MRS. FORD.   Why, it is my maid's aunt of Brentford.[10]

FORD.[11]   A witch, a quean, an old cozening quean! Have I not forbid her my house? She comes of errands, does she? We are simple men ; we do not know what's brought to pass under the profession of fortune-telling.[12] [She works by charms, by spells, by the figure, and such daubery as this is, beyond our element : we know nothing.][13] Come down, you witch, you hag, you ; come down, I say!

MRS. FORD.   Nay, good, sweet husband![14] Good gentlemen, let him not strike the old woman.

Re-enter FALSTAFF *in woman's clothes, and* MISTRESS PAGE.[15]

MRS. PAGE.   Come, Mother Prat ; come, give me your hand.

FORD.   I'll prat her. [*Beating him.*] Out of my door, you witch, you hag, you baggage, you pole-cat, you ronyon! out, out! I'll conjure you, I'll fortune-tell you.   [*Exit* FALSTAFF.

MRS. PAGE.   Are you not ashamed? I think you have killed the poor woman.

MRS. FORD.   Nay, he will do it. 'Tis a goodly credit for you.

FORD.   Hang her, witch!

EVANS.   By yea and no, I think the 'oman is a witch indeed : I like not when a 'oman has a great peard ; I spy a great peard under his muffler.[16]

[17] FORD.   Will you follow, gentlemen? I beseech you, follow ; see but the issue of my jealousy : if I cry out thus upon no trail, never trust me when I open again.

[1] *He lets himself go, again, in this speech, because he thinks he has caught her in her own trick. Then, having pinned her down, he proceeds to show her up and madly attacks the clothes.*

[2] *PAGE grapples his arms and lifts him clear of the basket. Everyone is laughing—except* FORD.

[3] *Almost screaming, but still helpless in* PAGE'S *grip.*

[4] *Frees himself and speaks, wrought up to a state of tears.*

[5] *Dives into the basket, sends the linen all over the place.*

[6] *Again lifting him out of the basket. This time* FORD *is almost on the point of collapse.* MRS. FORD *has gone up to the stairs ready to call the others down.* CAIUS, NYM *and* PISTOL *make way for her as she goes up, but close together again after she has passed.*

[7] *Making one last effort.*

[8] *Substitute " lover."*

[9] *Just going up when* MRS. FORD *calls out to* MRS. PAGE *from the foot of the stairs where she has been waiting.* CAIUS *and others open the stage so that she is seen.*

[10] *Comes down to him quite calmly.*

[11] *Grips her* R. *arm.*

[12] *Throws her across to* L.
[13] *Goes up to stairs.*
[14] *Remaining where she is.*

[15] MRS. PAGE *deliberately leads* FALSTAFF *into the room, past* FORD, *she being on* FALSTAFF'S R. *As soon as she comes* C. FORD *gets to work behind and drives* FALSTAFF *forward round in front of the basket. As he is coming across* EVANS *who is down* R., *looks him full in the face and then turns to audience with his hand on his chin and his eyes wide open.* FORD *beats* FALSTAFF *off through arch* R. *and kicks him off.* MRS. PAGE, *as soon as she leaves* FALSTAFF, *goes to her husband who is just at her* R. FORD *returns to* C.

[16] *The two wives stifle a laugh. Everybody has taken delight at the beating. Witches were not popular.*

[17] *Goes up to stairs and exit at end of speech.*

D

ACT II, SC. V

[1] *They all go up the stairs.*
[2] *The two wives come together C. and renew their appreciation of what has just passed.*

[3] *Up stairs L.*

SCENE VI

See Illustration No. 4, p. 22.

As soon as the curtain drops, the tabs are drawn and shouting and booing is heard.
As the curtain rises FALSTAFF *comes on from* R., *chased by the children, who will be fairies later on, and they are booing and throwing paper balls at him. A dog or two, on strong leads, would help the scene. They pass across* R. *to* L.

SCENE VII

A room in FORD'S *house*
See Illustration No. 6, p. 28.

[5] *Curtain opens on* FORD'S *house. The table is placed* L.C. *lengthways across the stage.*
[6] *Enter* EVANS *from* C. *and comes down to chair below fireplace, and turns it round and half-round to fire which is alight. He speaks as he enters, and is followed by* PAGE *and* MRS. PAGE, PAGE *being* L. *of* MRS. PAGE. *They come down to* L. *of table round back.* FORD *and* MRS. FORD *follow and come down* C., FORD *on the* R. *of his wife. They remain* C. *for a while. His arm is round her.*
[7] *Kiss her.*
[8] *Coming a little to the* R. *so that* MRS. PAGE *is by the table and sits against it.* EVANS *sits on chair down* L. *after warming his knees and hands.*
[9] MRS. FORD *turns to her husband and laughs. He also laughs and they both move over to the table so that* MRS. FORD *can sit against it like* MRS. PAGE *and beside her.*

PAGE. Let's obey his humour a little further : come, gentlemen.
[*Exeunt* FORD, PAGE, SHALLOW, CAIUS, *and* EVANS.[1]
MRS. PAGE. Trust me, he beat him most pitifully.[2]
MRS. FORD. Nay, by the mass, that he did not ; he beat him most unpitifully, methought.
MRS. PAGE. I'll have the cudgel hallowed and hung o'er the altar ; it hath done meritorious service.
MRS. FORD. What think you? may we, with the warrant of womanhood and the witness of a good conscience, pursue him with any further revenge?
MRS. PAGE. The spirit of wantonness is, sure, scared out of him : if the devil have him not in fee-simple, with fine and recovery, he will never, I think, in the way of waste, attempt us again.
MRS. FORD. Shall we tell our husbands how we have served him?
MRS. PAGE. Yes, by all means ; if it be but to scrape the figures out of your husband's brains. If they can find in their hearts the poor unvirtuous fat knight shall be any further afflicted, we two will still be the ministers.
MRS. FORD. I'll warrant they'll have him publicly shamed : and methinks there would be no period to the jest, should he not be publicly shamed.
MRS. PAGE. Come, to the forge with it then ; shape it : I would not have things cool.   [*Exeunt.*[3]

SCENE VI[4]

SCENE VII

A room in FORD'S *house.*[5]

Enter PAGE, FORD, MISTRESS PAGE, MISTRESS FORD, *and* SIR HUGH EVANS.[6]

EVANS. 'Tis one of the best discretions of a 'oman as ever I did look upon.
PAGE. And did he send you both these letters at an instant?
MRS. PAGE. Within a quarter of an hour.
FORD. Pardon me, wife. Henceforth do what thou wilt ;
I rather will suspect the sun with cold
Than thee with wantonness : now doth thy honour stand,
In him that was of late an heretic,
As firm as faith.[7]
PAGE.   [8] 'Tis well, 'tis well ; no more :
But let our plot go forward : let our wives
Yet once again, to make us public sport,
Appoint a meeting with this old fat fellow,
Where we may take him and disgrace him for it.[9]
FORD. There is no better way than that they spoke of.
PAGE. How? to send him word they'll meet him in the park at midnight? Fie, fie! he'll never come.
EVANS. [You say he has been thrown in the rivers and has been grievously peaten as an old 'oman : methinks there should be terrors in him that he should not come ; methinks his flesh is punished, he shall have no desires.
PAGE. So think I too.]
MRS. FORD. Devise but how you'll use him when he comes,
And let us two devise to bring him thither.

MRS. PAGE.   There is an old tale goes that Herne the hunter,
Sometime a keeper here in Windsor forest,
Doth all the winter-time, at still midnight,
Walk round about an oak, with great ragg'd horns ;
And there he blasts the tree and takes the cattle
And makes milch-kine yield blood and shakes a chain
In a most hideous and dreadful manner :
You have heard of such a spirit, and well you know
The superstitious idle-headed eld
Received and did deliver to our age
This tale of Herne the hunter for a truth.
     PAGE.   Why, yet there want not many that do fear
In deep of night to walk by this Herne's oak :
But what of this?
     MRS. FORD.   Marry, this is our device ;
That Falstaff at that oak shall meet with us.
     PAGE.   Well, let it not be doubted but he'll come :
And in this shape when you have brought him thither,
What shall be done with him? what is your plot?
     MRS. PAGE.   That likewise have we thought upon, and thus :
Nan Page my daughter and my little son
And three or four more of their growth we'll dress
Like urchins, ouphes and fairies, green and white,
With rounds of waxen tapers on their heads,
And rattles in their hands : upon a sudden,
As Falstaff, she and I, are newly met,
Let them from forth a sawpit rush at once
With some diffused song : upon their sight,
We two in great amazedness will fly :
Then let them all encircle him about
And, fairy-like, to pinch the unclean knight,
And ask him why, that hour of fairy revel,
In their so sacred paths he dares to tread
In shape profane.
     MRS. FORD.   And till he tell the truth,
Let the supposed fairies pinch him sound
And burn him with their tapers.
     MRS. PAGE.   The truth being known,
We'll all present ourselves, dis-horn the spirit,
And mock him home to Windsor.
     FORD.   The children must
Be practised well to this, or they'll ne'er do 't.
     EVANS.[1]   I will teach the children their behaviours ; and I will
be like a jack-an-apes also, to burn [2] the knight with my taber.
     FORD.[3]   That will be excellent.   I'll go and buy them vizards.
     MRS. PAGE.[4]   My Nan shall be the queen of all the fairies,
Finely attired in a robe of white.
     PAGE.   That silk will I go buy.[5]   [Aside.]   [6] And in that time
Shall Master Slender steal my Nan away
And marry her at Eton.[7]   Go send to Falstaff straight.
     FORD.   Nay, I'll to him again in name of Brook : [8]
He'll tell me all his purpose : sure, he'll come.
     MRS. PAGE.   Fear not you that.   Go get us properties
And tricking for our fairies.[9]
     EVANS.   Let us about it : it is admirable pleasures and fery honest
knaveries.

                    [Exeunt PAGE, FORD, and EVANS.

[1] Rises and pushes chair back to L. He
is very delighted with the whole idea, and
suits the action to the word at [2].
[3] FORD moves over to R.
[4] Both the women come C.

[5] EVANS moves up L. going to door and
practising his steps on the way.
[6] To audience.
[7] Turns to FORD.

[8] All laugh.

[9] FORD goes up R. PAGE up L. and they
exeunt with EVANS at back. EVANS is
very full of excitement.

ACT II, SC. VII

[1] *Taking her up to* C.

[2] C.

[3] *Comes down stage a little and speaks to audience. Curtain falls as she turns up stage to exit.*
Music as before.

MRS. PAGE. Go, Mistress Ford,[1]
Send quickly to Sir John, to know his mind.   [*Exit* MRS. FORD.[2]
[3] I'll to the doctor : he hath my good will,
And none but he, to marry with Nan Page.
[That Slender, though well landed, is an idiot ;
And he my husband best of all affects.
The doctor is well money'd, and his friends
Potent at court : he, none but he, shall have her,
Though twenty thousand worthier come to crave her.]   [*Exit.*

SCENE VIII

A room in the Garter Inn
See Illustration No. 2, p. 7.

[4] *Enter* HOST, *followed by* SIMPLE. *They come from up* R. HOST *speaks as he enters. They come down* R.

SCENE VIII

A room in the Garter Inn.

Enter HOST *and* SIMPLE.[4]

HOST. What wouldst thou have, boor? what, thick-skin? speak, breathe, discuss ; brief, short, quick, snap.

SIMPLE. Marry, sir, I come to speak with Sir John Falstaff from Master Slender.

HOST. There's his chamber, his house,[5] his castle, his standing-bed and truckle-bed ; 'tis painted about with the story of the Prodigal, fresh and new. Go knock and call ; he'll speak like an Anthropophaginian unto thee : knock, I say.

[5] *Points off* L. *up the stairs which are above the fireplace* L.

SIMPLE. There's an old woman, a fat woman, gone [6] up into his chamber : I'll be so bold as stay, sir, till she come down ; I come to speak with her, indeed.

[6] *Look of surprise from* HOST.

HOST. Ha! a fat woman! the knight may be robbed : I'll call.[7] Bully knight! bully Sir John! speak from thy lungs military : [8] art thou there? [9] it is thine host, thine Ephesian, calls.

[7] *Going up to stairs.*

[8], *and* [9] *Slight pauses.*

FALSTAFF [*above*]. How now, mine host!

HOST. Here's a Bohemian-Tartar tarries the coming down of thy fat woman. Let her descend, bully, let her descend ; my chambers are honourable : fie! privacy? fie!

Enter FALSTAFF.[10]

[10] *Down stairs.*

[11] *Speaks to him.*

[12] *Turns away and comes down to chair in front of fire.*

[13] SIMPLE *moves to* C. *and stands with his mouth open after his speech.*

[14] FALSTAFF *turns and takes notice of him for the first time.*

[15] *Accent "you."*
HOST *remains up at back, amused.*

FALSTAFF.[11] There was, mine host, an old fat woman even now with me ; [12] but she's gone.

[13] SIMPLE. Pray you, sir, was't not the wise woman of Brentford?

FALSTAFF.[14] Ay, marry, was it, mussel-shell : what would you[15] with her?

SIMPLE. My master, sir, Master Slender, sent to her, seeing her go through the streets, to know, sir, whether one Nym, sir, that beguiled him of a chain, had the chain or no.

FALSTAFF. I spake with the old woman about it.

SIMPLE. And what says she, I pray, sir?

FALSTAFF. Marry, she says that the very same man that beguiled Master Slender of his chain cozened him of it.

SIMPLE. I would I could have spoken with the woman herself ; I had other things to have spoken with her too from him.

FALSTAFF. What are they? let us know.

HOST. [Ay, come ; quick.

SIMPLE. I may not conceal them, sir.

HOST. Conceal them, or thou diest.]

SIMPLE. Why, sir, they were nothing but about Mistress Anne Page ; to know if it were my master's fortune to have her or no.

FALSTAFF. 'Tis, 'tis his fortune.

SIMPLE. What, sir?

FALSTAFF. To have her, or no. Go ; say the woman told me so.

SIMPLE. May I be bold to say so, sir?[1]

FALSTAFF. Ay, sir ; like who more bold.

SIMPLE. I thank your worship : I shall make my master glad with these tidings.   [Exit.

HOST.[2] Thou art clerkly, thou art clerkly, Sir John. Was there a wise woman with thee?

FALSTAFF. Ay, that there was, mine host ; one that hath taught me more wit than ever I learned before in my life ; and I paid nothing for it neither, but was paid for my learning.[3] I would all the world might be cozened ; for I have been cozened and beaten too. If it should come to the ear of the court, how I have been transformed and how my transformation hath been washed and cudgelled, they would melt me out of my fat drop by drop and liquor fishermen's boots with me : I warrant they would whip me with their fine wits till I were as crest-fallen as a dried pear. I never prospered since I forswore myself at primero. Well, if my wind were but long enough to say my prayers, I would repent.[4]

Enter MISTRESS QUICKLY.

Now, whence come you?

QUICKLY.[5] From the two parties, forsooth.

[6] FALSTAFF. The devil take one party and his dam the other! and so they shall be both bestowed.[7] I have suffered more for their sakes, more than the villanous inconstancy of man's disposition is able to bear.

QUICKLY.[8] And have not they suffered? Yes, I warrant ; speciously one of them ; Mistress Ford, good heart, is beaten black and blue, that you cannot see a white spot about her.

FALSTAFF. What tellest thou me of black and blue? I was beaten myself into all the colours of the rainbow ; and I was like to be apprehended for the witch of Brentford : but that my admirable dexterity of wit, my counterfeiting the action of an old woman, delivered me, the knave constable had set me i' the stocks, i' the common stocks, for a witch.

QUICKLY. Sir, let me speak with you in your chamber : [9] you shall hear how things go ; and, I warrant, to your content. Here is a letter will say somewhat.[10] Good hearts, what ado here is to bring you together! Sure, one of you does not serve heaven well, that you are so crossed.

FALSTAFF. Come up into my chamber.[11]   [Exeunt.

Enter FENTON *and* HOST.[12]

[HOST. Master Fenton talk not to me ; my mind is heavy : I will give over all.

FENTON. Yet hear me speak. Assist me in my purpose,
And, as I am a gentleman, I'll give thee
A hundred pound in gold more than your loss.

HOST. I will hear you, Master Fenton ; and I will at the least keep your counsel.]

FENTON. From time to time I have acquainted you
With the dear love I bear to fair Anne Page ;
Who mutually hath answer'd my affection,
[So far forth as herself might be her chooser]
Even to my wish : [I have a letter from her

[1] BARDOLPH *comes on and speaks to* HOST, *indicating that* FENTON *is waiting below to speak with him.* BARDOLPH *exits after* SIMPLE.

[2] *Going across to* R. *Turns and asks the question with a sly grin. Accent "was."*

[3] HOST *exits, still grinning.*

[4] *Rises at the end of his speech. As he does so,* QUICKLY *enters up* R. *He turns and is confronted with her. She very complacent and sweet. He looks at her for a moment, then bellows out his line.*

[5] *Sweetly and with a nice bob.*

[6] *Going up to the stairs.*

[7] *Turns to her at the foot of stairs*

[8] *Comes up to him speaking in extenuation of "both parties."*

[9] FALSTAFF *is not so receptive to her manner or suggestions as he was.*

[10] *Gives letter to him and he opens it and reads.*

[11] *A moment or two whilst he reads. Then the letter apparently alters his decision. He invites her up, but not completely restored in temper. She sighs, very pleased, and goes up.*

[12] *Speak as they enter from up* R., FENTON *on* HOST'S L. *They cross to chair over* L. *and* FENTON *sits on its* R. *arm.*

ACT II, SC. VIII

Of such contents as you will wonder at ;
The mirth whereof so larded with my matter,
That neither singly can be manifested,
Without the show of both ; fat Falstaff
Hath a great scene : the image of the jest
I'll show you here at large.] Hark, good mine host.
To-night at Herne's oak, just 'twixt twelve and one,
Must my sweet Nan present the Fairy Queen ;
The purpose why, is here : in which disguise,
[While other jests are something rank on foot.]
Her father hath commanded her to slip
Away with Slender and with him at Eton
Immediately to marry : she hath consented :
Now sir,
Her mother, ever strong against that match
And firm for Doctor Caius, hath appointed
That he shall likewise shuffle her away,
While other sports are tasking of their minds,
And at the deanery, where a priest attends,
Straight marry her : to this her mother's plot
She seemingly obedient likewise hath
Made promise to the doctor. Now, thus it rests :
Her father means she shall be all in white,
And in that habit, when Slender sees his time
To take her by the hand and bid her go,
She shall go with him : her mother hath intended,
The better to denote her to the doctor,
For they must all be mask'd and vizarded,
That quaint in green she shall be loose enrobed,
[With ribands pendent, flaring 'bout her head ;]
And when the doctor spies his vantage ripe,
To pinch her by the hand, and, on that token,
The maid hath given consent to go with him.
    HOST.   Which means she to deceive, father or mother ?

[1] *Accent " both," and " me." Rise on this line and take* HOST *to* C.

    FENTON.   Both,[1] my good host, to go along with me :[1]
And here it rests, that you'll procure the vicar
To stay for me at church 'twixt twelve and one,
And, in the lawful name of marrying,
To give our hearts united ceremony.

[2] *Going to* R.
[3] *Turn.*
[4] *Going up to him.*
[5] *Giving him money. They both laugh and go off* R.
    A few bars of music can be played here just to work the lapse of time, and ceasing as FALSTAFF *appears.*

    HOST.   Well, husband your device ; I'll to the vicar :[2]
[3] Bring you the maid, you shall not lack a priest.
    FENTON.   So shall I evermore be bound to thee ;[4]
Besides, I'll make a present recompense.[5]   *[Exeunt.*

[6] *From the stairs.* FALSTAFF *first.*

[7] *Stopping* QUICKLY'S *long speeches.*
[8] *Emphatic.*
[9] *She is about to speak, and he sees it coming.*

[10] *Bawls it.*

Enter FALSTAFF *and* MISTRESS QUICKLY.[6]

    FALSTAFF.   Prithee, no more prattling :[7] go.[8] I'll hold. This is the third time ; I hope good luck lies in odd numbers.[9] Away ! go. They say there is divinity in odd numbers, either in nativity, chance, or death. Away.[10]
    QUICKLY.   I'll provide you a chain ; and I'll do what I can to get you a pair of horns.

FALSTAFF.[1]   Away, I say ; time wears : hold up your head, and mince.   [*Exit* MRS. QUICKLY.

Enter FORD.

How now, Master Brook! Master Brook, the matter will be known to-night, or never. Be you in the Park about midnight, at Herne's oak, and you shall see wonders.[2]

FORD.   Went you not to her yesterday, sir, as you told me you had appointed? [3]

FALSTAFF.   I went to her, Master Brook, as you see, like a poor old man : but I came from her, Master Brook, like a poor old woman. That same knave Ford, her husband, hath the finest mad devil of jealousy in him, Master Brook, that ever governed frenzy. I will tell you : he beat me grievously, in the shape of a woman ; for in the shape of man, Master Brook, I fear not Goliath with a weaver's beam ; because I know also life is a shuttle.[4] I am in haste ;[5] go along with me : I'll tell you all, Master Brook. Since I plucked geese, played truant and whipped top, I knew not what 'twas to be beaten till lately. Follow[6] me : I'll tell you strange things of this knave Ford, on whom to-night I will be revenged, and[7] I will deliver his wife into your hand. Follow. [8] Strange things in hand, Master Brook! Follow.   [*Exeunt.*[9]

SCENE IX [10]

Windsor Park.[11]

Enter PAGE, SHALLOW, *and* SLENDER.

PAGE.   Come, come ; we'll couch i' the castle-ditch **till** we see the light of our fairies. Remember, son Slender, my daughter.

SLENDER.   Ay, forsooth ; I have spoke with her and we have a nay-word how to know one another : I come to her in white, and cry " mum " ; she cries " budget " ; and by that we know one another.

SHALLOW.   That's good too : but what needs either your " mum " or her " budget? " the white will decipher her well enough. It hath struck ten o'clock.

PAGE.   The night is dark ; lights and spirits will become it well. Heaven prosper our sport! No man means evil but the devil, and we shall know him by his horns. Let's away ; follow me. [*Exeunt.*[12]

Enter MISTRESS PAGE, MISTRESS FORD, *and* DOCTOR CAIUS.[13]

MRS. PAGE.   Master doctor, my daughter is in green : when you see your time, take her by the hand, away with her to the deanery, and dispatch it quickly. Go before into the Park : we two must go together.

CAIUS.[14]   I know vat I have to do. Adieu.

MRS. PAGE.   Fare you well, sir. [*Exit* CAIUS.] [15] My husband will not rejoice so much at the abuse of Falstaff as he will chafe at the doctor's marrying my daughter : but 'tis no matter ; better a little chiding than a great deal of heart-break.

MRS. FORD.   Where is Nan now and her troop of fairies, and the Welsh devil Hugh?

ACT II, SC. VIII

[1] *Sends her out with sheer sound. FALSTAFF comes down to get his hat which is on the back of chair, and stick, leaning against it. As he does so,* FORD *enters and meets* QUICKLY. *She whispers to him that* FALSTAFF *is coming and slips out. By this time* FALSTAFF *has secured his things and turns to see* FORD *advancing to him.*

[2] *Speaks with profound meaning.*

[3] *Coming down to* C.

[4] *Suddenly remembers all that he has to do, and crosses* FORD.
[5] *Turns to him.*
[6] *Takes his* R. *arm and they go up* R.
[7] *Stop and turns to him.*
[8] *Makes this very mysterious and full of great meaning.*
[9] FALSTAFF *goes off.* FORD *turns to audience and bursts out laughing and then exits.*
Fairy music begins at fall of curtain.

SCENE IX
Windsor Park
See Illustration No. 4, p. 22.

[10] *The fairy music can be heard going all through the scenes, swelling up just for a moment or so between the different exits and entrances and then dying down again, but still audible.*
[11] *Enter from* R. PAGE, SLENDER *and* SHALLOW. *They all wear light-coloured cloaks.*

[12] L.

[13] *Enter* R. MRS. PAGE, CAIUS *and* FORD.

[14] *Crosses to* L.
[15] *Exit* L.

ACT II, SC. IX

[1] L.

[2] *Music swells up as* FAIRIES, *headed by* EVANS, *enter* R. *They all dance right across without stopping,* EVANS *speaking his lines during his tripping. As they exit the music dies down to complete silence. The lights dim out and the front tabs fall. The inner curtains are taken away and the lights set. During this pause the Windsor Bell is heard strike twelve, as far away as it can be made to appear. Then the curtain rises.*

MRS. PAGE.   They are all couched in a pit hard by Herne's oak, with obscured lights ; which, at the very instant of Falstaff's and our meeting, they will at once display to the night.

MRS. FORD.   That cannot choose but amaze him.

MRS. PAGE.   If he be not amazed, he will be mocked ; if he be amazed, he will every way be mocked.

MRS. FORD.   [We'll betray him finely.

MRS. PAGE.   Against such lewdsters and their lechery Those that betray them do no treachery.]

MRS. FORD.   The hour draws on. To the oak, to the oak!

                                     [*Exeunt.*[1]

     Enter SIR HUGH EVANS *disguised, with others as Fairies.*[2]

EVANS.   Trib, trib, fairies ; come ; and remember your parts : be pold, I pray you ; follow me into the pit ; and when I give the watch-'ords, do as I pid you : come, come ; trib, trib.   [*Exeunt.*

ILLUSTRATION No. 7
Act II, Scene X

SCENE X [1]

Another part of the Park.

Enter FALSTAFF *disguised as Herne.*

FALSTAFF. The Windsor bell hath struck twelve ; the minute draws on. Now, the hot-blooded gods assist me ! Remember, Jove, thou wast a bull for thy Europa ; love set on thy horns. O powerful love ! that, in some respects, makes a beast a man, in some other, a man a beast. You were also, Jupiter, a swan for the love of Leda. O omnipotent Love ! [2] how near the god drew to the complexion of a goose. [A fault done first in the form of a beast. O Jove, a beastly fault ! And then another fault in the semblance of a fowl ; think on't, Jove ; a foul fault ! When gods have hot backs, what shall poor men do ?] For me, I am here a Windsor stag ; and the fattest, I think, i' the forest.[3] [Send me a cool rut-time, Jove, or who can blame me to piss my tallow ?] Who comes here ? my doe ?

Enter MISTRESS FORD *and* MISTRESS PAGE.

MRS. FORD. Sir John ! art thou there, my deer ? [my male deer ?]
FALSTAFF. My doe with the black scut ! Let the sky rain potatoes ; let it thunder to the tune of Green Sleeves, [hail kissing-comfits and snow eringoes]: let there come a tempest of provocation,[4] I will shelter me here.
MRS. FORD. Mistress Page is come with me,[5] sweetheart.[6]
FALSTAFF. Divide me like a bribe buck, each a haunch : [I will keep my sides to myself, my shoulders for the fellow of this walk, and my horns I bequeath your husbands.] Am I a woodman, ha ? Speak I like Herne the hunter ? Why, now is Cupid a child of conscience ; he makes restitution. As I am a true spirit, welcome ! [7]

[Noise within.

ACT II, SC. X

SCENE X

Another part of the Park

[1] *A sound of clanking chains is heard, getting gradually nearer until in the blue moonlight appears, not Herne the Hunter, but* FALSTAFF. *With horns and chains and, out of breath, he comes and stands in front of the oak.*

[2] MRS. FORD *and* MRS. PAGE *steal on from* L. MRS. PAGE *runs behind the tree to* R., *and* MRS. FORD *times it so that she drops down* L. *at* [3] .

[4] *About here* MRS. PAGE *comes into view down* R.

[5] *Very sweetly just as* FALSTAFF *is about to embrace—and doesn't.*

[6] *Groan of disappointment from* FALSTAFF, *signifying " That woman again."*

[7] *Both arms out to take them both when the noise is made off stage.*

D*

ACT II, SC. X

[1] *Both run off* L.

[2] FALSTAFF *thumps his stick on the ground. His pleasure is always snatched from his lips.*
Fairy music starts. EVANS *leads on from up* R. *and comes down* R. *with fairies running after him. All holloaing. From the other side comes* QUICKLY *and her contingent as in the figure.* ANNE, *who follows in* QUICKLY'S *group, comes* C. *behind* FALSTAFF, *who has gone down on his knees at the strange sound and gathering.* HOST *and his two boys dressed one in white, the other in green, remain up at back.*
FALSTAFF *simply stares straight out in front of him. As he kneels down he must come forward a step or two to leave room behind him for* ANNE.

[3] *Speaks in hoarse whisper, lies down.*
In the grouping, bring the characters as far down as possible so that PISTOL *is almost on a level with the oak.*
The fairy music continues to play softly through the entire scene until cue comes for it to stop.
[4] *Bottom fairy steps forward.*

[5] FAIRY *exits up* R.

[6] *The group joins up:* EVANS *and* QUICKLY *meeting in* C. *in front of* FALSTAFF. *They do not actually meet, but stop just before they reach* FALSTAFF.
[7] *Going up to him and above him.*

MRS. PAGE.   Alas, what noise?
MRS. FORD.   Heaven forgive our sins!
FALSTAFF.   What should this be?
MRS. FORD. }
MRS. PAGE. } Away, away!   [*They run off.*[1]
FALSTAFF.[2]   I think the devil will not have me damned, lest the oil that's in me should set hell on fire; he would never else cross me thus.

Enter SIR HUGH EVANS, *disguised as before;* PISTOL, *as Hobgoblin;* MISTRESS QUICKLY, ANNE PAGE, *and others, as Fairies, with tapers.*

[ANNE.]   Fairies, black, grey, green, and white,
You moonshine revellers, and shades of night,
You orphan heirs of fixed destiny,
Attend your office and your quality.
Crier Hobgoblin, make the fairy oyes.
    PISTOL.   Elves, list your names; silence, you airy toys.
Cricket, to Windsor chimneys shalt thou leap:
Where fires thou find'st unraked and hearths unswept,
There pinch the maids as blue as bilberry:
Our radiant queen hates sluts and sluttery.
    [3] FALSTAFF.   They are fairies; he that speaks to them shall die:
I'll wink and couch: no man their works must eye.
                    [*Lies down upon his face.*
    EVANS.   Where's Bede? [4] Go you, and where you find a maid
That, ere she sleep, has thrice her prayers said,
Raise up the organs of her fantasy;
Sleep she as sound as careless infancy:
But those as sleep and think not on their sins,
Pinch them, arms, legs, backs, shoulders, sides and [5] shins.
    ANNE.   About, about;
Search Windsor Castle, elves, within and out:
Strew good luck, ouphes, on every sacred room:
That it may stand till the perpetual doom,
In state as wholesome as in state 'tis fit,
Worthy the owner, and the owner it.
The several chairs of order look you scour
With juice of balm and every precious flower:
Each fair instalment, coat, and several crest,
With loyal blazon, evermore be blest!
And nightly, meadow-fairies, look you sing,
Like to the Garter's compass, in a ring:
The expressure that it bears, green let it be,
More fertile-fresh than all the field to see;
And 'Honi soit qui mal y pense' write
In emerald tufts, flowers purple, blue, and white;
Like sapphire, pearl and rich embroidery,
Buckled below fair knighthood's bending knee:
Fairies use flowers for their charactery.
Away; disperse: but till 'tis one o'clock,
Our dance of custom round about the oak
Of Herne the hunter, let us not forget.
    EVANS.   Pray you, lock hand in hand; [6] yourselves in order set;
And twenty glow-worms shall our lanterns be,
To guide our measure round about the tree.
But, stay; I smell a man of middle-earth.[7]

FALSTAFF.   Heavens defend me from that Welsh fairy,
lest he transform me to a piece of cheese!

PISTOL.   Vile worm, thou wast o'erlook'd even in [1] thy birth.

QUICKLY.   With trial-fire touch me his finger-end : [2]
If he be chaste, the flame will back descend
And turn him to no pain ; but if he start,
It is the flesh of a corrupted heart.

PISTOL.   A trial, come.

EVANS.   Come, will this wood take fire?
                    [*They burn him with their tapers.*

FALSTAFF.   Oh, Oh, Oh!

QUICKLY.   Corrupt, corrupt, and tainted in desire!
About him, fairies ; sing a scornful rhyme ;
And, as you trip, still pinch him to your time.[3]

SONG.

Fie on sinful fantasy !
Fie on lust and luxury !
Lust is but a bloody fire,
Kindled with unchaste desire,
Fed in heart, whose flames aspire
As thoughts do blow them, higher and higher.
Pinch him, fairies, mutually ;
Pinch him for his villany ;
Pinch him, and burn him, and turn him about,
Till candles and starlight and moonshine be out.

Enter PAGE, FORD, MISTRESS PAGE *and* MISTRESS FORD.

PAGE.   Nay, do not fly ; I think we have watch'd you now :
Will none but Herne the hunter serve your turn?

MRS. PAGE.   I pray you, come, hold up the jest no higher.
Now, good Sir John, how like you Windsor wives?
[See you these, husband? do not these fair yokes
Become the forest better than the town?]

FORD.   Now, sir, who's a cuckold now?   Master Brook, Falstaff's
a knave, a cuckoldly knave ; here are his horns, Master Brook : and,
Master Brook, he hath enjoyed nothing of Ford's but his buck-basket,
his cudgel, and twenty pounds of money, which must be paid to
Master Brook ; his horses are arrested for it, Master Brook.

MRS. FORD.   Sir John, we have had ill luck ; we could never
meet.   I will never take you for my love again ; but I will always
count you my deer.

FALSTAFF.   I do begin to perceive that I am made an ass.

FORD.   Ay, and an ox [4] too : both the proofs are extant.

FALSTAFF.   And these are not fairies? [5]   I was three or four times
in the thought they were not fairies ; [and yet the guiltiness of my
mind, the sudden surprise of my powers, drove the grossness of the
foppery into a received belief, in despite of the teeth of all rhyme and
reason, that they were fairies.]   See now how wit may be made a
Jack-a-Lent, when 'tis upon ill employment!

EVANS.   Sir John Falstaff, serve Got, and leave [6] your desires, and
fairies will not pinse you.

FORD.   Well said, fairy Hugh.

EVANS.   And leave your jealousies too, I pray you.

FORD.   I will never mistrust my wife again, till thou art able to
woo her in good English.

ACT II, SC. X

[1] *Coming down above him.*

[2] *Here the* FAIRIES *can light their candles by applying them to their lanterns.*

[3] *They all join up and commence their dance.* ANNE *joins up with them, next to* PISTOL. *As the group closes in it should be able to join at the back behind the tree. A sufficient number of* FAIRIES *must be provided to ensure this.*
    As the dance begins CAIUS *comes on from proscenium entrance down* L. HOST, *who is up at back, watching, sends the* SERVANT, *dressed in green, down* R. *and he skips across from* R. *to* L. *where* CAIUS *is standing.* CAIUS *takes his hand and squeezes it. The boy giggles ;* CAIUS *does the same and they trip off* L. (*proscenium entrance*) *very happy.*
    SLENDER *appears from down* R. (*proscenium entrance*). *The other* SERVANT *repeats the former business.* SLENDER *cries "Mum," the* SERVANT, *"Budget" : both giggle and go off* R. (*proscenium entrance*).
    HOST *then joins in the dance, taking* ANNE'S *right hand and joining his other with that of* PISTOL. FENTON *appears from* L.1 *or* L.2 E. *and comes down* L. *looking anxiously for* ANNE. *As* HOST *reaches him he leads* ANNE *out of the circle, gives her to* FENTON, *and they continue their dance across the front of the stage round the back and up off top* L., *followed by* HOST *still dancing to the music.*
    When he leaves the circle, the rest immediately close in on FALSTAFF *and pinch him. As soon as* FENTON, ANNE, *and* HOST *have gone off, they all run off up* R., *making the same noise as when they entered.*
    FALSTAFF *lies dead still, then cautiously raises his head and looks about. Seeing that he is alone, he rises, groaning and takes off his horns. As he does so* FORD *and* MRS. FORD *appear from the* R. *wings and come round behind the tree to* L. *just as* FALSTAFF *makes a move to go in that direction. As they come down, they too make the same noise as the* FAIRIES *and* FALSTAFF *groans with fright and turns to go* R., *where he encounters* MR. *and* MRS. PAGE, *who have followed the other two on from the wings. Simultaneously* EVANS *and the rest re-appear and fill the stage, uttering their cries.* FALSTAFF *goes down on his knees.*

[4] *Pointing to the horns.*

[5] *Laugh and " No " from all. He then struggles to his feet very relieved.*

[6] *Laugh from all.* EVANS *comes down to him at this line.*

FALSTAFF. Have I laid my brain in the sun and dried it, that it wants matter to prevent so gross o'er-reaching as this? Am I ridden with a Welsh goat too? shall I have a coxcomb of frize? 'Tis time I were choked with a piece of toasted cheese.

EVANS. Seese is not good to give putter ; your belly is all putter.

FALSTAFF. "Seese" and "putter"! have I lived to stand at the taunt of one that makes fritters of English? [This is enough to be the decay of lust and late-walking through the realm.]

MRS. PAGE. Why, Sir John, do you think, though we would have thrust virtue out of our hearts by the head and shoulders and have given ourselves without scruple to hell, that ever the devil could have made you our delight?

FORD. What, a hodge-pudding? a bag of flax?

MRS. PAGE. A puffed man?

PAGE. [Old, cold, withered and of intolerable entrails?]

FORD. And one that is as slanderous as Satan?

PAGE. And as poor as Job?

FORD. And as wicked as his wife?]

EVANS. And given to fornications, and to taverns and sack and wine and [metheglins], and to drinkings and swearings and starings, pribbles and prabbles?

FALSTAFF. Well, I am your theme : you have the start of me ; I am dejected ; I am not able to answer the Welsh flannel ; [1] ignorance itself is a plummet o'er me : use me as you will.

FORD. [Marry, sir, we'll bring you to Windsor, to one Master Brook, that you have cozened of money, to whom you should have been a pander : over and above that you have suffered, I think to repay that money will be a biting affliction.]

PAGE.[2] Yet be cheerful, knight : thou shalt eat a posset to-night at my house ; where I will desire thee to laugh at my wife, that now laughs at thee : tell her Master Slender hath married her daughter.

MRS. PAGE.[3] [aside]. Doctors doubt that : if Anne Page be my daughter, she is, by this, Doctor Caius' wife.

Enter SLENDER.[4]

SLENDER. Whoa, ho! ho, father Page!

PAGE. Son, how now! how now, son! have you dispatched?

SLENDER. Dispatched! I'll make the best in Gloucestershire know on 't ; would I were hanged, la, else!

PAGE. Of what, son?

SLENDER. I came yonder at Eton to marry Mistress Anne Page, and she's a great lubberly boy. If it had not been i' the church, I would have swinged him, or he should have swinged me. If I did not think it had been Anne Page, would I might never stir!—and 'tis a postmaster's boy.

PAGE. Upon my life, then, you took the wrong.

SLENDER. What need you tell me that? I think so, when I took a boy for a girl. [If I had been married to him, for all he was in woman's apparel, I would not have had him.]

PAGE. Why, this is your own folly. Did not I tell you how you should know my daughter by her garments?

SLENDER. I went to her in white, and cried "mum," and she cried "budget," as Anne and I had appointed ; and yet it was not Anne, but a postmaster's boy.[5]

MRS. PAGE. Good George, be not angry : I knew of your purpose ;

[1] EVANS *goes up stage laughing heartily.*

[2] *Goes up to* FALSTAFF.

[3] *Aside to audience.*

[4] SLENDER *runs on from* R. *(proscenium entrance) and across.* PAGE, *not knowing where he is until he hears his voice, then he turns to him. He is blubbering.*

[5] PAGE *makes as if to hit him and he runs off* R., *blubbering hard.*

turned my daughter into green ; and, indeed, she is now with the doctor at the deanery, and there married.

Enter CAIUS.[1]

CAIUS. Vere is Mistress Page? By gar, I am cozened : I ha' married un garçon, a boy ; un paysan, by gar, a boy ; it is not Anne Page : by gar, I am cozened.

[1] CAIUS *enters from down* L. *and comes to* L. *of* FALSTAFF.

MRS. PAGE. Why, did you take her in green?

CAIUS. Ay, by gar, and 'tis a boy : by gar, I'll raise all Windsor.
                                                    [*Exit.*[2]

FORD. This is strange. Who hath got the right Anne?

PAGE. My heart misgives me : here comes Master Fenton.

[2] *He moves over to the exit, turns and gives one fierce "Ah" and leaps into the air, and exits. All laugh.*

Enter FENTON *and* ANNE PAGE.[3]

How now, Master Fenton!

[3] *Up* L.

ANNE.[4] Pardon, good father! good my mother, pardon!

PAGE. Now, mistress, how chance you went not with Master Slender?

[4] ANNE *comes over to her father and then to her mother.* FENTON *follows and stands* L. *of* PAGE.

MRS. PAGE. Why went you not with master doctor, maid?

FENTON.[5] You do amaze her : hear the truth of it.
You would have married her most shamefully,
Where there was no proportion held in love.
The truth is, she and I, long since contracted,
Are now so sure that nothing can dissolve us.
The offence is holy that she hath committed ;
[And this deceit loses the name of craft,
Of disobedience, or unduteous title,
Since therein she doth evitate and shun
A thousand irreligious cursed hours,
Which forced marriage would have brought upon her.]

[5] FENTON *goes to her and takes her in his arms.*

FORD. Stand not amazed ; here is no remedy :
In love the heavens themselves do guide the state ;
Money buys lands, and wives are sold by fate.

FALSTAFF. I am glad, though you have ta'en a special stand to strike at me, that your arrow hath glanced.

PAGE. Well, what remedy? Fenton,[6] heaven give thee joy!
What cannot be eschew'd must be embraced.[7]

[6] *Puts his hands on* FENTON'S *shoulders, who has turned to him.*

[7] ANNE *turns to her mother, who kisses her.*

FALSTAFF. When night-dogs run, all sorts of deer are chased.

MRS. PAGE. Well, I will muse no further. Master Fenton,[8]
Heaven give you many, many merry days!
Good husband, let us every one go home,
And laugh this sport o'er by a country fire ;
Sir John and all.[9]

[8] *Passes* ANNE *to him.*

FORD.   [Let it be so. Sir John,
To Master Brook you yet shall hold your word ;
For he to-night shall lie with Mistress Ford.]   [*Exeunt.*

[9] *She crosses to* FALSTAFF *and both she and* MRS. FORD *do a deep curtesy.*

Curtain.

THE MERRY WIVES OF WINDSOR

FOREWORD

The happy mood of *The Merry Wives of Windsor*, the neat balance of its quaint characters ; the restrained erotic element converted into entertainment and free from noxious grossness ; the skilful use of bye-plots of which there are five in the play, woven so smoothly into the general composition ; the modified weight of FALSTAFF adjusted to the requirements of the action : these, among other characteristics, show with certainty the art of Shakespeare in its specific nature as the anatomy of the leaf or blossom, rightly seen, shares the same organizing genius that creates the star. Shakespeare cannot help but work in fine measures ; and they assert themselves equally in his every exploitation of human nature whether it shudders, stretches, sobs or breaks in the contest of principalities and powers, or revels in the saving grace of innocuous humour. The sparkling waves are still the waters of the deep, and the breeze the light touch of quiescent gales.

Predominant among the poet's faculties is that of temperance, of control. In the moments of greatest turbulence where strength of movement is titanic, there is a presiding authority determining its career, an unassailable technique which is the conscious director of that dramatic operation, the responsible agent by means of which it accomplishes its compelling effect. It is stronger than the steeds that prance the high ether of imagination, and preserves assurance of the day ; and it ordains its characters, orders their words, designs their company so that each perfectly models the personality of the other ; and in every tissue of the play's substance, gives the unexpected turn of growth, the precise organization of form, the modulation of subject-matter that brings it into the captivity of propriety and directs it to an ultimate wholesomeness.

These observations are justified by the fact that because the play is a light comedy it cannot be taken in a trivial way. If this is the method of approach, nothing notable will be achieved. It is very high art indeed to be able to create eccentric characters and keep them human, and ridicule without distorting it into absurdity : and it requires the same strictness of discipline of the actor to represent it with conviction—discipline and its derivative, good taste. He will achieve more by sober art than licentious liberty, and give greater delight. He will find his own work either enhanced as a complement, or rebuked by the persistent integrity of the things he ignores, according to his choice of behaviour. Whatever is done as a development of a part or situation, and it is the actor's function as an artist to do this, must be a spontaneous enlargement of the fundamental matter itself, not an imposition of some form of clever ' originality '. The best form of individuality is the submission to truth to enable it to use each vessel in that peculiar capacity which is given to it by the universal law of varied condition by means of which no two things of the same kind are made alike, so that each may add a slight revelation of its own however modest it may be. Shakespeare is real in everything he creates, and anything contrary to that reality, whether in tragedy or comedy, is neither common-sense nor art. It does not carry any conviction even in its moment of being. Shakespeare has been convincing for nearly four centuries and he is worth obedience.

Planned then first on a serious basis, this play will rise in a wealth of intriguing life, richly varied, alive with temperament and lovable souls.

Our poet is essentially the same in every exercise of his art, whether dealing with life as a throe of immortal birth, or as a poem upon the lips of youth, or as a smile or satire. Had he not been able to write *The Merry Wives of Windsor*, he could not have written *King Lear*. The creative principles are in each case the same.

COMMENTARY

ACT I SCENE I

This play, being light in texture and in plot, is, nevertheless, fully alive with a rich assortment of characters, and almost all of them slightly eccentric in the drawing. They are perfectly natural and plainly human, but each is vital with pronounced characteristics developed by each other's assertiveness. It is this which gives the play its great delight and brings the engaging complement to the slight substance of the main action. The incensed SHALLOW, the simple-minded SLENDER, the contriving, direct EVANS making ' fritters of English ', the good-humoured PAGE, the jovial FALSTAFF, the explosive PISTOL and belligerent BARDOLPH, the venomous and furtive NYM, the charming but very collected ANNE PAGE; all these are deftly and dramatically constructed in the typically concentrated style of Shakespeare and skilfully introduced and combined in action so as to enable the economy of their employment to be exploited to that perfection which is the quality we know as Shakespeare.

Thus, then, in this opening scene especially, carefully watch these different characteristics of the persons concerned, and take advantage of the judicious combinations which bring these qualities into action so as to exercise the right balance of their differences which alone constitutes the action : for as yet we have no plot to engage our attention, only people ; and they are all very interesting. Play closely. Don't allow gaps between speeches. The play is a swiftly moving comedy and it must begin with virility. There is nothing to linger over or to think about. Too much delay will weaken the virtue of the characters, since they have no resources but themselves as yet and no story to support them.

GLOSSARY OF WORDS

1. **Star-chamber.** 1,1–2. Court of Star-chamber. A court developed in the 15th c. out of one already bearing that name. It was a Supreme Court and, through it, the king could wield arbitrary and oppressive power. It was abolished in 1641. It is probable, but not certain, that it took its name from the fact that the roof was decked with stars.
2. **Esquire.** 1,3. See note 7.
3. **Coram.** 1,5. ' justice of peace and " Coram "'. A Latin preposition meaning ' before, in the presence of ', occurring in various legal and other phrases. But it is misused, by SLENDER for *quorum*, which means *lit.* ' of whom ', from the wording of commissions in which certain persons were specially designated as members of a body.
4. **Custalorum.** 1,6. See note 5.
5. **Rato-lorum.** 1,7. SLENDER's blunder for ' Rotulorum '. The full title is *Custos rotulorum*, the principal Justice of the Peace in a county, who has the custody of the rolls and records of the sessions of the peace. Between them, SHALLOW and SLENDER completely mutilate it.
6. **Gentleman.** 1,7. ' and a gentleman born, Master parson ;' A distinct rank given to a man of noble or gentle family who, though not of the nobility, is entitled to bear arms.
7. **Armigero.** 1,8. SHALLOW's romanticism for ' armiger ', L. for an esquire. He comes next to a knight in rank, and the precedence still exists because the rank survives although the courtesy title is applied in writing to man of common status.
8. **Quittance.** 1,9. A document signifying a discharge from debt.
9. **Luces.** 1,14. Adopt. from OFr. *lus* pike-fish. The ref. is to the arms of Sir T. Lucy whom Shakespeare caricatures as SHALLOW. He bore, among other charges, three luces standing upright. The dozen referred to in the next line but one is merely a fanciful exaggeration, in keeping with the satire. There is also a pun on ' luce ' and ' louse '. The coat is ' lousy '.
10. **Passant.** 2,1. ' it agrees well, passant ;' In heraldic language, said of an animal facing dexter, the right side of the shield, and walking, looking forward, and having one paw raised. EVANS adds that it is very apt—walking. (The actual charge is in an upright position. See note 9.)
11. **Py'r lady.** 2,8. A variant of ' By Our Lady '.
12. **Council.** 2,13. See note 1.
13. **Vizaments.** 2,16. ' take your vizaments in that.' An alteration of VISEMENT—ADVISEMENT, deliberations. EVANS advises SHALLOW that the council of Star-chamber is not for hearing riots or petty quarrels such as that between the Justice and FALSTAFF. Actually such cases were sometimes heard there.
14. **Motion.** 2,29. Suggestion.
15. **Fallow.** 2,54. ' How does your fallow greyhound, sir ? ' Of pale brownish or reddish yellow colour. OE. *falu, fealu, fealo.*
16. **Cotsall.** 2,55. A corruption of Cotswold.
17. **Pauca verba.** 3,28. ' Pauca verba, Sir John ;' Few words, and to the point.
18. **Worts.** 3,29. ' Good worts ! good cabbage.' A general name for any plant of the cabbage kind. OE. *wyrt* root. FALSTAFF puns on EVANS' ' goot worts ', *good words.*
19. **Cony-catching.** 3,32. *Lit.* rabbit-catching, and used synonymously for ' cheating ', ' knavish '. The word *cony* is from L. *cunicul-us* rabbit, this word formerly being used for the young animals only.
20. **Nym.** 3,32. The name of ' Nym ' is a variant of *nim* to take, steal.
21. **Banbury cheese.** 3,33. ' You Banbury cheese ! ' Banbury cheese was proverbially thin, or as one quot. states, ' Nothing but paring '. The allusion is to SLENDER's ' weedy ' appearance.
22. **Slice.** 3,37. ' Slice, I say ! ' A thin slice of a man ; NYM's notion of SLENDER. His following *pauca, pauca* is his own peculiar way of saying ' in short '.
23. **Fidelicet.** 3,41. EVANS' version of *videlicet*, that is to say ; *lit.* it is permissible to see.
24. **Great chamber.** 3,53. The principal room of the house, formerly the hall.
25. **Groats.** 3,53. A coin of general European use. The English groat coined in 1351-2 was made equal to fourpence. It is used to indicate a very small sum.
26. **Mill-sixpences.** 3,53-4. Old English coins, milled in 1561, the earliest that were milled (i.e. having serrated edges) in this country.
27. **Edward shovel-boards.** 3,54. A broad shilling of Edward VI, frequently used in the game of Shovel-board.
28. **Yead Miller.** 3,55. Edward, or rather Yedward.
29. **Mountain-foreigner.** 4,3. ' Ha, thou mountain-foreigner ! ' PISTOL's lofty definition of EVANS' Welsh origin.
30. **Latten bilbo.** 4,5. ' I combat challenge of this latten bilbo.' A mixed metal of yellow colour, either identical with, or closely resembling brass ; an inferior metal to finely tempered steel.
31. **Bilbo.** 4,5. Bilbao steel, notably fine.
32. **Labras.** 4,6. ' Word of denial in thy labras here ! ' PISTOL's blunder for L. *labra*, plural of *labrum* lip.
33. **Avised.** 4,9. ' Be avised, sir, and pass good humours :' Cautioned. It is an early form of ADVISED which is from late L. *advisum* view, opinion—*ad* to + *visum* seen. NYM, being accused by SLENDER of stealing his gloves, cautions the latter to cultivate better feelings. See following note.
34. **Humours.** 4,9. A ' humour ' was anciently one of the four chief fluids of the human body by whose relative proportions the temperament was supposed to be determined ; hence *mood, temperament.* It was a subject of great popular interest and was satirically treated by Shakespeare and others at great length.
35. **Marry trap.** 4,9-10. ' I will say " marry trap " with you . . .' Apparently a kind of proverbial exclamation, as much as to say ' By Mary ' you are caught—Nares.

36. **Nuthooks.** 4,10. A cant term for a beadle or constable, probably because he carried a hooked stick like the one used by persons to pull down branches when nutting.

37. **Note.** 4,11. '...the very note of it.' The idea as expressed.

38. **Scarlet and John.** 4,15. 'What say you, Scarlet and John?' A reference to BARDOLPH's red face. There was probably an old ballad containing the line 'And Robin Hood, Scarlet, and John' (see *Henry IV*, 2: V.3.107).

39. **Fap.** 4,19. Drunk.

40. **Cashiered.** 4,19. Deprived of consciousness. This word is of Flemish or Dutch origin meaning *to rescind, make void*.

41. **Conclusions.** 4,20. Powers of reasoning. See note 67.

42. **Careires.** 4,20. The ground on which a race is run; a variant of *career*, adopt. from Fr. *carrière* racecourse. See note 67.

43. **All-hallowmas.** 4,41. The feast of All Saints, Nov. 1; OE. *halʒa*, holy (man), saint.

44. **Michaelmas.** 4,41. The feast of St Michael, Sept. 29.

45. **Tender.** 4,44. 'there is ... a tender ... made afar off by Sir Hugh'. A proposal suggested on SLENDER's behalf. SIR HUGH has advanced the idea of SLENDER's marrying ANNE, to Page, acting 'afar off', i.e. as an intermediary not as a principal.

46. **Capacity.** 4,51. 'if you be capacity of it.' If SLENDER is able to understand.

47. **Parcel.** 5,12. '...the lips is parcel of the mouth.' EVANS evidently means 'part'.

48. **Possitable.** 5,17–18. 'you must speak possitable...' EVANS' version of 'positive', 'positively'.

49. **Conceive.** 5,23. Understand.

50. **Decrease.** 5,26. SLENDER's corruption of 'increase'.

51. **Contempt.** 5,28. SLENDER's blunder for 'content'.

52. **Fall.** 5,31. EVANS' version of 'fault'.

53. **Veneys.** 6,3. 'three veneys for a dish of stewed prunes;' A hit or thrust in fencing; a wound or blow; a bout in fencing. It is an alteration of VENUE, adopt. from OFr. *venue* coming —a coming on to strike.

54. **Sackerson.** 6,12. The name of a famous bear, probably kept for performing and therefore tame.

55. **Cock and pie.** 6,18. An oath, a perversion of the word God (an intermediate form being 'gock') + *Pie* a collection of rules in the R.C. Church of the pre-Reformation period dealing with the rearrangements of moveable feast-days.

56. **Nurse.** 6,30. One who looks after him, housekeeper. EVANS adds 'dry nurse', to make sure.

57. **Pippins.** 6,37. The names of a great variety of appies now raised from pips.

GLOSSARY OF PHRASES

58. **They may give the dozen white luces in their coat.** 1,13–14. They may show this as a charge on their shield. See note 9.

59. **The dozen white louses do become an old coat well.** 1,16. A quibble upon 'luces' and 'louses' and an 'old coat', since it refers both to an ancient heraldic coat and to an old suiting, in which 'louses' in multiple quantities are to be found. See following quot.

60. **It is a familiar beast to man, and signifies love.** 2,1–2. It is unpleasantly familiar and its love for man is not of the wholesome kind.

61. **The luce is the fresh fish; the salt fish is an old coat.** 2,3. No satisfactory explanation of this passage has yet been made. The pun lies in the second half of it. *Salt* may represent 'saltant', a current word for *jumping*. The jumping 'fish' are (part of) an old coat, the latter bearing the same double meaning as in 1,19. There is no heraldic fact to support any pre-existing surplus of luces.

62. **I may quarter, coz.** 2,4. SLENDER is proudly stating that his coat is a quarterly one, i.e. bearing the composite arms of his antecedents in the quarters. SHALLOW seizes the opportunity to introduce his cherished idea of his nephew (ANNE PAGE being the rich prospective bride) and tells SLENDER that he can do the same thing by *marrying*, although, strictly speaking, he would bear her arms on a small shield of pretence imposed on his own. His offspring would then incorporate her arms as quarters.

63. **It is marring indeed, if you quarter it.** 2,6. A pun on 'marring' and 'marrying'. Then in line 8: *if he has a quarter of your coat, there is but three skirts for yourself*, he develops his point by punning on 'coat'. SHALLOW would bear the same paternal arms as his nephew SLENDER, i.e. the arms of SLENDER's grandfather, in the first quarter, hence *your coat*. This leads to the quip about SHALLOW losing a quarter of his garment. See note 62.

64. **She has good gifts.** 2,33. She is well accomplished in looks.

65. **It could not be judged.** 3,1. It was uncertain whether it won or not. PAGE is embarrassed when SLENDER tells him that he heard of his dog having been defeated in a race.

66. **'Twere better for you if it were known in counsel.** 3,26. In private; kept a secret. FALSTAFF suggests to SHALLOW that the latter's threat to take FALSTAFF to the Star-Chamber Council for deer-stealing would be better if left alone. The pun is on 'council' and 'counsel'.

67. **And so conclusions passed the careires.** 4,20. And in consequence of SLENDER's being drunk, his power of reaching proper conclusions was non-existent. See note 42. BARDOLPH's accounting for SLENDER's accusing him of theft brings out this statement.

68. **My Book of Songs and Sonnets.** 4,36–7. This was probably of the Earl of Surrey's authorship and which was popular at this time—Malone.

69. **Book of Riddles.** 4,39. A popular book of the time—Malone.

70. **And, by my troth, I cannot abide the smell of hot meat since.** 6,3–4. J. Dover Wilson points out that the usual omission, before *and, by my troth*, of *and I with my ward defending my head, he hot my shin*, which is in the Quarto, deprives this line of its essential pun. 'Stewed prunes' was also a cant term for *prostitutes* because formerly the STEWS, or hot-air baths, were frequently used for immoral purposes. *Hot* was the old p.pple. of *hit*, hence SLENDER's unconscious quibble and (unconscious) oblique reference to the p. as 'hot meat'.

71. **But I shall as soon quarrel at it as any man in England.** 6,7–8. Criticize the sport of bear-baiting from the point of view of humaneness. SLENDER loves the sport one moment as a young blood should, and then suddenly advertises his sensitivity, all for ANNE's benefit.

72. **So cried and shrieked at it, that it passed.** 6,13–14. Passed all description. SLENDER shows up his own courage in recapturing the (tame) bear, against the fear of the public.

COMMENTARY

ACT I SCENE II

Here we touch the beginning of the main plot of the play where FALSTAFF is driven by straitened circumstances to devise means to obtain money; and after discharging BARDOLPH into the service of the HOST, explains his designs on MRS FORD and MRS PAGE as a means of raising some money from them. At the opening of the scene he is obviously under the shadow of his needs, and this must be manifested in order to enable him to show his happier feelings when balancing the promise of fortune in his conceit about the favours which the two ladies have already shown to him. His moroseness, however, is balanced by the jovial qualities of the HOST so that the scene does not open without vigour. He has his purpose, short as his appearance may be, and it must be allowed to do its proper function accordingly. Then after a short diversion, FALSTAFF leads into his subject. His enquiry as to which of his two remaining followers knows FORD is made the beginning of a major development; and it is for this purpose that the short preceding passage is devised: it enables him to make a pronounced change which would not be so effective were it to take place immediately after the HOST's exit.

From here he begins to move forward on the

definite development of his subject. His treatment of MRS FORD's favours towards him savours of satisfied conceit and expanding egotism which gives action and character in its growth. Again, with the same inflated self-evaluation, he announces his conquest of MRS PAGE's admiration and, happily assured of his prosperity, hands out his letters to PISTOL and NYM for delivery to the respective Wives. But his knavish followers are not taken in by his glamorous fairy-tale and he gets a shock as they throw them back to him. Thus we must have the grandiloquent ascent built up from the earlier despondency and then the sharp counter-action that discloses the pompous conceit for what it is. This is followed by a resounding display of rage, and summary dismissal of his discerning followers. The remaining episodes must be played fast and furiously, otherwise the action will drop. Therefore watch the various movements in the scene and bring to each its own character and quality ; so that, by combination, they give an effective and complete dramatic development.

GLOSSARY OF WORDS

73. **Bully-rook.** 7,2. *Bully* was a term of endearment, possibly derived from Du. meaning ' lover ' (of either sex), ' brother '.
74. **Wag.** 7,5. ' let them wag ;' Get moving. ME. *wagge* from root of OE. *wagian* to oscillate, shake.
75. **Entertain.** 7,9. ' I will entertain Bardolph ;' Take him into service. This is a now obsolete use of the word : late ME. adapt. from Fr. Late L. *inter* among + *tenēre* to hold.
76. **Hector.** 7,10. Son of Priam, King of Troy and one of the most valiant of all the heroes who fought against the Greeks.
77. **Froth and lime.** 7,13. Make a tankard foam.
78. **Wight.** 7,18. ' O base Hungarian wight ! ' A creature of despicable nature. It could mean a man or a woman ; OE. *wiht* thing, a living creature, demon. It was used to denote a living being in general and was sometimes specifically used for either good or (as here) unpleasant qualification.
79. **Spigot.** 7,18. ' wilt thou the spigot wield ? ' A vent-peg on a barrel, and another used to regulate the flow of liquor.
80. **Conceited.** 7,19. ' He was gotten in drink : is not the humour conceited ? ' BARDOLPH has just been made a tapster, and NYM comments upon the fact that the whole idea of BARDOLPH's new appointment is conceived in a very appropriate way.
81. **Tinderbox.** 7,20. A box containing the tinder or inflammable substance used for igniting a flame. A spark was produced by flint and steel usually kept in the same box. The reference is to BARDOLPH probably on account of his red nose. See also *Henry IV*, 1 : III.3.23
82. **Convey.** 8,1. ' " Convey ", the wise it call.' This word was used euphemistically for ' steal ', proceeding from a derived meaning of taking or removing in a secret way. PISTOL thus loftily corrects NYM.
83. **Fico.** 8,1. It. for *Fig*, from L. *ficus* ; a term of contempt.
84. **Kibes.** 8,4. Ulcerated chilblains especially on the heel. The word is of uncertain origin.
85. **Cony-catch.** 8,5. See note 19.
86. **Shift.** 8,5. ' I must shift.' Do something in order to avoid impending disaster ; from OE. *sciftan* to determine. FALSTAFF informs his followers of his impecuniosity and the need for amending it.
87. **Wight.** 8,8. See note 78.
88. **Discourses.** 8,14. ' She discourses, she carves, she gives the leer of invitation :' Talks meaningly, with a persuasive purpose. The word is commonly used to denote ' talking ', ' conversation ' etc. ; but FALSTAFF's deliberate and lewd assessment of MRS FORD's inclinations towards him gives this word a more than ordinary significance, and he pronounces it somewhat artfully.
89. **Carves.** 8,14. See above quot. Probably, talks with elegance that carves into FALSTAFF's desires with subtle suggestion.
90. **Leer of invitation.** 8,14. See above quot. The sensual glance that invites indulgence, and more probably one given from sideways. The early uses of the verb well suit the explanation ' to glance over one's cheek '.
91. **Construe.** 8,15. ' I can construe the action of her familiar style ;' Interpret the familiarity that lies in her method of address : ME. adapt. from L. *construēre* to pile together, build up.
92. **Angels.** 8,22. ' he hath a legion of angels.' A play upon the meaning of the word in its biblical sense and as applied to a gold coin bearing the figure of the archangel Michael standing upon, and piercing the dragon. It varied in value at different times from 6s. 8d. to 10s. It was first coined by Edward IV in 1465.
93. **Judicious œillades.** 8,27. Expert and appreciating amorous glances ; adopt. from Fr. *œillade*, from *œil* eye + *ade* the action (of the eye).
94. **Beam.** 8,27. Bright passionate glance.
95. **Guiana.** 8,34. A South American country rich in gold.
96. **Cheater.** 8,35. ' I will be cheater to them both '. *Cheater* is an aphetic form of ESCHEATOR, an officer of the Exchequer employed to exact forfeitures. The word comes from ME. *eschete*, adopt. from OFr.-Late L. meaning ' to fall to a person's share '. The abuse of the office led to the opprobrious use of the word.
97. **Exchequers.** 8,35. Sources of revenue, the Exchequer being the royal treasury. Originally this office contained a table covered with squares. The accounts were kept by means of counters placed on these squares.
98. **Pandarus.** 8,39. ' Shall I Sir Pandarus of Troy become . . . ? ' One of the Trojan chiefs who was fabled to have procured the love of Cressida (Chryseis) who was with her father in the Grecian camp. Hence, PISTOL refers to himself as a go-between in FALSTAFF's love-making, and that it is beneath the dignity of a soldier to do it.
99. **Humour.** 8,41. See note 34.
100. **Humour-letter.** 8,41. NYM's contemptuous reference to FALSTAFF's ' love '-letter. See note 34.
101. **Tightly.** 8,43. Safely, securely.
102. **Pinnace.** 8,44. ' Sail like my pinnace to these golden shores.' A light vessel. FALSTAFF thus addresses his page when giving him the letters to carry to the two rich Wives from whom he hopes to obtain generous gifts of money—his ' East and West Indies ' as he calls them in l. 36.
103. **Avaunt.** 8,45. Be gone. Adopt. from F. *avant* to the front, forward, and *lit.* meaning ' Onward ! '
104. **French thrift.** 8,48. The meaning of this is unknown.
105. **Skirted.** 8,48. ' myself and skirted page.' Probably, as the play is set in winter-time, the boy might be wearing a long loose gown or cloak over his doublet.
106. **Gourd and fullam.** 8,49. Each word means a species of false dice. PISTOL, in abject self-sympathy, is declaiming against the triumph of dishonesty over virtue.
107. **Tester.** 8,51. Colloquial slang for a sixpence.
108. **Phrygian Turk.** 8,52. Phrygia was a country of Asia Minor. The word Turk was used in a more general way than at present, and PISTOL with his usual extravagance, and supplemented by the resounding phrases of some of the bombastic dramas of the time, either coins or borrows the epithet to describe certain barbaric or unprincipled qualities evidenced in FALSTAFF in his mercenary approaches to both MRS PAGE and MRS FORD, or a double emphasis upon his inebriative qualities.
109. **Operations.** 8,53. ' I have operations which be humours of revenge.' Ideas. The First Folio adds ' in my head ' after ' operations '. Note that in the text *he* is a misprint for *be*.
110. **Welkin.** 8,55. ' By welkin and her star ! ' The heavens : OE. *wolcen* a cloud and thus *the sky, heavens.* As the sentence is obviously derived from some old play, its meaning is lost. ' Star ' may originally have been plural, or the ref. may be to the sun, or the moon, or pole-star.
111. **Eke.** 9,3. Also, in addition. OE. *éac.*
112. **Varlet.** 9,4. A contemptuous name given to a rascal. It is a var. of VALET, which is probably related to VASSEL, and meant a man-servant attending on a gentleman. The meaning eventually degenerated into an opprobrious sense—menial—low-born —and thence to *vile.*
113. **Yellowness.** 9,8. ' I will possess him with yellowness '. Jealousy, on account of the yellow appearance and (reputed) yellow vision of jaundiced people, *jaundiced* being used figuratively for ' being jealous '.
114. **Mars of malcontents.** 9,10. The perfect and god-like champion of those disaffected by (supposedly) ill-usage. Mars was the god of war. It is PISTOL's high-flown approximation of NYM's unlicensed venom and proposed vengeance against FALSTAFF.

GLOSSARY OF PHRASES

115. **I sit at ten pounds a week.** 7,7. FALSTAFF's way of saying that he is living at the rate of ten pounds per week, and needs to economize.

116. **Thou'rt an emperor, Caesar, Keisar, and Pheezar.** 7,8. The HOST's way of telling FALSTAFF that he is living like an emperor, like Caesar, and the rest which are simply his own elaborate variations. J. Dover Wilson quotes Hart as interpreting ' Pheezar ' as ' Vizier '. There was a verb TO FEEZE (Pheese), meaning to drive away, put to flight. The HOST, with customary creativeness, may have intended the sense of ' almightiness '. SLY uses the word in a debased sense in ' *Taming of the Shrew* ' I.1. (Induction) ' *I'll pheeze* (give you what for) *in faith* '.

117. **I am at a word.** 7,13. I have given my word ; the HOST's confirmation of his bond to engage BARDOLPH as a tapster.

118. **A withered serving-man a fresh tapster.** 7,15-16. A man who has finished his career as a serving-man begins a new one as a tapster.

119. **O base Hungarian wight !** 7,18. J. Dover Wilson states

that the ref. is to discarded soldiers after the war between Hungary and the Turks. See note 78.

120. **His filching was like an unskilful singer ; he kept not time.** 7,21-2. He was not careful in his methods, his timing.

121. **The good humour is to steal at a minute's rest.** 7,23. The proper idea or frame of mind is to take as little time as possible—be strict in keeping to this. NYM stretches the meaning of HUMOUR somewhat, but he plays with the word a great deal in his part, exaggerating it for purposes of ridicule. See note 34.

122. **He hath . . . translated her will, out of honesty into English.** 8,18-19. Perhaps a gibe at some of the tricks played with the language at this time.

123. **The anchor is deep: will that humour pass ?** 8,20. That is an equivocal remark : will it be understood ?

124. **Plod away o' the hoof.** 8,46. Go on wearily in poverty (since they refuse to help him to get rich).

125. **High and low beguiles the rich and poor.** 8,50. Dice loaded so as to fall with high or low numbers as required.

COMMENTARY

ACT I   SCENE III

This scene keeps the play going in liveliness of movement through the somewhat highly charged temperament of DR CAIUS. He is a new character and his vigour is different in quality from those who have preceded him. This is necessary, because in bringing the required vitality necessary to maintain our interest he adds a new version to it. In order to enable him to be fully effective, a short scene precedes his introduction, which by its character gives him the advantage of contrast and emphasis which would not be his were he to appear as an opening personality. This preparatory episode, however, is enlivened by an equally new and entertaining type in MRS QUICKLY, so that we are interested as well as technically prepared for our further surprise. She gains our attention by her combination of kindliness and a tongue that is not gravelled for lack of matter, but which has its own peculiar methods of interpreting that matter, and which, joined with her warmth of feeling, gives her a unique quality of character. She is balanced by a very simple SIMPLE, just the antithesis of herself, and between them they make an interesting little picture of SLENDER by their two distinct ideas of him, she taking SIMPLE's facts and converting them into her own truer and not too flattering representation.

This constitutes the action of this slight opening

scene, character in contrast with character. CAIUS is obviously a man to be humoured in his own house, and his Latin temperament creates a tempest indeed when he discovers SIMPLE in his closet and finds that the latter is a messenger from his rival in love for ANNE PAGE. This raises the scene to amusing intensity with MRS QUICKLY making an energetic attempt to preserve a rational balance. Being used to this kind of thing she becomes quite herself after CAUIS has gone to write his letter and delivers herself of her mind and matter with undisturbed and entertaining fullness of character. The Doctor sends SIMPLE away with his challenge to SLENDER, and is still stung with the discovery of the threat to his romance, but is balanced by the unsubdued MRS QUICKLY, who immediately on CAIUS' exit plainly discloses her own ideas about that romance. Her scene with FENTON is carried through with pleasantness which, though artfully encouraging FENTON's hopes of ANNE's love, avoids all compromise. Then, alone, she shows herself to be as deceptive as she is affable and so we have a sketch of a singular character, complete in all its details and placed in conjunction with others equally abnormal though still natural, and each by its due proportion adding the right effect to the composition of the whole.

GLOSSARY OF WORDS

126. **Posset.** 10,6. A drink composed of hot milk curdled with ale, wine or other liquor, often with sugar or spices.

127. **Sea-coal.** 10,7. Mineral coal (coal in the ordinary sense) as opposed to charcoal. Although commonly explained as meaning ' coal brought by sea ' it may more probably have originally taken its name from the fact that the first sources of supply may have been beds exposed on the coasts of Northumberland and South Wales.

128. **Breed-bate.** 10,9. Mischief-maker,

' bate ' being an aphetic form of ' abate ', to strike or beat down.

129. **Peevish.** 10,10. ' he is something peevish that way :' *Eccentric, a little mad.* The derivation is unknown.

130. **Paring-knife.** 10,17. A knife for paring leather.

131. **Cain-coloured.** [10,19. ' a Cain-coloured beard.' Cain's beard was traditionally supposed to be red.

132. **Softly-sprighted.** 10,20. ' A softly-sprighted man . . .' Having made one error in describing SLENDER as wearing

a ' great round beard ' she seems more cautious in her further identification ; and so we have a gentle way of saying that he is weak in spirit.

133. **Tall.** 10,21. Valiant, capable, etc. The word is of obscure origin, and primarily meant *quick, prompt, seemly, elegant, brave,* etc. See note 151.

134. **Warrener.** 10,23. An officer appointed to watch over a game preserve, or WARREN, a piece of land guarding game.

135. **Strut.** 11,2. ' does he not . . . strut

in his gait ?' Walk with affected bold-
ness. MRS QUICKLY reaches SLENDER's
true description at last. SIMPLE reads
the meaning more as manly stride, and
QUICKLY adds that fortune should not
send ANNE a worse fortune.

136. **Shent.** 11,8. Utterly disgraced. It
eventually comes from OE. meaning
shame, disgrace, ignominy, etc.

137. **Closet.** 11,9. A private room used
for any purpose of seclusion.

138. **Horn-mad.** 11,19. ' he would have
been horn-mad . . .' Madness or
mental disturbance caused through
having been made a cuckold. See
note 237.

139. **Simples.** 11,31. ' dere is some
simples in my closet'. Medicines of
elementary nature, probably herbal.
Note the pun, as SIMPLE is in the closet.

140. **Phlegmatic.** 11,41. A word actually
meaning *dull, sluggish,* and entirely
misapplied by MRS QUICKLY to CAIUS

when violently angry at finding
SIMPLE in the closet.

141. **Melancholy.** 12,5. ' you should have
heard him so loud and so melancholy.'
MRS QUICKLY makes a blunder here
by misusing the word for the interpretation of CAIUS' ability in excessive
emotional explosions when fully
roused above what already seems to
have been his limit. It may also be
an author's satire on the ' humour ',
melancholy. See note 34.

142. **Jack'nape.** 12,18. Monkey, ape,
applied opprobriously to a man. The
actual origin is uncertain. It first
appears as an opprobrious nickname
for W. de la Pole, Duke of Suffolk
(d. 1450), whose badge was a clog and
a chain such as was attached to a tame
ape.—See OED.

143. **Meddle or make.** 12,20. Interfere.

144. **Prate.** 12,29. ' We must give folks
leave to prate :' Gossip, talk idly.

MRS QUICKLY is reassuring CAIUS that
any rumours likely to question ANNE's
love for *him* are groundless.

145. **Good-jer.** 12,29. ' what, the good-
jer !' Good-year, an expletive, probably arising from the elliptical use
of *good year* as an exclamation—' as
I hope for a good year '. MRS
QUICKLY is remonstrating with CAIUS
over his intolerance.

146. **Trow.** 12,38. ' Who's there, I trow !'
An enquiry (as I believe someone to
be). It comes from OE. meaning
faith, belief. It sometimes reaches to
' imagine '.

147. **Detest.** 12,54. MRS QUICKLY's
blunder for ' protest '.

148. **Allicholy.** 13,1. MRS QUICKLY's
solecism for ' melancholy '.

149. **Musing.** 13,2. ' she is given . . .
to musing :' Sombre reflectiveness.

150. **Confidence.** 13,7. MRS QUICKLY's
blunder for ' conference '.

GLOSSARY OF PHRASES

151. **He is as tall a man of his hands as any is between this
and his head.** 10,21-2. *Tall of his hands* means ' active,
ready, or valiant with arms or weapons '. He is as valiant
as anyone between his skilful arm and his equally skilful heel.

152. **It is no matter-a ver dat.** 12,24. CAIUS' rendering of
It is no matter for that—' that does not matter '.

153. **You shall have An fool's-head of your own.** 12,33. A
play upon the word ' An '. The only ANNE that CAIUS will
get is an (his own) fool's head.

154. **Good faith, it is such another Nan.** 12,53-4. It is so
like her. MRS QUICKLY comments about ANNE after a

reference to FENTON's wart, which has been the amusing
subject of conversation between the two women at some time.

155. **I shall never laugh but in that maid's company ! But
indeed she is given . . . to allicholy.** 12,55-13,1. MRS
QUICKLY is going to keep her laughter only for ANNE because
she becomes so moody (through suppressed love for FENTON).
BUT needs special attention because it is frequently used in
its more literal sense than at present. It is OE. *be-ūtan,
būtan, būta,* ' on the outside ', ' without '. Thus we have
various senses of *exceptiveness*—' only ', ' because ', as well
as the adversative sense.

COMMENTARY

ACT I   SCENE IV

The main plot of the play now advances a step
further. The Wives have received their letters
from FALSTAFF and their contents awaken the two
women's wits to teach the knight a purging lesson.
The scene must be played with the fullness of
opportunities provided to create liveliness of
amazement, amusement, censure and then an
energetic resolve to invent the reward for such
unwarranted audacity. Watch for these various
phrases and give each a distinction of its own with
the ripeness of treatment that it requires. This
creates the action ; and without such treatment
the matter will become trivial and we shall have
nothing to anticipate.

FORD appears for the first time, attentive to
PISTOL's insinuations concerning FALSTAFF's intentions towards his wife, but as yet only thought-
ful. This is prepared for by the contrasting vigorous background of the consultations between the
two Wives. He intensifies his feelings at PISTOL's
suggestion that he may be made a cuckold, and
shows a stiffness of suspicion against PAGE's
complete lack of concern over NYM's attempt to
scare him with the same threat. Balance this
effect with care because it begins to shape FORD
into relief without undue strain. After a slight
conflict with his genial wife which establishes his

character a little further, we see his circumspection
about her become more intensified, but as yet he
does not betray any violence of feeling. A short
interval provided by the HOST and SHALLOW with
lighter material announcing the forthcoming duel
between CAIUS and EVANS, provides a pause to
enable FORD to resume his activities again, this
time increased by decisive action ; and after a
further short and intervening incident awakened
by SHALLOW and the HOST concerning certain
' sport in hand ', FORD, left alone, openly announces his doubt about his wife's loyalty and his
determination to make proof of it by practical
means.

These, in brief, are the various sections of the
scene, each with their own character and purpose,
which must be faithfully fulfilled in order to create
the dramatic movement of the scene and establish
its total effect with successful emphasis. FORD
begins as a believer in his wife's innocence :—
' Why, sir, my wife is not young.' He ends, strong
enough in his doubts about her to warrant a test.
The carefully appointed variations of incidents in
the scene, skilfully cultivate this development,
give time for growth of idea and by contrast relieve
each progression, so as to enable the final result to
be achieved with economy of means.

GLOSSARY OF WORDS

156. **Holiday-time.** 13,13. ' in the holi-day-time of my beauty '. MRS PAGE's reference to her somewhat late middle-age.

157. **Sack.** 13,18. A general name for a class of white wines formerly imported from Spain and the Canaries : adapt. from Fr. *vin sec*, ' dry wine '.

158. **Herod of Jewry.** 13,28. MRS PAGE is referring to FALSTAFF, not to the letter. It means *concentrated iniquity*.

159. **Flemish drunkard.** 13,30. The Flemish were proverbially hard drinkers.

160. **Assay.** 13,32. ' he dares in this manner assay me . . .' Try to take a liberty. Adopt. from OFr.-L. *exagium* ' weighing ', but used in Romanic in the wider sense of ' exam-ination ', ' trial ', ' testing '. Thus comes the meaning of ' advancing towards a thing or person in order to attempt to execute one's will or desire upon it.

161. **Frugal.** 13,33. ' frugal of my mirth :' Restrained or temperate in her jocu-larity. The basic meaning of the word is *economical, saving*.

162. **Puddings.** 13,36. Food of a coarse, thick nature—grossness of feeding ; a reference to FALSTAFF's indulgencie.

163. **Eternal.** 14,3. ' an eternal moment or so . . .' A moment that might lead to eternal damnation. MRS FORD is alluding to FALSTAFF's ' invitation ' as made in his letter to her.

164. **Hack.** 14,6. ' These knights will hack ;' The meaning has never been satisfactorily solved. Steevens sug-gests that it may mean ' to do mis-chief '. Staunton says that it is generally understood to be an allusion to the extravagant creation of knights by James I. This does not seem to apply at all. Perhaps it means that they are uncertain, hesitant or de-

ceitful meanings now obsolete. See note 188.

165. **Green Sleeves.** 14,14. MRS FORD compares FALSTAFF's former mani-festations of modest talk with this present exhibition of lewdness and remarks that the one no more agrees with the other than the comparison she now makes. ' Green Sleeves ' was a popular ballad, published in 1580. It deals with an inconstant lady who is hardly likely to be com-patible with the 100th Psalm—*Jubilate Deo*.

166. **Trow.** 14,15. ' What tempest, I trow . . .' As I imagine it to be. See note 146.

167. **Inherit.** 14,21. ' let thine inherit first ;' MRS PAGE says that MRS FORD can take the opportunity offered in her letter, but she (MRS PAGE) will never do so. She will not inherit any offers of love from FALSTAFF.

168. **Turtles.** 14,27. Turtle-doves, the emblems of conjugal fidelity.

169. **Entertain.** 14,32. ' I'll entertain myself like one that I am not ac-quainted with . . .' MRS PAGE will accommodate herself to a (loose) char-acter unlike herself. See note 75.

170. **Curtal dog.** 14,53. A dog with its tail docked. See note 192.

171. **Affects.** 14,54. ' Sir John affects my wife.' Has a love for ; from L. meaning *to endeavour, have, aim at*.

172. **Gallimaufry.** 15,3. A dish made up of varied remnants of food : adapt. from Fr. but of unknown origin.

173. **Perpend.** 15,3. Consider, weigh carefully or exactly : L. *perpendĕre* to weigh exactly, ponder.

174. **Actæon.** 15,6. ' Sir Actæon he, with Ringwood at thy heels :' A huntsman who saw Diana when she was bathing, and was changed into a stag and de-voured by his hounds. RINGWOOD was the name of one of FORD's dogs.

175. **Humour.** 15,23. See note 34.

176. **Cataian.** 15,28. A variant of CATHAIAN, a man of Cathay or China, ' used also to signify a sharper, from the dextrous thieving of these people ' (Nares).

177. **Melancholy.** 15,33. An amused use of the word. See note 34.

178. **Crotchets.** 15,35. MRS FORD tells her husband that he is bitten with foolish ideas : warped, twisted.

179. **Paltry.** 15,39. Worthless, despic-able.

180. **Yoke.** 15,53. ' a yoke of his dis-carded men ;' A pair, coupled like animals. PAGE refers contemptuously to NYM and PISTOL.

181. **Bully-rook.** 16,15. See note 73.

182. **Cavaliero-justice.** 16,15–16. Portu-guese, from Spanish, meaning ' cheva-lier ', ' gallant ', and, about 1600, ' roistering, swaggering fellow '. Here the meaning is a more respectful one, addressed as it is to Justice SHALLOW.

183. **Pottle.** 16,30. A measure of two quarts.

184. **Egress and regress.** 16,33. Abil-ity to come and go ; orig. a legal phrase.

185. **An-heires.** 16,35. ' Will you go, An-heires ? ' This is a corruption that has never been satisfactorily solved. ' Mynheers '; ' on, here '; ' on hearts '; are some of the solutions that have been offered. The text is obviously corrupt and does not approximate to any possible meaning as it stands. *An* might possibly mean *and* here.

186. **Stoccadoes.** 16,39. A thrust with a pointed weapon : corruptly adapt. from It. *stoccata*, from *stocco* point of a sword or dagger.

187. **Secure.** 16,45. ' Though Page be a secure fool . . .' Fool enough to feel secure in his wife's honesty.

GLOSSARY OF PHRASES

188. **These knights will hack ; and so thou shouldst not alter the article of thy gentry.** 14,5–6. The suggestion made here is that as these knights are not always trustworthy there will not be any cause for MRS FORD to change her title of ' mistress ' for that of ' lady ', Mrs being the rightful title or article of her state as a gentlewoman. Cf. note 6.

189. **As long as I have an eye to make difference of men's liking.** 14,8–9. As long as she has the power to be able to distinguish between man and man.

190. **This mystery of ill opinions.** 14,20. This strange mani-festation of gross opinions about MRS FORD's loose morals. MRS PAGE shows the letter that she had herself received from FALSTAFF, in the same vein, as a comfort to her friend.

191. **Lead him on with a fine-baited delay.** 14,40–1. MRS PAGE plans to keep FALSTAFF running after them with care-fully phrased promises that will induce him to persist in his love-making until he has pawned his horses to the HOST, because of having exhausted his means.

192. **Hope is a curtal dog in some affairs.** 14,53. PISTOL informs FORD that in some things hope is not as adequate as it might be ; circumstances, such as the love of FALSTAFF for MRS FORD, having more than normal power in their threats.

193. **I love not the humour of bread and cheese.** 15,21. NYM is not attracted by the frugal life, now that he has been cashiered by FALSTAFF.

194. **I would have nothing lie on my head.** 16,9–10. This is FORD's retort to PAGE who has quite openly stated that if FALSTAFF gets anything more than sharp words from his wife, may it lie on his head—may it be his fault. FORD replies with the familiar allusion to the horns of the cuckold. See note 237.

195. **Good even and twenty.** 16,17. A common greeting, mean-ing ' twenty more besides '. ' Evening ' was used any time after noon.

COMMENTARY

ACT I SCENE V

There are four elemental incidents in this scene : (a) FALSTAFF's harangue to PISTOL on the subject of his alleged gross lack of co-operation with FALSTAFF ; (b) MRS QUICKLY's ' invitation ' on behalf of the two Wives, to FALSTAFF to visit them, the one at a specified time, the other less definite but hopeful ; (c) FORD's interview with FALSTAFF, disguised as BROOK ; (d) FORD's com-plete degeneration in the grip of jealousy.

The main part of the action commences with the second episode, but in order to prepare for this, the opening incident is necessary, otherwise MRS QUICKLY's entrance and her mission would be too abrupt and less effective. FALSTAFF is just indulging in a violent fit of temperament because of his poverty and PISTOL's appeal for money. It gives the scene a forceful opening, a facet to FALSTAFF's character and a contrast for what is

E

to come. Make it strong and full in gross ani-
mosity, contempt and censure.

The whole of the scene between FALSTAFF and
MRS QUICKLY must be played with careful
treatment on the part of MRS QUICKLY. Shakespeare's love of acting for acting's sake displays
itself in her construction, because she is playing
a part all the time and so each speech has to be
applied in order to lure FALSTAFF into a false
belief that the doors are open to his desires. She
is very sly in the way she first introduces MRS
FORD's name : ' There is one Mistress Ford, sir ' :
and is the same again in her last speech below,
where in two lines she artfully presents the facts
of MRS FORD's being a ' good creature ' and
FALSTAFF a wanton, and that heaven must forgive them all, as a subtle opening to the purpose
of her visit. Let that purpose animate everything
she does, otherwise the scene will lose its nature.
Her following long speech must be to the same end,
although she is carried away by her own eloquence
and so adds the touch of eccentric humour which
gives her character and the scene its engaging
flavour. She delivers MRS FORD's message of
thanks for the letter with ardent gratitude and then
gently but significantly adds that the lady will be
alone between ten and eleven, continuing with
whole-hearted laughter that it will give FALSTAFF
an opportunity to come and see the picture he
knows of. Then with very deep sighs she re-
counts the (fictitious) awful life MRS FORD has to
lead with her husband and his jealous disposition, every fact being fully demonstrated, and *not
merely told*. Space does not allow of any further
detailed treatment of this scene, but it should be
exercised in the light of observations already
made.

In contrast with the event just passed, but
similar in the fact that FORD is also acting a part,
the next episode is played between the two men
with earnestness. FORD, like MRS QUICKLY, has
to work hard to gain his end and, like her, must not
merely state facts, but add the elaboration of
feeling to persuade FALSTAFF of his (FORD's) love
for MRS FORD, his despair at apparent failure, his
flattery of the knight, and his final and carefully
reserved inducement of payment, presented there
and then to FALSTAFF. It is in doing this that he
works up to full vehemence of effort, having kept
his former treatment confined in crafty falsehoods
and dissolving flattery, and by these means preparing for his final and winning temptation of jingling
money. Watch all these various processes and
vary them according to their natures so as to
achieve the ultimate effects in a well-planned
management of approach.

Throughout this scene FALSTAFF is cautious.
He is too cunning to betray himself, and even
when accepting FORD's money, does so almost with
an air of doing him a favour and as a matter of
business. But the promise of further sums of
money dissipates his reserve, and FORD has the
whole situation opened to him, with a final boastful assurance that he is to be made a cuckold.

In his soliloquy after FALSTAFF's departure,
FORD must handle his matter with care. He must
not rush headlong through the lines, but develop
the individuality of the different details. This
will prove more effective than a protracted and
gabbled sameness of treatment. Grow steady by
intensifying the language, and feeling its content,
and keep the full rhetorical power for the very
last line : ' better three hours too soon than a
minute too late.'

GLOSSARY OF WORDS

196. **Countenance.** 17,5. Credit. *Lit.*,
the manner of holding oneself—hence
' demeanour ', ' looks ', ' behaviour ',
' integrity ', ' credit '.

197. **Grated.** 17,5. ' I have grated upon
my good friends . . .' Brought persistent and troublesome pressure to
bear upon good friends.

198. **Coach-fellow.** 17,6. A horse yoked
together with another.

199. **Geminy.** 17,7. ' . . . a geminy of
baboons.' A pair : a form of *gemini*
adopt. from L. (pl. of *geminus*) twins.

200. **Gibbet.** 17,13. Gallows, but specifically one with a projecting arm from
which the bodies of criminals were
hung after execution : adopt. from
OFr. *gibet* gallows.

201. **Pickthatch.** 17,15. A disreputable
quarter of London.

202. **Unconfinable.** 17,16. ' thou unconfinable baseness,' Possessing baseness
of character without limit, and so
completely without moral sense of
obligation.

203. **Fain.** 17,19. Gladly. OE. *fæʒnian,
fæʒenian* fain, glad.

204. **Ensconce.** 17,20. Conceal. en +
sconce, ' a small fortification ', and
probably adapt. from OFr. *esconce*
hiding-place, shelter.

205. **Cat-a-mountain.** 17,21. The name
applied originally to the leopard or
panther.

206. **Red-lattice.** 17,21. ' your red-lattice
phrases '. Tavern slang, taverns formerly having red lattices.

207. **Bold-beating.** 17,21. ' bold-beating
oaths . . .' Apparently a confusion of
bold-faced adapt. and *brow-beating*. It is a
nonce compound.

208. **Wanton.** 17,47. ' your worship's a
wanton ! ' ' Naughty boy '. The word
is from ME. *wantowen* and *lit.* means
' undisciplined '.

209. **Canaries.** 18,2. MRS QUICKLY's
substitute for ' quandary '.

210. **Alligant.** 18,7. MRS QUICKLY's
solecism for ' elegant '.

211. **Pensioners.** 18,14. The body of
gentlemen, instituted by Henry VIII
as a royal bodyguard within the
palace.

212. **She-Murcury.** 18,16–17. Mercury
was the messenger to the gods, and
FALSTAFF likens MRS QUICKLY to him
as the go-between in his affairs with
the Wives.

213. **Frampold.** 18,25. Quarrelsome. The
origin of the word is obscure.

214. **Fartuous.** 18,31. MRS QUICKLY's
blunder for ' virtuous '.

215. **Infection.** 18,45. MRS QUICKLY's
blunder for ' affection '.

216. **Nay-word.** 18,53. A catch-word ;
a secret word for mutual recognition.
It is of obscure formation and has
no obvious connection with NAY or
AY.

217. **Discretion.** 18,56. ' old folks, you
know, have discretion . . .' In modern
colloquial English, ' are broad-
minded '. MRS QUICKLY treats the
word with sly emphasis, artfully im-
plying its *sophisticated* meaning, as
being distinct from the conventional
one of ' understanding ', ' perception ',
' intelligence '.

218. **Punk.** 19,4. Harlot. Its origin is
unknown.

219. **Fights.** 19,5. ' up with your fights :'
A species of protective covering erected
to protect the crew in a naval action.

220. **Fain.** 19,13. See note 203.

221. **Sack.** 19,14. See note 157.
222. **Via.** 19,19. Onward. A term of encouragement, from L. meaning *a road or way*.
223. **Sith.** 19,49. 'sith you yourself know . . .' Since, but with the sense of 'because of that same failing in yourself'. It is a reduced form of OE. *siððan* sithen = subsequent to that.
224. **Engrossed.** 20,2. 'engrossed opportunities to meet her;' FORD (alias Brook) says he has contrived to create opportunities to meet with MRS FORD. The word, ultimately from L. and there meaning *to put into stout or thick form*, originally meant *to write large* and then became almost exclusively applied to the special form of writing used in legal documents: thus, *to express in legal form, to arrange.*
225. **Fee'd.** 20,3. 'fee'd every slight occasion . . .' Spent money (on servants) to gain every small opportunity of getting a sight of MRS FORD.
226. **Niggardly.** 20,4. Scarcely, in the meanest measure. The etymology of the word is obscure, but it has the meaning of *mean, parsimonious, miserly.*
227. **Meed.** 20,8. Reward. The word is OE. *méd.*
228. **Importuned.** 20,16. Urged: ultimately from L. meaning 'inconvenient', 'troublesome', 'grievous'; hence, 'seeking something with great intensiveness'.
229. **Enlargeth.** 20,23. 'she enlargeth her mirth so far . . .' FORD says his wife is laughing so inordinately at him behind his back that she is arousing doubts about her fidelity towards him, her authentic husband.

Thus as 'Brook' he feels that he may be able to gain her favour since her honesty is only apparent.
230. **Admittance.** 20,26. 'a gentleman . . . of great admittance'. FORD flatters FALSTAFF by inferring that he is admitted to distinguished society.
231. **Authentic.** 20,26. 'authentic in your place and person'. Fully qualified and real in noble condition of character.
232. **Preparations.** 20,28. 'a gentleman . . . of learned preparations'. Accomplishments, prepared by study and purpose.
233. **Prescribe.** 20,36. Order or arrange things.
234. **Preposterously.** 20,37. In a ridiculous manner.
235. **Ward.** 20,43. Stronghold.
236. **Speed.** 20,57. Prosper. OE. *spéd*, prosperity, abundance. Speed in matters of pace means abundance, or quantity.
237. **Cuckoldly.** 21,3. A cuckold is a derisive name for the husband of an unfaithful wife. The origin of the sense is supposed to be found in the cuckoo's habit of laying its eggs in another bird's nest. A cuckold was fancifully supposed to wear horns on his brow. The origin of this is due to the practice of planting the spurs of a castrated cock on the root of the excised comb, where they grew and became horns, sometimes several inches long.
238. **Wittolly.** 21,4. One who is complacently aware of his wife's infidelity: late ME. *wetewold*, apparently formed after CUCKOLD with substitution of *wit* for the first part of the word.
239. **Cuckold.** 21,12. See note 237.

240. **Aggravate.** 21,15. 'I will aggravate his style;' Enlarge FORD's reputation in the respect of his being a knave. The word is from L. meaning *to make heavy or heavier, to increase the weight of.*
241. **Style.** 21,15. See previous note.
242. **Epicurean.** 21,17. Gluttonous. The philosophy of Epicurus taught that happiness was derived from the pursuit of the pleasures of the mind and the sweets of virtue. This eventually became perverted into sensual indulgence.
243. **Improvident.** 21,18. Blind, unforeseeing.
244. **Adoption.** 21,23. 'stand under the adoption of abominable terms'. These terms will adopt FORD as fitting them unless FALSTAFF is unmasked.
245. **Amaimon.** 21,24. The name of a devil.
246. **Barbason.** 21,25. Another name of a devil.
247. **Wittol.** 21,26. See note 238.
248. **Aqua-vitæ.** 21,30. A general term for any spirituous liquor : L., *water of life.*
249. **Gelding.** 21,31. A castrated animal, especially a horse.
250. **Devises.** 21,32. Makes her calculations, assorts her facts in detail. The word as used here contains something of its original meaning, *to divide, arrange, order*, following the process of MRS FORD's development of her ideas as expressed in 'plots' and 'ruminates'. The process of 'invention', which is the modern meaning of the word, is now given practical means of fulfilment : adapt. from OFr. *devise-r* to divide—late pop. L. *dīvīsāre* frequentative of *dīvīdĕre* to divide.

GLOSSARY OF PHRASES

251. **Why, then the world's my oyster, Which I with sword will open.** 17,2-3. The world is PISTOL's treasure-house, where he will find his wealth by force of sword.
252. **A short life and a throng!** 17,14. FALSTAFF advises PISTOL to try his chances as a cut-purse in a crowd.
253. **And in such wine and sugar of the best and fairest.** 18,8. MRS QUICKLY's epithet for the choicest of the most choice of suitors that have sought the favours of MRS FORD.
254. **This news distracts me.** 19,3. FALSTAFF implies that he is rather confounded by the news supplied by MRS QUICKLY that MRS FORD and MRS PAGE both love him. Will they tell each other and so complicate matters ? Schmidt defines it as meaning 'distracted with joy'.
255. **Let them say 'tis grossly done ; so it be fairly done, no matter.** 19,10-11. FALSTAFF comments upon the good promise succeeding upon his overtures to the two Wives,

by saying that anyone can criticize his methods as being coarse so long as they lead to profit.
256. **Good Sir John, I sue for yours : not to charge you.** 19,29. FORD, visiting FALSTAFF for the first time as Brook, asks to be better known to FALSTAFF, but in sueing for this, he has not come to borrow money from him.
257. **Mechanical salt-butter rogue.** 21,10. A derisive reference of FALSTAFF's, *Mechanical*= a common workman and *salt-butter* = a tradesman of low reputation.
258. **It shall hang like a meteor o'er the cuckold's horns.** 21,11-12. Something that conspicuously points down as a continual threat.
259. **I will predominate over the peasant.** 21,13. FALSTAFF is probably making a contemptuous comparison between himself as a knight and FORD as a mere gentleman or even as the 'mechanical salt-butter rogue' referred to three lines previously.

COMMENTARY

ACT I   SCENE VI

In presenting this scene, keep each character well defined so that in the general joviality the identities do not become obscured. It is the individual differences that help to make the interest, and not the matter alone. Well-defined details, even though not concerned in a scene of great dramatic nature, will add a quality to it that will give it a surprising turn of interest. The action must be maintained in its attractiveness through the succession of various scenes, whether they be concerned with the main or the sub-plot : and in this play in particular, so much does depend upon the activities of the characters themselves as

characters. The elderly but virile SHALLOW, kindly and hearty PAGE, poor EVANS, at first in pitiable fear of the coming conflict with CAIUS and yet striving with himself to maintain spasms of courage, and rising to sudden fury when told that CAIUS is nearby, all these form a delightful mixture of human nature and are made so by the oblivious SLENDER sighing out his wistful worship of ANNE, completely unattached to the scene. Also EVANS, by following up his outburst against the approaching CAIUS, and then immediately, upon his appearing, trying to arrange a private settlement whilst still exhibiting a public challenge, gives a happy touch of humour. The reconciliation of these two men after the others have gone, each finding a common foe in the HOST, is quaintly told and must be quaintly done. The scene is thus made up of a series of happy little episodes, all depending upon the exact touch of character in order to provide a charming chapter of entertainment in which we are not only amused, but feel a love for all concerned.

GLOSSARY OF WORDS

260. **Foin.** 22,20. To thrust with a sharp weapon; apparently from OFr. meaning ' a three-pronged fish-spear '.
261. **Traverse.** 22,20. In fencing, to move from side to side; short for ' traverse thy ground '.
262. **Punto.** 22,21. A thrust with the point of the rapier. Italian or Spanish.
263. **Stock.** 22,22. A thrusting sword: adopt. from Fr.-It. *stocco*.
264. **Reverse.** 22,22. In fencing, a back-handed stroke.
265. **Distance.** 22,22. The definite interval of space to be observed between two combatants.
266. **Montant.** 22,22. An old fencing term, meaning ' an upright blow or thrust '.
267. **Ethiopian.** 22,23. ' Is he dead, my Ethiopian ? ' The HOST's jocular

address to CAIUS, possibly because of his habitual black garments.
268. **Francisco.** 22,23. The HOST's substitute for Frenchman.
269. **Æsculapius.** 23,1. The Roman god of medicine.
270. **Galen.** 23,1. A celebrated physician of the 2nd c. A.D.
271. **Stale.** 23,2. The HOST's epithet for CAIUS. The word means ' urine '. See note 275.
272. **Castalion-King-Urinal.** 23,5. Castalia was the proper name of a spring on Mount Parnassus, sacred to the Muses. See note 275.
273. **Hector.** 23,5. See note 76.
274. **Bodykins.** 23,14. A diminutive of BODY and a shortened form of ' God's bodikins ' = God's dear body (*lit.*

little body). -KIN is a diminutive in continental origin and has no trace of OE.
275. **Mockwater.** 23,23. One of the HOST's jocularities towards CAIUS. Nares declares that it is an allusion to the mockery of the judging of diseases by the water or urine, as practised by the doctors of the time; thus—' you pretending water-doctor '.
276. **Clapper-claw.** 23,28. To claw or scratch with the open hand or nails; to beat, thrash. It apparently means to CLAW with a CLAPPER, though in what sense it is not clear. The HOST advises the kind of treatment he will receive from EVANS unless he makes friends with him.
277. **Eke.** 23,36. See note 111.
278. **Humour.** 23,39. See note 34.

GLOSSARY OF PHRASES

279. **My heart of elder.** 23,1. The heart of CAIUS is somewhat insubstantial, like the elder tree whose stems are hollow. The Doctor would not understand the HOST's inference.
280. **You go against the hair of your professions.** 23,10–11.

SHALLOW warns CAIUS the doctor and EVANS the parson that to quarrel and fight and possibly injure or kill is contrary to their callings as healer and divine.

COMMENTARY

ACT I SCENE VII

None

GLOSSARY OF WORDS

281. **Pittie-ward.** 24,4. Petty-ward, but otherwise inexplicable.
282. **Costard.** 24,10. *Lit.*, an apple of a large size, the original species being ribbed—perhaps from OFr. and AFr. *coste* rib; but sometimes humorously used for ' the top of the head '.
283. **Madrigals.** 24,13. ' Melodious birds sings madrigals '. Part songs of rather an elaborate nature, but also simply *songs*. EVANS is quoting one of Marlowe's poems where the word is used in the simpler sense. It is adapt. from It. *madrigale* but the origin is obscure. The primitive

sense may possibly be ' pastoral song '.
284. **Vagram.** 24,20. EVANS' confusion for ' fragrant '.
285. **Mess.** 25,32. ' a mess of porridge .' A prepared dish of porridge. The word means ' a portion of food ': adopt. from OFr. *mes*—late L. *missum* p.pple. of *mittĕre* to send.
286. **Hibocrates.** 25,34. EVANS' version of Hippocrates, a famous Greek physician born about 460 B.C.
287. **Galen.** 25,34. See note 270.
288. **Potions.** 26,12. See next note.
289. **Motions.** 26,12. ' he gives me the

potions and the motions '. Medicine and its effects.
290. **Proverbs.** 26,13. See next note.
291. **No-verbs.** 26,13. ' he gives me the proverbs and the no-verbs '. What to do and what not to do.
292. **Celestial.** 26,14. EVANS is addressed thus by the HOST because he is a parson.
293. **Vlouting-stog.** 26,23. EVANS' corruption of ' flouting-stock ', an object of mockery.
294. **Scall.** 26,25. ' . . . this same scall . . . companion '. Scalled, scabby ; an abusive term. SCALL is a scaly or scabby disease of the skin, especially of the scalp.

GLOSSARY OF PHRASES

295. **Is at most odds with his own gravity and patience.** 25,23-4. PAGE alludes to EVANS as acting so contrary to his customary demeanour.

296. **Come, lay their swords to pawn.** 26,17. Take them away for the time being and create a pledge that CAIUS and EVANS are to remain friends.

COMMENTARY

ACT II SCENE I

In this scene, MRS PAGE organizes her material and behaviour for FORD's benefit. She is extremely charming and enjoys her own thrust at FORD on her line ' Be sure of that,—two other husbands.' She also very cleverly ' forgets ' FALSTAFF's name in order to develop it to greater effect by a ' build-up ' for FORD's increased discomfiture. This must apparently be really searched for, but with a slight excess of effort in order to enable us to realize the intention of what is being done. It also enables FORD's succeeding passion to appear the more ridiculous, seeing that it has been deliberately cultivated by MRS PAGE's charming and subtle deceptiveness and management of her matter.

FORD's consternation is more concentrated than vehement. He must not start off at full pitch. Each detail is weighed with intensive incredulity. Each phrase is worked at in order to realize its almost impossible significance. To him, such things can hardly be true, but they are so. By degrees his intensity rises in higher pitch of voice until it reaches 'And Falstaff's boy with her !' Thus the effect is governed by using different styles of treatment, and intensity is preserved throughout and given a climax without any over-strain. After this climax he proceeds rapidly but without any loss of the point of what he is saying, slowing up somewhat but adding more power to his voice at

' all my neighbours shall cry aim '. This treatment is necessary in order to prevent an anti-climax after the middle of the speech and to make the matter dramatically convincing. The clock striking gives a necessary pause in order for the action to take a slight change, and so resume with a little more definite note of resolve. The cut imposed in the text should be ignored.

Thus we find the governing principles of this short scene which will make it equal in workmanship to what has gone before, and which must be observed in order to create its proper value and so continue to keep the play in its lively excellence.

As this is an acting edition of the play, a portion of the scene has been omitted, in order to concentrate upon the principal subject, and it closes with the final speech of FORD's. Normally, PAGE, the HOST, SLENDER, etc., enter to FORD after his speech and a short diversionary passage follows.

GLOSSARY OF WORDS

297. **Idle.** 27,10. 'and as idle as she may hang together'. Moody, illtempered. The basic meaning of the word is *empty* and FORD is describing his wife's condition through lack of any interest, perhaps in himself—as he imagines.

298. **Dickens.** 27,15. 'I cannot tell what the dickens his name is ...' Apparently a substitution for 'the devil' owing to the same identity of the initial letters. *Dickin* or *Dickon*, dim. of *Dick*, was in use long before the earliest known instance of this, and *Dickens* as a surname was prob-

ably also already in existence—see OED.

299. **League.** 27,20. Bond of friendship. The word is ultimately from L. meaning 'to bind'.

300. **Twelve score.** 27,27. 'as easy as a cannon will shoot . . . twelve score'. Twelve score paces.

301. **Take.** 27,32. 'I will take him'. Catch him in the act. *Take* has a variety of meanings in Shakespeare. It is from OE. *tacan* to grasp, seize, lay hold of. Other meanings include *assume, understand, choose.* It is an extremely interesting word and

occupies over thirteen pages of the OED.

302. **Actæon.** 27,34. See note 174.

303. **Cry aim.** 27,35. 'and to these violent proceedings all my neighbours shall cry aim'. An expression borrowed from archery, used to encourage the archers by crying out *aim*, when they were about to shoot, and then in a general sense *to applaud, to encourage with cheers*—Schmidt. It is in this latter sense that FORD uses it, anticipating what his friends will say after he has at length disclosed the infidelity of his own wife and MRS PAGE.

GLOSSARY OF PHRASES

304. **He pieces out his wife's inclination.** 27,27. FORD declares that PAGE, by his unconcern about his wife's amours, only encourages her inclination for them. *To piece out* means to add to.

305. **A man may hear this shower sing in the wind.** 27,29–30. FORD, seeing MRS PAGE and FALSTAFF's page on the way to

MRS FORD, says that what is going to happen soon declares itself in their action, and that MRS FORD, and possibly MRS PAGE, and FALSTAFF will soon be together.

306. **Good plots, they are laid.** 27,30–1. The ingenious plots are prepared ; PAGE's extension of the facts as revealed in the preceding ref.

COMMENTARY

ACT II SCENE II

The opening of this scene must be incisive and close. We are to feel that something intensely vital is being prepared for ; but though concise and quick, the elements must not lose ripeness of substance. The scene between FALSTAFF and MRS FORD explains its own treatment. It rests upon the convincing assumption of a demure but attractive MRS FORD, who nevertheless is very cautious in all she says and whose effect is completed by our knowledge of the deception which is taking place. This encouraging but also evasive woman enables FALSTAFF to roll out his preliminary admiration and compliment until the timely announcement of MRS PAGE's arrival. The scene

which follows must be played in all its fullness, with the various points all slightly overplayed. This will demand care, since to overwork them will distort the natural element and substitute farce for comedy. Thus when MRS FORD reaches her speech ' What shall I do . . .', she is a woman in a great dilemma just a little over-emphasized. The moment when MRS PAGE indicates the basket must be measured out with individuality. MRS FORD's line ' He's too big to go in there ' must also be brought out with strong and pained frustration. FALSTAFF's voluntary commitment to the confines of the basket, the covering of him with the clothes and the address of the servants to their task must be urgent, but planned so as not to lose its value in confusion. Stage effects are always planned, no matter how chaotic they are intended to be, otherwise meaningless muddle will be the only result. FORD, in his short, violent appearance, lifts the action to a sudden sharp climax, and after his exit the two Wives spend a short time in exuberant relish over what has taken place, and then begin new plots to involve FALSTAFF in further troubles. Keep the pitch of the scene vigorous and well-developed, otherwise after the high-pressured moments just passed the power may weaken. This is always a danger where dialogue follows sharp action. We need the less strenuous respite, but it must not be a collapse of the action. Vitality of treatment of the subject-matter of the dialogue is essential in order to maintain the grip.

The final episode offers plain evidence of treatment required. Again, the various distinctions of character supply the main substance of interest in their novel temperaments and methods of expressing themselves. FORD has had a set-back, and only snaps to begin with, becoming conciliatory and apologetic as he seems to realize that he has made a mistake. This calls for lively exercise of character on the part of the others so as not to allow the scene to sink to nothing.

GLOSSARY OF WORDS

307. **Buck-basket.** 28,2. A basket for carrying clothes to and from the place of laundering.

308. **Whitsters.** 28,11. Bleachers.

309. **Eyas-musket.** 28,17. A young hawk taken from the nest for the purposes of training; a term used playfully for a child: adopt. from Fr. L. *nĭdus* nest. MUSKET was originally adopt. from O.Norm.Fr. meaning *a small species of sparrow-hawk*.

310. **Jack-a-Lent.** 28,20. MRS PAGE's playful designation of ROBIN, perhaps on account of his size and appearance: the name of a figure set up to be pelted at, the game taking place during Lent.

311. **Use.** 29,7. 'we'll use this unwholesome humidity'. Deal with. The Wives prepare to meet FALSTAFF and treat him as they think fit.

312. **Humidity.** 29,7. See above quot. MRS FORD's epithet for FALSTAFF on account of his perpetual perspiration: from L. *hŭmid-us, ūmid-us*, from *ūmēre* to be moist.

313. **Pumpion.** 29,8. Melon, large pumpkin: Fr.-L.-Gk. Another appellation for FALSTAFF.

314. **Period.** 29,11. 'this is the period of my ambition:' Ultimate end, that which he has striven to reach: adopt. from Fr.-L.-Gk. meaning *going round, circuit*.

315. **Cog.** 29,14. Deceive: the verb TO COG is of unknown origin, but it meant 'to cheat at dice or cards by means of fraudulent manipulation'.

316. **Emulate.** 29,20. Equal, from L. *aemŭlā-ri* to rival.

317. **Ship-tire.** 29,21. 'beauty of the brow that becomes the ship-tire'. A head-dress shaped like a ship or having a ship-like ornament. The editor is not aware of any forms of head-dress of this kind until the 18th c. when waggons were used for the purpose. TIRE = head-dress, aphetic form of OFr. *atir* apparatus, equipment, accoutrement.

318. **Tire-valiant.** 29,21. Highly ornamental head-dress. See previous note.

319. **Admittance.** 29,22. 'of Venetian admittance'. Venetian design; *lit.* 'admitted' or created by Venetian milliners.

320. **Farthingale.** 29,27. The hooped petticoat formerly worn by women, and by means of which the dress was made to stand well out. The semicircled type mentioned here would probably be hooped only from the back to the sides.

321. **Counter-gate.** 29,39-40. The gate of certain prisons for debtors, etc., in London, Southwark, and some other cities and boroughs. The name COUNTER comes from the fact that such prisons were attached to the *Counter*, or office or hall of justice of a mayor.

322. **Presently.** 29,48. At once; always the correct meaning in Shakespeare.

323. **Arras.** 29,50. The hangings suspended from tenterhooks against the walls. They take their name from Arras in Artois, famous for the making of this textile.

324. **Tattling.** 29,51. 'she's a very tattling woman'. One who chatters in an irrepressible and inconsequential way, specifically concerned with petty evils.

325. **Bucking.** 30,31. Washing; ME. *bouken, bowken* to wash linen. See note 330.

326. **Whiting-time.** 30,31. Bleaching time.

327. **Dissembling.** 30,41. 'You dissembling knight!' Deceiving; the literal meaning is 'to alter the appearance (of a character or action) so as to deceive'.

328. **Cowl-staff.** 30,43. A staff used to carry a 'cowl', a tub or similar large vessel used for water etc. It was thrust through the two handles of the cowl and borne on the shoulders of two men.

329. **Drumble.** 30,44. 'look, how you drumble!' In modern colloquiality, 'dither'. It is a verb meaning 'to move sluggishly', from the noun which is a variant of 'dumble'; DUMMEL, dumb, stupid.

330. **Buck.** 30,52. 'Buck! I would I could wash myself of the buck!' FORD quibbles on the double meaning of the word as 'washing' and the 'male deer', because of its horns. Cf. note 237.

331. **To-night.** 31,3. 'I have dreamed to-night;' Last night. It was probably used in the following morning, when it would be near enough to be recognized as emphasizing the night just passed, as we speak of *today* during the succeeding night.

332. **Unkennel.** 31,5. 'we'll unkennel the fox.' Dislodge a fox from its hole.

333. **Uncape.** 31,6. 'So, now uncape.' Probably 'prepare to catch the fox'. FORD, having as he thinks sealed off every means of FALSTAFF's escape, is now ready to pounce. There is no known authentic explanation of the word, which is used for the only time in the language.

334. **Anon.** 31,10. Straightway, at once: OE. *on án* into one, *on áne* in one body, state, way, movement, moment.

335. **Gross.** 31,22. 'so gross in his jealousy . . .' Acute, violent, excessive. MRS FORD has never seen her husband so overcome by his passion—*lit.*, enlarged.

336. **Dissolute.** 31,28. 'his dissolute disease will scarce obey this medicine'. Disease of dissolute character. MRS PAGE is referring to FALSTAFF and asserting that immersion in the Thames will not altogether cure him.

337. **Presses.** 31,45. Large shelved cupboards for holding clothes, books, etc.

338. **Distemper.** 31,49. Disordered state of mind; 'want of due balance between contraries'—Johnson.

339. **A-birding.** 32,8. Fowling or bird-catching.

GLOSSARY OF PHRASES

340. **We'll teach him to know turtles from jays.** 29,8-9. Turtle-doves were the emblems of love; jays are chattering birds resembling magpies, with plumage of striking appearance. Hence the name became extended to an irresponsible chatterer, and then to a flashy and loose woman.

341. **I see what thou wert, if Fortune thy foe were not, Nature thy friend.** 29,28. This passage is enigmatical. Staunton suggests substituting 'but' for 'not'. FALSTAFF by context is suggesting the refined nature of MRS FORD and how she is lower than her natural dignity, as the wife of FORD.

342. **Like a many of these lisping hawthorn-buds.** 29,33. Young gaily-dressed dandies speaking in childlike manner. *To lisp* is derived from OE. and the meaning is primarily 'to stammer, falter in speaking'.

343. **Ay, buck; I warrant you, buck; and of the season too, it shall appear.** 31,1-2. FORD is quibbling on the word 'buck', and infers that this particular animal (FALSTAFF) is very much in (mating) season. See note 330.

344. **I have a fine hawk for the bush.** 32,8. The hawk hunts low as opposed to the falcon with longer pointed wings and loftier flight.

COMMENTARY

ACT II   SCENE III

The slight romance of the play has a brief period to itself in the opening of this scene. As short as it is, it must be played with sincerity and depth as far as the material allows. It is a link in the dramatic chain and must not be weak, but enabled to receive what strength it allows for.

The succeeding episode is another once more dependent upon character portrayal, chiefly the sharp ambitious promptings of the confused and stupid SLENDER. This is followed by the conflict between PAGE and MRS PAGE combined against the earnest endeavours of FENTON, and the pleadings of ANNE herself against her parents' obstinacy.

Make this action as real as possible, and the more hopeful turn of MRS PAGE's final speech a little pleasant surprise in the slight drama of love's baffled progress. And once again the charming duplicity of MRS QUICKLY offers her variability of favours, engaging FENTON with hope, and then after his leaving her, dispensing her promises to do what she can for all three suitors. The whole scene thus grows together from separate incidents, all made pleasantly different and all highly engaging by the assembly of (mostly) quaint characters making life a little unusual, but also very real.

GLOSSARY OF WORDS

345. **Gall'd.** 32,23. Weakened; *lit., injured, oppressed, made sore with rubbing.* From *gall,* a sore on a horse.

346. **Property.** 32,28. A means of bringing money to his (FENTON's) needs.

347. **Stamps in gold.** 32,34. Gold coins bearing stampings, probably of angels. See note 92.

348. **Jointure.** 33,17. 'He will make you a hundred and fifty pounds jointure.' SLENDER is worth this sum of money as his income and will join it with ANNE's dowry.

349. **'Od's heartlings.** 33,24. A minor oath—'God's little heart'.

350. **Pretty.** 33,24. 'that's a pretty jest indeed!' Witty, clever, apt:

OE. *prættig,* from *prætt, prat* (see note 408). Its early meaning was *cunning, crafty,* etc.; then it developed into signifying *clever, skilful, apt,* and thence to something *daintily attractive,* which is its modern meaning.

351. **Motions.** 33,29. Suggestions.

352. **Speciously.** 34,18. MRS QUICKLY's blunder for 'specially'.

GLOSSARY OF PHRASES

353. **I'll make a shaft or a bolt on 't : 'slid, 'tis but venturing.** 32,43. A proverbial phrase meaning 'to risk making something out of a circumstance or event'.

354. **Come cut and long-tail.** 33,15. *Lit.,* horses or dogs with cut tails and with long tails ; hence, *fig.* all sorts of people.

355. **Happy man be his dole.** 33,30. *Lit.,* let the share or lot dealt to a man be his happiness. SLENDER consoles himself with this proverb if his suit to ANNE should fail.

COMMENTARY

ACT II   SCENE IV

FALSTAFF's opening line ' Bardolph, I say,—' is almost a sudden roar. He is in a vile temper. It gives the scene a notable introduction and we realize something of FALSTAFF's reaction to his late experiences, something of his character as well. Then he settles down to a series of minor explosions, each one alive with the gross iniquity and humiliation still working with its acute intention upon him. The speech is thus made alive with experience upon his feelings and is not just a relating of facts. This constitutes dramatic action and gives life, not merely talk.

MRS QUICKLY has a minimum of means in which to do her work. She must nurse these means carefully. Her attitude must be one of deep concern. 'Marry, sir, I come to your worship from Mistress Ford ' is not just announcing a fact, but contains a certain demure and apologetic note, as though realizing that the difficulty of her mission requires a gentle introduction of this necessary fact, but, perhaps, not without a real pleasure at the touching of a sore spot. The soreness is made very

evident by FALSTAFF's reply, but she goes on with a broad emphasis in her treatment which will develop the scarcity of her matter into its most effective capacity. It needs to be slightly overdrawn, but the situation as we know it will give it propriety. It also enables the changes of subject to find their values since they will be enlarged and more emphatic. Having expressed MRS FORD's ' yearning ' with adequate fullness, she then leans over to FALSTAFF and very slyly informs him that FORD is going ' a-birding '. This change made between acutely varied and intentionally highly-developed facts expands the economy of means and satisfies the interest without loss, and a slight pause after it, in which FALSTAFF is able to show a relenting of anger, helps still further in the process. MRS QUICKLY then proceeds with artful exploitation of FALSTAFF's stirring desire. She takes her time and handles her invitation with all the insinuating amiability that she can command. A further slight pause after this, carefully waiting for the effect to operate, and for FALSTAFF to respond with signs of obviously weakening inclination, followed by a gentle but well-placed urge by stating that time is short, and finally a very warm assurance that Mrs Ford will make amends, these carefully applied items of treatment will operate the dramatic movement of this concise incident into its complete proportions.

In dealing with the events of his story, FALSTAFF at first is touched with anger, characteristically repressed to begin with, but opening out on his speech beginning with ' No, Master Brook . . .' FORD's reply is one of real incredulity and not merely a simple question, since he had searched and could not find any sign of FALSTAFF. The latter's confirmation is a bold affirmative since it emphasizes the situation. He proceeds without dwelling too much on the facts, and so saving himself for expansion on the final one of all : ' They conveyed *me* into a ' (slight pause) ' buck-basket '. FORD's reaction to this is almost a momentary loss of self-control, stifled however, but still somewhat evident in his forceful repetition of ' A buck-basket ! ' ; and from this elevation of pitch, FALSTAFF roars on at full strength which subdues itself in the deep disgust arising from his filthy surroundings. From then onward, he is quicker, less forceful, but not losing any of the essential meaning of the details of his facts. From ' But mark the sequel, Master Brook ' however, he

underlines the details, with slower pace and more graphic emphasis, working up to ' think of that . . .' Then as he commences with ' in the height of this bath ' his intensity increases to its fullest, intensity weighed out in each phrase with the climax arriving at ' horse-shoe '.

His next speech begins with collected determination, passing to a significant and knowing statement of fact that makes his way clear ; and he ends his meeting with FORD full of cheerful confidence. Thus we have a series of varied incidents all deftly constructed and each requiring the careful modelling of their constituent technical requirements in order to give them their due effectiveness.

FORD brings the scene to a close by first breaking out of his stupefaction throe by throe from the first ' Hum ! ha ! is this a vision ? ' up to the explosive ' this 'tis to have linen and buck-baskets : ' Then he hurries on intensively and finally works up to his concluding frantic resolve to be ' horn-mad '. Make it all just a little absurd, because his own condition is such ; but never allow the treatment to reach any distorting form of caricature. It will lose its conviction if it does this.

The scene which follows this one in the orthodox editions is omitted. It is of no dramatic interest and concerns PAGE's young son doing his Latin homework.

GLOSSARY OF WORDS

356. **Toast.** 34,23. ' put a toast in 't '. A piece of toast, which was frequently put in wine or other drinks.
357. **Slighted.** 34,28. ' slighted me into the river . . .' Threw contemptuously.
358. **Mummy.** 34,34. ' a mountain of mummy '. A mountain of a corpse.
359. **Reins.** 34,38. ' to cool the reigns '. The loins ; adapt. from OFr. *reins*— L. *renes* kidneys. It is used in the Bible in the sense of the seat of the feelings.
360. **Chalices.** 34,42. Cups. The word comes from L. *calix*, *calic-em* cup, and appeared in English in various forms.
361. **Pullet-sperm.** 34,45. FALSTAFF's name for the chicken in its egg condition.
362. **Erection.** 35,6. MRS QUICKLY's blunder for ' direction ' (instruction).
363. **Yearn.** 35,9. ' that it would yearn your heart . . .' *Lit.* to desire earnestly. Here it means that it would cause FALSTAFF's heart to feel or cry out very strongly for MRS FORD, and is adopt. from the term used when hounds cry out eagerly. It is obsolete.

364. **Sped.** 35,30. See note 236.
365. **Peaking.** 35,33. ' the peaking Cornuto her husband '. Nosey, prying.
366. **Cornuto.** 35,33. See previous quot. From It.—L. *cornutus* cornute, to give horns to, i.e. to make a cuckold of. See note 237.
367. **Protested.** 35, 36. ' after we had . . . protested '. After they had declared their love for each other : PROTEST is from L. meaning ' to declare formally, testify as a witness '.
368. **Instigated.** 35,38. Urged.
369. **Hinds.** 35,55. Household servants : early ME. *hine*.
370. **Bell-wether.** 36,9. The leading sheep in a flock, who carries a bell around its neck. FALSTAFF uses the name in a derisive sense because of FORD's loud use of his voice when entering his house in search of FALSTAFF.
371. **Bilbo.** 36,10. See note 31.
372. **Peck.** 36,10. ' in the circumference of a peck '. A vessel used to measure a peck of dry goods, the size of two gallons, dry measure ; but it varied greatly in England according to circumstances.

373. **Distillation.** 36,11. Something distilled, being treated as so to exclude drops of moisture. FALSTAFF is alluding to the perspiration that resulted from his being crammed in the basket.
374. **Fretted.** 36,12. Rotted. The basic meaning of the verb To FRET is ' to eat away'.
375. **Dutch dish.** 36,16. A reference to some form of Dutch preparation now no longer identifiable.
376. **Lecher.** 36,37. A man given to sensual indulgence : adopt. from OFr. *lecheor* from *lechier* meaning ' to live in debauchery or gluttony ', and ultimately derived from OTeut. *likkôjan* to lick. ModFr. *lécher* to lick.
337. **Halfpenny purse.** 36,38–39. Something very small.
378. **Horn-mad.** 36,43. ' I'll be horn-mad '. See note 138. FORD quotes this as a proverb here, which probably originated from the fact of horned beasts becoming enraged. He assumes that he is a cuckold and that he will therefore become ' horn-mad '. See also note 379.

GLOSSARY OF PHRASES

379. **Though what I am I cannot avoid, yet to be what I would not shall not make me tamc.** 36,40–42. FORD, after FALSTAFF's revelations of the preliminary love passages between MRS FORD and himself before he (FORD) entered the house, imagines that he has been cuckolded. He cannot avoid it now, but to be in that unenviable condition will not dispirit him. No, on the contrary, he will be as mad as a mad beast.

COMMENTARY

ACT II Scene V

Falstaff opens the scene with completely restored faith in Mrs Ford, and exhibits a fulsome gallantry on his own part. Then comes the carefully asked question about their (his own and Mrs Ford's) immunity from any interference, which is answered by Mrs Ford's delightful reply 'He's a-birding, sweet Sir John.' Give this opening passage its proper consideration, because it does help to enhance the abrupt interruption of Mrs Page's voice. If there is nothing of value to break, the break itself has no point in it.

The following scenes between the two Wives, and then with Falstaff, are very clearly defined. Give them their full demands in large-scale treatment. To make them just ordinarily conversational would cause them completely to lose their rich effect. After the disappearance of Falstaff in order to become the fat woman of Brentford, keep the dialogue animated and so avoid a slump after the more practical action.

In the succeeding scene, don't obscure the points through headlong passion. These kind of scenes require a studied government to begin with so that the apparent disjointedness and erratic fluctuations of passions proceed from a deliberate plan on the part of the actor. Play closely with line almost overlapping the cue, and the characters sharp and well assertive in delivery. Ford begins his speech 'Master Page, as I am a man', with a complete drop from his mad passion into a short-breathed measured-out intensity, couched in strenuous colloquial tones, but rising again to the uncontrolled pitch. Thus we have a necessary change, needed to rest the prevailing high tension for a moment in order to give it a fresh power; but the interim period *must not lose the grip*. It is remarkable what Shakespeare is able to do with small measures. Ford's speech 'Help to search my house this one time' is less violent, but it is charged with urgent pleading so that it has its own specific variety of strength. Then comes a new turn to the scene as Mrs Ford calls out to Mrs Page to bring the 'old woman' down from the chamber. This is addressed in a long and featured manner because it is a point of change in the action and attracts everyone's attention, especially our own, as indicating some important development. This also enables Ford to start off again in biting sarcasm which twists his voice in exaggerated tones of bitter ridicule. Make this prominent in order to preserve the 'body' of the speech and prevent an unmeaning gabble.

Finally, after the exit of the male characters, let the two Wives have a good laugh and then enter upon their own scene with sustained virility so that there is no anti-climax after the displays of energetic action that have just passed. Keep them full-blooded in their comments and deliberations and brimming with merriment over their exploits both past and anticipated, remembering that they 'would not have things cool'.

GLOSSARY OF WORDS

380. **Sufferance.** 36,44–45. 'your sorrow hath eaten up my sufferance'. That which he has suffered. Her grief at what he has suffered for her sake has balanced events.
381. **Obsequious.** 36,45. Responsive: adapt. from L. *obsequiōs-us* compliant, obedient.
382. **Requital.** 36,45. Equal devotion.
383. **Accoutrement.** 36,47. 'in all the accoutrement, complement and ceremony of it'. Trappings. From MFr. and probably from *à* to + *coustre, coutre* a sacristan who robed the clergyman.
384. **Complement.** 36,47. See previous quot. Falstaff is assuring Mrs Ford of his complete attention to the details of his love-making, sparing nothing to make it devoted to her. This word implies this fullness of effort and comes from L. meaning 'to fill up'; thus, 'to complete'.
385. **Gossip.** 37,2. 'What, ho, gossip Ford!' This word is from OE. *godsibb*, God + *sib* akin, related. It was formerly applied to a sponsor at baptism, then became the synonym for a colloquial friend and especially for the women who attended a birth: thus, women who talked together,

women who talked idly or dangerously. Here the word is applied in a pleasant and friendly use.
386. **Lunes.** 37,11. Fits of irrational passion: adapt. from Med.L. *luna* lit. 'moon', hence 'fit of lunacy'.
387. **Takes on.** 37,12. 'he so takes on ... with my husband;' Behaves in a wild, unrestrained way; an idiomatic use of the word not easy to analyse. It probably means that he takes hold of his trouble in a violent way—exercises his feelings passionately. See note 301.
388. **Rails.** 37,12. Coarse abusive, violent language: from Fr. *raillier*, of uncertain origin.
389. **Complexion.** 37,13. 'curses Eve's daughters, of what complexion soever;' This word hovers between 'features' and 'nature'. It originally meant the combination of the 'humours' of a man into the nature of his temperament; and this is still a frequently used meaning in Shakespeare. The word is adopt. from Fr.-L. meaning 'combination', 'connection', 'association', and later 'physical constitution or conformation'.
390. **Peer out.** 37,14. Search out.
391. **Bestow.** 37,30. 'how should I

bestow him?' Dispose of; lit. 'to find a place for': BE + *stowen* to place.
392. **Kiln-hole.** 37,39. The fire-hole of a kiln.
393. **Abstract.** 37,42. 'he hath an abstract ... of such places'. A natural thought, idea. It is an obsolete meaning. The word is adopt. from L. *abstractus* 'drawn away', and came to mean among other things 'that which was drawn away or isolated from the concrete', thus *thought, idea*.
394. **Thrummed.** 38,4. Covered with coarse ends or tufts. OE. *þrum* end-piece, remnant.
395. **Presently.** 38,21. At once.
396. **Draff.** 38,30. The residue of malt after brewing.
307. **Lief.** 38,36. Rather. OE. *léof, líof* love. It was used adjectively as *beloved, agreeable, precious, etc.* In Shakespeare it is always used to denote preference—'I had rather', or 'gladly', derived meanings then in current use.
398. **Panderly.** 38,39. See note 98.
399. **Knot.** 38,40. 'a knot, a ging, a pack, a conspiracy'. A collection of people.
400. **Ging.** 38,40. See previous quot. A confederacy. The word probably

originally meant ' a going together ' and was used to denote ' a company of armed men ', ' a host ', ' a gang '. FORD uses it in the latter sense with the specific meaning of ' a band of plotters '.

401. **Pack.** 38,40. See previous quot. FORD is duplicating his meaning by using different words in order to give intensity to it.

402. **Table-sport.** 39,25. ' let me ... be your table-sport ; ' Subject of amusing conversation at table. FORD is willing to be made the subject of ridicule if he is proved wrong in suspecting FALSTAFF's presence in the house a second time.

403. **Leman.** 39,26. ' his wife's leman '. Lover. The word was used equally in good and bad senses and applied to both sexes : Early ME. *leofman* from *léof, lief* dear + MAN.

404. **Quean.** 39,32. Harlot : OE. *quene* a woman : from Early ME. a term of

disparagement or abuse. This particular sense was especially applied in the 16–17th c.

405. **Cozening.** 39,32. ' an old cozening quean ! ' Cheating, deceiving ; explained by Cotgrove, 1611, as ' to clayme kindred for aduantage, or particular ends ; as he, who to saue charges in travelling, goes from house to house, as cosin to the owner of euery one '.

406. **Figure.** 39,36. ' She works . . . by the figure '. A scheme or table showing the disposition of the heavens at a given time. One quote in the OED is dated 1393.

407. **Daubery.** 39,36. Crude devices.

408. **Prat.** 39,42. ' I'll prat her.' OE *praett*, guile, trick : a play by FORD upon the name of the old woman. The OED also gives a quote, 1567, as *Rogues cant* : *prat*, a buttocke.

409. **Pole-cat.** 39,43. A title for vile,

immoral persons. It is a small carnivorous European animal.

410. **Ronyon.** 39,43. An abusive term, the origin of which is obscure.

411. **Warrant.** 40.7. ' the warrant of womanhood . . .' Privilege because of FALSTAFF's advances towards them, *or* because it is in a woman's nature to be revenged.

412. **Fee-simple.** 40,11. ' if the devil have him not in fee-simple '. In absolute possession. It was an estate in land etc. belonging to the owner and his heirs for ever.

413. **Fine and recovery.** 40,11. A sum of money paid by a tenant to his lord in order to be able to transfer his lands to another.

414. **Figures.** 40,15. ' scrape the figures out of your husband's brains '. Evil imaginations.

415. **Methinks.** 40,20. It seems to me : ME + *thincan* to seem.

416. **Period.** 40,20. See note 314.

GLOSSARY OF PHRASES

417. **Youth in a basket !** 38,39. A proverbial saying for ' a fortunate lover '—J. Dover Wilson.

418. **If I cry out thus upon no trail, never trust me when I open again.** 39,53–54. After his second failure to find

FALSTAFF in his house, FORD declares that if, like a hunting-dog, he has started on a false trail, he must never be trusted if he ever institutes another.

COMMENTARY

ACT II   SCENE VIII

This scene is quite straightforward. It needs to be kept as active as possible and not retire into mere pleasantries or plots without the stimulus of great relish. MRS PAGE, in particular, must devise the facts of the forthcoming exposure of FALSTAFF with quick imagination and *create* the details as opposed to unassisted announcement of them, and everyone must be keen with delight and anticipation. The scene will not play itself, and it is necessary that vitality must be brought to it by the actors.

GLOSSARY OF WORDS

419. **Heretic.** 40,31. One who believes something contrary to the teaching of orthodox religion : ultimately from Gk. meaning ' able to choose '.

420. **Herne.** 41,1. ' Herne the hunter . . .' According to tradition, the spectre of one of the former keepers of Windsor Forest who hanged himself for fear of disgrace due to some offence that he had committed. A family of that name was living in Windsor in the 16th c.

421. **Takes.** 41,5. ' takes the cattle . . .' Puts under an evil influence. See note 301.

422. **Milch-kine.** 41,6. Cows in milk.

423. **Idle-headed eld.** 41,9. The ignorant people of old or former times.

424. **Urchins.** 41,23. Goblins : a variant of HERCHEON, IRCHIN ; adopt. from O.Norm.Fr.-L. meaning ' a hedgehog '. Goblins and elves were supposed occasionally to assume the forms of these animals.

425. **Ouphes.** 41,23. ' ouphes and fairies '. Perhaps a variant of *ouf, oaf*, or a scribal or typographical error for *auph* or *oaph*, an elf's child, goblin child, one deformed or an idiot. It first appears in this Shakespearean instance. Cf. note 463.

426. **Rattles.** 41,25. ' rattles in their hands : ' These were probably made of small bladders or old parchment or ' dooble papers ' containing pebbles or dried peas.

427. **Sawpit.** 41,27. A pit where wood is sawn.

428. **Diffused.** 41,28. ' With some diffused song : ' Treated so as to mystify, perplex and cause distraction to FALSTAFF.

429. **Vizards.** 41,45. Masks, false faces.

430. **Potent.** 42,8. Influential ; lit. powerful : *potens* powerful.

COMMENTARY

ACT II   SCENE VIII

The opening scene with SIMPLE is mostly a piece of filling-out matter, but it has its function in connecting the last scene but one with the arrival of FALSTAFF at the Inn in the clothes of the old woman of Brentford. Again, the interest is aroused by the interpretation of character and the wide contrast between the foolish SIMPLE and the boisterous, blunt HOST. FALSTAFF amuses us by his nimble trickery of the stupid servant, and then reveals his chastened spirit in subdued misery. This treatment is necessary because he suddenly rises in a spasm of rage when MRS QUICKLY announces that she comes ' From the two parties, forsooth.' But MRS QUICKLY is not at a loss to keep hold of him, and vigorously presents the picture of MRS FORD's fellow-suffering. FALSTAFF, however, is not appeased and bounds back with more than equal retort that though she is black and blue, he is all the colours of the rainbow, and had run the near risk of being put in the stocks as a witch. This is a passage of broad strength shared equally by FALSTAFF and MRS QUICKLY. Then she comes in immediately with *great earnestness* and emphasizes that he will hear from her things to his content. She thrusts the letter into his hand and immediately sighs out against the adverse fate striving to frustrate the mutual happiness of the two concerned. See that this treatment is properly observed because it is the means by which FALSTAFF is brought round from his gross resentment against his misfortunes. These means are not great, but with careful application of the measures suggested it can be accomplished.

FENTON'S scene with the HOST is earnest, careful and fairly rapid without losing any point in the details which he develops. Particularize somewhat more precisely from 'Now, thus it rests :' so that he is able to lead up to the answer to the HOST's question, 'Which means she to deceive, father or mother ? ', with a big 'Both'.

FALSTAFF after his secret session with MRS QUICKLY is reassured and his speech to FORD begins in this vein. He is still feeling somewhat beaten, but he is not in a hurry because he has a chance to have his revenge on FORD. The speech must be taken with this sense of urgency since it is leading on to some development, some mysterious development as FORD is informed and bid follow to hear the details. The action is no longer being developed by degrees in these scenes, but it is running on to the final one of the play.

GLOSSARY OF WORDS

431. **Standing-bed.** 42,14. A bed supported by legs, as opposed to a truckle-bed. See next note.
432. **Truckle-bed.** 42,15. A small bed that was wheeled under and from beneath a standing-bed : AFr.-L. equiv. to Gk. meaning ' sheaf of a pulley, the "grip" in which the pulley is inserted '.
433. **Anthropophaginian.** 42,16–17. Cannibal : from Gk. ' man-eating '.
434. **Ephesian.** 42,23. A boon companion. It was purely a cant term.
435. **Bohemian-Tartar.** 42,25. ' Tartar ' was an old cant name for a strolling vagabond. The Tartars were natives of a region of Central Asia. The

HOST's compound is an original description of SIMPLE to supply a picturesque apostrophe to a man most unlikely to suit it. Bohemia was a kingdom of Central Europe, forming part of the Austrian empire.
436. **Cozened.** 42,39. See note 405.
437. **Clerkly.** 43,8. ' Thou art clerkly Sir John.' Skilful in phrasing the answers so as to satisfy in a non-committal way.
438. **Transformed.** 43,14–15. Turned into dirty linen.
439. **Primero.** 43,19. A gambling card-game, very fashionable from about 1530-1640.

440. **Apprehended.** 43,32. Arrested : from L. meaning ' to seize '.
441. **Rank.** 44,10 ' something rank on foot'. In full swing.
442. **Mince.** 45,2. Walk with short precise steps like a lady.
443. **Weaver's beam.** 45,13–14. That part of a loom, a wooden roller or cylinder, on which weavers wind the warp. Also a similar roller on which the cloth is wound as it is woven.
444. **Plucked geese.** 45,15–16. A reference by FALSTAFF to one of his boyish occupations when given the job of plucking a goose's feathers.

GLOSSARY OF PHRASES

445. **Like who more bold.** 43,5. This is the Folio reading. The Quarto reads ' Ay, tike . . .' *tike* meaning ' clown ' or ' clod-pole '—see Staunton. Thus the meaning becomes *who more bold than a fool ?*
446. **Than the villanous inconstancy of man's disposition is able to bear.** 43,25–26. FALSTAFF, after his two experiences in FORD's house, declares to MRS QUICKLY that he has suffered more than the treacherous uncertainty of man's endurance is able to stand up to.
447. **The mirth whereof so larded with the matter, That neither singly can be manifested, Without the show of both ; fat Falstaff Hath a great scene.** 44,2–5. FENTON is persuading the HOST to help him in his endeavours to marry

ANNE, and produces a letter explaining the proposed trick that is to be played on FALSTAFF. The humour of the whole affair is so involved that it closely concerns his own private plot as well and neither one can be distinguished separately from the other. FALSTAFF is to play a greatly amusing part as the central character in the episode.
448. **They say there is divinity in odd numbers, either in nativity, chance, or death.** 44,46–47. A Latin quotation from Ovid—' numero deus impare gaudet ' : God takes pleasure in odd numbers, i.e. God works in the unexpected. After two ill-favoured attempts by FALSTAFF to woo MRS FORD, perhaps this odd one will prove fortunate.

COMMENTARY

ACT II SCENE IX

Simple as it is, this scene must be kept lively and each character vigorous in its particular motive. It helps to anticipate the exciting things that are to come.

GLOSSARY OF WORDS

449. **Nay-word.** 45,24. See note 216.
450. **Mum.** 45,25. ' I . . . cry " mum " ; she cries " budget " ; ' ¡Mumbudget

was probably some child's game in which silence was required as indicated by ' mum '.

451. **Budget.** 45,25. See previous note.
452. **Lewdsters.** 46,8. Lewd persons.

GLOSSARY OF PHRASES

None.

COMMENTARY

ACT II SCENE X

FALSTAFF, now assured of final victory, invokes the aid of the amorous gods to stir his own escapade to success. He welcomes MRS FORD as his doe with expansive greeting and defies any intervention whatever as he surrenders himself to his bliss. But, alas, the same sweet voice that greeted him as 'my dear' tells him with equal sweetness that MRS PAGE has come too. FALSTAFF accepts the situation in a hearty congenial way only to have his serenity disturbed by the flight of the two 'does' at a sudden unearthly noise. FALSTAFF then makes a characteristically pungent summary of the event and the disguised principals enter with their fairy company.

ANNE issues her orders with a clear declaration of the supernatural nature of the visitors. This, together with PISTOL's more grotesque demonstrativeness, is purposely done to convince FALSTAFF of the unearthly presences and practices around him, and this should be borne in mind and acted accordingly. Their speeches are not merely opening incidents in the episode, but have this other purpose in their treatment. FALSTAFF is overawed by the well-contrived deception and sinks down in real fear.

ANNE must take her long speech with liveliness, but also touch the only poetic passage in the play with the virtue of completeness in the words and rhythm. It is a delightful issue of the finer elements of language and seasons the whole scene with a touch of fantasy, helping its nature to keep its pleasant charm by giving the comedy an easing companion of alternative merit.

The remainder of the scene is in the hands of the characters and the final deployment of the issue happily and plainly unfolded without difficulty, and the play closes on a concert of good humour, from 'Sir John and all'.

GLOSSARY OF WORDS

453. **Rut-time.** 47,11. The annual recurring sexual excitement of deer—and, by extension, in other animals as well: adopt. from OFr.-L. to roar.

454. **Scut.** 47,14. 'My doe with the black scut !' A short erect tail; the precise application is obscure.

455. **Potatoes.** 47,14. 'Let the sky rain potatoes ;' Yams (not the modern potato) ; considered provocative—J. Dover Wilson.

456. **Kissing-comfits.** 47,15. A perfumed sweet for making the breath pleasant.

457. **Eringoes.** 47,16. The candied root of the Sea-Holly, formerly used as a sweetmeat.

458. **Bribe.** 47,19. 'Divide me like a bribe buck'. A buck obtained by poaching and immediately divided up among those who have conspired to obtain it. The early sense of the word meant *theft, robbery*, etc.

459. **Buck.** 47,19. See previous quot. The male of several animals, but used in this instance with ref. to the male deer ; OE. *bucca* a he-goat.

460. **Restitution.** 47,23. ' now is Cupid a child of conscience ; he makes restitution '. Having deprived FALSTAFF of his hopes in the past, he (Cupid) is now about to fulfil them.

461. **Hobgoblin.** 48,12. A frightening apparition ; usually another name for Puck or Robin Goodfellow, HOB being a familiar by-form of *Rob* = Robert or Robin.

462. **Oyes.** 48,12. The call by the public crier to command attention : OFr. *oiez, oyez* hear ye ! The pronunciation in this instance is—*o-ise*.

463. **Elves.** 48,13. The name of a class of supernatural beings, in early Teutonic belief supposed to possess formidable magical powers, exercised variously for the benefit or the injury of mankind.

464. **Airy toys.** 48,13. Objects of dainty quality whose element is in the air.

465. **Bilberry.** 48,16. The fruit of a small shrub growing in exposed places. It is blue-black in colour.

466. **Radiant.** 48,17. ' Our radiant queen . . .' ANNE, addressing the fairies, alludes to Titania radiating light and purity.

467. **Sluts.** 48,17. Lazy women of dirty habits.

468. **Fantasy.** 48,22. Imagination. This word comes from Gk. meaning *a making visible* and in modern use conveys the sense of 'fancifulness', 'whimsicality', 'capriciousness'. PHANTASY, although basically the same word, is now used to denote 'imagination', 'visionary notion'. As the context implies the more wholesome nature of *fancy*, it is nearer to 'imagination' of true things than to whimsical or fantastic creations.

469. **Ouphes.** 48,28. Used here in the sense of the elf's child. See note 425.

470. **Balm.** 48,33. A natural product of certain trees, possessing a sweet fragrance and medicinal properties.

471. **Blazon.** 48,35. The heraldic terms expressed on a banner or shield.

472. **Expressure.** 48,38. 'The expressure that it bears'. That which is expressed—the motto of the Garter.

473. **Charactery.** 48,44. Writing or means of symbolization.

474. **Middle-earth.** 48,51. The earth, as lying between heaven and hell ; the material world : a perversion of MIDDELERD, erd = OE. *ead*, dwelling, the land where one dwells.

475. **O'erlook'd.** 49,3. ' thou wast o'erlook'd even in thy birth '. Bewitched, looked upon with the evil eye. Obsolete meaning, but very common at the time and until the end of the 19th c.

476. **Extant.** 49,39. Very evident, stand-out very clearly : from L. meaning ' to stand out '.

477. **Jack-a-Lent.** 49,45. See note 310.

478. **O'er-reaching.** 50,2. ' so gross o'er-reaching . . .' FALSTAFF feels that he is unable to prevent, by retort, the gibes that are aimed at him from all sides with overpowering, ' o'er-reaching ' unanimity.

479. **Ridden.** 50,2. ' Am I ridden with a Welsh goat too ? ' Made a fool of by a Welsh goat ; a derisive epithet for EVANS as the native of a mountainous country.

480. **Hodge-pudding.** 50,14. A pudding made of a mixture of odd ingredients.

481. **Puffed.** 50,15. ' A puffed man ?' A man blown out like a bladder.

482. **Metheglins.** 50,21. ' wine and metheglins '. A spiced or medicated variety of mead, originally peculiar to Wales. Coming from EVANS in his list of FALSTAFF's indulgences, it is obviously an addition of his own. It is Welsh in origin, meaning ' healing ', ' medicinal ': adapt. from L. *medicus* + *llyn* liquor.

483. **Posset.** 50,30. See note 126.

484. **Dispatched.** 50,37. ' have you dispatched ?' Have you carried the plan into effect ? This offers SLENDER a chance to quibble in his reply, using the word in its other meaning of ' putting to death '.

485. **Swinged.** 50,43. Beaten, thrashed : a p.pple. and ME. form of SWENGE, OE. *swengan* to shake, shatter.

486. **Evitate.** 51,23. Avoid, escape from ; adapt. from Fr. *éviter*—L. *évitāre*, from *ē* out + *vitāre* to shun.

487. **Eschew'd.** 51,32. Avoided : adopt. from OFr. *eschiver, eschever*. The root meaning appears to be *to dread, avoid, shun*, whence also SHY.

488. **Muse.** 51,34. Wonder.

GLOSSARY OF PHRASES

489. **Jove, thou wast a bull for thy Europa.** 47,2-3. Jove, in love with Europa, changed himself into a bull, which she in admiration caressed, and then mounted its back. The animal bore her across the sea to Crete and there revealed itself as Jove. She had three children by him.

490. **You were also, Jupiter, a swan for the love of Leda.** 47,5. The god fell in love with Leda while she was bathing. He persuaded Venus to change herself into an eagle, while he became a swan. Pretending to escape from the eagle's attacks, he flew to Leda's bosom and converted the situation to his own advantage.

491. **Let there come a tempest of provocation.** 47,16. A whole host of confounding circumstances, provoking disappointment. FALSTAFF has made up his mind that nothing whatever is going to interfere with his happiness with MRS FORD.

492. **I will keep my sides to myself, my shoulders for the fellow of this walk.** 47,19-20. FALSTAFF divides himself up like a buck. Having parted with his haunches to the Wives, he lasciviously keeps his own sides or thighs for himself, gives his shoulders, as is customary, to the forester patrolling that particular 'walk' or division, and so leads to the important concluding item, the horns, with which he laughingly makes cuckolds of the two husbands, although this is rather more wishful thinking than fact.

493. **As I am a true spirit, welcome!** 47,23. FALSTAFF, wearing the horns and chains of the spectral Herne, assures the two Wives that he is a wholesome 'spirit', a 'spirit' of truth and reality.

494. **You orphan heirs of fixed destiny.** 48,10. This line has never been satisfactorily explained. It may mean that they, as spirits, are without natural parents and the purposes of their being are determined for them as agents of superior powers, without wills of their own. The word *fairy* ultimately comes from L. *fāta* the Fates.

495. **They are fairies ; he that speaks to them shall die.** 48,18. This is the survival of an old superstition.

496. **The several chairs of order.** 48,32. The stalls of the Knights of the Garter in the chapel.

497. **Each fair instalment, coat, and several crest, With loyal blazon, evermore be blest!** 48,34-35. Each honourable seat and the distinction it brings, together with the coat of arms, crest of the holder of the seat, each of which displays the heraldic insignia of a loyal subject.

498. **Honi soit qui mal y pense.** 48,40. Evil be to him who evil thinks ; the motto of the Order of the Garter.

499. **Do not these fair yokes Become the forest better than the town ?** 49,28-29. This passage is doubtful, but it seems reasonable to attribute the meaning to FALSTAFF's antlers which are yoked together. MRS FORD points to these and suggests that such things belong to the forest and not domestic life and that she is not interested in making her husband a cuckold.

500. **Ay, and an ox too: both the proofs are extant.** 49,39. This is FORD's reply to FALSTAFF's observation that he has been made an ass in the practical joke played upon him. FORD uses a quibble in the word 'ox'. To make an ox of anyone was to make a fool of him ; and a coarser meaning may very probably be implied as well, where ox is evidently meant for a castrated bull. FALSTAFF has been prevented in his purposes. The 'proofs' are the two Wives.

501. **Drove the grossness of the foppery into a received belief.** 49,42-43. The grotesque nature of the nonsense. FALSTAFF is excusing his being deceived because of the confused state of his mind and the sudden surprise.

502. **A coxcomb of frize.** 50,3. A foolscap which was made in the shape of the comb of a cockerel. 'Frize' is another form of *frieze*, a kind of coarse woollen cloth. Wales was celebrated for this kind of cloth and the epithet is addressed to EVANS.

503. **I am not able to answer the Welsh flannel.** 50,24. FALSTAFF is so humiliated and exhausted mentally that he cannot retort even to the cheap unrefined gibes of EVANS, cheap as the material out of which his disguise is made.

504. **Ignorance itself is a plummet o'er me.** 50,24-25. A passage never clearly defined. FALSTAFF is too exhausted to find any resources against his situation and tormentors and he is thus being proved completely ignorant of any means of self-defence, *plummet* being a sounding-lead used by seamen to find the depth of water and prove the sufficiency for the ship's passage.

505. **The truth is, she and I, long since contracted.** 51,18. FENTON tells of the fact that they have plighted troth or in modern language 'become engaged'.

506. **In love the heavens themselves do guide the state.** 51,27. In love, matters are determined by heavenly ordinance.

507. **Wives are sold by fate.** 51,28. Wives are not bought or determined by anything but the mutual inclination of both parties concerned.

508. **When night-dogs run, all sorts of deer are chased.** 51,33. Things that happen in the dark are unpredictable.

1970.

G. S.

INDEX

Rocannon's
World

Books by Ursula K. Le Guin

NOVELS:

Rocannon's World
Planet of Exile
City of Illusions
The Left Hand of Darkness
A Wizard of Earthsea
The Tombs of Atuan
The Farthest Shore
The Lathe of Heaven
The Dispossessed

SHORT STORIES:

The Wind's Twelve Quarters
Orsinian Tales

POETRY:

Wild Angels

Rocannon's World

Ursula K. Le Guin

HARPER & ROW, PUBLISHERS
NEW YORK, HAGERSTOWN, SAN FRANCISCO, LONDON

Part of this novel appeared in *Amazing Stories,* September, 1964, as a short story. Copyright © 1964 by Ziff-Davis Publications, Inc.

ISBN 0–06–012568-3

LIBRARY OF CONGRESS CATALOG CARD NUMBER: 76–47250

77 78 79 80 81 10 9 8 7 6 5 4 3 2 1

Introduction to the 1977 Edition

W<small>HEN I SET OUT</small> to write my first science-fiction novel, in the century's mid-sixties and my own mid-thirties, I had written several novels, but I had never before invented a planet. It is a mysterious business, creating worlds out of words. I hope I can say without irreverence that anyone who has done it knows why Jehovah took Sunday off. Looking back on this first effort of mine, I can see the timidity, and the rashness, and the beginner's luck, of the apprentice demiurge.

When asked to "define the difference between fantasy and science fiction," I mouth and mumble and always end up talking about the spectrum, that very useful spectrum, along which one thing shades into another. Definitions are for grammar, not literature, I say, and boxes are for bones. — But of course fantasy and science fiction *are* different, just as red and blue are different; they have different frequencies; if you mix them (on paper—I work on paper) you get purple, something else again. *Rocannon's World* is definitely purple.

I knew very little about science fiction when I wrote it. I had read a good deal of science fiction, in the early forties and in the early sixties, and that was absolutely all I knew about it: the stories and novels I had read. Not many knew very much more about it, in 1964. Many had read more; and there was Fandom; but very few besides James Blish and Damon Knight had *thought* much about science fiction. It was reviewed, in fanzines, as I soon discovered, and in a very few—mainly *SFR* and *ASFR*—criticized; outside the

v

science fiction magazines it was seldom reviewed and never criticized. It was not studied. It was not taught. There were no schools—in any sense. There were no theories: only the opinions of editors. There was no aesthetic. All that—the New Wave, the academic discovery, Clarion, theses, countertheses, journals of criticism, books of theory, the big words, the exciting experiments—was just, as it were, poised to descend upon us. but it hadn't yet, or at least it hadn't reached my backwater. All I knew was that there was a kind of magazine and book labeled SF by the publishers, a category, into which I had fallen, impelled by a mixture of synchronicity and desperation.

So there I was, getting published at last, and I was supposed to be writing science fiction. How?

I think there may have already existed a book or two on How to Write SF, but I have always avoided all manuals except Fowler's *English Usage* since being exposed to a course in Creative Writing at Harvard and realizing that I was allergic to Creative Writing. How do you write science fiction? Who knows? cried the cheerful demiurge, and started right in to do it.

Demi has learned a few things since then. We all have. One thing he learned (if Muses are female, I guess demiurges are male) was that red is red and blue is blue and if you want either red or blue, don't mix them. There is a lot of promiscuous mixing going on in *Rocannon's World*. We have NAFAL and FTL space ships, we also have Brisingamen's necklace, windsteeds, and some imbecilic angels. We have an extremely useful garment called an impermasuit, resistant to "foreign elements, extreme temperatures, radioactivity, shocks, and blows of moderate velocity and weight such as swordstrokes or bullets," and inside which the wearer would die of suffocation within five minutes. The impermasuit is a good example of where fantasy and science fiction *don't* shade gracefully into one another. A symbol from collective fantasy—the Cloak of Protection (invisibility, etc.)—is decked out with some pseudo-scientific verbiage and a bit of vivid description, and passed off as a marvel of Future Technology. This can be done triumphantly if the symbol goes deep enough (Wells's Time Machine), but if it's merely decorative or convenient, it's cheating. It degrades both symbol and science; it confuses possibility with probability, and ends up with neither. The impermasuit is a lost item of engineering, which you won't find in any of my books written after *Rocannon's World*. Maybe it got taken up by the people who ride in the Chariots of the Gods.

This sort of thing is beginner's rashness, the glorious freedom of ignorance. It's my world, I can do anything! Only, of course, you can't. Exactly as each word of a sentence limits the choice of subsequent words, so that by the end of the sentence you have little or no choice at all, so (you see what I mean? having said "exactly as," I must now say "so") each word, sentence, paragraph, chapter, character, description, speech, invention and event in a novel determines and limits the rest of the novel—but no, I am not going to end this sentence as I expected to, because my parallel is *not* exact: the spoken sentence works forward only in time, while the novel, which is not conceived or said all at once, works both ways, forward and back. The beginning is implied in the end, as much as the end is in the beginning. (This is not circularity. Fascinating circular novels exist —*Finnegans Wake, Gravity's Rainbow, Dhalgren*—but if all novels achieved or even attempted circularity, novel readers would rightly rebel; the normal, run-of-the-mill novel begins in one "place" and ends somewhere else, following a pattern— line, zigzag, spiral, hopscotch, trajectory—which has what the circle in its perfection does not have: direction.) Each part shapes every other part. So, even in science fiction, all that wonderful freedom to invent worlds and creatures and sexes and devices has, by about page 12 of the manuscript, become strangely limited. You have to be sure all the things you invented, even if you haven't mentioned them or even thought of them yet, hang together; or they will all hang separately. As freedom increases, so, alas, does responsibility.

As for the timidity I mentioned, the overcaution in exploring my brave new world: though I sent my protagonist Rocannon unprotected (he does finally lose his impermasuit) into the unknown, I was inclined to take refuge myself in the very-well-known-indeed. My use of fragments of the Norse mythology, for instance: I lacked the courage of experience, which says, Go on, make up your own damn myth, it'll turn out to be one of the Old Ones anyhow. Instead of drawing on my own unconscious, I borrowed from legend. It didn't make very much difference in this case, because I had heard Norse myths before I could read, and read *The Children of Odin* and later the Eddas many, many times, so that that mythos was a shaping influence on both my conscious and unconscious mind (which is why I hate Wagner). I'm not really sorry I borrowed from the Norse; it certainly did them no harm; but still, Odin in an impermasuit—it's a bit silly. The borrowing interfered, too, with the tentative exploration of my own personal mythology, which this book inaugurated. That is why Rocannon was so much braver than I was. He knew jolly well he wasn't Odin, but simply a piece of me, and that my job was to go toward the shared, collective ground of myth, the root, the source—by nobody's road but my own. It's the only way anybody gets there.

Timidity, again, in the peopling of my world. Elves and dwarves. Heroes and servants. Male-dominated feudalism. The never-never-Bronze Age of sword and sorcery. A League of Worlds. I didn't know yet that the science in my fiction was mostly going to be social science, psychology, anthropology, history, etc., and that I had to figure out how to use all that, and work hard at it too, because nobody else had yet done much along those lines. I just took what came to hand, the FTL drive and the Bronze Age, and used them without much thinking about it, saving the courage of real invention for pure fantasies—the Winged Ones, the windsteeds, the Kiemhrir. A lesser courage, but a delight; one I have pretty much lost. You can't take everything with you, as you go on.

I hope this doesn't read as if I were knocking the book, or worse, trying to defuse criticism by anticipating it, a very slimy trick in the Art of Literary Self-Defense. I like this book. Like Bilbo, I like rather more than half of it nearly twice as much as it deserves. I certainly couldn't write it now, but I can read it; and the thirteen-year distance lets me see, peacefully, what isn't very good in it, and what is—the Kiemhrir, for instance, and Semley, and some of the things Kyo says, and that gorge where they camp near a waterfall. And it has a good shape.

May I record my heartfelt joy at the final disappearance in this edition of the typographical errors which, plentiful in the first edition, have been multiplying like gerbils ever since. One of them—Clayfish for Clayfolk—even got translated into French. The Clayfolk, euphoniously, became Argiliens, but the misprint, "the burrowing Clayfish," became "ces poissons d'argilière qui fouissaient le sol," which I consider one of the great triumphs of French Reason in the service of pure madness. There may be some typos in this edition, but I positively look forward to them. At least, with any luck at all, they'll be new ones.

Ursula K. Le Guin

Portland
January 1977

Rocannon's
World

PROLOGUE: THE NECKLACE

How can you tell the legend from the fact on these worlds that lie so many years away?—planets without names, called by their people simply The World, planets without history, where the past is the matter of myth, and a returning explorer finds his own doings of a few years back have become the gestures of a god. Unreason darkens that gap of time bridged by our lightspeed ships, and in the darkness uncertainty and disproportion grow like weeds.

In trying to tell the story of a man, an ordinary League scientist, who went to such a nameless half-known world not many years ago, one feels like an archeologist amid millennial ruins, now struggling through choked tangles of leaf, flower, branch and vine to the sudden bright geometry of a wheel or a polished cornerstone, and now entering some commonplace, sunlit doorway to find inside it the darkness, the impossible flicker of a flame, the glitter of a jewel, the half-glimpsed movement of a woman's arm.

How can you tell fact from legend, truth from truth?

Through Rocannon's story the jewel, the blue glitter seen briefly, returns. With it let us begin, here:

Galactic Area 8, No. 62: FOMALHAUT II.
High-Intelligence Life Forms: Species Contacted:
Species I.

A) Gdemiar (singular Gdem): Highly intelligent, fully hominoid nocturnal troglodytes, 120-135 cm. in height, light skin, dark head-hair. When contacted these cave-dwellers possessed a rigidly stratified oli-

garchic urban society modified by partial colonial telephathy, and a technologically oriented Early Steel culture. Technology enhanced to Industrial, Point C, during League Mission of 252-254. In 254 an Automatic Drive ship (to-from New South Georgia) was presented to oligarchs of the Kiriensea Area community. Status C-Prime.

B) Fiia (singular Fian): Highly intelligent, fully hominoid, diurnal, av. ca. 130 cm. in height, observed individuals generally light in skin and hair. Brief contacts indicated village and nomadic communal societies, partial colonial telepathy, also some indication of short-range TK. The race appears a-technological and evasive, with minimal and fluid culture-patterns. Currently untaxable. Status E-Query.

Species II.
Liuar (singular Liu): Highly intelligent, fully hominoid, diurnal, av. height above 170 cm., this species possesses a fortress/village, clan-descent society, a blocked technology (Bronze), and feudal-heroic culture. Note horizontal social cleavage into 2 pseudoraces: (a: Olgyior, "midmen," light-skinned and dark-haired; (b: Angyar, "lords," very tall, dark-skinned, yellow-haired—

"That's her," said Rocannon, looking up from the *Abridged Handy Pocket Guide to Intelligent Life-forms* at the very tall, dark-skinned, yellow-haired woman who stood halfway down the long museum hall. She stood still and erect, crowned with bright hair, gazing at something in a display case. Around her fidgeted four uneasy and unattractive dwarves.

"I didn't know Fomalhaut II had all those people besides the trogs," said Ketho, the curator.

"I didn't either. There are even some "Unconfirmed" species listed here, that they never contacted. Sounds like

6

time for a more thorough survey mission to the place. Well, now at least we know what she is."

"I wish there were some way of knowing *who* she is. . . ."

She was of an ancient family, a descendant of the first kings of the Angyar, and for all her poverty her hair shone with the pure, steadfast gold of her inheritance. The little people, the Fiia, bowed when she passed them, even when she was a barefoot child running in the fields, the light and fiery comet of her hair brightening the troubled winds of Kirien.

She was still very young when Durhal of Hallan saw her, courted her, and carried her away from the ruined towers and windy halls of her childhood to his own high home. In Hallan on the mountainside there was no comfort either, though splendor endured. The windows were unglassed, the stone floors bare; in coldyear one might wake to see the night's snow in long, low drifts beneath each window. Durhal's bride stood with narrow bare feet on the snowy floor, braiding up the fire of her hair and laughing at her young husband in the silver mirror that hung in their room. That mirror, and his mother's bridal-gown sewn with a thousand tiny crystals, were all his wealth. Some of his lesser kinfolk of Hallan still possessed wardrobes of brocaded clothing, furniture of gilded wood, silver harness for their steeds, armor and silver-mounted swords, jewels and jewelry—and on these last Durhal's bride looked enviously, glancing back at a gemmed coronet or a golden brooch even when the wearer of the ornament stood aside to let her pass, deferent to her birth and marriage-rank.

Fourth from the High Seat of Hallan Revel sat Durhal and his bride Semley, so close to Hallanlord that the old man often poured wine for Semley with his own hand, and spoke of hunting with his nephew and heir Durhal, looking on the young pair with a grim, unhopeful love. Hope came hard to the Angyar of Hallan and all the Western Lands, since the Starlords had appeared with their houses

7

that leaped about on pillars of fire and their awful weapons that could level hills. They had interfered with all the old ways and wars, and though the sums were small there was terrible shame to the Angyar in having to pay a tax to them, a tribute for the Starlord's war that was to be fought with some strange enemy, somewhere in the hollow places between the stars, at the end of years. "It will be your war too," they said, but for a generation now the Angyar had sat in idle shame in their revelhalls, watching their double swords rust, their sons grow up without ever striking a blow in battle, their daughters marry poor men, even midmen, having no dowry of heroic loot to bring a noble husband. Hallanlord's face was bleak when he watched the fair-haired couple and heard their laughter as they drank bitter wine and joked together in the cold, ruinous, resplendent fortress of their race.

Semley's own face hardened when she looked down the hall and saw, in seats far below hers, even down among the halfbreeds and the midmen, against white skins and black hair, the gleam and flash of precious stones. She herself had brought nothing in dowry to her husband, not even a silver hairpin. The dress of a thousand crystals she had put away in a chest for the wedding-day of her daughter, if daughter it was to be.

It was, and they called her Haldre, and when the fuzz on her little brown skull grew longer it shone with steadfast gold, the inheritance of the lordly generations, the only gold she would ever possess. . . .

Semley did not speak to her husband of her discontent. For all his gentleness to her, Durhal in his hard lordly pride had only contempt for envy, for vain wishing, and she dreaded his contempt. But she spoke to Durhal's sister Durossa.

"My family had a great treasure once," she said. "It was a necklace all of gold, with the blue jewel set in the center—sapphire?"

Durossa shook her head, smiling, not sure of the name either. It was late in warmyear, as these Northern Angyar

8

called the summer of the eight-hundred-day year, beginning the cycle of months anew at each equinox; to Semley it seemed an outlandish calendar, a midmannish reckoning. Her family was at an end, but it had been older and purer than the race of any of these northwestern marchlanders, who mixed too freely with the Olgyior. She sat with Durossa in the sunlight on a stone windowseat high up in the Great Tower, where the older woman's apartment was. Widowed young, childless, Durossa had been given in second marriage to Hallanlord, who was her father's brother. Since it was a kinmarriage and a second marriage on both sides she had not taken the title of Hallanlady, which Semley would some day bear; but she sat with the old lord in the High Seat and ruled with him his domains. Older than her brother Durhal, she was fond of his young wife, and delighted in the bright-haired baby Haldre.

"It was bought," Semley went on, "with all the money my forebear Leynen got when he conquered the Southern Fiefs—all the money from a whole kingdom, think of it, for one jewel! Oh, it would outshine anything here in Hallan, surely, even those crystals like koob-eggs your cousin Issar wears. It was so beautiful they gave it a name of its own; they called it the Eye of the Sea. My great-grandmother wore it."

"You never saw it?" the older woman asked lazily, gazing down at the green mountainslopes where long, long summer sent its hot and restless winds straying among the forests and whirling down white roads to the seacoast far away.

"It was lost before I was born."

"No, my father said it was stolen before the Starlords ever came to our realm. He wouldn't talk of it, but there was an old midwoman full of tales who always told me the Fiia would know where it was."

"Ah, the Fiia I should like to see!" said Durossa. "They're in so many songs and tales; why do they never come to the Western Lands?"

"Too high, too cold in winter, I think. They like the sunlight of the valleys of the south."

"Are they like the Clayfolk?"

"Those I've never seen; they keep away from us in the south. Aren't they white like midmen, and misformed? The Fiia are fair; they look like children, only thinner, and wiser. Oh, I wonder if they know where the necklace is, who stole it and where he hid it! Think, Durossa—if I could come into Hallan Revel and sit down by my husband with the wealth of a kingdom round my neck, and out-shine the other women as he outshines all men!"

Durossa bent her head above the baby, who sat studying her own brown toes on a fur rug between her mother and aunt. "Semley is foolish," she murmured to the baby; "Semley who shines like a falling star, Semley whose husband loves no gold but the gold of her. . . ."

And Semley, looking out over the green slopes of summer toward the distant sea, was silent.

But when another coldyear had passed, and the Star-lords had come again to collect their taxes for the war against the world's end—this time using a couple of dwarvish Clayfolk as interpreters, and so leaving all the Angyar humiliated to the point of rebellion—and another warmyear too was gone, and Haldre had grown into a lovely, chattering child, Semley brought her one morning to Durossa's sunlit room in the tower. Semley wore an old cloak of blue, and the hood covered her hair.

"Keep Haldre for me these few days, Durossa," she said, quick and calm. "I'm going south to Kirien."

"To see your father?"

"To find my inheritance. Your cousins of Harget Fief have been taunting Durhal. Even that halfbreed Parna can torment him, because Parna's wife has a satin coverlet for her bed, and a diamond earring, and three gowns, the dough-faced black-haired trollop! while Durhal's wife must patch her gown—"

"Is Durhal's pride in his wife, or what she wears?"

But Semley was not to be moved. "The Lords of Hallan

10

are becoming poor men in their own hall. I am going to bring my dowry to my lord, as one of my lineage should."

"Semley! Does Durhal know you're going?"

"My return will be a happy one—that much let him know," said young Semley, breaking for a moment into her joyful laugh; then she bent to kiss her daughter, turned and before Durossa could speak, was gone like a quick wind over the floors of sunlit stone.

Married women of the Angyar never rode for sport, and Semley had not been from Hallan since her marriage; so now, mounting the high saddle of a windsteed, she felt like a girl again, like the wild maiden she had been, riding half-broken steeds on the north wind over the fields of Kirien. The beast that bore her now down from the hills of Hallan was of finer breed, striped coat fitting sleek over hollow, buoyant bones, green eyes slitted against the wind, light and mighty wings sweeping up and down to either side of Semley, revealing and hiding, revealing and hiding the clouds above her and the hills below.

On the third morning she came to Kirien and stood again in the ruined courts. Her father had been drinking all night, and, just as in the old days, the morning sunlight poking through his fallen ceilings annoyed him, and the sight of his daughter only increased his annoyance. "What are you back for?" he growled, his swollen eyes glancing at her and away. The fiery hair of his youth was quenched, gray strands tangled on his skull. "Did the young Halla not marry you, and you've come sneaking home?"

"I am Durhal's wife. I came to get my dowry, father."

The drunkard growled in disgust; but she laughed at him so gently that he had to look at her again, wincing.

"Is it true, father, that the Fiia stole the necklace Eye of the Sea?"

"How do I know? Old tales. The thing was lost before I was born, I think. I wish I never had been. Ask the Fiia if you want to know. Go to them, go back to your husband. Leave me alone here. There's no room at Kirien for girls and gold and all the rest of the story. The story's

11

over here; this is the fallen place, this is the empty hall. The sons of Leynen all are dead, their treasures are all lost. Go on your way, girl."

Gray and swollen as the web-spinner of ruined houses, he turned and went blundering toward the cellars where he hid from daylight.

Leading the striped windsteed of Hallan, Semley left her old home and walked down the steep hill, past the village of the midmen, who greeted her with sullen respect, on over fields and pastures where the great, wing-clipped, half-wild herilor grazed, to a valley that was green as a painted bowl and full to the brim with sunlight. In the deep of the valley lay the village of the Fiia, and as she descended leading her steed the little, slight people ran up toward her from their huts and gardens, laughing, calling out in faint, thin voices.

"Hail Halla's bride, Kirienlady, Windborne, Semley the Fair!"

They gave her lovely names and she liked to hear them, minding not at all their laughter; for they laughed at all they said. That was her own way, to speak and laugh. She stood tall in her long blue cloak among their swirling welcome.

"Hail Lightfolk, Sundwellers, Fiia friends of men!"

They took her down into the village and brought her into one of their airy houses, the tiny children chasing along behind. There was no telling the age of a Fian once he was grown; it was hard even to tell one from another and be sure, as they moved about quick as moths around a candle, that she spoke always to the same one. But it seemed that one of them talked with her for a while, as the others fed and petted her steed, and brought water for her to drink, and bowls of fruit from their gardens of little trees. "It was never the Fiia that stole the necklace of the Lords of Kirien!" cried the little man. "What would the Fiia do with gold, Lady? For us there is sunlight in warmyear, and in coldyear the remembrance of sunlight; the

12

yellow fruit, the yellow leaves in end-season, the yellow hair of our lady of Kirien; no other gold."

"Then it was some midman stole the thing?"

Laughter rang long and faint about her. "How would a midman dare? O Lady of Kirien, how the great jewel was stolen no mortal knows, not man nor midman nor Fian nor any among the Seven Folk. Only dead minds know how it was lost, long ago when Kireley the Proud whose great-granddaughter is Semley walked alone by the caves of the sea. But it may be found perhaps among the Sunhaters."

"The Clayfolk?"

A louder burst of laughter, nervous.

"Sit with us, Semley, sunhaired, returned to us from the north." She sat with them to eat, and they were as pleased with her graciousness as she with theirs. But when they heard her repeat that she would go to the Clayfolk to find her inheritance, if it was there, they began not to laugh; and little by little there were fewer of them around her. She was alone at last with perhaps the one she had spoken with before the meal. "Do not go among the Clayfolk, Semley," he said, and for a moment her heart failed her. The Fian, drawing his hand down slowly over his eyes, had darkened all the air about them. Fruit lay ash-white on the plate; all the bowls of clear water were empty.

"In the mountains of the far land the Fiia and the Gdemiar parted. Long ago we parted," said the slight, still man of the Fiia. "Longer ago we were one. What we are not, they are. What we are, they are not. Think of the sunlight and the grass and the trees that bear fruit, Semley; think that not all roads that lead down lead up as well."

The Fian bowed, laughing a little.

Outside the village she mounted her striped windsteed, and, calling farewell in answer to their calling, rose up into the wind of afternoon and flew southwestward toward the caves down by the rocky shores of Kiriensea.

She feared she might have to walk far into those tunnel-caves to find the people she sought, for it was said the

13

Clayfolk never came out of their caves into the light of the sun, and feared even the Greatstar and the moons. It was a long ride; she landed once to let her steed hunt tree-rats while she ate a little bread from her saddle-bag. The bread was hard and dry by now and tasted of leather, yet kept a faint savor of its making, so that for a moment, eating it alone in a glade of the southern forests, she heard the quiet tone of a voice and saw Durhal's face turned to her in the light of the candles of Hallan. For a while she sat daydreaming of that stern and vivid young face, and of what she would say to him when she came home with a kingdom's ransom around her neck: "I wanted a gift worthy of my husband, Lord . . ." Then she pressed on, but when she reached the coast the sun had set, with the Greatstar sinking behind it. A mean wind had come up from the west, starting and gusting and veering, and her windsteed was weary fighting it. She let him glide down on the sand. At once he folded his wings and curled his thick, light limbs under him with a thrum of purring. Semley stood holding her cloak close at her throat, stroking the steed's neck so that he flicked his ears and purred again. The warm fur comforted her hand, but all that met her eyes was gray sky full of smears of cloud, gray sea, dark sand. And then running over the sand a low, dark creature—another—a group of them, squatting and running and stopping.

She called aloud to them. Though they had not seemed to see her, now in a moment they were all around her. They kept a distance from her windsteed; he had stopped purring, and his fur rose a little under Semley's hand. She took up the reins, glad of his protection but afraid of the nervous ferocity he might display. The strange folk stood silent, staring, their thick bare feet planted in the sand. There was no mistaking them: they were the height of the Fiia and in all else a shadow, a black image of those laughing people. Naked, squat, stiff, with lank black hair and gray-white skins, dampish looking like the skins of grubs; eyes like rocks.

14

"You are the Clayfolk?"

"Gdemiar are we, people of the Lords of the Realms of Night." The voice was unexpectedly loud and deep, and rang out pompous through the salt, blowing dusk; but, as with the Fiia, Semley was not sure which one had spoken.

"I greet you, Nightlords. I am Semley of Kirien, Durhal's wife of Hallan. I come to you seeking my inheritance, the necklace called Eye of the Sea, lost long ago."

"Why do you seek it here, Angya? Here is only sand and salt and night."

"Because lost things are known of in deep places," said Semley, quite ready for a play of wits, "and gold that came from earth has a way of going back to the earth. And sometimes the made, they say, returns to the maker." This last was a guess; it hit the mark.

"It is true the necklace Eye of the Sea is known to us by name. It was made in our caves long ago, and sold by us to the Angyar. And the blue stone came from the Clayfields of our kin to the east. But these are very old tales, Angya."

"May I listen to them in the places where they are told?"

The squat people were silent a while, as if in doubt. The gray wind blew by over the sand, darkening as the Greatstar set; the sound of the sea loudened and lessened. The deep voice spoke again: "Yes, lady of the Angyar. You may enter the Deep Halls. Come with us now." There was a changed note in his voice, wheedling. Semley would not hear it. She followed the Claymen over the sand, leading on a short rein her sharp-taloned steed.

At the cave-mouth, a toothless, yawning mouth from which a stinking warmth sighed out, one of the Claymen said, "The air-beast cannot come in."

"Yes," said Semley.

"No," said the squat people.

"Yes, I will not leave him here. He is not mine to leave. He will not harm you, so long as I hold his reins."

"No," deep voices repeated; but others broke in, "As

15

you will," and after a moment of hesitation they went on. The cave-mouth seemed to snap shut behind them, so dark was it under the stone. They went in single file, Semley last.

The darkness of the tunnel lightened, and they came under a ball of weak white fire hanging from the roof. Farther on was another, and another; between them long black worms hung in festoons from the rock. As they went on these fire-globes were set closer, so that all the tunnel was lit with a bright, cold light.

Semley's guides stopped at a parting of three tunnels, all blocked by doors that looked to be of iron. "We shall wait, Angya," they said, and eight of them stayed with her, while three others unlocked one of the doors and passed through. It fell to behind them with a clash.

Straight and still stood the daughter of the Angyar in the white, blank light of the lamps; her windsteed crouched beside her, flicking the tip of his striped tail, his great folded wings stirring again and again with the checked impulse to fly. In the tunnel behind Semley the eight Claymen squatted on their hams, muttering to one another in their deep voices, in their own tongue.

The central door swung clanging open. "Let the Angya enter the Realm of Night!" cried a new voice, booming and boastful. A Clayman who wore some clothing on his thick gray body stood in the doorway beckoning to her. "Enter and behold the wonders of our lands, the marvels made by hands, the works of the Nightlords!"

Silent, with a tug at her steed's reins, Semley bowed her head and followed him under the low doorway made for dwarfish fold. Another glaring tunnel stretched ahead, dank walls dazzling in the white light, but, instead of a way to walk upon, its floor carried two bars of polished iron stretching off side as far as she could see. On the bars rested some kind of cart with metal wheels. Obeying her new guide's gestures, with no hesitation and no trace of wonder on her face, Semley stepped into the cart and made the windsteed crouch beside her. The Clayman got

16

in and sat down in front of her, moving bars and wheels about. A loud grinding noise arose, and a screaming of metal on metal, and then the walls of the tunnel began to jerk by. Faster and faster the walls slid past, till the fire-globes overhead ran into a blur, and the stale warm air became a foul wind blowing the hood back off her hair.

The cart stopped. Semley followed the guide up basalt steps into a vast anteroom and then a still vaster hall, carved by ancient waters or by the burrowing Clayfolk out of the rock, its darkness that had never known sunlight lit with the uncanny cold brilliance of the globes. In grilles cut in the walls huge blades turned and turned, changing the stale air. The great closed space hummed and boomed with noise, the loud voices of the Clayfolk, the grinding and shrill buzzing and vibration of turning blades and wheels, the echoes and re-echoes of all this from the rock. Here all the stumpy figures of the Claymen were clothed in garments imitating those of the Starlords—divided trousers, soft boots, and hooded tunics—though the few women to be seen, hurrying servile dwarves, were naked. Of the males many were soldiers, bearing at their sides weapons shaped like the terrible light-throwers of the Star-lords, though even Semley could see these were merely shaped iron clubs. What she saw, she saw without look-ing. She followed where she was led, turning her head neither to left nor right. When she came before a group of Claymen who wore iron circlets on their black hair her guide halted, bowed, boomed out, "The High Lords of the Gdemiar!"

There were seven of them, and all looked up at her with such arrogance on their lumpy gray faces that she wanted to laugh.

"I come among you seeking the lost treasure of my family, O Lords of the Dark Realm," she said gravely to them. "I seek Leynen's prize, the Eye of the Sea." Her voice was faint in the racket of the huge vault.

"So said our messengers, Lady Semley." This time she could pick out the one who spoke, one even shorter than

17

the others, hardly reaching Semley's breast, with a white, powerful, fierce face. "We do not have this thing you seek."

"Once you had it, it is said."

"Much is said, up there where the sun blinks."

"And words are borne off by the winds, where there are winds to blow. I do not ask how the necklace was lost to us and returned to you, its makers of old. Those are old tales, old grudges. I only seek to find it now. You do not have it now; but it may be you know where it is."

"It is not here."

"Then it is elsewhere."

"It is where you cannot come to it. Never, unless we help you."

"Then help me. I ask this as your guest."

"It is said, *The Angyar take; the Fiia give; the Gdemiar give and take.* If we do this for you, what will you give us?"

"My thanks, Nightlord."

She stood tall and bright among them, smiling. They all stared at her with a heavy, grudging wonder, a sullen yearning.

"Listen, Angya, this is a great favor you ask of us. You do not know how great a favor. You cannot understand. You are of a race that will not understand, that cares for nothing but windriding and crop-raising and sword-fighting and shouting together. But who made your swords of the bright steel? We, the Gdemiar! Your lords come to us here and in Clayfields and buy their swords and go away, not looking, not understanding. But you are here now, you will look, you can see a few of our endless marvels, the lights that burn forever, the car that pulls itself, the machines that make our clothes and cook our food and sweeten our air and serve us in all things. Know that all these things are beyond your understanding. And know this: we, the Gdemiar, are the friends of those you call the Starlords! We came with them to Hallan, to Reohan, to Hul-Orren, to all your castles, to help them speak to you. The lords to whom you, the proud Angyar, pay tribute,

18

are our friends. They do us favors as we do them favors! Now, what do your thanks mean to us?"

"That is your question to answer," said Semley, "not mine. I have asked my question. Answer it, Lord."

For a while the seven conferred together, by word and silence. They would glance at her and look away, and mutter and be still. A crowd grew around them, drawn slowly and silently, one after another till Semley was encircled by hundreds of the matted black heads, and all the great booming cavern floor was covered with people, except a little space directly around her. Her windsteed was quivering with fear and irritation too long controlled, and his eyes had gone very wide and pale, like the eyes of a steed forced to fly at night. She stroked the warm fur of his head, whispering, "Quietly now, brave one, bright one, windlord. . . ."

"Angya, we will take you to the place where the treasure lies." The Clayman with the white face and iron crown had turned to her once more. "More than that we cannot do. You must come with us to claim the necklace where it lies, from those who keep it. The air-beast cannot come with you. You must come alone."

"How far a journey, Lord?"

His lips drew back and back. "A very far journey, Lady. Yet it will last only one long night."

"I thank you for your courtesy. Will my steed be well cared for this night? No ill must come to him."

"He will sleep till you return. A greater windsteed you will have ridden, when you see that beast again! Will you not ask where we take you?"

"Can we go soon on this journey? I would not stay long away from my home."

"Yes. Soon." Again the gray lips widened as he stared up into her face.

What was done in those next hours Semley could not have retold; it was all haste, jumble, noise, strangeness. While she held her steed's head a Clayman stuck a long needle into the golden-striped haunch. She nearly cried

19

out at the sight, but her steed merely twitched and then, purring, fell asleep. He was carried off by a group of Clayfolk who clearly had to summon up their courage to touch his warm fur. Later on she had to see a needle driven into her own arm—perhaps to test her courage, she thought, for it did not seem to make her sleep; though she was not quite sure. There were times she had to travel in the rail-carts, passing iron doors and vaulted caverns by the hundred and hundred; once the rail-cart ran through a cavern that stretched off on either hand measureless into the dark, and all that darkness was full of great flocks of herilor. She could hear their cooing, husky calls, and glimpse the flocks in the front-lights of the cart; then she saw some more clearly in the white light, and saw that they were all wingless, and all blind. At that she shut her eyes. But there were more tunnels to go through, and always more caverns, more gray lumpy bodies and fierce faces and booming boasting voices, until at last they led her suddenly out into the open air. It was full night; she raised her eyes joyfully to the stars and the single moon shining, little Heliki brightening in the west. But the Clayfolk were all about her still, making her climb now into some new kind of cart or cave, she did not know which. It was small, full of little blinking lights like rushlights, very narrow and shining after the great dank caverns and the starlit night. Now another needle was stuck in her, and they told her she would have to be tied down in a sort of flat chair, tied down head and hand and foot.

"I will not," said Semley.

But when she saw that the four Claymen who were to be her guides let themselves be tied down first, she submitted. The others left. There was a roaring sound, and a long silence; a great weight that could not be seen pressed upon her. Then there was no weight; no sound; nothing at all.

"Am I dead?" asked Semley.

"Oh no, Lady," said a voice she did not like.

Opening her eyes, she saw the white face bent over her,

the wide lips pulled back, the eyes like little stones. Her bonds had fallen away from her, and she leaped up. She was weightless, bodiless; she felt herself only a gust of terror on the wind.

"We will not hurt you," said the sullen voice or voices. "Only let us touch you, Lady. We would like to touch your hair. Let us touch your hair. . . ."

The round cart they were in trembled a little. Outside its one window lay blank night, or was it mist, or nothing at all? One long night, they had said. Very long. She sat motionless and endured the touch of their heavy gray hands on her hair. Later they would touch her hands and feet and arms, and one her throat: at that she set her teeth and stood up, and they drew back.

"We have not hurt you, Lady," they said. She shook her head.

When they bade her, she lay down again in the chair that bound her down; and when light flashed golden, at the window, she would have wept at the sight, but fainted first.

"Well," said Rocannon, "now at least we know what she is."

"I wish there were some way of knowing *who* she is," the curator mumbled. "She wants something we've got here in the Museum, is that what the trogs say?"

"Now, don't call 'em trogs," Rocannon said conscientiously; as a hilfer, an ethnologist of the High Intelligence Life Forms, he was supposed to resist such words. "They're not pretty, but they're Status C Allies . . . I wonder why the Commission picked them to develop? Before even contacting all the HILF species? I'll bet the survey was from Centaurus—Centaurans always like nocturnals and cave-dwellers. I'd have backed Species II, here, I think."

The troglodytes seem to be rather in awe of her."

"Aren't you?"

Ketho glanced at the tall woman again, then reddened and laughed. "Well, in a way. I never saw such a beautiful alien type in eighteen years here on New South Georgia. I never saw such a beautiful woman anywhere, in fact. She looks like a goddess." The red now reached the top of his bald head, for Ketho was a shy curator, not given to hyperbole. But Rocannon nodded soberly, agreeing.

"I wish we could talk to her without those tr— Gdemiar as interpreters. But there's no help for it." Rocannon went toward their visitor, and when she turned her splendid face to him he bowed down very deeply, going right down to to the floor on one knee, his head bowed and his eyes shut. This was what he called his All-purpose Intercultural Curtsey, and he performed it with some grace. When he came erect again the beautiful woman smiled and spoke.

"She say, Hail, Lord of Stars," growled one of her squat escorts in Pidgin-Galactic.

"Hail, Lady of the Angyar," Rocannon replied. "In what way can we of the Museum serve the lady?"

Across the troglodytes' growling her voice ran like a brief silver wind.

"She say, Please give her necklace which treasure her blood-kin-forebears long long."

"Which necklace?" he asked, and understanding him, she pointed to the central display of the case before them, a magnificent thing, a chain of yellow gold, massive but very delicate in workmanship, set with one big hot-blue sapphire. Rocannon's eyebrows went up, and Ketho at his shoulder murmured, "She's got good taste. That's the Fomalhaut Necklace—famous bit of work."

She smiled at the two men, and again spoke to them over the heads of the troglodytes.

"She say, O Starlords, Elder and Younger Dwellers in House of Treasures, this treasure her one. Long long time. Thank you."

"How did we get the thing, Ketho?"

"Wait; let me look it up in the catalogue. I've got it here. Here. It came from these trogs—trolls—whatever they are: Gdemiar. They have a bargain-obsession, it says;

22

we had to let 'em buy the ship they came here on, an AD-4. This was part payment. It's their own handiwork."

"And I'll bet they can't do this kind of work anymore, since they've been steered to Industrial."

"But they seem to feel the thing is hers, not theirs or ours. It must be important, Rocanno, or they wouldn't have given up this time-span to her errand. Why, the objective lapse between here and Fomalhaut must be considerable!"

"Several years, no doubt," said the hilfer, who was used to starjumping. "Not very far. Well, neither the *Handbook* nor the *Guide* gives me enough data to base a decent guess on. These species obviously haven't been properly studied at all. The little fellows may be showing her simple courtesy. Or an interspecies war may depend on this damn sapphire. Perhaps her desire rules them, because they consider themselves totally inferior to her. Or despite appearances she may be their prisoner, their decoy. How can we tell? . . . Can you give the thing away, Ketho?"

"Oh yes. All the Exotica are technically on loan, not our property, since these claims come up now and then. We seldom argue. Peace above all, until the War comes. . . ."

"Then I'd say give it to her."

Ketho smiled. "It's a privilege," he said. Unlocking the case, he lifted out the great golden chain; then, in his shyness, he held it out to Rocannon, saying, "You give it to her."

So the blue jewel first lay, for a moment, in Rocannon's hand.

His mind was not on it; he turned straight to the beautiful, alien woman, with his handful of blue fire and gold. She did not raise her hands to take it, but bent her head, and he slipped the necklace over her hair. It lay like a burning fuse along her golden-brown throat. She looked up from it with such pride, delight, and gratitude in her face that Rocannon stood wordless, and the little curator murmured hurriedly in his own language, "You're welcome, you're very welcome." She bowed her golden head

23

to him and to Rocannon. Then, turning, she nodded to her squat guards—or captors?—and, drawing her worn blue cloak about her, paced down the long hall and was gone. Ketho and Rocannon stood looking after her.

"What I feel . . ." Rocannon began.

"Well?" Ketho inquired hoarsely, after a long pause.

"What I feel sometimes is that I . . . meeting these people from worlds we know so little of, you know, sometimes . . . that I have as it were blundered through the corner of a legend, of a tragic myth, maybe, which I do not understand. . . ."

"Yes," said the curator, clearing his throat. "I wonder . . . I wonder what her name is."

Semley the Fair, Semley the Golden, Semley of the Necklace. The Clayfolk had bent to her will, and so had even the Starlords in that terrible place where the Clayfolk had taken her, the city at the end of the night. They had bowed to her, and given her gladly her treasure from amongst their own.

But she could not yet shake off the feeling of those caverns about her where rock lowered overhead, where you could not tell who spoke or what they did, where voices boomed and gray hands reached out—Enough of that. She had paid for the necklace; very well. Now it was hers. The price was paid, the past was the past.

Her windsteed had crept out of some kind of box, with his eyes filmy and his fur rimed with ice, and at first when they had left the caves of the Gdemiar he would not fly. Now he seemed all right again, riding a smooth south wind through the bright sky toward Hallan. "Go quick, go quick," she told him, beginning to laugh as the wind cleared away her mind's darkness. "I want to see Durhal soon, soon. . . ."

And swiftly they flew, coming to Hallan by dusk of the second day. Now the caves of the Clayfolk seemed no more than last year's nightmare, as the steed swooped with her up the thousand steps of Hallan and across the

Chasmbridge where the forests fell away for a thousand feet. In the gold light of evening in the flightcourt she dismounted and walked up the last steps between the stiff carven figures of heroes and the two gatewards, who bowed to her, staring at the beautiful, fiery thing around her neck.

In the Forehall she stopped a passing girl, a very pretty girl, by her looks one of Durhal's close kin, though Semley could not call to mind her name. "Do you know me, maiden? I am Semley Durhal's wife. Will you go tell the Lady Durossa that I have come back?"

For she was afraid to go on in and perhaps face Durhal at once, alone; she wanted Durossa's support.

The girl was gazing at her, her face very strange. But she murmured, "Yes, Lady," and darted off toward the Tower.

Semley stood waiting in the gilt, ruinous hall. No one came by; were they all at table in the Revelhall? The silence was uneasy. After a minute Semley started toward the stairs to the Tower. But an old woman was coming to her across the stone floor, holding her arms out, weeping.

"Oh Semley, Semley!"

She had never seen the gray-haired woman, and shrank back.

"But Lady, who are you?"

"I am Durossa, Semley."

She was quiet and still, all the time that Durossa embraced her and wept, and asked if it were true the Clayfolk had captured her and kept her under a spell all these long years, or had it been the Fiia with their strange arts? Then, drawing back a little, Durossa ceased to weep.

"You're still young, Semley. Young as the day you left here. And you wear round your neck the necklace. . . ."

"I have brought my gift to my husband Durhal. Where is he?"

"Durhal is dead."

Semley stood unmoving.

"Your husband, my brother, Durhal Hallanlord was killed seven years ago in battle. Nine years you had been

25

gone. The Starlords came no more. We fell to warning with the Eastern Halls, with the Angyar of Log and Hul-Orren. Durhal, fighting, was killed by a midman's spear, for he had little armor for his body, and none at all for his spirit. He lies buried in the fields above Orren Marsh."

Semley turned away. "I will go to him, then," she said, putting her hand on the gold chain that weighed down her neck. "I will give him my gift."

"Wait, Semley! Durhal's daughter, your daughter, see her now, Haldre the Beautiful!"

It was the girl she had first spoken to and sent to Durossa, a girl of nineteen or so, with eyes like Durhal's eyes, dark blue. She stood beside Durossa, gazing with those steady eyes at this woman Semley who was her mother and was her own age. Their age was the same, and their gold hair, and their beauty. Only Semley was a little taller, and wore the blue stone on her breast.

"Take it, take it. It was for Durhal and Haldre that I brought it from the end of the long night!" Semley cried this aloud, twisting and bowing her head to get the heavy chain off, dropping the necklace so it fell on the stones with a cold, liquid clash. "O take it, Haldre!" she cried again, and then, weeping aloud, turned and ran from Hallan, over the bridge and down the long, broad steps, and, darting off eastward into the forest of the mountainside like some wild thing escaping, was gone.

PART ONE: The Starlord

I

So ENDS the first part of the legend; and all of it is true. Now for some facts, which are equally true, from the League *Handbook for Galactic Area Eight.*
Number 62: FOMALHAUT II.

Type AE—Carbon Life. An iron-core planet, diameter 6600 miles, with heavy oxygen-rich atmosphere. Revolution: 800 Earthdays 8 hrs. 11 min. 42 sec. Rotation: 29 hrs. 51 min. 02 sec. Mean distance from sun 3.2 AU, orbital eccentricity slight. Obliquity of ecliptic 27° 20′ 20″ causing marked seasonal change. Gravity .86 Standard.

Four major landmasses, Northwest, Southwest, East and Antarctic Continents, occupy 38% of planetary surface.

Four satellites (types Perner, Loklik, R-2 and Phobos). The Companion of Fomalhaut is visible as a superbright star.

Nearest League World: New South Georgia, capital Kerguelen (7.88 lt. yrs.).

History: The planet was charted by the Elieson Expedition in 202, robot-probed in 218.

First Geographical Survey, 235-6. Director: J. Kiolaf. The major landmasses were surveyed by air (see maps 3114-a, b, c, 3115-a, b.). Landings, geological and biological studies and HILF contacts were made only on East and Northwest Continents (see description of intelligent species below).

27

Technological Enhancement Mission to Species I-A, 252-4. Director: J. Kiolaf (Northwest Continent only.)

Control and Taxation Missions to Species I-A and II were carried out under auspices of the Area Foundation in Kerguelen, N.S.Ga., in 254, 258, 262, 266, 270; in 275 the planet was placed under Interdict by the Allworld HILF Authority, pending more adequate study of its intelligent species.

First Ethnographic Survey, 321. Director: G. Rocannon.

A high tree of blinding white grew quickly, soundlessly up the sky from behind South Ridge. Guards on the towers of Hallan Castle cried out, striking bronze on bronze. Their small voices and clangor of warning were swallowed by the roar of sound, the hammerstroke of wind, the staggering of the forest.

Mogien of Hallan met his guest the Starlord on the run, heading for the flightcourt of the castle. "Was your ship behind South Ridge, Starlord?"

Very white in the face, but quiet-voiced as usual, the other said, "It was."

"Come with me." Mogien took his guest on the postillion saddle of the windsteed that waited ready saddled in the flightcourt. Down the thousand steps, across the Chasmbridge, off over the sloping forests of the domain of Hallan the steed flew like a gray leaf on the wind.

As it crossed over South Ridge the riders saw smoke rise blue through the level gold lances of the first sunlight. A forest fire was fizzling out among damp, cool thickets in the streambed of the mountainside.

Suddenly beneath them a hole dropped away in the side of the hills, a black pit filled with smoking black dust. At the edge of the wide circle of annihilation lay trees burnt to long smears of charcoal, all pointing their fallen tops away from the pit of blackness.

The young Lord of Hallan held his gray steed steady on the updraft from the wrecked valley and stared down, saying nothing. There were old tales from his grandfather's and great-grandfather's time of the first coming of the Starlords, how they had burnt away hills and made the sea boil with their terrible weapons, and with the threat of those weapons had forced all the Lords of Angien to pledge them fealty and tribute. For the first time now Mogien believed those tales. His breath was stuck in his throat for a second. "Your ship was . . ."

"The ship was here. I was to meet the others here, today. Lord Mogien, tell your people to avoid this place. For a while. Till after the rains, next coldyear."

"A spell?"

"A poison. Rain will rid the land of it." The Starlord's voice was still quiet, but he was looking down, and all at once he began to speak again, not to Mogien but to that black pit beneath them, now striped with the bright early sunlight. Mogien understood no word he said, for he spoke in his own tongue, the speech of the Starlords; and there was no man now in Angien or all the world who spoke that tongue.

The young Angya checked his nervous mount. Behind him the Starlord drew a deep breath and said, "Let's go back to Hallan. There is nothing here. . . ."

The steed wheeled over the smoking slopes. "Lord Rokanan, if your people are at war now among the stars, I pledge in your defense the swords of Hallan!"

"I thank you, Lord Mogien," said the Starlord, clinging to the saddle, the wind of their flight whipping at his bowed graying head.

The long day passed. The night wind gusted at the casements of his room in the tower of Hallan Castle, making the fire in the wide hearth flicker. Coldyear was nearly over; the restlessness of spring was in the wind. When he raised his head he smelled the sweet musty fragrance of grass tapestries hung on the walls and the sweet fresh fragrance of night in the forests outside. He

29

spoke into his transmitter once more: "Rocannon here. This is Rocannon. Can you answer?" He listened to the silence of the receiver a long time, then once more tried ship frequency: "Rocannon here . . ." When he noticed how low he was speaking, almost whispering, he stopped and cut off the set. They were dead, all fourteen of them, his companions and his friends. They had all been on Fomalhaut II for half one of the planet's long years, and it had been time for them to confer and compare notes. So Smate and his crew had come around from East Continent, and picked up the Antarctic crew on the way, and ended up back here to meet with Rocannon, the Director of the First Ethnographic Survey, the man who had brought them all here. And now they were dead.

And their work—all their notes, pictures, tapes, all that would have justified their death to them—that was all gone too, blown to dust with them, wasted with them.

Rocannon turned on his radio again to Emergency frequency; but he did not pick up the transmitter. To call was only to tell the enemy that there was a survivor. He sat still. When a resounding knock came at his door he said in the strange tongue he would have to speak from now on, "Come in!"

In strode the young Lord of Hallan, Mogien, who had been his best informant for the culture and mores of Species II, and who now controlled his fate. Mogien was very tall, like all his people, bright-haired and dark-skinned, his handsome face schooled to a stern calm through which sometimes broke the lightning of powerful emotions: anger, ambition, joy. He was followed by his Olgyior servant Raho, who set down a yellow flask and two cups on a chest, poured the cups full, and withdrew. The heir of Hallan spoke: "I would drink with you, Starlord."

"And my kin with yours and our sons together, Lord," replied the ethnologist, who had not lived on nine different exotic planets without learning the value of good manners.

30

He and Mogien raised their wooden cups bound with silver and drank.

"The wordbox," Mogien said, looking at the radio, "it will not speak again?"

"Not with my friends' voices."

Mogien's walnut-dark face showed no feeling, but he said, "Lord Rokanan, the weapon that killed them, this is beyond all imagining."

"The League of All Worlds keeps such weapons for use in the War To Come. Not against our own worlds."

"Is this the War, then?"

"I think not. Yaddam, whom you knew, was staying with the ship; he would have heard news of that on the ansible in the ship, and radioed me at once. There would have been warning. This must be a rebellion against the League. There was rebellion brewing on a world called Faraday when I left Kerguelen, and by sun's time that was nine years ago."

"This little wordbox cannot speak to the City Kerguelen?"

"No; and even if it did, it would take the words eight years to go there, and the answer eight years to come back to me." Rocannon spoke with his usual grave and simple politeness, but his voice was a little dull as he explained his exile. "You remember the ansible, the machine I showed you in the ship, which can speak instantly to other worlds, with no loss of years—it was that that they were after, I expect. It was only bad luck that my friends were all at the ship with it. Without it I can do nothing."

"But if your kinfolk, your friends, in the City Kerguelen, call you on the ansible, and there is no answer, will they not come to see—" Mogien saw the answer as Rocannon said it:

"In eight years. . . ."

When he had shown Mogien over the Survey ship, and shown him the instantaneous trasmitter, the ansible, Rocannon had told him also about the new kind of ship that could go from one star to another in no time at all.

31

"Was the ship that killed your friends an FTL?" inquired the Angyar warlord.

"No. It was manned. There are enemies here, on this world, now."

This became clear to Mogien when he recalled that Rocannon had told him that living creatures could not ride the FTL ships and live; they were used only as robot-bombers, weapons that could appear and strike and vanish all within a moment. It was a queer story, but no queerer than the story Mogien knew to be true: that, though the kind of ship Rocannon had come here on took years and years to ride the night between the worlds, those years to the men in the ship seemed only a few hours. In the City Kerguelen on the star Forrosul this man Rocannon had spoken to Semley of Hallan and given her the jewel Eye of the Sea, nearly half a hundred years ago. Semley who had lived sixteen years in one night was long dead, her daughter Haldre was an old woman, her grandson Mogien a grown man; yet here sat Rocannon, who was not old. Those years had passed, for him, in riding between the stars. It was very strange, but there were other tales stranger yet.

"When my mother's mother Semley rode across the night . . ." Mogien began, and paused.

"There was never so fair a lady in all the worlds," said the Starlord, his face less sorrowful for a moment.

"The lord who befriended her is welcome among her kinfolk," said Mogien. "But I meant to ask, Lord, what ship she rode. Was it ever taken from the Clayfolk? Does it have the ansible on it, so you could tell your kinfolk of this enemy?"

For a second Rocannon looked thunderstruck, then he calmed down. "No," he said, "it doesn't. It was given to the Clayfolk seventy years ago; there was no instantaneous transmission then. And it would not have been installed recently, because the planet's been under Interdict for forty-five years now. Due to me. Because I interfered. Because, after I met Lady Semley, I went to my people and said, what are we doing on this world we don't know anything about? Why are we taking their money and pushing them about? What right have we? But if I'd left the situation alone at least there'd be someone coming here every couple of years; you wouldn't be completely at the mercy of this invader—"

"What does an invader want with us?" Mogien inquired, not modestly, but curiously.

"He wants your planet, I suppose. Your world. Your earth. Perhaps yourselves as slaves. I don't know."

"If the Clayfolk still have that ship, Rokanan, and if the ship goes to the City, you could go, and rejoin your people."

The Starlord looked at him a minute. "I suppose I could," he said. His tone was dull again. There was silence between them for a minute longer, and then Rocannon spoke with passion: "I left you people open to this. I brought my own people into it and they're dead. I'm not going to run off eight years into the future and find out what happened next! Listen, Lord Mogien, if you could help me get south to the Clayfolk, I might get the ship and use it here on the planet, scout about with it. At least, if I can't change its automatic drive, I can send it off to Kerguelen with a message. But I'll stay here."

"Semley found it, the tale tells, in the caves of the Gdemiar near the Kiriensea."

"Will you lend me a windsteed, Lord Mogien?"

"And my company, if you will."

"With thanks!"

"The Clayfolk are bad hosts to lone guests," said Mogien, looking pleased. Not even the thought of that ghastly black hole blown in the mountainside could quell the itch in the two long swords hitched to Mogien's belt. It had been a long time since the last foray.

"May our enemy die without sons," the Angya said gravely, raising his refilled cup.

Rocannon, whose friends had been killed without warn-

33

ing in an unarmed ship, did not hesitate. "May they die without sons," he said, and drank with Mogien, there in the yellow light of rushlights and double moon, in the High Tower of Hallan.

II

By EVENING of the second Rocannon was stiff and wind-burned, but had learned to sit easy in the high saddle and to guide with some skill the great flying beast from Hallan stables. Now the pink air of the long, slow sunset stretched above and beneath him, levels of rose-crystal light. The windsteeds were flying high to stay as long as they could in sunlight, for like great cats they loved warmth. Mogien on his black hunter—a stallion, would you call it, Rocannon wondered, or a tom?—was looking down, seeking a camping place, for windsteeds would not fly in darkness. Two midmen soared behind on smaller white mounts, pink-winged in the after-glow of the great sun Fomalhaut.

"Look there, Starlord!"

Rocannon's steed checked and snarled, seeing what Mogien was pointing to: a little black object moving low across the sky ahead of them, dragging behind it through the evening quiet a faint rattling noise. Rocannon gestured that they land at once. In the forest glade where they alighted, Mogien asked, "Was that a ship like yours, Starlord?"

"No. It was a planet-bound ship, a helicopter. It could only have been brought here on a ship much larger than mine was, a starfrigate or a transport. They must be coming here in force. And they must have started out before I did. What are they doing here anyhow, with bombers and helicopters? . . . They could shoot us right out of the sky from a long way off. We'll have to watch out for them, Lord Mogien."

"The thing was flying up from the Clayfields. I hope they were not there before us."

35

Rocannon only nodded, heavy with anger at the sight of that black spot on the sunset, that roach on a clean world. Whoever these people were that had bombed an unarmed Survey ship at sight, they evidently meant to survey this planet and take it over for colonization or for some military use. The High-Intelligence Life Forms of the planet, of which there were at least three species, all of low technological achievement, they would ignore or enslave or extirpate, whichever was most convenient. For to an aggressive people only technology mattered.

And there, Rocannon said to himself as he watched the midmen unsaddle the windsteeds and loose them for their night's hunting, right there perhaps was the League's own weak spot. Only technology mattered. The two missions to this world in the last century had started pushing one of the species toward a pre-atomic technology before they had even explored the other continents or contacted all intelligent races. He had called a halt to that, and had finally managed to bring his own Ethnographic Survey here to learn something about the planet; but he did not fool himself. Even his work here would finally have served only as an informational basis for encouraging technological advance in the most likely species or culture. This was how the League of All Worlds prepared to meet its ultimate enemy. A hundred worlds had been trained and armed, a thousand more were being schooled in the uses of steel and wheel and tractor and reactor. But Rocannon the hilfer, whose job was learning, not teaching, and who had lived on quite a few backward worlds, doubted the wisdom of staking everything on weapons and the uses of machines. Dominated by the aggressive, tool-making humanoid species of Centaurus, Earth, and the Cetians, the League had slighted certain skills and powers and potentialities of intelligent life, and judged by too narrow a standard.

This world, which did not even have a name yet beyond Formalhaut II, would probably never get much attention paid to it, for before the League's arrival none of its species seemed to have got beyond the lever and the forge. Other races on other worlds could be pushed ahead faster, to help when the extra-galactic enemy returned at last. No doubt this was inevitable. He thought of Mogien offering to fight a fleet of lightspeed bombers with the swords of Hallan. But what if lightspeed or even FTL bombers were very much like bronze swords, compared to the weapons of the Enemy? What if the weapons of the Enemy were things of the mind? Would it not be well to learn a little of the different shapes minds come in, and their powers? The League's policy was too narrow; it led to too much waste, and now evidently it had led to re-bellion. If the storm brewing on Faraday ten years ago had broken, it meant that a young League world, having learned war promptly and been armed, was now out to carve its own empire from the stars.

He and Mogien and the two dark-haired servants gnawed hunks of good hard bread from the kitchens of Hallan, drank yellow *vaskan* from a skin flask, and soon settled to sleep. Very high all around their small fire stood the trees, dark branches laden with sharp, dark, closed cones. In the night a cold, fine rain whispered through the forest. Rocannon pulled the feathery herilo-fur bedroll up over his head and slept all the long night in the whisper of the rain. The windsteeds came back at daybreak, and before sunrise they were aloft again, windriding toward the pale lands near the gulf where the Clayfolk dwelt.

Landing about noon in a field of ray clay, Rocannon and the two servants, Raho and Yahan, looked about blankly, seeing no sign of life. Mogien said with the absolute confidence of his caste, "They'll come."

And they came: the squat hominoids Rocannon had seen in the museum years ago, six of them, not much taller than Rocannon's chest or Mogien's belt. They were naked, a whitish-gray color like their clay-fields, a sin-gularly earthy-looking lot. When they spoke, they were uncanny, for there was no telling which one spoke; it seemed they all did, but with one harsh voice. *Partial colonial telepathy,* Rocannon recalled from the *Handbook,* and looked with increased respect at the ugly little men with their rare gift. His three tall companions evinced no such feeling. They looked grim.

"What do the Angyar and the servants of the Angyar wish in the field of the Lords of Night?" one of the Claymen, or all of them, was or were asking in the Common Tongue, an Angyar dialect used by all species.

"I am the Lord of Hallan," said Mogien, looking gigantic. "With me stands Rokanan, master of stars and the ways between the night, servant of the League of All Worlds, guest and friend of the Kinfolk of Hallan. High honor is due him! Take us to those fit to parley with us. There are words to be spoken, for soon there will be snow in warmyear and winds blowing backward and trees growing upside down!" The way the Angyar talked was a real pleasure, Rocannon thought, though its tact was not what struck you.

The Claymen stood about in dubious silence. "Truly this is so?" they or one of them asked at last.

"Yes, and the sea will turn to wood, and stones will grow toes! Take us to your chiefs, who know what a Starlord is, and waste no time!"

More silence. Standing among the little troglodytes, Rocannon had an uneasy sense as of mothwings brushing past his ears. A decision was being reached.

"Come," said the Claymen aloud, and led off across the sticky field. They gathered hurriedly around a patch of earth, stooped, then stood aside, revealing a hole in the ground and a ladder sticking out of it: the entrance to the Domain of Night.

While the midmen waited aboveground with the steeds, Mogien and Rocannon climbed down the ladder into a cave-world of crossing, branching tunnels cut in the clay and lined with coarse cement, electric-lighted, smelling of sweat and stale food. Padding on flat gray feet behind them, the guards took them to a half-lit, round chamber

38

like a bubble in a great rock stratum, and left them there alone.

They waited. They waited longer.

Why the devil had the first surveys picked these people to encourage for League membership? Rocannon had a perhaps unworthy explanation: those first surveys had been from cold Centaurus, and the explorers had dived rejoicing into the caves of the Gdemiar, escaping the blinding floods of light and heat from the great A-3 sun. To them, sensible people lived underground on a world like this. To Rocannon, the hot white sun and the bright nights of quadruple moonlight, the intense weather-changes and ceaseless winds, the rich air and light gravity that permitted so many air-borne species, were all not only compatible but enjoyable. But, he reminded himself, just by that he was less well qualified than the Centaurans to judge these cave-folk. They were certainly clever. They were also telepathic—a power much rarer and much less well understood than electricity—but the first surveys had not made anything of that. They had given the Gdemiar a generator and a lock-drive ship and some math and some pats on the back, and left them. What had the little men done since? He asked a question along this line of Mogien.

The young lord, who had certainly never seen anything but a candle or a resin-torch in his life, glanced without the least interest at the electric light-bulb over his head. "They have always been good at making things," he said, with his extraordinary, straightforward arrogance.

"Have they made new sorts of things lately?"

"We buy our steel swords from the Clayfolk; they had smiths who could work steel in my grandfather's time; but before that I don't know. My people have lived a long time with Clayfolk, suffering them to tunnel beneath our border-lands, trading them silver for their swords. They are said to be rich, but forays on them are tabu. Wars between two breeds are evil matters—as you know. Even when my grandfather Durhal sought his wife here, thinking they had stolen her, he would not break the tabu to

39

force them to speak. They will neither lie nor speak truth if they can help it. We do not love them, and they do not love us; I think they remember old days before the tabu. They are not brave."

A mighty voice boomed out behind their backs: "Bow down before the presence of the Lords of Night!" Rocannon had his hand on his lasergun and Mogien both hands on his sword-hilts as they turned; but Rocannon immediately spotted the speaker set in the curving wall, and murmured to Mogien, "Don't answer."

"Speak, O strangers in the Caverns of the Nightlords!" The sheer blare of sound was intimidating, but Mogien stood there without a blink, his high-arching eyebrows indolently raised. Presently he said, "Now you've wind-ridden three days, Lord Rokanan, do you begin to see the pleasure of it?"

"Speak and you shall be heard!"

"I do. And the striped steed goes light as the west wind in warmyear," Rocannon said, quoting a compliment overheard at table in the Revelhall.

"He's of very good stock."

"Speak! You are heard!"

They discussed windsteed-breeding while the wall bellowed at them. Eventually two Claymen appeared in the tunnel. "Come," they said stolidly. They led the strangers through further mazes to a very neat little electric-train system, like a giant but effective toy, on which they rode several miles more at a good clip, leaving the clay tunnels for what appeared to be a limestone-cave area. The last station was at the mouth of a fiercely-lighted hall, at the far end of which three troglodytes stood waiting on a dais. At first, to Rocannon's shame as an ethnologist, they all looked alike. As Chinamen had to the Dutch, as Russians had to the Centaurans. . . . Then he picked out the individuality of the central Clayman, whose face was lined, white, and powerful under an iron crown.

"What does the Starlord seek in the Caverns of the Mighty?"

The formality of the Common Tongue suited Rocannon's need precisely as he answered, "I had hoped to come as a guest to these caverns, to learn the ways of the Nightlords and see the wonders of their making. I hope yet to do so. But ill doings are afoot and I come now in haste and need. I am an officer of the League of All Worlds. I ask you to bring me to the starship which you keep as a pledge of the League's confidence in you."

The three stared impassively. The dais put them on a level with Rocannon; seen thus on a level, their broad, ageless faces and rock-hard eyes were impressive. Then, grotesquely, the left-hand one spoke in Pidgin-Galactic: "No ship," he said.

"There is a ship."

After a minute the one repeated ambiguously, "No ship."

"Speak the Common Tongue. I ask your help. There is an enemy to the League on this world. It will be your world no longer if you admit that enemy."

"No ship," said the left-hand Clayman. The other two stood like stalagmites.

"Then must I tell the other Lords of the League that the Clayfolk have betrayed their trust, and are unworthy to fight in the War To Come?"

Silence.

"Trust is on both sides, or neither," the iron-crowned Clayman in the center said in the Common Tongue.

"Would I ask your help if I did not trust you? Will you do this at least for me: send the ship with a message to Kerguelen? No one need ride it and lose the years; it will go itself."

Silence again.

"No ship," said the left-hand one in his gravel voice.

"Come, Lord Mogien," said Rocannon, and turned his back on them.

"Those who betray the Starlords," said Mogien in his clear arrogant voice, "betray older pacts. You made our swords of old, Clayfolk. They have not got rusty." And he

41

strode out beside Rocannon, following the stump gray guides who led them in silence back to the railway, and through the maze of dank, glaring corridors, and up at last into the light of day.

They windrode a few miles west to get clear of Clayfolk territory, and landed on the bank of a forest river to take counsel.

Mogien felt he had let his guest down; he was not used to being thwarted in his generosity, and his self-possession was a little shaken. "Cave-grubs," he said. "Cowardly vermin! They will never say straight out what they have done or will do. All the Small Folk are like that, even the Fiia. But the Fiia can be trusted. Do you think the Clay-folk gave the ship to the enemy?"

"How can we tell?"

"I know this: they would give it to no one unless they were paid its price twice over. Things, things—they think of nothing but heaping up things. What did the old one mean, trust must be on both sides?"

"I think he meant that his people feel that we—the League—betrayed them. First we encourage them, then suddenly for forty-five years we drop them, send them no messages, discourage their coming, tell them to look after themselves. And that was my doing, though they don't know it. Why should they do me a favor, after all? I doubt they've talked with the enemy yet. But it would make no difference if they did bargain away the ship. The enemy could do even less with it than I could have done." Rocannon stood looking down at the bright river, his shoulders stooped.

"Rokanan," said Mogien, for the first time speaking to him as to a kinsman, "near this forest live my cousins of Kyodor, a strong castle, thirty Angyar swordsmen and three villages of midmen. They will help us punish the Clayfolk for their insolence—"

"No." Rocannon spoke heavily. "Tell your people to keep an eye on the Clayfolk, yes; they might be bought over by this enemy. But there will be no tabus broken or

42

wars fought on my account. There is no point to it. In times like this, Mogien, one man's fate is not important."

"If it is not," said Mogien, raising his dark face, "what is?"

"Lords," said the slender young midman Yahan, "someone's over there among the trees." He pointed across the river to a flicker of color among the dark conifers.

"Fiia!" said Mogien. "Look at the windsteeds." All four of the big beasts were looking across the river, ears pricked.

"Mogien Hallanlord walks the Fiia's ways in friendship!" Mogien's voice rang over the broad, shallow, clattering water, and presently in mixed light and shadow under the trees on the other shore a small figure appeared. It seemed to dance a little as spots of sunlight played over it making it flicker and change, hard to keep the eyes on. When it moved, Rocannon thought it was walking on the surface of the river, so lightly it came, not stirring the sunlit shallows. The striped windsteed rose and stalked softly on thick, hollow-boned legs to the water's edge. As the Fian waded out of the water the big beast bowed its head, and the Fian reached up and scratched the striped, furry ears. Then he came toward them.

"Hail Mogien Halla's heir, sunhaired, swordbearer!" The voice was thin and sweet as a child's, the figure short and light as a child's, but it was no child's face. "Hail Hallan-guest, Starlord, Wanderer!" Strange, large, light eyes turned for a moment full on Rocannon.

"The Fiia know all names and news," said Mogien, smiling; but the little Fian did not smile in response. Even to Rocannon, who had only briefly visited one village of the species with the Survey team, this was startling.

"O Starlord," said the sweet, shaking voice, "who rides the windships that come and kill?"

"Kill—your people?"

"All my village," the little man said. "I was with the flocks out on the hills. I mindheard my people call, and I came, and they were in the flames burning and crying out.

43

There were two ships with turning wings. They spat out fire. Now I am alone and must speak aloud. Where my people were in my mind there is only fire and silence. Why was this done, Lords?"

He looked from Rocannon to Mogien. Both were silent. He bent over like a man mortally hurt, crouching, and hid his face.

Mogien stood over him, his hands on the hilts of his swords, shaking with anger. "Now I swear vengeance on those who harmed the Fiia! Rokanan, how can this be? The Fiia have no swords, they have no riches, they have no enemy! Look, his people are all dead, those he speaks to without words, his tribesmen. No Fian lives alone. He will die alone. Why would they harm his people?"

"To make their power known," Rocannon said harshly. "Let us bring him to Hallan, Mogien."

The tall lord knelt down by the little crouching figure. "Fian, man's-friend, ride with me. I cannot speak in your mind as your kinsmen spoke, but airborne works are not all hollow."

In silence they mounted, the Fian riding the high saddle in front of Mogien like a child, and the four steeds rose up again on the air. A rainy south wind favored their flight, and late the next day under the beating of his steed's wing Rocannon saw the marble stairway up through the forest, the Chasmbridge across the green abyss, and the towers of Hallan in the long western light.

The people of the castle, blond lords and dark-haired servants, gathered around them in the flightcourt, full of the news of the burning of the castle nearest them to the east, Reohan, and the murder of all its people. Again it had been a couple of helicopters and a few men armed with laser-guns; the warriors and farmers of Reohan had been slaughtered without giving one stroke in return. The people of Hallan were half berserk with anger and defiance, into which came an element of awe when they saw the Fian riding with their young lord and heard why he was there. Many of them, dwellers in this northermost fortress of Angien, had never seen one of the Fiia before, but all knew them as the stuff of legends and the subject of a powerful tabu. An attack, however bloody, on one of their own castles fit into their warrior outlook; but an attack on the Fiia was desecration. Awe and rage worked together in them. Late that evening in his tower room Rocannon heard the tumult from the Revelhall below, where the Angyar of Hallan all were gathered swearing destruction and extinction to the enemy in a torrent of metaphor and a thunder of hyperbole. They were a boastful race, the Angyar: vengeful, overweening, obstinate, illiterate, and lacking any first-person forms for the verb "to be unable." There were no gods in their legends, only heroes.

Through their distant racket a near voice broke in, startling Rocannon so his hand jumped on the radio tuner. He had at last found the enemy's communication band. A voice rattled on, speaking a language Rocannon did not know. Luck would have been too good if the enemy had spoken Galactic; there were hundreds of thousands of languages among the Worlds of the League, let alone the recognized planets such as this one and the planets still unknown. The voice began reading a list of numbers, which Rocannon understood, for they were in Cetian, the language of a race whose mathematical attainments had led to the general use throughout the League of Cetian mathematics and therefore Cetian numerals. He listened with strained attention, but it was no good, a mere string of numbers.

The voice stopped suddenly, leaving only the hiss of static.

Rocannon looked across the room to the little Fian, who had asked to stay with him, and now sat cross-legged and silent on the floor near the casement window.

"That was the enemy, Kyo."

The Fian's face was very still.

"Kyo," said Rocannon—it was the custom to address a Fian by the Angyar name of his village, since individuals of the species perhaps did and perhaps did not have individual names—"Kyo, if you tried, could you mindhear the enemies?"

In the brief notes from his one visit to a Fian village Rocannon had commented that Species 1-B seldom answered direct questions directly; and he well remembered their smiling elusiveness. But Kyo, left desolate in the alien country of speech, answered what Rocannon asked him. "No, Lord," he said submissively.

"Can you mindhear others of your own kind, in other villages?"

"A little. If I lived among them, perhaps . . . Fiia go sometimes to live in other villages than their own. It is said even that once the Fiia and the Gdemiar mindspoke together as one people, but that was very long ago. It is said . . ." He stopped.

"Your people and the Clayfolk are indeed one race, though you follow very different ways now. What more, Kyo?"

"It is said that very long ago, in the south, in the high places, the gray places, lived those who mindspoke with all creatures. All thoughts they could hear, the Old Ones, the Most Ancient. . . . But we came down from the mountains, and lived in the valleys and the caves, and have forgotten the harder way."

Rocannon pondered a moment. There were no mountains on the continent south of Hallan. He rose to get his *Handbook for Galactic Area Eight,* with its maps, when the radio, still hissing on the same band, stopped him short. A voice was coming through, much fainter, remote, rising and falling on billows of static, but speaking in Galactic. "Number Six, come in. Number Six, come in. This is Foyer. Come in, Number Six." After endless repetitions and pauses it continued: "This is Friday. No, this is Friday. . . . This is Foyer; are you there, Number Six? The FTLs are due tomorrow and I want a full report on the Seven Six sidings and the nets. Leave the staggering plan to the Eastern Detachment. Are you getting me, Number Six? We are going to be in ansible communication with

Base tomorrow. Will you get me that information on the sidings at once. Seven Six sidings. Unnecessary—" A surge of starnoise swallowed the voice, and when it reemerged it was audible only in snatches. Ten long minutes went by in static, silence, and snatches of speech, then a nearer voice cut in, speaking quickly in the unknown language used before. It went on and on; moveless, minute after minute, his hand still on the cover of his *Handbook,* Rocannon listened. As moveless, the Fian sat in the shadows across the room. A double pair of numbers was spoken, then repeated; the second time Rocannon caught the Cetian word for "degrees." He flipped his notebook open and scribbled the numbers down; then at last, though he still listened, he opened the *Handbook* to the maps of Fomalhaut II.

The numbers he had noted were 28° 28—121° 40. If they were coördinates of latitude and longitude . . . He brooded over the maps a while, setting the point of his pencil down a couple of times on blank open sea. Then, trying 121 West with 28 North, he came down just south of a range of mountains, halfway down the Southwest Continent. He sat gazing at the map. The radio voice had fallen silent.

"Starlord?"

"I think they told me where they are. Maybe. And they've got an ansible there." He looked up at Kyo unseeingly, then back at the map. "If they're down there—if I could get there and wreck their game, if I could get just one message out on their ansible to the League, if I could . . ."

Southwest Continent had been mapped only from the air, and nothing but the mountains and major rivers were sketched inside the coastlines: hundreds of kilometers of blank, of unknown. And a goal merely guessed at.

"But I can't just sit here," Rocannon said. He looked up again, and met the little man's clear, uncomprehending gaze.

47

He paced down the stone-floored room and back. The radio hissed and whispered.

There was one thing in his favor: the fact that the enemy would not be expecting him. They thought they had the planet all to themselves. But it was the only thing in his favor.

"I'd like to use their weapons against them," he said. "I think I'll try to find them. In the land to the south. . . . My people were killed by these strangers, like yours, Kyo. You and I are both alone, speaking a language not our own. I would rejoice in your companionship."

He hardly knew what moved him to the suggestion.

The shadow of a smile went across the Fian's face. He raised his hands, parallel and apart. Rushlight in sconces on the walls bowed and flickered and changed. "It was foretold that the Wanderer would choose companions," he said. "For a while."

"The Wanderer?" Rocannon asked, but this time the Fian did not answer.

III

THE LADY OF THE CASTLE crossed the high hall slowly, skirts rustling over stone. Her dark skin was deepened with age to the black of an ikon; her fair hair was white. Still she kept the beauty of her lineage. Rocannon bowed and spoke a greeting in the fashion of her people: "Hail Hallanlady, Durhal's daughter, Haldre the Fair!"

"Hail Rokanan, my guest," she said, looking calmly down at him. Like most Angyar women and all Angyar men she was considerably taller than he. "Tell me why you go south." She continued to pace slowly across the hall, and Rocannon walked beside her. Around them was dark air and stone, dark tapestry hung on high walls, the cool light of morning from clerestory windows slanting across the black of rafters overhead.

"I go to find my enemy, Lady."

"And when you have found them?"

"I hope to enter their . . . their castle, and make use of their . . . message-sender, to tell the League they are here, on this world. They are hiding here, and there is very little chance of their being found: the worlds are thick as sand on the sea-beach. But they must be found. They have done harm here, and they would do much worse on other worlds."

Haldre nodded her head once. "Is it true you wish to go lightly, with few men?"

"Yes, Lady. It is a long way, and the sea must be crossed. And craft, not strength, is my only hope against their strength."

"You will need more than craft, Starlord," said the old woman. "Well, I'll send with you four loyal midmen, if

49

that suffices you, and two windsteeds laden and six saddled, and a piece or two of silver in case barbarians in the foreign lands want payment for lodging you, and my son Mogien."

"Mogien will come with me? These are great gifts, Lady, but that is the greatest!"

She looked at him a minute with her clear, sad, inexorable gaze. "I am glad it pleases you, Starlord." She resumed her slow walking, and he beside her. "Mogien desires to go, for love of you and for adventure; and you, a great lord on a very perilous mission, desire his company. So I think it is surely his way to follow. But I tell you now, this morning in the Long Hall, so that you may remember and not fear my blame if you return: I do not think he will come back with you."

"But Lady, he is the heir of Hallan."

She went in silence a while, turned at the end of the room under a time-darkened tapestry of winged giants fighting fair-haired men, and finally spoke again. "Hallan will find others heirs." Her voice was calm and bitter cold. "You Starlords are among us again, bringing new ways and wars. Reohan is dust; how long will Hallan stand? The world itself has become a grain of sand on the shore of night. All things change now. But I am certain still of one thing: that there is darkness over my lineage. My mother, whom you knew, was lost in the forests in her madness; my father was killed in battle, my husband by treachery; and when I bore a son my spirit grieved amid my joy, foreseeing his life would be short. That is no grief to him; he is an Angya, he wears the double swords. But my part of the darkness is to rule a failing domain alone, to live and live and outlive them all. . . ."

She was silent again a minute. "You may need more treasure than I can give you, to buy your life or your way. Take this. To you I give it, Rokanan, not to Mogien. There is no darkness on it to you. Was it not yours once, in the city across the night? To us it has been only a burden and a shadow. Take it back, Starlord; use it for a ransom or a

50

gift." She unclasped from her neck the gold and the great blue stone of the necklace that had cost her mother's life, and held it out in her hand to Rocannon. He took it, hearing almost with terror the soft, cold clash of the golden links, and lifted his eyes to Haldre. She faced him, very tall, her blue eyes dark in the dark clear air of the hall. "Now take my son with you, Starlord, and follow your way. May your enemy die without sons."

Torchlight and smoke and hurrying shadows in the castle flightcourt, voices of beasts and men, racket and confusion, all dropped away in a few wingbeats of the striped steed Rocannon rode. Behind them now Hallan lay, a faint spot of light on the dark sweep of the hills, and there was no sound but a rushing of air as the wide half-seen wings lifted and beat down. The east was pale behind them, and the Greatstar burned like a bright crystal, heralding the sun, but it was long before daybreak. Day and night and the twilights were stately and unhurried on this planet that took thirty hours to turn. And the pace of the seasons also was large; this was the dawn of the vernal equinox, and four hundred days of spring and summer lay ahead.

"They'll sing songs of us in the high castles," said Kyo, riding postillion behind Rocannon. "They'll sing how the Wanderer and his companions rode south across the sky in the darkness before the spring. . . ." He laughed a little. Beneath them the hills and rich plains of Angien unfolded like a landscape painted on gray silk, brightening little by little, at last glowing vivid with colors and shadows as the lordly sun rose behind them.

At noon they rested a couple of hours by the river whose southwest course they were following to the sea; at dusk they flew down to a little castle, on a hilltop like all Angyar castles, near a bend of the same river. There they were made welcome by the lord of the place and his household. Curiosity obviously itched in him at the sight of a Fian traveling by windsteed, along with the Lord of Hallan, four midmen, and one who spoke with a queer accent, dressed like a lord, but wore no swords and was white-

51

faced like a midman. To be sure, there was more inter-mingling between the two castes, the Angyar and Olgyior, than most Angyar like to admit; there were light-skinned warriors, and gold-haired servants; but this "Wanderer" was altogether too anomalous. Wanting no further rumor of his presence on the planet, Rocannon said nothing, and their host dared ask no questions of the heir of Hallan; so if he ever found out who his strange guests had been, it was from minstrels singing the tale, years later.

The next day passed the same for the seven travelers, riding the wind above the lovely land. They spent that night in an Olgyior village by the river, and on the third day came over country new even to Mogien. The river, curv-ing away to the south, lay in loops and oxbows, the hills ran out into long plains, and far ahead was a mirrored pale brightness in the sky. Late in the day they came to a castle set alone on a white bluff, beyond which lay a long reach of lagoons and gray sand, and the open sea.

Dismounting, stiff and tired and his head ringing from wind and motion, Rocannon thought it the sorriest Angyar stronghold he had yet seen: a cluster of huts like wet chick-ens bunched under the wings of a squat, seedy-looking fort. Midmen, pale and short-bodied, peered at them from the straggling lanes. "They look as if they'd bred with Clayfolk," said Mogien. "This is the gate, and the place is called Tolen, if the wind hasn't carried us astray. Ho! Lords of Tolen, the guest is at your gate!"

There was no sound within the castle.

"The gate of Tolen swings in the wind," said Kyo, and they saw that indeed the portal of bronze-bound wood sagged on its hinges, knocking in the cold sea-wind that blew up through the town. Mogien pushed it open with his swordpoint. Inside was darkness, a scuttering rustle of wings, and a dank smell.

"The Lords of Tolen did not wait for their guests," said Mogien. "Well, Yahan, talk to these ugly fellows and find us lodging for the night."

The young midman turned to speak to the townsfolk

who had gathered at the far end of the castle forecourt to stare. One of them got up the courage to hitch himself forward, bowing and going sideways like some seaweedy beach-creature, and spoke humbly to Yahan. Rocannon could partly follow the Olgyior dialect, and gathered that the old man was pleading that the village had no proper housing for *pedanar,* whatever they were. The tall midman Raho joined Yahan and spoke fiercely, but the old man only hitched and bowed and mumbled, till at last Mogien strode forward. He could not by the Angyar code speak to the serfs of a strange domain, but he unsheathed one of his swords and held it up shining in the cold sea turned and shuffled down into the darkening alleys of the village. The travelers followed, the furled wings of their steeds brushing the low reed roofs on both sides.

"Kyo, what are pedanar?"

The little man smiled.

"Yahan, what is that word, pedanar?"

The young midman, a goodnatured, candid fellow, looked uneasy. "Well, Lord, a pedan is . . . one who walks among men . . ."

Rocannon nodded, snapping up even this scrap. While he had been a student of the species instead of its ally, he had kept seeking for their religion; they seemed to have no creeds at all. Yet they were quite credulous. They took spells, curses, and strange powers as matter of fact, and their relation to nature was intensely animistic; but they had no gods. This word, at last, smelled of the supernatural. It did not occur to him at the time that the word had been applied to himself.

It took three of the sorry huts to lodge the seven of them, and the windsteeds, too big to fit any house of the village, had to be tied outside. The beast huddled together, ruffling their fur against the sharp sea-wind. Rocannon's striped steed scratched at the wall and complained in a mewing snarl till Kyo went out and scratched its ears. "Worse awaits him soon, poor beast," said Mogien, sitting

53

beside Rocannon by the stove-pit that warmed the hut. "They hate water."

"You said at Hallan that they wouldn't fly over the sea, and these villagers surely have no ships that would carry them. How are we going to cross the channel?"

"Have you your picture of the land?" Mogien inquired. The Angyar had no maps, and Mogien was fascinated by the Geographic Survey's maps in the *Handbook*. Rocannon got the book out of the old leather pouch he had carried from world to world, and which contained the little equipment he had had with him in Hallan when the ship had been bombed—*Handbook* and notebooks, suit and gun, medical kit and radio, a Terran chess-set and a battered volume of Hainish poetry. At first he had kept the necklace with its sapphire in with this stuff, but last night, oppressed by the value of the thing, he had sewn the sapphire pendant up in a little bag of soft barilor-hide and strung the necklace around his own neck, under his shirt and cloak, so that it looked like an amulet and could not be lost unless his head was too.

Mogien followed with a long, hard forefinger the contours of the two Western Continents where they faced each other: the far south of Angien, with its two deep gulfs and a fat promontory between them reaching south; and across the channel, the northermost cape of the Southwest Continent, which Mogien called Fiern. "Here we are," Rocannon said, setting a fish vertebra from their supper on the tip of the promontory.

"And here, if these cringing fish-eating yokels speak truth, is a castle called Plenot." Mogien put a second vertebra a half-inch east of the first one, and admired it. "A tower looks very like that from above. When I get back to Hallan, I'll send out a hundred men on steeds to look down on the land, and from their pictures we'll carve in stone a great picture of all Angien. Now at Plenot there will be ships—probably the ships of this place, Tolen, as well as their own. There was a feud between these two poor lords, and that's why Tolen stands now full of wind and night. So the old man told Yahan."

"Will Plenot lend us ships?"

"Plenot will *lend* us nothing. The lord of Plenot is an Errant." This meant, in the complex code of relationships among Angyar domains, a lord banned by the rest, an outlaw, not bound by the rules of hospitality, reprisal, or restitution.

"He has only two windsteeds," said Mogien, unbuckling his swordbelt for the night. "And his castle, they say, is built of wood."

Next morning as they flew down the wind to that wooden castle a guard spotted them almost as they spotted the tower. The two steeds of the castle were soon aloft, circling the tower; presently they could make out little figures with bows leaning from window-slits. Clearly an Errant Lord expected no friends. Rocannon also realized now why Angyar castles were roofed over, making them cavernous and dark inside, but protecting them from an airborne enemy. Plenot was a little place, ruder even than Tolen, lacking a village of midmen, perched out on a spit of black boulders above the sea; but poor as it was, Mogien's confidence that six men could subdue it seemed excessive. Rocannon checked the thighstraps of his saddle, shifted his grip on the long air-combat lance Mogien had given him, and cursed his luck and himself. This was no place for an ethnologist of forty-three.

Mogien, flying well ahead on his black steed, raised his lance and yelled. Rocannon's mount put down its head and beat into full flight. The black-and-gray wings flashed up and down like vans; the long, thick, light body was tense, thrumming with the powerful heartbeat. As the wind whistled past, the thatched tower of Plenot seemed to hurtle toward them, circled by two rearing gryphons. Rocannon crouched down on the windsteed's back, his long lance couched ready. A happiness, an old delight was swelling in him; he laughed a little, riding the wind. Closer and closer came the rocking tower and its two winged guards, and suddenly with a piercing falsetto shout Mogien hurled his lance, a bolt of silver through the air. It hit one rider square in the chest, breaking his thighstraps with the force of the blow, and hurled him over his steed's haunches in a clear, seemingly slow arc three hundred feet down to the breakers creaming quietly on the rocks. Mogien shot straight on past the riderless steed and opened combat with the other guard, fighting in close, trying to get a sword-stroke past the lance which his opponent did not throw but used for jabbing and parrying. The four midmen on their white and gray mounts hovered nearby like terrible pigeons, ready to help but not interfering with their lord's duel, circling just high enough that the archers below could not pierce the steeds' leathern bellymail. But all at once all four of them, with that nerve-rending falsetto yell, closed in on the duel. For a moment there was a knot of white wings and glittering steel hanging in midair. From the knot dropped a figure that seemed to be trying to lie down on the air, turning this way and that with loose limbs seeking comfort, till it struck the castle roof and slid to a hard bed of rock below.

Now Rocannon saw why they had joined in the duel: the guard had broken its rules and struck at the steed instead of the rider. Mogien's mount, purple blood staining one black wing, was straining inland to the dunes. Ahead of him shot the midmen, chasing the two riderless steeds, which kept circling back, trying to get to their safe stables in the castle. Rocannon headed them off, driving his steed right at them over the castle roofs. He saw Raho catch one with a long cast of his rope, and at the same moment felt something sting his leg. His jump startled his excited steed; he reined in too hard, and the steed arched up its back and for the first time since he had ridden it began to buck, dancing and prancing all over the wind above the castle. Arrows played around him like reversed rain. The midmen and Mogien mounted on a wild-eyed yellow steed shot past him, yelling and laughing. His mount straightened out and followed them. "Catch, Starlord!" Yahan yelled, and a comet with a black tail came arching at him. He caught it in self-defense, found it is lighted resin-torch, and joined the others in circling the tower at close range, trying to set its thatch roof and wooden beams alight.

"You've got an arrow in your left leg," Mogien called as he passed Rocannon, who laughed hilariously and hurled his torch straight into a window-slit from which an archer leaned. "Good shot!" cried Mogien, and came plummeting down onto the tower roof, re-arising from it in a rush of flame.

Yahan and Raho were back with more sheaves of smoking torches they had set alight on the dunes, and were dropping these wherever they saw reed or wood to set afire. The tower was going up now in a roaring fountain of sparks, and the windsteeds, infuriated by constant reining-in and by the sparks stinging their coats, kept plunging down toward the roofs of the castle, making a coughing roar very horrible to hear. The upward rain of arrows had ceased, and now a man scurried out into the forecourt, wearing what looked like a wooden salad bowl on his head, and holding up in his hands what Rocannon first took for a mirror, then saw was a bowl full of water. Jerking at the reins of the yellow beast, which was still trying to get back down to its stable, Mogien rode over the man and called, "Speak quick! My men are lighting new torches!"

"Of what domain, Lord?"

"Hallan!"

"The Lord-Errant of Plenot craves time to put out the fires, Hallanlord!"

"In return for the lives and treasures of the men of Tolen, I grant it."

"So be it," cried the man, and, still holding up the full bowl of water, he trotted back into the castle. The attackers withdrew to the dunes and watched the Plenot folk rush out to man their pump and set up a bucket-brigade from the sea. The tower burned out, but they kept the walls and hall standing. There were only a couple of dozen of them, counting some women. When the fires were out, a group of them came on foot from the gate, over the rocky spit and up the dunes. In front walked a tall, thin man with the walnut skin and fiery hair of the Angyar; behind him came two soldiers still wearing their salad-bowl helmets, and behind them six ragged men and women staring about sheepishly. The tall man raised in his two hands the clay bowl filled with water. "I am Ogoren of Plenot, Lord-Errant of this domain."

"I am Mogien Halla's heir."

"The lives of the Tolenfolk are yours, Lord." He nodded to the ragged group behind him. "No treasure was in Tolen."

"There were two longships, Errant."

"From the north the dragon flies, seeing all things," Ogoren said rather sourly. "The ships of Tolen are yours."

"And you will have your windsteeds back, when the ships are at Tolen wharf," said Mogien, magnanimous.

"By what other lord had I the honor to be defeated?" Ogoren asked with a glance at Rocannon, who wore all the gear and bronze armor of an Angyar warrior, but no swords. Mogien too looked at his friend, and Rocannon responded with the first alias that came to mind, the name Kyo called him by—"Olhor," the Wanderer.

Ogoren gazed at him curiously, then bowed to both and said, "The bowl is full, Lords."

"Let the water not be spilled and the pact not be broken!"

Ogoren turned and strode with his two men back to his smouldering fort, not giving a glance to the freed prisoners huddled on the dune. To these Mogien said only, "Lead home my windsteed; his wing was hurt," and, remounting the yellow beast from Plenot, he took off. Rocannon followed, looking back at the sad little group as they began their trudge home to their own ruinous domain.

By the time he reached Tolen his battle-spirits had flagged and he was cursing himself again. There had in fact been an arrow sticking out of his left calf when he dismounted on the dune, painless till he had pulled it out without stopping to see if the point were barbed, which it was. The Angyar certainly did not use poison; but there was always blood poisoning. Swayed by his companions' genuine courage, he had been ashamed to wear his protective and almost invisible impermasuit for this foray. Owning armor that could withstand a laser-gun, he might die in this damned hovel from the scratch of a bronze-headed arrow. And he had set off to save a planet, when he could not even save his own skin.

The oldest midman from Hallan, a quiet stocky fellow named Iot, came in and almost wordlessly, gentle-mannered, knelt and washed and bandaged Rocannon's hurt. Mogien followed, still in battle dress, looking ten feet tall with his crested helmet, and five feet wide across the shoulders exaggerated by the stiff winglike shoulderboard of his cape. Behind him came Kyo, silent as a child among the warriors of a stronger race. Then Yahan came in, and Raho, and young Bien, so that the hut creaked at the seams when they all squatted around the stove-pit. Yahan filled seven silver-bound cups, which Mogien gravely passed around. They drank. Rocannon began to feel better. Mogien inquired of his wound, and Rocannon felt much better. They drank more vaskan, while scared and admiring faces of villagers peered momentarily in the doorway from the twilit lane outside. Rocannon felt benevolent and heroic. They ate, and drank more, and then in the airless hut reeking with smoke and fried fish and harness-grease and sweat, Yahan stood up with a lyre of bronze with silver strings, and sang. He sang of Durholde of Hallan who set free the prisoners of Korhalt, in the days of the Red Lord, by the marshes of Born; and when he had sung the lineage of every warrior in that battle and every stroke he struck, he sang straight on the freeing of the Tolenfolk and the burning of Plenot Tower, of the Wanderer's torch blazing through a rain of arrows, of the great stroke struck by Mogien Halla's heir, the lance cast across the wind finding its mark like the unerring lance of Hendin in the days of old. Rocannon sat drunk and contented, riding the river of song, feeling himself now wholly committed, sealed by his shed blood to this world to which he had come a stranger across the gulfs of night. Only beside him now and then he sensed the presence of the little Fian, smiling, alien, serene.

IV

THE SEA STRETCHED in long misty swells under a smoking rain. No color was left in the world. Two windsteeds, wingbound and chained in the stern of the boat, lamented and yowled, and over the swells through rain and mist came a doleful echo from the other boat.

They had spent many days at Tolen, waiting till Rocannon' leg healed, and till the black windsteed could fly again. Though these were reasons to wait, the truth was that Mogien was reluctant to leave, to cross the sea they must cross. He roamed the gray sands among the lagoons below Tolen all alone, struggling perhaps with the premonition that had visited his mother Haldre. All he could say to Rocannon was that the sound and sight of the sea made his heart heavy. When at last the black steed was fully cured, he abruptly decided to send it back to Hallan in Bien's care, as if saving one valuable thing from peril. They had also agreed to leave the two packsteeds and most of their load to the old Lord of Tolen and his nephews, who were still creeping about trying to patch their drafty castle. So now in the two dragon-headed boats on the rainy sea were only six travelers and five steeds, all of them wet and most of them complaining.

Two morose fishermen of Tolen sailed the boat. Yahan was trying to comfort the chained steeds with a long and monotonous lament for a long-dead lord; Rocannon and the Fian, cloaked and with hoods pulled over their heads, were in the bow. "Kyo, once you spoke of mountains to the south."

"Oh yes," said the little man, looking quickly northward, at the lost coast of Angien.

"Do you know anything of the people that live in the southern land—in Fiern?"

His *Handbook* was not much help; after all, it was to fill the vast gaps in the *Handbook* that he had brought his Survey here. It postulated five High-Intelligence Life Forms for the planet, but described only three: the Angyar/Olgyior; the Fiia and Gdemiar; and a non-humanoid species found on the great Eastern Continent on the other side of the planet. The geographers' notes on Southwest Continent were mere hearsay: *Unconfirmed species ?4: Large humanoids said to inhabit extensive towns (?). Unconfirmed Species ?5: Winged marsupials.* All in all, it was about as helpful as Kyo, who often seemed to believe that Rocannon knew the answers to all the questions he asked, and now replied like a schoolchild, "In Fiern live the Old Races, is it not so?" Rocannon had to content himself with gazing southward into the mist that hid the questionable land, while the great bound beasts howled and the rain crept chilly down his neck.

Once during the crossing he thought he heard the racket of a helicopter overhead, and was glad the fog hid them; then he shrugged. Why hide? The army using this planet as their base for interstellar warfare were not going to be very badly scared by the sight of ten men and five overgrown housecats bobbing in the rain in a pair of leaky boats. . . .

They sailed on in a changeless circle of rain and waves. Misty darkness rose from the water. A long, cold night went by. Gray light grew, showing mist, and rain, and waves. Then suddenly the two glum sailors in each boat came alive, steering and staring anxiously ahead. A cliff loomed all at once above the boats, fragmentary in the writhing fog. As they skirted its base, boulders and wind-dwarfed trees hung high over their sails.

Yahan had been questioning one of the sailors. "He says we'll sail past the mouth of a big river here, and on the other side is the only landingplace for a long way." Even as he spoke the overhanging rocks dropped back into mist and a thicker fog swirled over the boat, which creaked as a new current struck her keel. The grinning dragon head at the bow rocked and turned. The air was white and opaque; the water breaking and boiling at the sides was opaque and red. The sailors yelled to each other and to the other boat. "The river's in flood," Yahan said. "They're trying to turn— Hang on!" Rocannon caught Kyo's arm as the boat yawed and then pitched and spun on crosscurrents, doing a kind of crazy dance while the sailors fought to hold her steady, and blind mist hid the water, and the windsteeds struggled to free their wings, snarling with terror.

The dragonhead seemed to be going forward steady again, when in a gust of fog-laden wind the unhandy boat jibbed and heeled over. The sail hit water with a slap, caught as if in glue, and pulled the boat right over on her side. Red, warm water quietly came up to Rocannon's face, filled his mouth, filled his eyes. He held on to whatever he was holding and struggled to find the air again. It was Kyo's arm he had hold of, and the two of them floundered in the wild sea warm as blood that swung them and rolled them and tugged them farther from the capsized boat. Rocannon yelled for help, and his voice fell dead in the blank silence of fog over the waters. Was there a shore— which way, how far? He swam after the dimming hulk of the boat, Kyo dragging on his arm.

"Rokanan!"

The dragonhead prow of the other boat loomed grinning out of the white chaos. Mogien was overboard, fighting the current beside him, getting a rope into his hands and around Kyo's chest. Rocannon saw Mogien's face vividly, the arched eyebrows and yellow hair dark with water. They were hauled up into the boat, Mogien last.

Yahan and one of the fishermen from Tolen had been picked up right away. The other sailor and the two windsteeds were drowned, caught under the boat. They were far enough out in the bay now that the flood-currents and winds from the river-gorge were weaker. Crowded with

63

soaked, silent men, the boat rocked on through the red water and the wreathing fog.

"Rokanan, how comes it you're not wet?"

Still dazed, Rocannon looked down at his sodden clothing and did not understand. Kyo, smiling, shaking with cold, answered for him: "The Wanderer wears a second skin." of his impermasuit, which he had put on for warmth in the damp cold last night, leaving only head and hands bare. So he still had it, and the Eye of the Sea still lay hidden on his breast; but his radio, his maps, his gun, all other links with his own civilization, were gone.

"Yahan, you will go back to Hallan."

The servant and his master stood face to face on the shore of the southern land, in the fog, surf hissing at their feet. Yahan did not reply.

They were six riders now, with three windsteeds. Kyo could ride with one midman and Rocannon with another, but Mogien was too heavy a man to ride double for long distances; to spare the windsteeds, the third midman must go back with the boat to Tolen. Mogien had decided Yahan, the youngest, should go.

"I do not send you back for anything ill done or undone, Yahan. Now go—the sailors are waiting."

The servant did not move. Behind him the sailors were kicking apart the fire they had eaten by. Pale sparks flew up briefly in the fog.

"Lord Mogien," Yahan whispered, "send Iot back."

Mogien's face got dark, and he put a hand on his swordhilt.

"Go, Yahan!"

"I will not go, Lord."

The sword came hissing out of its sheath, and Yahan with a cry of despair dodged backward, turned, and disappeared into the fog.

"Wait for him a while," Mogien said to the sailors, his face impassive. "Then go on your way. We must seek our way now. Small Lord, will you ride my steed while he walks?" Kyo sat huddled up as if very cold; he had not

64

eaten, and had not spoken a word since they landed on the coast of Fiern. Mogien set him on the gray steed's saddle and walked at the beast's head, leading them up the beach away from the sea. Rocannon followed glancing back after Yahan and ahead at Mogien, wondering at the strange being, his friend, who one moment would have killed a man in cold wrath and the next moment spoke with simple kindness. Arrogant and loyal, ruthless and kind, in his very disharmony Mogien was lordly.

The fisherman had said there was a settlement east of this cove, so they went east now in the pallid fog that surrounded them in a soft dome of blindness. On windsteeds they might have got above the fog-blanket, but the big animals, worn out and sullen after being tied two days in the boat, would not fly. Mogien, Iot and Raho led them, and Rocannon followed behind, keeping a surreptitious lookout for Yahan, of whom he was fond. He had kept on his impermasuit for warmth, though not the headpiece, which insulated him entirely from the world. Even so, he felt uneasy in the blind mist walking an unknown shore, and he searched the sand as he went for any kind of staff or stick. Between the grooves of the windsteeds' dragging wings and ribbons of seaweed and dried salt scum he saw a long white stick of driftwood; he worked it free of the sand and felt easier, armed. But by stopping he had fallen far behind. He hurried after companions' tracks through the fog. A figure loomed up to his right. He knew at once it was none of his companions, and brought his stick up like a quarterstaff, but was grabbed from behind and pulled down backwards. Something like wet leather was slapped across his mouth. He wrestled free and was rewarded with a blow on his head that drove him into unconsciousness.

When sensation returned, painfully and a little at a time, he was lying on his back in the sand. High up above him two vast foggy figures were ponderously arguing. He understood only part of their Olgyior dialect. "Leave it here," one said, and the other said something like, "Kill it here,

65

it hasn't got anything." At this Rocannon rolled on his side and pulled the headmask of his suit up over his head and face and sealed it. One of the giants turned to peer down at him and he saw it was only a burly midman bundled in furs. "Take it to Zgama, maybe Zgama wants it," the other one said. After more discussion Rocannon was hauled up by the arms and dragged along at a jogging run. He struggled, but his head swam and the fog had got into his brain. He had some consciousness of the mist growing darker, of voices, of a wall of sticks and clay and interwoven reeds, and a torch flaring in a sconce. Then a roof overhead, and more voices, and the dark. And finally, face down on a stone floor, he came to and raised his head.

Near him a long fire blazed in a hearth the size of a hut. Bare legs and hems of ragged pelts made a fence in front of it. He raised his head farther and saw a man's face: a midman, white-skinned, black-haired, heavily bearded, clothed in green and black striped furs, a square fur hat on his head. "What are you?" he demanded in a harsh bass, glaring down at Rocannon.

"I . . . I ask the hospitality of this hall," Rocannon said when he had got himself onto his knees. He could not at the moment get any farther.

"You've had some of it," said the bearded man, watching him feel the lump on his occiput. "Want more?" The muddy legs and fur rags around him jigged, dark eyes peered, white faces grinned.

Rocannon got to his feet and straightened up. He stood silent and motionless till his balance was steady and the hammering of pain in his skull had lessened. Then he lifted his head and gazed into the bright black eyes of his captor. "You are Zgama," he said.

The bearded man stepped backwards, looking scared. Rocannon, who had been in trying situations on several worlds, followed up his advantage as well as he could. "I am Olhor, the Wanderer. I come from the north and from the sea, from the land behind the sun. I come in peace and I go in peace. Passing by the Hall of Zgama, I go south. Let no man stop me!"

"Ahh," said all the open mouths in the white faces, gazing at him. He kept his own eyes unwavering Zgama.

"I am master here," the big man said, his voice rough and uneasy. "None pass by me!"

Rocannon did not speak, or blink.

Zgama saw that in this battle of eyes he was losing: all his people still gazed with round eyes at the stranger. "Leave off your staring!" he bellowed. Rocannon did not move. He realized he was up against a defiant nature, but it was too late to change his tactics now. "Stop staring!" Zgama roared again, then whipped a sword from under his fur cloak, whirled it, and with a tremendous blow sheered off the stranger's head.

But the stranger's head did not come off. He staggered, but Zgama's swordstroke had rebounded as from rock. All the people around the fire whispered, "Ahhh!" The stranger steadied himself and stood unmoving, his eyes fixed on Zgama.

Zgama wavered; almost he stood back to let this weird prisoner go. But the obstinacy of his race won out over his bafflement and fear. "Catch him—grab his arms!" he roared, and when his men did not move he grabbed Rocannon's shoulders and spun him around. At that his men moved in, and Rocannon made no resistace. His suit protected him from foreign elements, extreme temperatures, radioactivity, shocks, and blows of moderate velocity and weight such as swordstrokes or bullets; but it could not get him out of the grasp of ten or fifteen strong men.

"No man passes by the Hall of Zgama, Master of the Long Bay!" The big man gave his rage full vent when his braver bullies had got Rocannon pinioned. "You're a spy for the Yellowheads of Angien. I know you! You come with your Angyar talk and spells and tricks, and dragonboats will follow you out of the north. Not to this place! I am the master of the masterless. Let the Yellowheads and their lickspittle slaves come here—we'll give 'em a taste of

67

bronze! You crawl up out of the sea asking a place by my fire, do you? I'll get you warm, spy. I'll give you roast meat, spy. Tie him to the post there!" His brutal bluster had heartened his people, and they jostled to help lash the stranger to one of the hearth-posts that supported a great spit over the fire, and to pile up wood around his legs.

Then they fell silent. Zgama strode up, grim and massive in his furs, took up a burning branch from the hearth and shook it in Rocannon's eyes, then set the pyre aflame. It blazed up hot. In a moment Rocannon's clothing, the brown cloak and tunic of Hallan, took fire and flamed up around his head, at his face.

"Ahhh," all the watchers whispered once more, but one of them cried, "Look!" As the blaze died down they saw through the smoke the figure stand motionless, flames licking up its legs, gazing straight at Zgama. On the naked breast, dropping from a chain of gold, shone a great jewel like an open eye.

"Pedan, pedan," whimpered the women, cowering in dark corners.

Zgama broke the hush of panic with his bellowing voice. "He'll burn! Let him burn! Deho, throw on more wood, the spy's not roasting quick enough!" He dragged a little boy out into the leaping, restless firelight and forced him to add wood to the pyre. "Is there nothing to eat? Get food, you women! You see our hospitality, you Olhor, see how we eat?" He grabbed a joint of meat off the trencher a woman offered him, and stood in front of Rocannon tearing at it and letting the juice run down his beard. A couple of his bullies imitated him, keeping a little farther away. Most of them did not come anywhere near that end of the hearth; but Zgama got them to eat and drink and shout, and some of the boys dared one another to come up close enough to add a stick to the pyre where the mute, calm man stood with flames playing along his red-lit, strangly shining skin.

Fire and noise died down at last. Men and women slept curled up in their fur rags on the floor, in corners, in the warm ashes. A couple of men watched, sword on knees and flask in hand.

Rocannon let his eyes close. By crossing two fingers he unsealed the headzone of his suit, and breathed fresh air again. The long night wore along and slowly the long dawn lightened. In gray daylight, through fog wreathing in the windowholes, Zgama came sliding on greasy spots on the floor and stepping over snoring bodies, and peered at his captive. The captive's gaze was grave and steady, the captor's impotently defiant. "Burn, burn!" Zgama growled, and went off.

Outside the rude hall Rocannon heard the cooing mutter of herilor, the fat and feathery domesticated meat-animals of the Angyar, kept wing-clipped and here pastured probably on the sea-cliffs. The hall emptied out except for a few babies and women, who kept well away from him even when it came time to roast the evening meat.

By then Rocannon had stood bound for thirty hours, and was suffering both pain and thirst. That was his deadline, thirst. He could go without eating for a long time, and supposed he could stand in chains at least as long, though his head was already light; but without water he could get through only one more of these long days.

Powerless as he was, there was nothing he could say to Zgama, threat or bribe, that would not simply increase the barbarian's obduracy.

That night as the fire danced in front of his eyes and through it he watched Zgama's bearded, heavy, white face, he kept seeing in his mind's eye a different face, bright-haired and dark: Mogien, whom he had come to love as a friend and somewhat as a son. As the night and the fire went on and on he thought also of the little Fian Kyo, childlike and uncanny, bound to him in a way he had not tried to understand; he saw Yahan singing of heroes; and Iot and Raho grumbling and laughing together as they curried the great-winged steeds; and Haldre unclasping the gold chain from her neck. Nothing came to him from all his earlier life, though he had lived many years on many

69

worlds, learned much, done much. It was all burnt away. He thought he stood in Hallan, in the long hall hung with tapestries of men fighting giants, and that Yahan was offering him a bowl of water.

"Drink it, Starlord. Drink."

And he drank.

V

FENI AND FELI, the two largest moons, danced in white reflections on the water as Yahan held a second bowlful for him to drink. The hearthfire glimmered only in a few coals. The hall was dark picked out with flecks and shafts of moonlight, silent except for the breathing and shifting of many sleepers.

As Yahan cautiously loosed the chains Rocannon leaned his full weight back against the post, for his legs were numb and he could not stand unsupported.

"They guard the outer gate all night," Yahan was whispering in his ear, "and those guards keep awake. Tomorrow when they take the flocks out—"

"Tomorrow night. I can't run. I'll have to bluff out. Hook the chain so I can lean my weight on it, Yahan. Get the hook here, by my hand." A sleeper nearby sat up pawning, and with a grin that flashed a moment in the moonlight Yahan sank down and seemed to melt in shadows.

Rocannon saw him at dawn going out with the other men to take the herilor to pasture, wearing a muddy pelt like the others, his black hair sticking out like a broom. Once again Zgama came up and scowled at his captive. Rocannon knew the man would have given half his flocks and wives to be rid of his unearthly guest, but was trapped in his own cruelty: the jailer is the prisoner's prisoner. Zgama had slept in the warm ashes and his hair was smeared with ash, so that he looked more the burned man than Rocannon, whose naked skin shone white. He stamped off, and again the hall was empty most of the day, though guards stayed at the door. Rocannon improved his time with surreptitious isometric exercises. When a passing woman caught him stretching, he stretched on, swaying and emitting a low, weird croon. She dropped to all fours and scuttled out, whimpering.

Twilit fog blew in the windows, sullen womenfolk boiled a stew of meat and seaweed, returning flocks cooed in hundreds outside, and Zgama and his men came in, fog-droplets glittering in their beards and furs. They sat on the floor to eat. The place rang and reeked and steamed. The strain of returning each night to the uncanny was showing; faces were grim, voices quarrelsome. "Build up the fire—he'll roast yet!" shouted Zgama, jumping up to push a burning log over onto the pyre. None of his men moved.

"I'll eat your heart, Olhor, when it fries out between your ribs! I'll wear that blue stone for a nosering!" Zgama was shaking with rage, frenzied by the silent steady gaze he had endured for two nights. "I'll make you shut your eyes!" he screamed, and snatching up a heavy stick from the floor he brought it down with a whistling crack on Rocannon's head, jumping back at the same moment as if afraid of what he handled. The stick fell among the burning logs and stuck up at an angle.

Slowly, Rocannon reached out his right hand, closed his fist about the stick and drew it out of the fire. Its end was ablaze. He raised it till it pointed at Zgama's eyes, and then, as slowly, he stepped forward. The chains fell away from him. The fire leaped up and broke apart in sparks and coals about his bare feet.

"Out!" he said, coming straight at Zgama, who fell back one step and then another. "You're not master here. The lawless man is a slave, and the cruel man is a slave, and the stupid man is a slave. You are my slave, and I drive you like a beast. Out!" Zgama caught both sides of the doorframe, but the blazing staff came at his eyes, and he cringed back into the courtyard. The guards crouched down, motionless. Resin-torches flaring beside the outer gate brightened the fog; there was no noise but the murmur of the herds in their byres and the hissing of the sea below

72

the cliffs. Step by step Zgama went backward till he reached the outer gate between the torches. His black- and-white face stared masklike as the fiery staff came closer. Dumb with fear, he clung to the log doorpost, filling the gateway with his bulky body. Rocannon, exhausted and vindictive, drove the flaming point hard against his chest, pushed him down, and strode over his body into the blackness and blowing fog outside the gate. He went about fifty paces into the dark, then stumbled, and could not get up.

No one pursued. No one came out of the compound behind him. He lay half-conscious in the dune-grass. After a long time the gate torches died out or were extinguished, and there was only darkness. Wind blew with voices in the grass, and the sea hissed down below.

As the fog thinned, letting the moons shine through, Yahan found him there near the cliff's edge. With his help, Rocannon got up and walked. Feeling their way, stumbling, crawling on hands and knees where the going was rough and dark, they worked eastward and southward away from the coast. A couple of times they stopped to get their breath and bearings, and Rocannon fell asleep almost as soon as they stopped. Yahan woke him and kept him going until, some time before dawn, they came down a valley under the eaves of a steep forest. The domain of trees was black in the misty dark. Yahan and Rocannon entered it along the streambed they had been following, but did not go far. Rocannon stopped and said in his own language, "I can't go any farther." Yahan found a sandy strip under the streambank where they could lie hidden at least from above; Rocannon crawled into it like an animal into its den, and slept.

When he woke fifteen hours later at dusk, Yahan was there with a small collection of green shoots and roots to eat. "It's too early in warmyear for fruit," he explained ruefully, "and the oafs in Oafscastle took my bow. I made some snares but they won't catch anything till tonight."

Rocannon consumed the salad avidly, and when he had drunk from the stream and stretched and could think again,

73

he asked, "Yahan, how did you happen to be there—in Oafscastle?"

The young midman looked down and buried a few inedible root-tips neatly in the sand. "Well, Lord, you know that I . . . defied my Lord Mogien. So after that, I thought I might join the Masterless."

"You'd heard of them before?"

"There are tales at home of places where we Olgyior are both lords and servants. It's even said that in old days only we midmen lived in Angien, and were hunters in the forests and had no masters; and the Angyar came from the south in dragonboats. . . . Well, I found the fort, and Zgama's fellows took me for a runaway from some other place down the coast. They grabbed my bow and put me to work and asked no questions. So I found you. Even if you hadn't been there I would have escaped. I would not be a lord among such oafs!"

"Do you know where our companions are?"

"No. Will you seek for them, Lord?"

"Call me by my name, Yahan. Yes, if there's any chance of finding them I'll seek them. We can't cross a continent alone, on foot, without clothes or weapons."

Yahan said nothing, smoothing the sand, watching the stream that ran dark and clear beneath the heavy branches of the conifers.

"You disagree?"

"If my Lord Mogien finds me he'll kill me. It is his right."

By the Angyar code, this was true; and if anyone would keep the code, it was Mogien.

"If you find a new master, the old one may not touch you: is that not true, Yahan?"

The boy nodded. "But a rebellious man finds no new master."

"That depends. Pledge your service to me, and I'll answer for you to Mogien—if we find him. I don't know what words you use."

"We say"—Yahan spoke very low—"*to my Lord I give the hours of my life and the use of my death.*"

"I accept them. And with them my own life which you gave back to me."

The little river ran noisily from the ridge above them, and the sky darkened solemnly. In late dusk Rocannon slipped off his impermasuit and, stretching out in the stream, let the cold water running all along his body wash away sweat and weariness and fear and the memory of the fire licking at his eyes. Off, the suit was a handful of transparent stuff and semivisible, hairthin tubes and wires and a couple of translucent cubes the size of a fingernail. Yahan watched him with an uncomfortable look as he put the suit on again (since he had no clothes, and Yahan had been forced to trade his Angyar clothing for a couple of dirty herilo fleeces). "Lord Olhor," he said at last, "it was . . . was it that skin that kept the fire from burning you? Or the . . . the jewel?"

The necklace was hidden now in Yahan's own amulet-bag, around Rocannon's neck. Rocannon answered gently, "The skin. No spells. It's a very strong kind of armor."

"And the white staff?"

He looked down at the driftwood stick, one end of it heavily charred; Yahan had picked it up from the grass of the sea-cliff, last night, just as Zgama's men had brought it along to the fort with him; they had seemed determined he should keep it. What was a wizard without his staff? "Well," he said, "it's a good walking-stick, if we've got to walk." He stretched again, and for want of more supper before they slept, drank once more from the dark, cold, noisy stream.

Late next morning when he woke, he was recovered, and ravenous. Yahan had gone off at dawn, to check his snares and because he was too cold to lie longer in their damp den. He returned with only a handful of herbs, and a piece of bad news. He had crossed over the forested ridge which they were on the seaward side of, and from its top had seen to the south another broad reach of the sea.

"Did those misbegotten fish-eaters from Tolen leave us on an island?" he growled, his usual optimism subverted by cold, hunger, and doubt.

Rocannon tried to recall the coastline on his drowned maps. A river running in from the west emptied on the north of a long tongue of land, itself part of a coastwise mountainchain running west to east; between that tongue and the mainland was a sound, long and wide enough to show up very clear on the maps and in his memory. A hundred, two hundred kilometers long? "How wide?" he asked Yahan, who answered glumly, "Very wide. I can't swim, Lord."

"We can walk. This ridge joins the mainland, west of here. Mogien will be looking for us along that way, probably." It was up to him to provide leadership—Yahan had certainly done more than his share—but his heart was low in him at the thought of that long detour through unknown and hostile country. Yahan had seen no one, but had crossed paths, and there must be men in these woods to make the game so scarce and shy.

But for there to be any hope of Mogien's find them—if Mogien was alive, and free, and still had the windsteeds—they would have to work southward, and if possible out into open country. He would look for them going south, for that was all the goal of their journey. "Let's go," Rocannon said, and they went.

A little after midday they looked down from the ridge across a broad inlet running east and west as far as eye could see, lead-gray under a low sky. Nothing of the southern shore could be made out but a line of low, dark, dim hills. The wind that blew up the sound was bitter cold at their backs as they worked down to the shore and started westward along it. Yahan looked up at the clouds, hunched his head down between his shoulders and said mournfully, "It's going to snow."

And presently the snow began, a wet windblown snow of spring, vanishing on the wet ground as quickly as on the dark water of the sound. Rocannon's suit kept the cold from him, but strain and hunger made him very weary; Yahan was also weary. and very cold. They slogged a'ong, for there was nothing else to do. They forded a creek, plugged up the bank through coarse grass and blowing snow, and at the top came face to face with a man.

"Houf!" he said staring in surprise and then in wonder. For what he saw was two men walking in a snowstorm, one blue-lipped and shivering in ragged furs. the other one stark naked. "Ha, Houf!" he said again. He was a tall, bony, bowed, bearded man with a w'd look in his dark eyes. "Ha you, there!" he said in the Olgyior speech, "you'll freeze to death!"

"We had to swim—our boat sank," Yahan improvised promptly. "Have you a house with a fire in it. hunter of pelliunur?"

"You were crossing the sound from the south?"

The man looked troubled, and Yahan replied with a vague gesture, "We're from the east—we came to buy pelliunfurs, but all our tradegoods went down in the water."

"Hanh, hanh," the wild man went, still troubled, but a genial streak in him seemed to win out over his fears. "Come on; I have fire and food," he said, and turning, he jigged off into the thin, gusting snow. Following. they came soon to his hut perched on a slope between the forested ridge and the sound. Inside and out it was like any winter hut of the midmen of the forests and hills of Angien, and Yahan squatter down before the fire with a sigh of frank relief, as if at home. That reassured their host better than any ingenious explanations. "Build up the fire, lad," he said, and he gave Rocannon a homespun cloak to wrap himself in.

Throwing off his own cloak, he set a clay bowl of stew in the ashes to warm. and hunkered down companionably with them, rolling his eyes at one and then the other. "Always snows this time of year, and it'll snow harder soon. Plenty of room for you; there's three of us winter here. The others will be in tonight or tomorrow or soon enough;

they'll be staying out this snowfall up on the ridge where they were hunting. Pelliun hunters we are, as you saw by my whistles, eh lad?" He touched the set of heavy wooden panpipes dangling at his belt, and grinned. He had a wild, fierce, foolish look to him, but his hospitality was tangible. He gave them their fill of meat stew, and when the evening darkened, told them to get their rest. Rocannon lost no time. He rolled himself up in the stinking furs of the bed-niche, and slept like a baby.

In the morning snow still fell, and the ground now was white and featureless. Their host's companions had not come back. "They'll have spent the night over across the Spine, in Timash village. They'll come along when it clears."

"The Spine—that's the arm of the sea there?"

"No, that's the sound—no villages across it! The Spine's the ridge, the hills up above us here. Where do you come from, anyhow? You talk like us here, mostly, but your uncle don't."

Yahan glanced apologetically at Rocannon, who had been asleep while acquiring a nephew. "Oh—he's from the Backlands; they talk differently. We call that water the sound, too. I wish I knew a fellow with a boat to bring us across it."

"You want to go south?"

"Well, now that all our goods are gone, we're nothing here but beggars. We'd better try to get home."

"There's a boat down on the shore, a ways from here. We'll see about that when the weather clears. I'll tell you, lad, when you talk so cool about going south my blood gets cold. There's no man dwelling between the sound and the great mountains, that ever I heard of, unless it's the Ones not talked of. And that's all old stories, and who's to say if there's any mountains even? I've been over on the other side of the sound—there's not many men can tell you that. Been there myself, hunting, in the hills. There's plenty of pelliunur there, near the water. But no villages. No men. None. And I wouldn't stay the night."

78

"We'll just follow the southern shore eastward," Yahan said indifferently, but with a perplexed look; his inventions were forced into further complexity with every question.

But his instinct to lie had been correct— "At least you didn't sail from the north!" their host, Piai, rambled on, sharpening his long, leaf-bladed knife on a whetstone as he talked. "No men at all across the sound, and across the sea only mangy fellows that serve as slaves to the Yellowheads. Don't your people know about them? In the north country over the sea there's a race of men with yellow heads. It's true. They say that they live in houses high as trees, and carry silver swords, and ride between the wings of windsteeds! I'll believe that when I see it. Windsteed fur brings a good price over on the coast, but the beasts are dangerous to hunt, let alone taming one and riding it. You can't believe all people tell in tales. I make a good enough living out of pelliun furs. I can bring the beasts from a day's flight around. Listen!" He put his panpipes to his hairy lips and blew, very faintly at first, a half-heard, halting plaint that swelled and changed, throbbing and breaking between notes, rising into an almost-melody that was a wild beast's cry. The chill went up Rocannon's back; he had heard that tune in the forests of Hallan. Yahan, who had been trained as a huntsman, grinned with excitement and cried out as if on the hunt and sighting the quarry, "Sing! sing! she rises there!" He and Piai spent the rest of the afternoon swapping hunting-stories, while outside the snow still fell, windless now and steady.

The next day dawned clear. As on a morning of coldyear, the sun's ruddy-white brilliance was blinding on the snow-whitened hills. Before midday Piai's two companions arrived with a few of the downy gray pelliun-furs. Black-browed, strapping men like all those southern Olgyior, they seemed still wilder than Piai, wary as animals of the strangers, avoiding them, glancing at them only sideways.

"They call my people slaves," Yahan said to Rocannon

when the others were outside the hut for a minute. "But I'd rather be a man serving men than a beast hunting beasts, like these." Rocannon raised his hand, and Yahan was silent as one of the Southerners came in, glancing sidelong at them, unspeaking.

"Let's go," Rocannon muttered in the Olgyior tongue, which he had mastered a little more of these last two days. He wished they had not waited till Piai's companions had come, and Yahan also was uneasy. He spoke to Piai, who had just come in:

"We'll be going now—this fair weather shou'd hold till we get around the inlet. If you hadn't sheltered us we'd never have lived through these two nights of cold. And I never would have heard the pelliun-song so played. May all your hunting be fortunate!"

But Piai stood still and said nothing. Finally he hawked, spat on the fire, rolled his eyes, and growled, "Around the inlet? Didn't you want to cross by boat? There's a boat. It's mine. Anyhow, I can use it. We'll take you over the water."

"Six days walking that'll save you," the shorter newcomer, Karmik, put in.

"It'll save you six days walking," Piai repeated. "We'll take you across in the boat. We can go now."

"All right," Yahan replied after glancing at Rocannon; there was nothing they could do.

"Then let's go," Piai grunted, and so abruptly, with no offer of provision for the way, they left the hut, Piai in the lead and his friends bringing up the rear. The wind was keen, the sun bright; though snow remained in sheltered places, the rest of the ground ran and squelched and glittered with the thaw. They followed the shore westward for a long way, and the sun was set when they reached a little cove where a rowboat lay among rocks and reeds out on the water. Red of sunset flushed the water and the western sky; above the red glow the little moon Heliki gleamed waxing, and in the darkening east the Greatstar, Fomalhaut's distant companion, shone like an opal. Under the brilliant sky, over the brilliant water, the long hilly shores ran featureless and dark.

"There's the boat," said Piai, stopping and facing them, his face red with the western light. The other two came and stood in silence beside Rocannon and Yahan.

"You'll be rowing back in darkness," Yahan said.

"Greatstar shines; it'll be a light night. Now, lad, there's the matter of paying us for our rowing you."

"Ah," said Yahan.

"Piai knows—we have nothing. This cloak is his gift," said Rocannon, who, seeing how the wind blew, did not care if his accent gave them away.

"We are poor hunters. We can't give gifts," said Karmik, who had a softer voice and a saner, meaner look than Piai and the other one.

"We have nothing," Rocannon repeated. "Nothing to pay for the rowing. Leave us here."

Yahan joined in, saying the same thing more fluently, but Karmik interrupted: "You're wearing a bag around your neck, stranger. What's in it?"

"My soul," said Rocannon promptly.

They all stared at him, even Yahan. But he was in a poor position to bluff, and the pause did not last. Karmik put his hand on his leaf-bladed hunting knife, and moved closer; Piai and the other imitated him. "You were in Zgama's fort," he said. "They told a long tale about it in Timash village. How a naked man stood in a burning fire, and burned Zgama with a white stick, and walked out of the fort wearing a great jewel on a gold chain around his neck. The said it was magic and spells. I think they are all fools. Maybe you can't be hurt. But this one—" He grabbed Yahan lightning-quick by his long hair, twisted his head back and sideways, and brought the knife up against his throat. "Boy, you tell this stranger you travel with to pay for your lodging—eh?"

They all stood still. The red dimmed on the water, the Greatstar brightened in the east, the cold wind blew past them down the shore.

"We won't hurt the lad," Piai growled, his fierce face twisted and frowning. "We'll do what I said, we'll row you over the sound—only pay us. You didn't say you had gold to pay with. You said you'd lost all your gold. You slept under my roof. Give us the thing and we'll row you across."

"I will give it—over there," Rocannon said, pointing across the sound.

"No," Karmik said.

Yahan, helpless in his hands, had not moved a muscle; Rocannon could see the beating of the artery in this throat, against which the knife-blade lay.

"Over there," he repeated grimly, and tilted his driftwood walking stick forward a little in case the sight of it might impress them. "Row us across; I give you the thing. This I tell you. But hurt him and you die here, now. This I tell you!"

"Karmik, he's a pedan," Piai muttered. "Do what he says. They were under the roof with me, two nights. Let the boy go. He promises the thing you want."

Karmik looked scowling from him to Rocannon and said at last, "Throw that white stick away. Then we'll take you across."

"First let the boy go," said Rocannon, and when Karmik released Yahan, he laughed in his face and tossed the stick high, end over end, out into the water.

Knives drawn, the three huntsmen herded him and Yahan to the boat; they had to wade out and climb in her from the slippery rocks on which dull-red ripples broke. Piai and the third man rowed, Karmik sat knife in hand behind the passengers.

"Will you give him the jewel?" Yahan whispered in the Common Tongue, which these Olgyior of the peninsula did not use.

Rocannon nodded.

Yahan's whisper was very hoarse and shaky. "You jump and swim with it, Lord. Near the south shore. They'll let me go, when it's gone—"

"They'd slit your throat. Shh."

"They're casting spells, Karmik," the third man was saying. "They're going to sink the boat—"

"Row, you rotten fish-spawn. You, be still, or I'll cut the boy's neck."

Rocannon sat patiently on the thwart, watching the water turn misty gray as the shores behind and before them receded into night. Their knives could not hurt him, but they could kill Yahan before he could do much to them. He could have swum for it easy enough, but Yahan could not swim. There was no choice. At least they were getting the ride they were paying for.

Slowly the dim hills of the southern shore rose and took on substance. Faint gray shadows dropped westward and few stars came out in the gray sky; the remote solar brilliance of the Greatstar dominated even the moon Heliki, now in its waning cycle. They could hear the sough of waves against the shore. "Quit rowing," Karmik ordered, and to Rocannon: "Give me the thing now."

"Closer to shore," Rocannon said impassively.

"I can make it from here, Lord," Yahan muttered shakily. "There are reeds sticking up ahead there—"

The boat moved a few oarstrokes ahead and halted again.

"Jump when I do," Rocannon said to Yahan, and then slowly rose and stood up on the thwart. He unsealed the neck of the suit he had worn so long now, broke the leather cord around his neck with a jerk, tossed the bag that held the sapphire and its chain into the bottom of the boat, resealed the suit and in the same instant dived.

He stood with Yahan a couple of minutes later among the rocks of the shore, watching the boat, a blackish blur in the gray quarter-light on the water, shrinking.

"Oh may they rot, may they have worms in their bowels and their bones turn to slime," Yahan said, and began to cry. He had been badly scared, but more than the reaction from fear broke down his self-control. To see a "lord" toss away a jewel worth a kingdom's ransom to save a

83

midman's life, his life, was to see all order subverted, admitting unbearable responsibility. "It was wrong, Lord!" he cried out. "It was wrong!"

"To buy your life with a rock? Come on, Yahan, get a hold of yourself. You'll freeze if we don't get a fire going. Have you got your drill? There's a lot of brushwood up this way. Get a move on!"

They managed to get a fire going there on the shore, and built it up till it drove back the night and the still, keen cold. Rocannon had given Yahan the huntsman's fur cape, and huddling in it the young man finally went to sleep. Rocannon sat keeping the fire burning, uneasy and with no wish to sleep. His own heart was heavy that he had had to throw away the necklace, not because it was valuable, but because once he had given it to Semley, whose remembered beauty had brought him, over all the years, to this world; because Haldre had given it to him, hoping, he knew, thus to buy off the shadow, the early death she feared for her son. Maybe it was as well the thing was gone, the weight, the danger of its beauty. And maybe, if worst came to worst, Mogien would never know that it was gone; because Mogien would not find him, or was already dead. . . . He put that thought aside. Mogien was looking for him and Yahan—that must be his assumption. He would look for them going south. For what plan had they ever had, except to go south—there to find the enemy, or, if all his guesses had been wrong, not to find the enemy? But with or without Mogien, he would go south.

They set out at dawn, climbing the shoreline hills in the twilight, reaching the top of them as the rising sun revealed a high, empty plain running sheer to the horizon, streaked with the long shadows of bushes. Piai had been right, apparently, when he said nobody lived south of the sound. At least Mogien would be able to see them from miles off. They started south.

It was cold, but mostly clear. Yahan wore what clothes they had, Rocannon his suit. They crossed creeks angling down toward the sound now and then, often enough to keep them from thirst. That day and next day they went on, living on the roots of a plant called peya and on a couple of stump-winged, hop-flying, coney-like creatures that Yahan knocked out of the air with a stick and cooked on a fire of twigs lit with his firedrill. They saw no other living thing. Clear to the sky the high grasslands stretched, level, treeless, roadless, silent.

Oppressed by immensity, the two men sat by their tiny fire in the vast dusk, saying nothing. Overhead at long intervals, like the beat of a pulse in the night, came a soft cry very high in the air. They were barilor, wild cousins of the tamed herilor, making their northward spring migration. The stars for a hand's breadth would be blotted out by the great flocks, but never more than a single voice called, brief, a pulse on the wind.

"Which of the stars do you come from, Olhor?" Yahan asked softly, gazing up.

"I was born on a world called Hain by my mother's people, and Davenant by my father's. You call its sun the Winter Crown. But I left it long ago. . . ."

"You're not all one people, then, the Starfolk?"

"Many hundred peoples. By blood I'm entirely of my mother's race; my father, who was a Terran, adopted me. This is the custom when people of different species, who cannot conceive children, marry. As if one of your kin should marry a Fian woman."

"This does not happen," Yahan said stiffly.

"I know. But Terran and Davenanter are as alike as you and I. Few worlds have so many different races as this one. Most often there is one, much like us, and the rest are beasts without speech."

"You've seen many worlds," the young man said dreamily, trying to conceive of it.

"Too many," said the older man. "I'm forty, by your years; but I was born a hundred and forty years ago. A hundred years I've lost without living them, between the worlds. If I went back to Davenant or Earth, the men and women I knew would be a hundred years dead. I can only go on; or stop, somewhere—What's that?" The sense of some presence seemed to silence even the hissing of wind through grass. Something moved at the edge of the firelight—a great shadow, a darkness. Rocannon knelt tensely; Yahan sprang away from the fire.

Nothing moved. Wind hissed in the grass in the gray starlight. Clear around the horizon the stars shone, unbroken by any shadow.

The two rejoined at the fire. "What was it?" Rocannon asked.

Yahan shook his head. "Piai talked of . . . something . . ."

They slept patchily, trying to spell each other keeping watch. When the slow dawn came they were very tired. They sought tracks or marks where the shadow had seemed to stand, but the young grass showed nothing. They stamped out their fire and went on, heading southward by the sun.

They had thought to cross a stream soon, but they did not. Either the stream-courses now were running north-south, or there simply were no more. The plain or pampa that seemed never to change as they walked had been becoming always a little dryer, a little grayer. This morning they saw none of the peya bushes, only the coarse gray-green grass going on and on.

At noon Rocannon stopped.

"It's no good, Yahan," he said.

Yahan rubbed his neck, looking around, then turned his gaunt, tired young face to Rocannon. "If you want to go on, Lord, I will."

"We can't make it without water or food. We'll steal a boat on the coast and go back to Hallan. This is no good. Come on."

Rocannon turned and walked northward. Yahan came along beside him. The high spring sky burned blue, the wind hissed endlessly in the endless grass. Rocannon went along steadily, his shoulders a little bent, going step by step into permanent exile and defeat. He did not turn when Yahan stopped.

"Windsteeds!"

Then he looked up and saw them, three great gryphon-cats circling down upon them, claws outstretched, wings black against the hot blue sky.

PART TWO: The Wanderer

VI

MOGIEN LEAPED OFF his steed before it had its feet on the ground, ran to Rocannon and hugged him like a brother. His voice rang with delight and relief. "By Hendin's lance, Starlord! why are you marching stark naked across this desert? How did you get so far south by walking north? Are you—" Mogien met Yahan's gaze, and stopped short.

Rocannon said, "Yahan is my bondsman."

Mogien said nothing. After a certain struggle with himself he began to grin, then he laughed out loud. "Did you learn our customs in order to steal my servants, Rokanan? But who stole your clothes?"

"Olhor wears more skins than one," said Kyo, coming with his light step over the grass. "Hail, Firelord! Last night I heard you in my mind."

"Kyo led us to you." Mogien confirmed. "Since we set foot on Fiern's shore ten days ago he never spoke a word, but last night, on the bank of the sound, when Lioka rose, he listened to the moonlight and said, 'There! Come daylight we flew where he had pointed, and so found you."

"Where is Iot?" Rocannon asked, seeing only Raho stand holding the windsteeds' reins. Mogien with unchanging face replied, "Dead. The Olgyior came on us in the fog on the beach. They had only stones for weapons, but they were many. Iot was killed, and you were lost. We hid in a cave in the seacliffs till the steeds would fly again. Raho went forth and heard tales of a stranger who stood in a burning fire unburnt, and wore a blue jewel. So when the

89

steeds would fly we went to Zgama's fort, and not finding
you we dropped fire on his wretched roofs and drove his
herds into the forests, and then began to look for you along
the banks of the sound."

"The jewel, Mogien," Rocannon interrupted; "the Eye
of Sea—I had to buy our lives with it. I gave it away."

"The jewel?" said Mogien, staring. "Semley's jewel—
you gave it away? Not to buy your life—who can harm
you? To buy that worthless life, that disobedient halfman?
You hold my heritage cheap! Here, take the thing; it's not
so easily lost!" He spun something up in the air with a
laugh, caught it, and tossed it glittering to Rocannon, who
stood and gaped at it, the blue stone burning in his hand,
the golden chain.

"Yesterday we met two Olgyior, and one dead one, on
the other shore of the sound, and we stopped to ask about
a naked traveler they might have seen going by with his
worthless servant. One of them groveled on his face and
told us the story, and so I took the jewel from the other
one. And his life along with it, because he fought. Then we
knew you had crossed the sound; and Kyo brought us
straight to you. But why were you going northward, Rokanan?"

"To—to find water."

"There's a stream to the west," Raho put in. "I saw it
just before we saw you."

"Let's go to it. Yahan and I haven't drunk since last
night."

They mounted the windsteeds, Yahan with Raho, Kyo
in his old place behind Rocannon. The wind-bowed grass
dropped away beneath them, and they skimmed southwestward between the vast plain and the sun.

They camped by the stream that wound clear and slow
among flowerless grasses. Rocannon could at last take off
the impermasuit, and dressed in Mogien's spare shirt and
cloak. They ate hardbread brought from Tolen, peya roots,
and four of the stump-winged coneys shot by Raho and by
Yahan, who was full of joy when he got his hands on a

bow again. The creatures out here on the plain almost flew upon the arrows, and let the windsteeds snap them up in flight, having no fear. Even the tiny green and violet and yellow creatures called kilar, insect-like with transparent buzzing wings, though they were actually tiny marsupials, here were fearless and curious, hovering about one's head peering with round gold eyes, lighting on one's hand or knee a moment and skimming distractingly off again. It looked as if all this immense grassland were void of intelligent life. Mogien said they had seen no sign of men or other beings as they had flown above the plain.

"We thought we saw some creature last night, near the fire," Rocannon said hesitantly, for what had they seen? Kyo looked around at him from the cooking-fire; Mogien, unbuckling his belt that held the double swords, said nothing.

They broke camp at first light and all day rode the wind between plain and sun. Flying above the plain was as pleasant as walking across it had been hard. So passed the following day, and just before evening, as they looked out for one of the small streams that rarely broke the expanse of grass, Yahan turned in his saddle and called across the wind, "Olhor! See ahead!" Very far ahead, due south, a faint ruffling or crimping of gray broke the smooth horizon.

"The mountains!" Rocannon said, and as he spoke he heard Kyo behind him draw breath sharply, as if in fear.

During the next day's flight the flat pampas gradually rose into low swells and rolls of land, vast waves on a quiet sea. High-piled clouds drifted northward above them now and then, and far ahead they could see the land tilting upward, growing dark and broken. By evening the mountains were clear; when the plain was dark the remote, tiny peaks in the south still shone bright gold for a long time. From those far peaks as they faded, the moon Lioka rose and sailed up like a great, hurrying, yellow star. Feni and Feli were already shining, moving in more stately fashion from east to west. Last of the four rose Heliki and pursued the others, brightening and dimming in a half-hour cycle,

91

brightening and dimming. Rocannon lay on his back and watched, through the high black stems of grass, the slow and radiant complexity of the lunar dance.

Next morning when he and Kyo went to mount the gray-striped windsteed Yahan cautioned him, standing at the beast's head: "Ride him with care today, Olhor." The windsteed agreed with a cough and a long snarl, echoed by Mogien's gray.

"What ails them?"

"Hunger!" said Raho, reining in his white steed hard. "They got their fill of Zgama's herilor, but since we started across this plain there's been no big game, and these hop-flyers are only a mouthful to 'em. Belt in your cloak, Lord Olhor—if it blows within reach of your steed's jaws you'll be his dinner." Raho, whose brown hair and skin testified to the attraction one of his grandmothers had exerted on some Angyar nobleman, was more brusque and mocking than most midmen. Mogien never rebuked him, and Raho's harshness did not hide his passionate loyalty to his lord. A man near middle age, he plainly thought this journey a fool's errand, and as plainly had never thought to do anything but go with his young lord into any peril.

Yahan handed up the reins and dodged back from Rocannon's steed, which leaped like a released spring into the air. All that day the three steeds flew wildly, tirelessly, toward the hunting-grounds they sensed or scented to the south, and a north wind hastened them on. Forested foothills rose always darker and clearer under the floating barrier of mountains. Now there were trees on the plain, clumps and groves like islands in the swelling sea of grass. The groves thickened into forests broken by green parkland. Before dusk they came down by a little sedgy lake among wooded hills. Working fast and gingerly, the two midmen stripped all packs and harness off the steeds, stood back and let them go. Up they shot, bellowing, wide wings beating, flew off in three different directions over the hills, and were gone.

"They'll come back when they've fed," Yahan told Rocannon, "or when Lord Mogien blows his still whistle."

"Sometimes they bring mates back with them—wild ones," Raho added, baiting the tenderfoot.

Mogien and the midmen scattered, hunting hop-flyers or whatever else turned up; Rocannon pulled some fat peya-roots and put them to roast wrapped in their leaves in the ashes of the campfire. He was expert at making do with what any land offered, and enjoyed it; and these days of great flights between dusk and dusk, of constant barely-assuaged hunger, of sleep on the bare ground in the wind of spring, had left him very fine-drawn, tuned and open to every sensation and impression. Rising, he saw that Kyo had wandered down to the lake-edge and was standing there, a slight figure no taller than the reeds that grew far out into the water. He was looking up at the mountains that towered gray across the south, gathering around their high heads all the clouds and silence of the sky. Rocannon, coming up beside him, saw in his face a look both desolate and eager. He said without turning, in his light hesitant voice, "Olhor, you have again the jewel."

"I keep trying to give it away," Rocannon said, grinning.

"Up there," the Fian said, "you must give more than gold and stones. . . . What will you give, Olhor, there in the cold, in the high place, the gray place? From the fire to the cold. . . ." Rocannon heard him, and watched him, yet did not see his lips move. A chill went through him and he closed his mind, retreating from the touch of a strange sense into his own humanity, his own identity. After a minute Kyo turned, calm and smiling as usual, and spoke in his usual voice. "There are Fiia beyond these foothills, beyond the forests, in green valleys. My people like the valleys, even here, the sunlight and the low places. We may find their villages in a few days' flight."

This was good news to the others when Rocannon reported it. "I thought we were going to find no speaking beings here. A fine, rich land to be so empty," Raho said.

Watching a pair of the dragonfly-like kilar dancing like

winged amethysts above the lake, Mogien said "It was not always empty. My people crossed it long ago, in the years before the heroes, before Hallan was built or high Oynhall, before Hendin struck the great stroke or Kirfiel died on Orren Hill. We came in boats with dragonheads from the south, and found in Angien a wild folk hiding in woods and sea-caves, a white-faced folk. You know the song, Yahan, the Lay of Orhogien—

> Riding the wind,
> walking the grass,
> skimming the sea,
> toward the star Brehen
> on Lioka's path . . .

Lioka's path is from the south to the north. And the battles in the song tell how we Angyar fought and conquered the wild hunters, the Olgyior, the only ones of our race in Angien; for we're all one race, the Liuar. But the song tells nothing of those mountains. It's an old song perhaps the beginning is lost. Or perhaps my people came from these foothills. This is a fair country—woods for hunting and hills for herds and heights for fortresses. Yet no men seem to live here now. . . ."

Yahan did not play his silver-strung lyre that night; and they all slept uneasily, maybe because the windsteeds were gone, and the hills were so deathly still, as if no creature dared move at all by night.

Agreeing that their camp by the lake was too boggy, they moved on next day, taking it easy and stopping often to hunt and gather fresh herbs. At dusk they came to a hill the top of which was humped and dented, as if under the grass lay the foundations of a fallen building. Nothing was left, yet they could trace or guess where the flightcourt of a little fortress had been, in years so long gone no legend told of it. They camped there, where the windsteeds would find them readily when they returned.

Late in the long night Rocannon woke and sat up. No

moon but little Lioka shone, and the fire was out. They had set no watch. Mogien was standing about fifteen feet away, motionless, a tall vague form in the starlight. Rocannon sleepily watched him, wondering why his cloak made him look so tall and narrow-shouldered. That was not right. The Angyar cloak flared out at the shoulders like a pagoda-roof, and even without his cloak Mogien was notably broad across the chest. Why was he standing there so tall and stooped and lean?

The face turned slowly, and it was not Mogien's face.

"Who's that?" Rocannon asked, starting up, his voice thick in the dead silence. Beside him Raho sat up, looked around grabbed his bow and scrambled to his feet. Behind the tall figure something moved slightly—another like it. All around them, all over the grass-grown ruins in the starlight, stood tall, lean, silent forms, heavily cloaked, with bowed heads. By the cold fire only he and Raho stood.

"Lord Mogien!" Raho shouted.

No answer.

"Where is Mogien? What people are you? Speak—"

They made no answer, but they began slowly to move forward. Raho nocked an arrow. Still they said nothing. but all at once they expanded weirdly, their cloaks sweeping out on both sides, and attacked from all directions at once, coming in slow, high leaps, As Rocannon fought them he fought to waken from the dream—it must be a dream; their slowness, their silence, it was all unreal, and he could not feel them strike him. But he was wearing his suit. He heard Raho cry out desperately, "Mogien!" The attackers had forced Rocannon down by sheer weight and numbers, and then before he could struggle free again he was lifted up head downward, with a sweeping, sickening movement. As he writhed, trying to get loose from the many hands holding him, he saw starlit hills and woods swinging and rocking beneath him—far beneath. His head swam and he gripped with both hands onto the thin limbs of the creatures that had lifted him. They were all about

95

him, their hands holding him, the air full of black wings beating.

It went on and on, and still sometimes he struggled to wake up from this monotony of fear, the soft hissing voices about him, the multiple laboring wing-beats jolting him endlessly on. Then all at once the flight changed to a long slanting glide. The brightening east slid horribly by him, the ground tilted up at him, the many soft, strong hands holding him let go, and he fell. Unhurt, but too sick and dizzy to sit up, he lay sprawling and stared about him.

Under him was a pavement of level, polished tile. To left and right above him rose wall, silvery in the early light, high and straight and clean as if cut of steel. Behind him rose the huge dome of a building, and ahead, through a topless gateway, he saw a street of windowless silvery houses, perfectly aligned, all alike, a pure geometric perspective in the unshadowed clarity of dawn. It was a city, not a stone-age village or a bronze-age fortress but a great city, severe and grandiose, powerful and exact, the product of a high technology. Rocannon sat up, his head still swimming.

As the light grew he made out certain shapes in the dimness of the court, bundles of something; the end of one gleamed yellow. With a shock that broke his trance he saw the dark face under the shock of yellow hair. Mogien's eyes were open, staring at the sky, and did not blink.

All four of his companions lay the same, rigid, eyes open. Raho's face was hideously convulsed. Even Kyo, who had seemed invulnerable in his very fragility, lay still with his great eyes reflecting the pale sky.

Yet they breathed, in long, quiet breaths seconds apart; he put his ear to Mogien's chest and heard the heartbeat very faint and slow, as if from far away.

A sibilance in the air behind him made him cower down instinctively and hold as still as the paralyzed bodies around him. Hands tugged at his shoulders and legs. He was turned over, and lay looking up into a face; a large, long face, somber and beautiful. The dark head was hairless, lacking even eyebrows. Eyes of clear gold looked out between wide, lashless lids. The mouth, small and delicately carved, was closed. The soft, strong hands were at his jaw, forcing his own mouth open. Another tall form bent over him, and he coughed and choked as something was poured down his throat—warm water, sickly and stale. The two great beings let him go. He got to his feet, spitting, and said, "I'm all right, let me be!" But their backs were already turned. They were stooping over Yahan, one forcing open his jaws, the other pouring in a mouthful of water from a long, silvery vase.

They were very tall, very thin, semi-humanoid; hard and delicate, moving rather awkwardly and slowly on the ground, which was not their element. Narrow chests projected between the shoulder-muscles of long, soft wings that fell curving down their backs like gray capes. The legs were thin and short, and the dark, noble heads seemed stooped forward by the upward jut of the wingblades.

Rocannon's *Handbook* lay under the fog-bound waters of the channel, but his memory shouted at him: *High Intelligence Life Forms, Unconfirmed Species* ?4: *Large humanoids said to inhabit extensive towns* (?). And he had the luck to confirm it, to get the first sight of a new species, a new high culture, a new member for the League. The clean, precise beauty of the buildings, the impersonal charity of the two great angelic figures who brought water, their kingly silence, it all awed him. He had never seen a race like this on any world. He came to the pair, who were giving Kyo water, and asked with diffident courtesy, "Do you speak the Common Tongue, winged lords?"

They did not heed him. They went quietly with their soft, slightly crippled ground-gait to Raho and forced water into his contorted mouth. It ran out again and down his cheeks. They moved on to Mogien, and Rocannon followed them. "Hear me!" he said, getting in front of them, but stopped: it came on him sickeningly that the wide golden eyes were blind, that they were blind and deaf. For they did not answer or glance at him, but walked

97

away, tall, aerial, the soft wings cloaking them from neck to heel. And the door fell softly to behind them.

Pulling himself together, Rocannon went to each of his companions, hoping an antidote to the paralysis might be working. There was no change. In each he confirmed the slow breath and faint heartbeat—in each except one. Raho's chest was still and his pitifully contorted face was cold. The water they had given him was still wet on his cheeks.

Anger broke through Rocannon's awed wonder. Why did the angel-men treat him and his friends like captured wild animals? He left his companions and strode across the court yard, out the topless gate into the street of the incredible city.

Nothing moved. All doors were shut. Tall and windowless, one after another, the silvery facades stood silent in the first light of the sun.

Rocannon counted six crossings before he came to the street's end: a wall. Five meters high it ran in both directions without a break; he did not follow the circumferential street to seek a gate, guessing there was none. What need had winged beings for city gates? He returned up the radial street to the central building from which he had come, the only building in the city different from and higher than the high silvery houses in their geometric rows. He reëntered the courtyard. The houses were all shut, the streets clean and empty, the sky empty, and there was no noise but that of his steps.

He hammered on the door at the inner end of the court. No response. He pushed, and it swung open.

Within was a warm darkness, a soft hissing and stirring, a sense of height and vastness. A tall form lurched past him, stopped and stood still. In the shaft of low early sunlight he had let in the door, Rocannon saw the winged being's yellow eyes close and reopen slowly. It was the sunlight that blinded them. They must fly abroad, and walk their silver streets, only in the dark.

Facing that unfathomable gaze, Rocannon took the attitude that hilfers called "GCO" for Generalised Communications Opener, a dramatic, receptive pose, and asked in Galactic, "Who is your leader?" Spoken impressively, the question usually got some response. None this time. The Winged One gazed straight at Rocannon, blinked once with an impassivity beyond disdain, shut his eyes, and stood there to all appearances sound asleep.

Rocannon's eyes had eased to the near-darkness, and he now saw, stretching off into the warm gloom under the vaults, rows and clumps and knots of the winged figures, hundreds of them, all unmoving, eyes shut.

He walked among them and they did not move.

Long ago, on Davenant, the planet of his birth, he had walked through a museum full of statues, a child looking up into the unmoving faces of the ancient Hainish gods.

Summoning his courage, he went up to one and touched him—her? they could as well be females—on the arm. The golden eyes opened, and the beautiful face turned to him, dark above him in the gloom. "Hassa!" said the Winged One, and, stooping quickly, kissed his shoulder, then took three steps away, refolded its cape of wings and stood still, eyes shut.

Rocannon gave them up and went on, groping his way through the peaceful, honeyed dusk of the huge room till he found a farther doorway, open from floor to lofty ceiling. The area beyond it was a little brighter, tiny roof holes allowing a dust of golden light to sift down. The walls curved away on either hand, rising to a narrow arched vault. It seemed to be a circular passage-room surrounding the central dome, the heart of the radial city. The inner wall was wonderfully decorated with a patter of intricately linked triangles and hexagons repeated clear up to the vault. Rocannon's puzzled ethnological enthusiasm revived. These people were master builders. Every surface in the vast building was smooth and every joint precise; the conception was splendid and the execution faultless. Only a high culture could have achieved this. But never had he met a highly-cultured race so unresponsive. After all, why had they brought him and the others here? Had they, in their silent angelic arrogance, saved the wanderers from some danger of the night? Or did they use other species as slaves? If so, it was queer how they had ignored his apparent immunity to their paralyzing agent. Perhaps they communicated entirely without words; but he inclined to believe, in this unbelievable palace, that the explanations might lie in the fact of an intelligence that was simply outside human scope. He went on, finding in the inner wall of the torus-passage a third door, this time very low, so that he had to stoop, and a Winged One must have to crawl.

Inside was the same warm, yellowish, sweet-smelling gloom, but here stirring, muttering, susurrating with a steady soft murmur of voices and slight motions of innumerable bodies and dragging wings. The eye of the dome, far up, was golden. A long ramp spiraled at a gentle slant around the wall clear up to the drum of the dome. Here and there on the ramp movement was visible, and twice a figure, tiny from below, spread its wings and flew soundlessly across the great cylinder of dusty golden air. As he started across the hall to the foot of the ramp, something fell from midway up the spiral, landing with a hard dry crack. He passed close by it. It was the corpse of one of the Winged Ones. Though the impact had smashed the skull, no blood was to be seen. The body was small, the wings apparently not fully formed.

He went doggedly on and started up the ramp.

Ten meters or so above the floor he came to a triangular niche in the wall in which Winged Ones crouched, again short and small ones, with wrinkled wings. There were nine of them, grouped regularly, three and three and three at even intervals, around a large pale bulk that Rocannon peered at a while before he made out the muzzle and the open, empty eyes. It was a windsteed, alive, paralyzed. The little delicately carved mouths of nine Winged Ones bent to it again and again, kissing it, kissing it.

Another crash on the floor across the hall. This Rocannon glanced at as he passed at a quiet run. It was the drained withered body of a barilo.

He crossed the high ornate torus-passage and threaded his way as quickly and softly as he could among the sleep-standing figures in the hall. He came out into the court-yard. It was empty. Slanting white sunlight shone on the pavement. His companions were gone. They had been dragged away from the larvae, there in the domed hall, to suck dry.

VII

ROCANNON'S KNEES gave way. He sat down on the polished red pavement, and tried to repress his sick fear enough to think what to do. What to do. He must go back into the dome and try to bring out Mogien and Yahan and Kyo. At the thought of going back in there among the tall angelic figures whose noble heads held brains degenerated or specialized to the level of insects, he felt a cold prickling at the back of his neck; but he had to do it. His friends were in there and he had to get them out. Were the larvae and their nurses in the dome sleepy enough to let him? He quit asking himself questions. But first he must check the outer wall all the way around, for if there was no gate, there was no use. He could not carry his friends over a fifteen-foot wall.

There were probably three castes, he thought as he went down the silent perfect street: nurses for the larvae in the dome, builders and hunters in the outer rooms, and in these houses perhaps the fertile ones, the egglayers and hatchers. The two that had given water would be nurses, keeping the paralyzed prey alive till the larvae sucked it dry. They had given water to dead Raho. How could he not have seen that they were mindless? He had wanted to think them intelligent because they looked so angelically human. *Strike Species* ?4, he told his drowned *Handbook,* savagely. Just then, something dashed across the street at the next crossing—a low, brown creature, whether large or small he could not tell in the unreal perspective of identical housefronts. It clearly was no part of the city. At least the angel-insects had vermin infesting their fine hive. He went on quickly and steadily through the utter

102

silence, reached the outer wall, and turned left along it.

A little way ahead of him, close to the jointless silvery base of the wall, crouched one of the brown animals. On all fours it came no higher than his knee. Unlike most low-intelligence animals on this planet, it was wingless. It crouched there looking terrified, and he simply detoured around it, trying not to frighten it into defiance, and went on. As far as he could see ahead there was no gate in the curving wall.

"Lord," cried a faint voice from nowhere. "Lord!"

"Kyo!" he shouted, turning, his voice clapping off the walls. Nothing moved. White walls, black shadows, straight lines, silence.

The little brown animal came hopping toward him. "Lord," it cried thinly, "Lord, O come, come. O come, Lord!"

Rocannon stood staring. The little creature sat down on its strong haunches in front of him. It panted, and its heartbeat shook its furry chest, against which tiny black hands were folded. Black, terrified eyes looked up at him. It repeated in quavering Common Speech, "Lord . . ."

Rocannon knelt. His thoughts raced as he regarded the creature; at last he said very gently, "I do not know what to call you."

"O come," said the little creature, quavering. "Lords—lords. Come!"

"The other lords—my friends?"

"Friends," said the brown creature. "Friends. Castle. Lords, castle, fire, windsteed, day, night, fire. O come!"

"I'll come," said Rocannon.

It hopped off at once, and he followed. Back down the radial street it went, then one side-street to the north, and in one of the twelve gates of the dome. There in the red-paved court lay his four companions as he had left them. Later on, when he had time to think, he realized that he had come out from the dome into a different courtyard and so missed them.

Five more of the brown creatures waited there, in a

rather ceremonious group near Yahan. Rocannon knelt again to minimize his height and made as good a bow as he could. "Hail, small lords," he said.

"Hail, hail," said all the furry little people. Then one, whose fur was black around the muzzle, said, "Kiemhrir."

"You are the Kiemhrir?" They bowed in quick imitation of his bow. "I am Rokanan Olhor. We come from the north, from Angien, from Hallan Castle."

"Castle," said Blackface. His tiny piping voice trembled with earnestness. He pondered, scratched his head. "Days, night, years, years," he said. "Lords go. Years, years, years. . . Kiemhrir ungo." He looked hopefully at Rocannon.

"The Kiemhrir . . . stayed here?" Rocannon asked.

"Stay!" cried Blackface with surprising volume. "Stay! Stay!" And the others all murmured as if in delight, "Stay. . ."

"Day," Blackface said decisively, pointing up at this day's sun, "lords come. Go?"

"Yes, we would go. Can you help us?"

"Help!" said the Kiemher, latching onto the word in the same delighted, avid way. "Help go. Lord, stay!"

So Rocannon stayed: sat and watched the Kiemhrir go to work. Blackface whistled, and soon about a dozen more came cautiously hopping in. Rocannon wondered where in the mathematical neatness of the hive-city they found places to hide and live; but plainly they did, and had storerooms too, for one came carrying in its little black hands a white spheroid that looked very like an egg. It was an eggshell used as a vial; Blackface took it and carefully loosened its top. In it was a thick, clear fluid. He spread a little of this on the puncture-wounds in the shoulders of the unconscious men; then, while others tenderly and fearfully lifted the men's heads, he poured a little of the fluid in their mouths. Raho he did not touch. The Kiemhrir did not speak among themselves, using only whistles and gestures, very quiet and with a touching air of courtesy.

104

Blackface came over to Rocannon and said reassuringly, "Lord, stay."

"Wait? Surely."

"Lord," said the Kiemher with a gesture towards Raho's body, and then stopped.

"Dead," Rocannon said.

"Dead, dead," said the little creature. He touched the base of his neck, and Rocannon nodded.

The silver-walled court brimmed with hot light. Yahan, lying near Rocannon, drew a long breath.

The Kiemhrir sat on their haunches in a half-circle behind their leader. To him Rocannon said, "Small lord, may I know your name?"

"Name," the black-faced one whispered. The others all were very still. "Liuar," he said, the old word Mogien had used to mean both nobles and midmen, or what the *Handbook* called Species II. "Liuar, Fiia, Gdemiar: names. Kiemhrir: unname."

Rocannon nodded, wondering what might be implied here. The word "kiemher, kiemhrir" was in fact, he realized, only an adjective, meaning lithe or swift.

Behind him Kyo caught his breath, stirred, sat up. Rocannon went to him. The little nameless people watched with their black eyes, attentive and quiet. Yahan roused, then finally Mogien, who must have got a heavy dose of the paralytic agent, for he could not even lift his hand at first. One of the Kiemhrir shyly showed Rocannon that he could do good by rubbing Mogien's arms and legs, which he did, meanwhile explaining what had happened and where they were.

"The tapestry," Mogien whispered.

"What's that?" Rocannon asked him gently, thinking he was still confused, and the young man whispered.

"The tapestry, at home—the winged giants."

Then Rocannon remembered how he had stood with Haldre beneath a woven picture of fair-haired warriors fighting winged figures, in the Long Hall of Hallan.

Kyo, who had been watching the Kiemhrir, held out his hand. Blackface hopped up to him and put his tiny, black, thumbless hand on Kyo's long, slender palm.

"Wordmasters," said the Fian softly. "Wordlovers, the eaters of words, the nameless ones, the lithe ones, long remembering. Still you remember the words of the Tall People, O Kiemhrir?"

"Still," said Blackface.

With Rocannon's help Mogien got to his feet, looking gaunt and stern. He stood a while beside Raho, whose face was terrible in the strong white sunlight. Then he greeted the Kiemhrir, and said, answering Rocannon, that he was all right again.

"If there are no gates, we can cut footholds and climb," Rocannon said.

"Whistle for the steeds, Lord," mumbled Yahan.

The question whether the whistle might wake the creatures in the dome was too complex to put across to the Kiemhrir. Since the Winged Ones seemed entirely nocturnal, they opted to take the chance. Mogien drew a little pipe on a chain from under his cloak, and blew a blast on it that Rocannon could not hear, but that made the Kiemhrir flinch. Within twenty minutes a great shadow shot over the dome, wheeled, darted off north, and before long returned with a companion. Both dropped with a mighty fanning of wings into the courtyard: the striped windsteed and Mogien's gray. The white one they never saw again. It might have been the one Rocannon had seen on the ramp in the musty, golden dusk of the dome, food for the larvae of the angels.

The Kiemhrir were afraid of the steeds. Blackface's gentle miniature courtesy was almost lost in barely controlled panic when Rocannon tried to thank him and bid him farewell. "O fly, Lord!" he said piteously, edging away from the great, taloned feet of the windsteeds; so they lost no time in going.

An hour's windride from the hive-city their packs and the spare cloaks and furs they used for bedding, lay

106

untouched beside the ashes of last night's fire. Partway down the hill lay three Winged Ones dead, and near them both Mogien's swords, one of them snapped off near the hilt. Mogien had waked to see the Winged Ones stooping over Yahan and Kyo. One of them had bitten him, "and I could not speak," he said. But he had fought and killed three before the paralysis brought him down. "I heard Raho call. He called to me three times, and I could not help him." He sat among the grassgrown ruins that had outlived all names and legends, his broken sword on his knees, and said nothing else.

They built up a pyre of branches and brushwood, and on it laid Raho, whom they had borne from the city, and beside him his hunting-bow and arrows. Yahan made a new fire, and Mogien set the wood alight. They mounted the windsteeds, Kyo behind Mogien and Yahan behind Rocannon, and rose spiraling around the smoke and heat of the fire that blazed in the sunlight of noon on a hilltop in the strange land.

For a long time they could see the thin pillar of smoke behind them as they flew.

The Kiemhrir had made it clear that they must move on, and keep under cover at night, or the Winged Ones would be after them again in the dark. So toward evening they came down to a stream in a deep, wooded gorge, making camp within earshot of a waterfall. It was damp, but the air was fragrant and musical, relaxing their spirits. They found a delicacy for dinner, a certain shelly, slow-moving water animal very good to eat; but Rocannon could not eat them. There was vestigial fur between the joints and on the tail; they were ovipoid mammals, like many animals here, like the Kiemhrir probably. "You eat them, Yahan. I can't shell something that might speak to me," he said, wrathful with hunger, and came to sit beside Kyo.

Kyo smiled, rubbing his sore shoulder. "If all things could be heard speaking . . ."

"I for one would starve."

"Well, the green creatures are silent," said the Fian,

patting a rough-trunked tree that leaned across the stream. Here in the south the trees, all conifers, were coming into bloom, and the forests were dusty and sweet with drifting pollen. All flowers here gave their pollen to the wind, grasses and conifers: there were no insects, no petaled flowers. Spring on the unnamed world was all in green, dark green and pale green, with great drifts of golden pollen.

Mogien and Yahan went to sleep as it grew dark, stretched out by the warm ashes; they kept no fire lest it draw the Winged Ones. As Rocannon had guessed, Kyo was tougher than the men when it came to poisons; he sat and talked with Rocannon, down on the streambank in the dark.

"You greeted the Kiemhrir as if you knew of them," Rocannon observed, and the Fian answered:

"What one of us in my village remembered, all remembered, Olhor. So many tales and whispers and lies and truths are known to us, and who knows how old some are. . . ."

"Yet you knew nothing of the Winged Ones?"

It looked as if Kyo would pass this one, but at last he said, "The Fiia have no memory for fear, Olhor. How should we? We chose. Night and caves and swords of metal we left to the Clayfolk, when our way parted from theirs, and we chose the green valleys, the sunlight, the bowl of wood. And therefore we are the Half-People. And we have forgotten, we have forgotten much!" His light voice was more decisive, more urgent this night than ever before, sounding clear through the noise of the stream below them and the noise of the falls at the head of the gorge. "Each day as we travel southward I ride into the tales that my people learn as little children, in the valleys of Angien. And all the tales I find true. But half of them all we have forgotten. The little Name-Eaters, the Kiemhrir, these are in old songs we sing from mind to mind; but not the Winged Ones. The friends, but not the enemies. The sunlight, not the dark. And I am the companion of Olhor who goes southward into the legends, bearing no sword. I ride with Olhor, who seeks to hear his enemy's voice, who has traveled through the great dark, who has seen the World hang like a blue jewel in the darkness. I am only a half-person. I cannot go farther than the hills. I cannot go into the high places with you, Olhor!"

Rocannon put his hand very lightly on Kyo's shoulder. At once the Fian fell still. They sat hearing the sound of the stream, of the falls in the night, and watching starlight gleam gray on water that ran, under drifts and whorls of blown pollen, icy cold from the mountains to the south.

Twice during the next day's flight they saw far to the east the domes and spoked streets of hive-cities. That night they kept double watch. By the next night they were high up in the hills, and a lashing cold rain beat at them all night long and all the next day as they flew. When the rain-clouds parted a little there were mountains looming over the hills now on both sides. One more rain-sodden, watch-broken night went by on the hilltops under the ruin of an ancient tower, and then in early afternoon of the next day they came down the far side of the pass into sunlight and a broad valley leading off southward into misty, mountain-fringed distances.

To their right now while they flew down the valley as if it were a great green roadway, the white peaks stood serried, remote and huge. The wind was keen and golden, and the windsteeds raced down it like blown leaves in the sunlight. Over the soft green concave below them, on which darker clumps of shrubs and trees seemed enameled, drifted a narrow veil of gray. Mogien's mount came circling back, Kyo pointing down, and they rode down the golden wind to the village that lay between hill and stream, sunlit, its small chimneys smoking. A herd of herilor grazed the slopes above it. In the center of the scattered circle of little houses, all stilts and screens and sunny porches, towered five great trees. By these the travelers landed, and the Fiia came to meet them, shy and laughing. These villagers spoke little of the Common Tongue, and were unused to speaking aloud at all. Yet it was like a homecoming to enter their airy houses, to eat from bowls of polished wood, to take refuge from wilderness and weather for one evening in their blithe hospitality. A strange little people, tangential, gracious, elusive: the Half-People, Kyo had called his own kind. Yet Kyo himself was no longer quite one of them. Though in the fresh clothing they gave him he looked like them, moved and gestured like them, in the group of them he stood out absolutely. Was it because as a stranger he could not freely mindspeak with them, or was it because he had. in this friendship with Rocannon, changed, having become another sort of being, more solitary, more sorrowful, more complete?

They could describe the lay of this land. Across the great range west of their valley was desert, they said; to continue south the travelers should follow the valley, keeping east of the mountains, a long way, until the range itself turned east. "Can we find passes across?" Mogien asked, and the little people smiled and said, "Surely, surely."

"And beyond the passes do you know what lies?"

"The passes are very high, very cold," said the Fiia, politely.

The travelers stayed two nights in the village to rest, and left with packs filled with waybread and dried meat given by the Fiia, who delighted in giving. After two days' flight they came to another village of the little folk, where they were again received with such friendliness that it might have been not a strangers' arrival, but a long-awaited return. As the steeds landed a group of Fian men and women came to meet them, greeting Rocannon, who was first to dismount, "Hail, Olhor!" It startled him, and still puzzled him a little after he thought that the word of course meant "wanderer," which he obviously was. Still, it was Kyo the Fian who had given him the name.

Later, farther down the valley after another long, calm

day's flight, he said to Kyo, "Among your people, Kyo, did you bear no name of your own?"

"They call me 'herdsman,' or 'younger brother,' or 'runner.' I was quick in our racing."

"But those are nicknames, descriptions—like Olhor or Kiemhrir. You're great namegivers, you Fiia. You greet each comer with a nickname, Starlord, Swordbearer, Sunhaired, Wordmaster—I think the Angyar learned their love of such nicknaming from you. And yet you have no names."

"Starlord, far-traveled, ashen-haired, jewel-bearer," said Kyo, smiling;—"what then is a name?"

"Ashen-haired? Have I turned gray?—I'm not sure what a name is. My name given me at birth was Gaverel Rocannon. When I've said that, I've described nothing, yet I've named myself. And when I see a new kind of tree in this land I ask you—or Yahan and Mogien, since you seldom answer—what its name it. It troubles me, until I know its name."

"Well, it is a tree; as I am a Fian; as you are a . . . what?"

"But there are distinctions, Kyo! At each village here I ask what are those western mountains called, the range that towers over their lives from birth to death, and they say, 'Those are mountains, Olhor.' "

"So they are," said Kyo.

"But there are other mountains—the lower range to the east, along this same valley! How do you know one range from another, one being from another, without names?

Clasping his knees, the Fian gazed at the sunset peaks burning high in the west. After a while Rocannon realized that he was not going to answer.

The winds grew warmer and the long days longer as warmyear advanced and they went each day farther south. As the windsteeds were double-loaded they did not push on fast, stopping often for a day or two to hunt and to let the steeds hunt; but at last they saw the mountains curving around in front of them to meet the coastal range to the

111

east, barring their way. The green of the valley ran up the knees of huge hills, and ceased. Much higher lay patches of green and brown-green, alpine valleys; then the gray of rock and talus; and finally, halfway up the sky, the luminous storm-ridden white of the peaks.

They came, high up in the hills, to a Fian village. Wind blew chill from the peaks across frail roofs, scattering blue smoke among the long evening light and shadows. As ever they were received with cheerful grace, given water and fresh meat and herbs in bowls of wood, in the warmth of a house, while their dusty clothes were cleaned, and their windsteeds fed and petted by tiny, quicksilver children. After supper four girls of the village danced for them, without music, their movements and footfalls so light and swift that they seemed bodiless, a play of light and dark in the glow of the fire, elusive, fleeting. Rocannon glanced with a smile of pleasure at Kyo, who as usual sat beside him. The Fian returned his look gravely and spoke: "I shall stay here, Olhor."

Rocannon checked his startled reply and for a while longer watched the dancers, the changing unsubstantial patterns of firelit forms in motion. They wove a music from silence, and a strangeness in the mind. The firelight on the wooden walls bowed and flickered and changed.

"It was foretold that the Wanderer would choose companions. For a while."

He did not know if he had spoken, or Kyo, or his memory. The words were in his mind and in Kyo's. The dancers broke apart, their shadows running quickly up the walls, the loosened hair of one swinging bright for a moment. The dance that had no music was ended, the dancers that had no more name than light and shadow were still. So between him and Kyo a pattern had come to its end, leaving quietness.

VIII

BELOW HIS WINDSTEED'S heavily beating wings Rocannon saw a slope of broken rock, a slanting chaos of boulders running down behind, tilted up ahead so that the steed's left wingtip almost brushed the rocks as it labored up and forward towards the col. He wore the battle-straps over his thighs, for updrafts and gusts sometimes blew the steeds off balance, and he wore his impermasuit for warmth. Riding behind him, wrapped in all the cloaks and furs the two of them had, Yahan was still so cold that he had strapped his wrists to the saddle, unable to trust his grip. Mogien, riding well ahead on his less burdened steed, bore the cold and altitude much better than Yahan, and met their battle with the heights with a harsh joy.

Fifteen days ago they had left the last Fian village, bidding farewell to Kyo, and set out over the foothills and lower ranges for what looked like the widest pass. The Fiia could give them no directions; at any mention of crossing the mountains they had fallen silent, with a cowering look.

The first days had gone well, but as they got high up the windsteeds began to tire quickly, the thinner air not supplying them with the rich oxygen intake they burned while flying. Higher still they met the cold and the treacherous weather of high altitudes. In the last three days they had covered perhaps fifteen kilometers, most of that distance on a blind lead. The men went hungry to give the steeds an extra ration of dried meat; this morning Rocannon had let them finish what was left in the sack, for if they did not get across the pass today they would have to drop back down to woodlands where they could hunt and rest, and start all over. They seemed now on the right way toward a

113

pass, but from the peaks to the east a terrible thin wind blew, and the sky was getting white and heavy. Still Mogien flew ahead, and Rocannon forced his mount to follow; for in this endless cruel passage of the great heights, Mogien was his leader and he followed. He had forgotten why he wanted to cross these mountains, remembering only that he had to, that he must go south. But for the courage to do it, he depended on Mogien. "I think this is your domain," he had said to the young man last evening when they had discussed their present course; and, looking out over the great, cold view of peak and abyss, rock and snow and sky, Mogien had answered with his quick lordly certainty, "This is my domain."

He was calling now, and Rocannon tried to encourage his steed, while he peered ahead through frozen lashes seeking a break in the endless slanting chaos. There it was, an angle, a jutting roofbeam of the planet: the slope of rock fell suddenly away and under them lay a waste of white, the pass. On either side wind-scoured peaks reared on up into the thickening snowclouds. Rocannon was close enough to see Mogien's untroubled face and hear his shout, the falsetto battle-yell of the victorious warrior. He kept following Mogien over the white valley under the white clouds. Snow began to dance about them, not falling, only dancing here in its habitat, its birthplace, a dry flickering dance. Half-starved and overladen, the wind-steed gasped at each lift and downbeat of its great barred wings. Mogien had dropped back so they would not lose him in the snowclouds, but still kept on, and they followed.

There was a glow in the flickering mist of snowflakes, and gradually there dawned a thin, clear radiance of gold. Pale gold, the sheer fields of snow reached downward. Then abruptly the world fell away, and the windsteeds floundered in a vast gulf of air. Far beneath, very far, clear and small, lay valleys, lakes, the glittering tongue of a glacier, green patches of forest. Rocannon's mount floundered and dropped, its wings raised, dropped like a stone so that

114

Yahan cried out in terror and Rocannon shut his eyes and held on.

The wings beat and thundered, beat again; the falling slowed, became again a laboring glide, and halted. The steed crouched trembling in a rocky valley. Nearby Mogien's gray beast was trying to lie down while Mogien, laughing, jumped off its back and called, "We're over, we did it!" He came up to them, his dark, vivid face bright with triumph. "Now both sides of the mountains are my domain, Rokanan! . . . This will do for our camp tonight. Tomorrow the steeds can hunt, farther down where trees grow, and we'll work down on foot. Come, Yahan."

Yahan crouched in the postillion-saddle, unable to move. Mogien lifted him from the saddle and helped him lie down in the shelter of a jutting boulder; for though the late afternoon sun shone here, it gave little more warmth than did the Greatstar, a tiny crumb of crystal in the southwestern sky; and the wind still blew bitter cold. While Rocannon unharnessed the steeds, the Angyar lord tried to help his servant, doing what he could to get him warm. There was nothing to build a fire with—they were still far above timberline. Rocannon stripped off the impermasuit and made Yahan put it on, ignoring the midman's weak and scared protests, then wrapped himself up in furs. The windsteeds and the men huddled together for mutual warmth, and shared a little water and Fian waybread. Night rose up from the vague lands below. Stars leaped out, released by darkness, and the two brighter moons shone within hand's reach.

Deep in the night Rocannon roused from blank sleep. Everything was starlit, silent, deathly cold. Yahan had hold of his arm and was whispering feverishly, shaking his arm and whispering. Rocannon looked where he pointed and saw standing on the boulder above them a shadow, an interruption in the stars.

Like the shadow he and Yahan had seen on the pampas, far back to northward, it was large and strangely vague. Even as he watched it the stars began to glimmer faintly

115

through the dark shape, and then there was no shadow, only black transparent air. To the left of where it had been Heliki shone, faint in its waning cycle.

"It was a trick of moonlight, Yahan," he whispered. "Go back to sleep, you've got a fever."

"No," said Mogien's quiet voice beside him. "It wasn't a trick, Rokanan. It was my death."

Yahan sat up, shaking with fever. "No, Lord! not yours; it couldn't be! I saw it before, on the plains when you weren't with us—so did Olhor!"

Summoning to his aid the last shreds of common sense, of scientific moderation, of the old life's rules, Rocannon tried to speak authoritatively: "Don't be absurd," he said.

Mogien paid no attention to him. "I saw it on the plains, where it was seeking me. And twice in the hills while we sought the pass. Whose death would it be if not mine? Yours, Yahan? Are you a lord, an Angya, do you wear the second sword?"

Sick and despairing, Yahan tried to plead with him, but Mogien went on, "It's not Rokanan's, for he still follows his way. A man can die anywhere, but his own death, his true death, a lord meets only in his domain. It waits for him in the place which is his, a battlefield or a hall or a road's ends. And this is my place. From these mountains my people came, and I have come back. My second sword was broken, fighting. But listen, my death: I am Halla's heir Mogien—do you know me now?"

The thin, frozen wind blew over the rocks. Stones loomed about them, stars glittering out beyond them. One of the windsteeds stirred and snarled.

"Be still," Rocannon said. "This is all foolishness. Be still and sleep. . . ."

But he could not sleep soundly after that, and whenever he roused he saw Mogien sitting by his steed's great flank, quiet and ready, watching over the night-darkened lands.

Come daylight they let the windsteeds free to hunt in the forests below, and started to work their way down on foot. They were still very high, far above timberline, and safe only so long as the weather held clear. But before they had gone an hour they saw Yahan could not make it; it was not a hard descent, but exposure and exhaustion had taken too much out of him and he could not keep walking, let alone scramble and cling as they sometimes must. Another day's rest in the protection of Rocannon's suit might give him the strength to go on; but that would mean another night up here without fire or shelter or enough food. Mogien weighed the risks without seeming to consider them at all, and suggested that Rocannon stay with Yahan on a sheltered and sunny ledge, while he sought a descent easy enough that they might carry Yahan down, or, failing that, a shelter that might keep off snow.

After he had gone, Yahan, lying in a half stupor, asked for water. Their flask was empty. Rocannon told him to lie still, and climbed up the slanting rockface to a boulder-shadowed ledge fifteen meters or so above, where he saw some packed snow glittering. The climb was rougher than he had judged, and he lay on the ledge gasping the bright, thin air, his heart going hard.

There was a noise in his ears which at first he took to be the singing of his own blood; then near his hand he saw water running. He sat up. A tiny stream, smoking as it ran, wound along the base of a drift of hard, shadowed snow. He looked for the stream's source and saw a dark gap under the overhanging cliff: a cave. A cave was their best hope of shelter, said his rational mind, but it spoke only on the very fringe of a dark non-rational rush of feeling—of panic. He sat there unmoving in the grip of the worst fear he had ever known.

All about him the unavailing sunlight shone on gray rock. The mountain peaks were hidden by the nearer cliffs, and the lands below to the south were hidden by unbroken cloud. There was nothing at all here on this bare gray ridgepole of the world but himself, and a dark opening between boulders.

After a long time he got to his feet, went forward stepping across the steaming rivulet, and spoke to the presence which he knew waited inside that shadowy gap. "I have come," he said.

The darkness moved a little, and the dweller in the cave stood at its mouth.

It was like the Clayfolk, dwarfish and pale; like the Fiia, frail and clear-eyed; like both, like neither. The hair was white. The voice was no voice, for it sounded within Rocannon's mind while all his ears heard was the faint whistle of the wind; and there were no words. Yet it asked him what he wished.

"I do not know," the man said aloud in terror, but his set will answered silently for him: *I will go south and find my enemy and destroy him.*

The wind blew whistling; the warm stream chuckled at his feet. Moving slowly and lightly, the dweller in the cave stood aside, and Rocannon, stooping down, entered the dark place.

What do you give for what I have given you?
What must I give, Ancient One?
That which you hold dearest and would least willingly give.
I have nothing of my own on this world. What thing can I give?
A thing, a life, a chance; an eye, a hope, a return: the name need not be known. But you will cry its name aloud when it is gone. Do you give it freely?
Freely, Ancient One.

Silence and the blowing of wind. Rocannon bowed his head and came out of the darkness. As he straightened up red light struck full in his eyes, a cold red sunrise over a gray-and-scarlet sea of cloud.

Yahan and Mogien slept huddled together on the lower ledge, a heap of furs and cloaks, unstirring as Rocannon climbed down to them. "Wake up," he said softly. Yahan sat up, his face pinched and childish in the hard red dawn.

"Olhor! We thought—you were gone—we thought you had fallen—"

Mogien shook his yellow-maned head to clear it of sleep, and looked up a minute at Rocannon. Then he said hoarsely and gently, "Welcome back, Starlord, companion. We waited here for you."

"I met . . . I spoke with . . ."

Mogien raised his hand. "You have come back; I rejoice in your return. Do we go south?"

"Yes."

"Good," said Mogien. In that moment it was not strange to Rocannon that Mogien, who for so long had seemed his leader, now spoke to him as a lesser to a greater lord.

Mogien blew his whistle, but though they waited long the windsteeds did not come. They finished the last of the hard, nourishing Fian bread, and set off once more on foot. The warmth of the impermasuit had done Yahan good, and Rocannon insisted he keep it on. The young midman needed food and real rest to get his strength back, but he could get on now, and they had to get on; behind that red sunrise would come heavy weather. It was not dangerous going, but slow and wearisome. Midway in the morning one of the steeds appeared: Mogien's gray, flitting up from the forests far below. They loaded it with the saddles and harness and furs—all they carried now—and it flew along above or below or beside them as it pleased, sometimes letting out a ringing yowl as if to call its striped mate, still hunting or feasting down in the forests.

About noon they came to a hard stretch: a cliff-face sticking out like a shield, over which they would have to crawl roped together. "From the air you might see a better path for us to follow, Mogien," Rocannon suggested. "I wish the other steed would come." He had a sense of urgency; he wanted to be off this bare gray mountainside and be hidden down among trees.

"The beast was tired out when we let it go; it may not have made a kill yet. This one carried less weight over the

119

pass. I'll see how wide this cliff is. Perhaps my steed can carry all three of us for a few bowshots." He whistled and the gray steed, with the loyal obedience that still amazed Rocannon in a beast so large and so carnivorous, wheeled around in the air and came looping gracefully up to the cliffside where they waited. Mogien swung up on it and with a shout sailed off, his bright hair catching the last shaft of sunlight that broke through thickening banks of cloud.

Still the thin, cold wind blew. Yahan crouched back in an angle of rock, his eyes closed. Rocannon sat looking out into the distance at the remotest edge of which could be sensed the fading brightness of the sea. He did not scan the immense, vague landscape that came and went between drifting clouds, but gazed at one point, south and a little east, one place. He shut his eyes. He listened, and heard.

It was a strange gift he had got from the dweller in the cave, the guardian of the warm well in the unnamed mountains; a gift that went all against his grain to ask. There in the dark by the deep warm spring he had been taught a skill of the senses that his race and the men of Earth had witnessed and studied in other races, but to which they were deaf and blind, save for brief glimpses and rare exceptions. Clinging to his humanity, he had drawn back from the totality of the power that the guardian of the well possessed and offered. He had learned to listen to the minds of one race, one kind of creature, among all the voices of all the worlds one voice: that of his enemy.

With Kyo he had had some beginnings of mindspeech; but he did not want to know his companions' minds when they were ignorant of his. Understanding must be mutual, when loyalty was, and love.

But those who had killed his friends and broken the bond of peace he spied upon, he overheard. He sat on the granite spur of a trackless mountain-peak and listened to the thoughts of men in buildings among rolling hills thousands of meters below and a hundred kilometers away. A dim chatter, a buzz and babble and confusion, a remote roil and storming of sensations and emotions. He did not know how to select voice from voice, and was dizzy among a hundred different places and positions; he listened as a young infant listens, undiscriminating. Those born with eyes and ears must learn to see and hear, to pick out a face from a double eyeful of upside-down world, to select meaning from a welter of noise. The guardian of the well had the gift, which Rocannon had only heard rumor of on one other planet, of unsealing the telepathic sense; and he had taught Rocannon how to limit and direct it, but there had been no time to learn its use, its practice. Rocannon's head spun with the impingement of alien thoughts and feelings, a thousand strangers crowded in his skull. No words came through. Mindhearing was the word the Angyar, the outsiders, used for the sense. What he "heard" was not speech but intentions, desires, emotions, the physical locations and sensual-mental directions of many different men jumbling and overlapping through his own nervous system, terrible gusts of fear and jealousy, drifts of contentment, abysses of sleep, a wild racking vertigo of half-understanding, half-sensation. And all at once out of the chaos something stood absolutely clear, a contact more definite than a hand laid on his naked flesh. Someone was coming toward him: a man whose mind had sensed his own. With this certainty came lesser impressions of speed, of confinement; of curiosity and fear.

Rocannon opened his eyes, staring ahead as if he would see before him the face of that man whose being he had sensed. He was close; Rocannon was sure he was close, and coming closer. But there was nothing to see but air and lowering clouds. A few dry, small flakes of snow whirled in the wind. To his left bulked the great bosse of rock that blocked their way. Yahan had come out beside him and was watching him, with a scared look. But he could not reassure Yahan, for that presence tugged at him

121

and he could not break the contact. "There is . . . there is a . . . an airship," he muttered thickly, like a sleeptalker. "There!"

There was nothing where he pointed; air, cloud.

"There," Rocannon whispered.

Yahan, looking again where he pointed, gave a cry. Mogien on the gray steed was riding the wind well out from the cliff; and beyond him, far out in a scud of cloud, a larger black shape had suddenly appeared, seeming to hover or to move very slowly. Mogien flashed on downwind without seeing it, his face turned to the mountain wall looking for his companions, two tiny figures on a tiny ledge in the sweep of rock and cloud.

The black shape grew larger, moving in, its vanes clacking and hammering in the silence of the heights. Rocannon saw it less clearly than he sensed the man inside it, the uncomprehending touch of mind on mind, the intense defiant fear. He whispered to Yahan, "Take cover!" but could not move himself. The helicopter nosed in unsteadily, rags of cloud catching in its whirring vanes. Even as he watched it approach, Rocannon watched from inside it, not knowing what he looked for, seeing two small figures on the mountainside, afraid, afraid—A flash of light, a hot shock of pain, pain in his own flesh, intolerable. The mind-contact was broken, blown clean away. He was himself, standing on the ledge pressing his right hand against his chest and gasping, seeing the helicopter creep still closer, its vanes whirring with a dry loud rattle, its laser-mounted nose pointing at him.

From the right, from the chasm of air and cloud, shot a gray winged beast ridden by a man who shouted in a voice like a high, triumphant laugh. One beat of the wide gray wings drove steed and rider forward straight against the hovering machine, full speed, head on. There was a tearing sound like the edge of a great scream, and then the air was empty.

The two on the cliff crouched staring. No sound came up

122

from below. Clouds wreathed and drifted across the abyss.

"Mogien!"

Rocannon cried the name aloud. There was no answer. There was only pain, and fear, and silence.

IX

RAIN PATTERED HARD on a raftered roof. The air of the room was dark and clear.

Near his couch stood a woman whose face he knew, a proud, gentle, dark face crowned with gold.

He wanted to tell her that Mogien was dead, but he could not say the words. He lay there sorely puzzled, for now he recalled that Haldre of Hallan was an old woman, white-haired; and the golden-haired woman he had known was long dead; and anyway he had seen her only once, on a planet eight lightyears away, a long time ago when he had been a man named Rocannon.

He tried again to speak. She hushed him, saying in the Common Tongue though with some difference in sounds, "Be still, my lord." She stayed beside him, and presently told him in her soft voice, "This is Breygna Castle. You came here with another man, in the snow, from the heights of the mountains. You were near death and still are hurt. There will be time. . . ."

There was much time, and it slipped by vaguely, peacefully in the sound of the rain.

The next day or perhaps the next, Yahan came in to him, Yahan very thin, a little lame, his face scarred with frostbite. But a less understandable change in him was his manner, subdued and submissive. After they had talked a while Rocannon asked uncomfortably, "Are you afraid of me, Yahan?"

"I will try not to be, Lord," the young man stammered.

When he was able to go down to the Revelhall of the castle, the same awe or dread was in all faces that turned to him, though they were brave and genial faces. Gold-haired, dark-skinned, a tall people, the old stock of which the Angyar were only a tribe that long ago had wandered north by sea: these were the Liuar, the Earthlords, living since before the memory of any race here in the foothills of the mountains and the rolling plains to the south.

At first he thought that they were unnerved simply by his difference in looks, his dark hair and pale skin: but Yahan was colored like him, and they had no dread of Yahan. They treated him as a lord among lords, which was a joy and a bewilderment to the ex-serf of Hallan. But Rocannon they treated as a lord above lords, one set apart.

There was one who spoke to him as to a man. The Lady Ganye, daughter-in-law and heiress of the castle's old lord, had been a widow for some months; her bright-haired little son was with her most of the day. Though shy, the child had no fear of Rocannon, but was rather drawn to him, and liked to ask him questions about the mountains and the northern lands and the sea. Rocannon answered whatever he asked. The mother would listen, serene and gentle as the sunlight, sometimes turning smiling to Rocannon her face that he had remembered even as he had seen it for the first time.

He asked her at last what it was they thought of him in Breygna Castle, and she answered candidly, "They think you are a god."

It was the word he had noted long since in Tolen village, *pedan*.

"I'm not," he said, dour.

She laughed a little.

"Why do they think so?" he demanded. "Do the gods of the Liuar come with gray hair and crippled hands?" The laserbeam from the helicopter had caught him in the right wrist, and he had lost the use of his right hand almost entirely.

"Why not?" said Ganye with her proud, candid smile. "But the reason is that you came *down* the mountain."

He absorbed this a while. "Tell me, Lady Ganye, do you know of . . . the guardian of the well?"

125

At this her face was grave. "We know tales of that people only. It is very long, nine generations of the Lords of Breygna, since Iollt the Tall went up into the high places and came down changed. We knew you had met with them, with the Most Ancient."

"How do you know?"

"In your sleep in fever you spoke always of the price, of the cost, of the gift given and its price. Iollt paid too. . . . The cost was your right hand, Lord Olhor?" she asked with sudden timidity, raising her eyes to his.

"No. I would give both my hands to have saved what I lost."

He got up and went to the window of the tower-room, looking out on the spacious country between the mountains and the distant sea. Down from the high foothills where Breygna Castle stood wound a river, widening and shining among lower hills, vanishing into hazy reaches where one could half make out villages, fields, castle towers, and once again the gleam of the river among blue rainstorms and shafts of sunlight.

"This is the fairest land I ever saw," he said. He was still thinking of Mogien, who would never see it.

"It's not so fair to me as it once was."

"Why, Lady Ganye?"

"Because of the Strangers!"

"Tell me of them, Lady."

"They came here late last winter, many of them riding in great windships, armed with weapons that burn. No one can say what land they come from; there are no tales of them at all. All the land between Viarn River and the sea is theirs now. They killed or drove out all the people of eight domains. We in the hills here are prisoners; we dare not go down even to the old pasturelands with our herds. We fought the Strangers, at first. My husband Ganhing was killed by their burning weapons." Her gaze went for a second to Rocannon's seared, crippled hand; for a second she paused. "In . . . in the time of the first thaw he was killed, and still we have no revenge. We bow our heads and avoid

126

their lands, we the Earthlords! And there is no man to make these Strangers pay for Ganhing's death."

O lovely wrath, Rocannon thought, hearing the trumpets of lost Hallan in her voice. "They will pay, Lady Ganye; they will pay a high price. Though you knew I was no god, did you take me for quite a common man?"

"No, Lord," said she. "Not quite."

The days went by, the long days of the yearlong summer. The white slopes of the peaks above Breygna turned blue, the grain-crops in Breygna fields ripened, were cut and re-sown, and were ripening again when one afternoon Rocannon sat down by Yahan in the courtyard where a pair of young windsteeds were being trained. "I'm off again to the south, Yahan. You stay here."

"No, Olhor! Let me come—"

Yahan stopped, remembering perhaps that foggy beach where in his longing for adventures he had disobeyed Mogien. Rocannon grinned and said, "I'll do best alone. It won't take long, one way or the other."

"But I am your vowed servant, Olhor. Please let me come."

"Vows break when names are lost. You swore your service to Rokanan, on the other side of the mountains. In this land there are no serfs, and there is no man named Rokanan. I ask you as my friend, Yahan, to say no more to me or to anyone here, but saddle the steed of Hallan for me at daybreak tomorrow."

Loyally, next morning before sunrise Yahan stood waiting for him in the flightcourt, holding the bridle of the one remaining windsteed from Hallan, the gray striped one. It had made its way a few days after them to Breygna, half frozen and starving. It was sleek and full of spirit now, snarling and lashing its striped tail.

"Do you wear the Second Skin, Olhor?" Yahan asked in a whisper, fastening the battle-straps on Rocannon's legs. "They say the Strangers shoot fire at any man who rides near their lands."

"I'm wearing it."

"But no sword? . . ."

"No. No sword. Listen, Yahan, if I don't return, look in the wallet I left in my room. There's some cloth in it, with —with markings in it, and pictures of the land; if any of my people ever come here, give them those, will you? And also the necklace is there." His face darkened and he looked away a moment. "Give that to the Lady Ganye. If I don't come back to do it myself. Goodbye, Yahan; wish me good luck."

"May your enemy die without sons," Yahan said fiercely, in tears, and let the windsteed go. It shot up into the warm, uncolored sky of summer dawn, turned with a great rowing beat of wings, and, catching the north wind, vanished above the hills. Yahan stood watching. From a window high up in Breygna Tower a soft, dark face also watched, for a long time after it was out of sight and the sun had risen.

It was a queer journey Rocannon made, to a place he had never seen and yet knew inside and out with the varying impressions of hundreds of different minds. For though there was no seeing with the mind-sense, there was tactile sensation and perception of space and spatial relationships, of time, motion, and position. From attending to such sensations over and over for hours on end in a hundred days of practice as he sat moveless in his room in Breygna Castle, he had acquired an exact though unvisualized and unverbalized knowledge of every building and area of the enemy base. And from direct sensation and extrapolation from it, he knew what the base was, and why it was here, and how to enter it, and where to find what he wanted from it.

But it was very hard, after the long intense practice, *not* to use the mind-sense as he approached his enemies: to cut it off, deaden it, using only his eyes and ears and intellect. The incident on the mountainside had warned him that at close range sensitive individuals might become aware of his presence, though in a vague way, as a hunch or premonition. He had drawn the helicopter pilot to the mountain like a fish on a line, though the pilot probably had never understood what had made him fly that way or why he had felt compelled to fire on the men he found. Now, entering the huge base alone, Rocannon did not want any attention drawn to himself, none at all, for he came as a thief in the night.

At sunset he had left his windsteed tethered in a hillside clearing, and now after several hours of walking was approaching a group of buildings across a vast, blank plain of cement, the rocket-field. There was only one field and seldom used, now that all men and materiel were here. War was not waged with lightspeed rockets when the nearest civilized planet was eight lightyears away.

The base was large, terrifyingly large when seen with one's own eyes, but most of the land and buildings went to housing men. The rebels now had almost their whole army here. While the League wasted its time searching and subduing their home planet, they were staking their gamble on the very high probability of their not being found on this one nameless world among all the worlds of the galaxy. Rocannon knew that some of the giant barracks were empty again; a contingent of soldiers and technicians had been sent out some days ago to take over, as he guessed, a planet they had conquered or had persuaded to join them as allies. Those soldiers would not arrive at that world for almost ten years. The Faradayans were very sure of themselves. They must be doing well in their war. All they had needed to wreck the safety of the League of All Worlds was a well-hidden base, and their six mighty weapons.

He had chosen a night when of all four moons only the little captured asteroid, Heliki, would be in the sky before midnight. It brightened over the hills as he neared a row of hangars, like a black reef on the gray sea of cement, but no one saw him, and he sensed no one near. There were no fences and few guards. Their watch was kept by machines that scanned space for lightyears around the Fomalhaut system. What had they to fear, after all, from the Bronze Age aborigines of the little nameless planet?

Heliki shone at its brightest as Rocannon left the shadow of the row of hangars. It was halfway through its waning cycle when he reached his goal: the six FTL ships. They sat like six immense ebony eggs side by side under a vague, high canopy, a camouflage net. Around the ships, looking like toys, stood a scattering of trees, the edge of Viarn Forest.

Now he had to use his mindhearing, safe or not. In the shadow of a group of trees he stood still and very cautiously, trying to keep his eyes and ears alert at the same time, reached out toward the ovoid ships, into them, around them. In each, he had learned at Breygna, a pilot sat ready day and night to move the ships out—probably to Faraday—in case of emergency.

Emergency, for the six pilots, meant only one thing: that the Control Room, four miles away at the east edge of the base, had been sabotaged or bombed out. In that case each was to move his ship out to safety by using its own controls, for these FTLs had controls like any spaceship, independent of any outside, vulnerable computers and power-sources. But to fly them was to commit suicide; no life survived a faster-than-light "trip." So each pilot was not only a highly trained polynomial mathematician, but a sacrificial fanatic. They were a picked lot. All the same, they got bored sitting and waiting for their unlikely blaze of glory. In one of the ships tonight Rocannan sensed the presence of two men. Both were deeply absorbed. Between them was a plane surface cut in squares. Rocannon had picked up the same impression on many earlier nights, and his rational mind registered *chessboard,* while his mindhearing moved on to the next ship. It was empty.

He went quickly across the dim gray field among scattered trees to the fifth ship in line, climbed its ramp and entered the open port. Inside it had no resemblance to a ship of any kind. It was all rocket-hangars and launching pads, computer banks, reactors, a kind of cramped and deathly labyrinth with corridors wide enough to roll citybuster missiles through. Since it did not proceed through space-time it had no forward or back end, no logic; and he could not read the language of the signs. There was no live mind to reach to as a guide. He spent twenty minutes searching for the control room, methodically, repressing panic, forcing himself not to use the mindhearing lest the absent pilot become uneasy.

Only for a moment, when he had located the control room and found the ansible and sat down before it, did he permit his mind-sense to drift over to the ship that sat east of this one. There he picked up a vivid sensation of a dubious hand hovering over a white Bishop. He withdrew at once. Noting the coordinates at which the ansible sender was set, he changed them to the coordinates of the League HILF Survey Base for Galactic Area 8, at Kerguelen, on the planet New South Georgia—the only coordinates he knew without reference to a handbook. He set the machine to transmit and began to type.

As his fingers (left hand only, awkwardly) struck each key, the letter appeared simultaneously on a small black screen in a room in a city on a planet eight lightyears distant:

URGENT TO LEAGUE PRESIDIUM. The FTL warship base of the Faradayan revolt is on Fomalhaut II, Southwest Continent, 28°28' North by 121°40' West, about 3 km. NE of a major river. Base blacked out but should be visible as 4 building-squares 28 barrack groups and hangar on rocket field running E-W. The 6 FTLs are not on the base but in open just SW of rocket field at edge of a forest and are camouflaged with net and light-absorbers. Do not attack indiscriminately as aborigines are not inculpated. This is Gaverel Rocannon of Fomalhaut Ethnographic Survey. I am the only survivor of the expedition. Am

131

*sending from ansible aboard grounded enemy FTL.
About 5 hours till daylight here.*

He had intended to add, "Give me a couple of hours to get clear," but did not. If he were caught as he left, the Faradayans would be warned and might move out the FTLs. He switched the transmitter off and reset the coordinates to their previous destination. As he made his way out along the catwalks in the huge corridors he checked the next ship again. The chess-players were up and moving about. He broke into a run, alone in the half-lit, meaningless rooms and corridors. He thought he had taken a wrong turning, but went straight to the port, down the ramp, and off at a dead run past the interminable length of the ship, past the interminable length of the next ship, and into the darkness of the forest.

Once under the trees he could run no more, for his breath burned in his chest, and the black branches let no moonlight through. He went on as fast as he could, working back around the edge of the base to the end of the rocket field and then back the way he had come across country, helped out by Heliki's next cycle of brightness and after another hour by Feni rising. He seemed to make no progress through the dark land, and time was running out. If they bombed the base while he was this close shockwave or firestorm would get him, and he struggled through the darkness with the irrepressible fear of the light that might break behind him and destroy him. But why did they not come, why were they so slow?

It was not yet daybreak when he got to the double-peaked hill where he had left his windsteed. The beast, annoyed at being tied up all night in good hunting country, growled at him. He leaned against its warm shoulder, scratching its ear a little, thinking of Kyo.

When he had got his breath he mounted and urged the steed to walk. For a long time it crouched sphinx-like and would not even rise. At last it got up, protesting in a sing-

132

song snarl, and paced northward with maddening slowness. Hills and fields, abandoned villages and hoary trees were now faint all about them, but not till the white of sunrise spilled over the eastern hills would the windsteed fly. Finally it soared up, found a convenient wind, and floated along through the pale, bright dawn. Now and then Rocannon looked back. Nothing was behind him but the peaceful land, mist lying in the riverbottom westward. He listened with the mind-sense, and felt the thoughts and motions and wakening dreams of his enemies, going on as usual.

He had done what he could do. He had been a fool to think he could do anything. What was one man alone, against a people bent on war? Worn out, chewing wearily on his defeat, he rode on toward Breygna, the only place he had to go. He wondered no longer why the League delayed their attack so long. They were not coming. They had thought his message a trick, a trap. Or, for all he knew, he had misremembered the coordinates: one figure wrong had sent his message out into the void where there was neither time nor space. And for that, Raho had died, Iot had died, Mogien had died: for a message that got nowhere. And he was exiled here for the rest of his life, useless, a stranger on an alien world.

It did not matter, after all. He was only one man. One man's fate is not important.

"If it is not, what is?"

He could not endure those remembered words. He looked back once more, to look away from the memory of Mogien's face—and with a cry threw up his crippled arm to shut out the intolerable light, the tall white tree of fire that sprang up, soundless, on the plains behind him.

In the noise and the blast of wind that followed, the windsteed screamed and bolted, then dropped down to earth in terror. Rocannon got free of the saddle and cowered down on the ground with his head in his arms. But he could not shut it out—not the light but the darkness, the darkness that blinded his mind, the knowledge in his

133

own flesh of the death of a thousand men all in one moment. Death, death, death over and over and yet all at once in one moment in his one body and brain. And after it, silence.

He lifted his head and listened, and heard silence.

EPILOGUE

RIDING DOWN the wind to the court of Breygna at sundown, he dismounted and stood by his windsteed, a tired man, his gray head bowed. They gathered quickly about him, all the bright-haired people of the castle, asking him what the great fire in the south had been, whether runners from the plains telling of the Strangers' destruction were telling the truth. It was strange how they gathered around him, knowing that he knew. He looked for Ganye among them. When he saw her face he found speech, and said haltingly, "The place of the enemy is destroyed. They will not come back here. Your Lord Ganhing has been avenged. And my Lord Mogien. And your brothers, Yahan; and Kyo's people; and my friends. They are all dead."

They made way for him, and he went on into the castle alone.

In the evening of a day some days after that, a clear blue twilight after thundershowers, he walked with Ganye on the rainwet terrace of the tower. She had asked him if he would leave Breygna now. He was a long time answering.

"I don't know. Yahan will go back to the north, to Hallan, I think. There are lads here who would like to make the voyage by sea. And the Lady of Hallan is waiting for news of her son. . . . But Hallan is not my home. I have none here. I am not of your people."

She knew something now of what he was, and asked, "Will your own people not come to seek you?"

He looked out over the lovely country, the river gleaming in the summer dusk far to the south. "They may," he said. "Eight years from now. They can send death at once, but life is slower. . . . Who are my people? I am not

135

what I was. I have changed; I have drunk from the well in the mountains. And I wish never to be again where I might hear the voices of my enemies."

They walked in silence side by side, seven steps to the parapet; then Ganye, looking up toward the blue, dim bulwark of the mountains, said, "Stay with us here."

Rocannon paused a little and then said, "I will. For a while."

But it was for the rest of his life. When ships of the League returned to the planet, and Yahan guided one of the surveys south to Breygna to find him, he was dead. The people of Breygna mourned their Lord, and his widow, tall and fair-haired, wearing a great blue jewel set in gold at her throat, greeted those who came seeking him. So he never knew that the League had given that world his name.